EPITAPH:
REVEILLE

BY

VICTOR NIEVES

EPITAPH: REVEILLE

Designed by Acorn Book Services

Publication Managed by Acorn Book Services
www.acornbookservices.com
acornbookservices@gmail.com
304-995-1295

Cover Design: Michelle Designs
http://melchelledesigns.com/

ISBN-10: 0990399206
ISBN-13: 978-0-9903992-0-9

Printed in the United States of America

To my family and friends, who believed in a wild dream,
and helped me turn that into a reality.
Their support and encouragement have kept me going since page one.
This is for you guys.

TABLE OF CONTENTS

ACKNOWLEDGMENTS

'd like to thank Molly, Maddie, Sarah, Amy, Katelyn, and Trevor for giving me unending support, encouragement, and for being always ready and willing to read anything I threw at them.

I'd also like to acknowledge Zach and Chris, who provided hours of sound, firsthand military advice and tireless hand-to-hand combat demonstrations. Your commitment to this project and the valuable insight you gave into what different science fiction readers expect, helped me to make this the best book possible.

Thank you, Sam, for all the medical consultation you provided and your uplifting support.

And Lauren: my mentor, my teacher, and my friend who stood by patiently and coached me through this whole process. Without all of our meetings, our pages and pages of emails, those enlightening talks you gave me, your wise counsel, and the opportunity you gave me, the *Epitaph* series would be nothing more than an unfinished manuscript collecting dust in a desk drawer.

Daniel, for your enthusiastic attitude and unbelievably excellent illustrations.

Mel, for the patience you displayed when working with the hardest person in the world for which to make a book cover.

Cindy, for all your wonderful marketing ideas.

Of course, I must mention Hannah and John, without whom this idea would have never come to light.

Thank you to my family, who was always willing to listen to the frustrated author, unsatisfied with his work, and who gave him so much wonderful support and encouragement, without which this book would never have been possible.

Lastly, to my grandfather, who's not only my best friend, but also the man who believed in me from the start.

INTRODUCTION

As a kid, I loved science fiction: books, movies, make-believe games—the works. I loved the originality of the genre. The places it could take you and the things the characters in those books did made me wish I was the commander of a starship, cruising through space, on a mission that, if successful, would save the entire galaxy.

As I got older, I realized I wanted to do something like that. I wanted to somehow, someway, share with other people the ideas, the journeys, and the adventures that were in my head. So, in June 2005, I finally came up with an idea. I turned on the computer, opened a word document, and started typing.

Seven years later, in January of 2013, I had finally completed the manuscript from start to epic finish that I had titled *Epitaph: Reveille*, the first book in the planned *Epitaph* trilogy.

For me, it was a monumental accomplishment. Not only had I written a book, but I also felt satisfied that I had successfully concocted a story, an idea, into something that bridged the vast expanse between my imagination and reality.

It was then I realized writing was what I wanted to do. Through it, I could express what I felt, what I wanted to feel, and put into words the vast sea of imagination in which I swam. I could take people through an epic journey, one that could span the length of any planet, battlefield, or realm I wanted; be they vast deserts, sprawling metropolis' where towers reached so high their peaks scraped the very stars, and beyond, on to the darkest, coldest, unexplored depths of space. It was the perfect place, the perfect playground, for me to express what I experienced in my imagination so that other people could join in the adventures with me.

Epitaph: Reveille is not only a book for science fiction fans, but also a gateway into the realm of science fiction itself. It's the perfect device, the perfect start, to guide you into a world where possibility is only hindered by the bounds of your own imagination.

I hope you enjoy reading this book as much as I've enjoyed writing it.

And rest assured: the adventures don't end here …

… *Epitaph: Reveille* is but the tip of the iceberg.

PROLOGUE

0100 hours, August 13, 2314

Omicron Roh System, planet Solomon

Kronus Experimental Weapons Development Lab

A Shadow slid out of the shaft and dropped soundlessly into the fourth floor elevator. He tapped a button on the holographic wall panel and the doors parted at the seams.

Kileeus Scales swept the corridor with his assault rifle.

No contacts.

With a slight flick of his cobalt eyes, his mind integrated with his armor's neural hardware and a holographic schematic of the lab snapped up in the right corner of the inside of his helmet's visor. He reviewed it quickly—his destination was one floor down. There were three ways he could go:

Stairs—too risky, far too much of a chance of being spotted.

Elevator—too loud, not enough cover, too exposed.

Air duct—perfect.

He sprinted down the corridor. When he reached the vent, his rock-solid arm muscles afforded him the strength to wrench the covering clean off the wall. His motion tracker blipped once—a proximity alert. Four targets were approaching his position.

He'd need to move fast before he was spotted.

He slipped into the duct and out of the hallway just as quietly as he'd come in.

Scales dropped a full eight meters down the duct and landed in another shaft, crouched on one knee. With a single fluid motion, he brought his MAR-4 to bear, shouldered it with one finger a mere twitch away from the trigger.

He glanced at his motion tracker—no contacts.

Time to move.

Scales scooted along the narrow shaft in a crouch for a dozen meters until he saw rays of light cutting across his path. To his right, another grating covered his exit.

He slid a fiber optic probe through the bars, and watched the video feedback via his HUD's small screen. He twisted it one hundred eighty degrees, taking in the whole room.

Floor to ceiling shelves were laden with food and other provisions. Two huge tanks against the far wall held thousands of gallons of fresh water. Large boxes and crates were stacked high.

There were too many places for an enemy to hide, but this was the Rendezvous Zone, so he'd have to risk it.

If all had gone according to plan, his partner would be waiting for him here.

He rewound the probe and tucked it into his armor's storage compartment. Scales firmly braced himself and knocked the vent cover free with a powerful kick. It went flying across the room and clattered against the wall.

Scales moved in and swept the room with his MAR.

Nothing.

He switched his visor's imaging to thermal.

No heat signatures registered.

Satisfied, he eased his grip on his MAR and clicked his com mic twice—the Shadow signal for "all clear."

He waited for a response.

One heartbeat.

Two.

Three.

Then it came: two clicks, a dash, then two more clicks—the counter response.

He caught movement in his peripheral vision and spun around to face it, weapon at the ready.

A being emerged from behind the water tanks.

It was his partner, a fellow Shadow.

Nakolus Aaragon.

"And I thought you'd never get here," Aaragon said with a chastising yet playful snort. "But just as well, it's nice to see you."

He gave a deep, respectful bow in the manner of the Vakari *Shirum*.

Scales answered with a bow of his own. "Likewise, Nakolus. Did you find us a shortcut?"

Aaragon jerked his head in the direction of the water tanks. Scales followed. Behind the tanks, a vent covering was bolted over another shaft. This one, however, was twice as thick as the others. It would take more than a few good kicks to loosen, so Scales had a better idea.

"We follow this for fifty meters," Aaragon said as he crouched down to inspect the grate. "It'll take us to the labs. A straight shot."

"Watch out."

Scales tapped a small device on his vambrace. Out of a miniature wrist-mounted diode, a needle-fine red beam shot forth. He guided the laser around the covering's rim, cutting through the steel bolts like they were paper. When he was finished he clicked it off and grabbed the vent. The weakened steel pulled free with almost no effort.

Aaragon knelt and pointed his MAR at the storeroom's entrance.

"Go," he said. "I've got your six."

Scales slung his assault rifle and dropped prone. When he'd crawled fifteen meters down the shaft, he heard a slight scraping sound through his helmet's enhanced audio suite—Aaragon crept in behind him.

They crept through the dusty, grimy aluminum chute—slowly, cautiously, for several minutes.

When Scales reached the end, he peered through the bars of the vent cover and found himself looking down at the labs, twelve meters below.

Scales snaked the fiber optic probe through to check for any contacts. There was no one there. At least, no one he could see. He carefully removed the grating as quietly as he could and dropped down out of the shaft. Aaragon followed close behind. They sprinted silently across the tiled floor and came to a halt before a large titanium bulkhead. Scales took position right, Aaragon left.

The B labs lay through the doorway. Their target, a human scientist spearheading the development of a new weapon for the Rebels, would be inside those labs.

Their mission was to sneak into the facility, eliminate their target, plant an explosive charge, quietly ex-filtrate, and then blow the place once they'd gotten clear.

The door before them was locked, sealed tight, but Aaragon was on it.

"Give me a moment." He typed in a few commands on the keypad, hacked the security codes via his TACTICOM pad, and the door slid open.

Scales went through first and took cover behind a bank of computer mainframes. He peered over the top and saw their target standing over a table with his back to them. The man was rapidly typing away at a terminal, completely unaware of the two assassins mere meters away.

"Target sighted," Scales said over the coms to Aaragon. His partner slunk through the door and expertly melted into the shadows.

"I've got our exit," Aaragon replied. "Doorway, far corner. It leads right outside."

"Acknowledged," Scales said. "Set the timer on the bomb for three minutes. Mark."

Scales took a steadying breath. He lined up the scientist in the sights of his MAR, and squeezed the trigger.

A single round hit the man square in the back, severing his spine. He slumped over the console and fell to the floor. Blood pooled around his body.

"Target eliminated," Scales said. "Let's get out of here."

There was a hiss of air, the screeching of un-oiled gears, and suddenly, a door opened across the lab.

In walked six scientists. It took them a moment to take it in, but when they saw the body of their comrade, they froze in horror.

"Shit," Scales muttered under his breath.

One of them broke rank and bolted for the alarm.

She pulled it just as Scales sighted down. He squeezed the trigger, and a three-round burst caught the woman between her shoulders. Blood spattered the wall.

But it was done. The alarm wailed, and their cover was blown.

"Bomb set," Aaragon said over the coms.

Scales put the rest of the scientists down with a sustained stream of gunfire right as Aaragon said, "Scales, I'm reading contacts headed this way. A dozen guards. We need to move. Now."

Scales stood up and sprinted for the exit. Aaragon was already hacking the security override when Scales approached.

"There," he said as the door opened. "Got it. Let's get—"

A sharp crackle of thunder resonated through the labs.

A high-caliber bullet hit Aaragon in the back. He crumpled to the ground.

"Nakolus!" Scales yelled.

He turned around in time to see a dozen guards burst into the lab with rifles blazing. Bullets zipped over his head as he threw himself prone and crawled for cover behind a row of computer consoles. On his HUD, Aaragon's bio signs flatlined.

Scales closed his eyes and cursed himself in his native tongue.

The timer readout from the bomb read 1:42.

Scales knew he had to make a run for it, out of the door Aaragon had given his life to open and into the snow covered fields to the pick-up point.

He steeled himself, stole one last glance at his fallen partner, and primed two smoke grenades. He lobbed them over the top of the console. In the few brief moments of confusion, the hail of bullets faltered. Scales arose and sprinted for the exit.

He'd made it across the field and into a forest of evergreens just as the timer ticked down to zero. The earth trembled. There was a deafening clash of thunder, and smoke roiled up high into the sky.

Scales didn't turn around. He kept on running through the forest. He knew he'd never be able to leave Aaragon's body behind if he looked back.

When he reached a grove four kilometers from the facility, he stopped. Panting, he flipped on the small homing beacon sheathed in his belt. All that was left was to wait for pickup. He melted into cover to avoid detection in case the Rebels had sent out a search party.

He exhaled.

As a Shadow, it was his duty to complete any mission, no matter the cost.

Although this time, the cost had been his *Shirum*, his bond-brother.

Epitaph: Reveille

WEAPON: MAR-5 ASSULT RIFLE

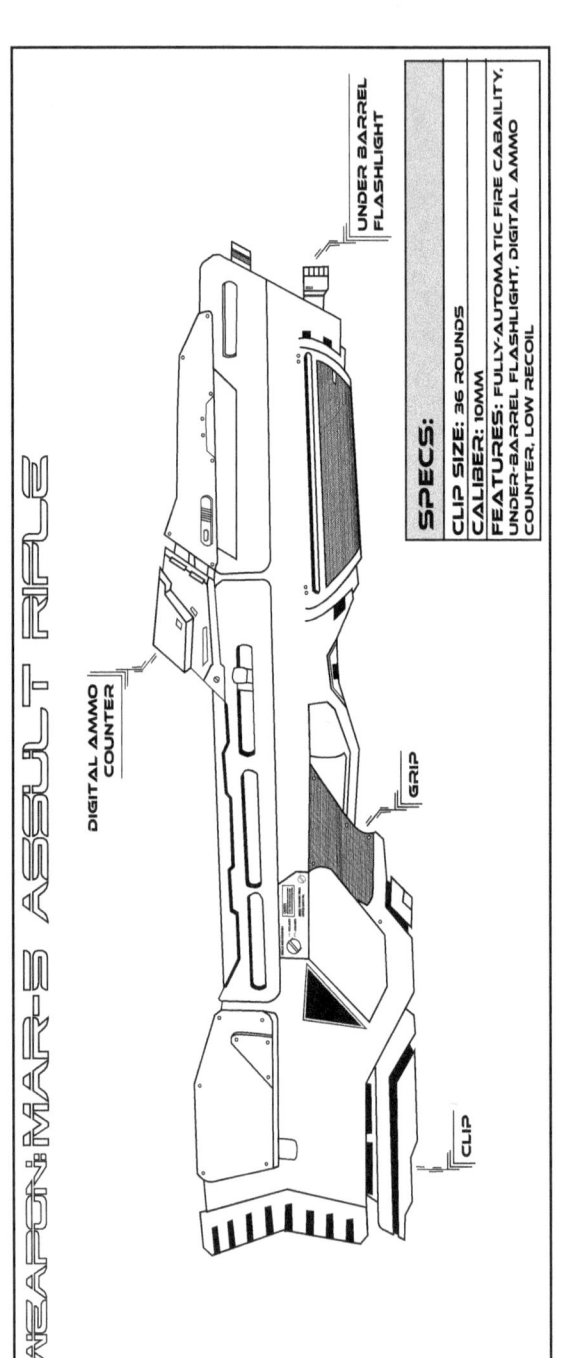

DIGITAL AMMO COUNTER

UNDER BARREL FLASHLIGHT

GRIP

CLIP

SPECS:

CLIP SIZE: 36 ROUNDS

CALIBER: 10MM

FEATURES: FULLY-AUTOMATIC FIRE CABAILITY, UNDER-BARREL FLASHLIGHT, DIGITAL AMMO COUNTER, LOW RECOIL

SECTION I:

THE COMING STORM

CHAPTER ONE

The sound of approaching footsteps broke Katherine Taylor's concentration. She blinked twice to clear her head as she dropped back into the real world.

"Commander?"

She glanced up from the mess table to see a young lieutenant standing rigidly at attention.

"Lieutenant," she asked, "what can I do for you?"

"Ma'am, a Captain Knight just arrived and is requesting to speak with you. He says it's urgent."

Katherine furrowed her brow. "I wasn't aware we were expecting any visitors today."

"To my knowledge, ma'am, we weren't. His arrival is unscheduled."

"Hmm." Katherine looked away and began organizing the papers scattered atop the table before her. "Well, tell him I'll be right there." She stuffed the documents back into the folder. "And give this to Lieutenant Fjoder. Tell her to take it to my quarters."

"Yes, ma'am." The lieutenant took the folder and slipped it under his arm. "Captain Knight is waiting for you in the observation room."

He snapped to attention, swiveled on his heel, and left. Once again, Katherine was alone.

"Great," she grumbled as she stood to her full height of five feet and nine inches.

It was never good for a superior officer to show up unannounced. She had a dreadful feeling this wasn't going to bode well for her.

She offered that thought an apprehensive sigh and quickly gulped down the rest of her coffee. The still-warm food on her tray was untouched when she took it over to the counter. Her stomach growled in protest, but she'd have to eat later. She left the mess and started briskly through the corridors to the observation room. The rapt clacking of her footfalls echoed throughout the facility's empty halls.

Knight. That has to be a human surname.

Personally, she didn't care what species Captain Knight was—be he human or alien. She was just as comfortable working around aliens as she was around her own kind.

It had been two hundred and sixty-five years since First Contact, since humanity had first encountered an alien race. Soon after, they had become a part of the United Galactic Coalition—a joint, multi-species galactic government— and working and living side-by-side with aliens had evolved into a natural way of life for the human race.

Since humanity's assimilation into the UGC, terraforming projects had transformed many of the barren planets and moons in the Sol system into major population centers.

Next to Earth, no other planet in the system held the population that Mars did. Terraforming had long ago transformed its red, barren rocks into a world of rich flora and sprawling mega-cities. Over the centuries, it had grown into one of the Sol system's largest trading hubs.

But Mars was more than a home to nine billion souls, at least as far as the Office of Military Intelligence (OMI) was concerned. Their interest was not in what thrived on its surface, but what lay buried beneath its crust.

At the roots of Olympus Mons—the system's largest volcano— archeologists had uncovered an unidentifiable relic, one that served as an interesting testament to previous inhabitants.

Katherine had several scientific degrees, so when the excavation on the artifact called "the Monolith" was completed, she had been contacted and asked to act as the supervising chief analyst at the facility codenamed "Leonidas" by Military Intelligence.

She had accepted the job without a moment's hesitation.

Katherine was a firm believer that there had been what she termed "precursor" races that had settled the galaxy and planted the seeds of life when the universe was only an infant. The Monolith could very well serve as a solid, corporeal testament to that belief.

As head analyst, it was her job to review all the data gathered on the artifact, as well as to order any tests she saw fit. She'd left herself little time for sleep this past month, but coffee was a wonderful invention, and, thankfully, one that had endured through the ages.

However, as much as she hated to admit it, her efforts—as well as the efforts of the other forty scientists—were yielding very little information as to what the Monolith actually was, what its function had been, and most importantly, what had happened to the race that had built it.

The folder Katherine had given to the lieutenant in the mess was unsatisfyingly light.

But she enjoyed a challenge, and the Monolith was proving to be just that.

Like the Monolith, Katherine was a rare find in the galaxy these days, at least as far as human genetics went. Her dark brown hair and deep blue eyes were a testament to that. Though sometimes she didn't always eat as healthy as she would have liked—sometimes work simply didn't allow for that—she worked hard to maintain her slim, curvy figure.

She rounded a corner and started down a long, dimly lit corridor. The observation room's cold, gunmetal-grey door laid forebodingly ahead. In her head, she pondered every possible reason for the nature of Captain Knight's visit. Every scenario ended with the same, disturbing conclusion: this was going to be trouble for her.

She was nervous, though she refused to let the anxiety of the unknown wreak havoc on her composure. She was going to treat the situation as professionally as her personality allowed, which was always *very* professional.

She halted and gave her uniform a quick check. She pulled her jacket taut and smoothed her sleeves. Satisfied, she exhaled sharply and stabbed the green holographic open button with her index finger.

The door slid open with a *hiss*.

Here we go.

Katherine stepped through the door.

A long, wooden conference table served as the room's centerpiece. There were a dozen empty chairs arranged neatly around it.

In one of them sat a human male; the gold bands on the sleeves of his black navy dress uniform indeed denoted the rank of captain.

He stood as she entered.

Katherine snapped to attention. "Sir," she said. "Commander Katherine Taylor reporting as requested."

"At ease, Commander," he said with a strong Scottish brogue.

Katherine eased her stance. She clasped her hands behind her back.

Knight extended his hand.

"Captain Elias Knight," he introduced himself as she shook his hand firmly. "It's a pleasure to finally meet you. You have quite the reputation, you know, even among the eggheads in OMI, and believe me, that's really saying something. There aren't many people that can hold claim to having over thirty published essays on the theoretical physics of our galaxy's many phenomena. You have quite a gift, Commander."

Katherine smiled. "Thank you, sir." She was somewhat flattered, and his tone sounded sincere, though she remained dubious. She pursed her lips. *You didn't come all this way just to tell me you think I'm smart.*

"Quite welcome." Knight then turned and drifted toward the observation window at the back of the room.

Out of the glass forty meters down, the Monolith sat ominously stoic, inert, jutting out from the roots of the volcano like a tooth protruding from red gums.

To Katherine, it served as an ancient guardian, a silent, lifeless warden, protecting perhaps the last vestige of the long forgotten history of its makers.

Katherine ventured over to the observation window and joined him. She and Knight stood silently for a few moments, gazing at the Monolith. The golden light cast from the bright floodlights stationed around the dig site was reflected in its glassy surface.

"Tell me," Knight asked, "what are all those symbols and shapes, those glyphs scrawled across the artifact?"

"They're mica inclusions embedded beneath the Monolith's surface," Katherine replied, "but we have no idea what they mean. No one seems to. At least, not yet. I have been piecing together a sort of alphabet from what little I could glean. I'm still working on it."

"How old is it?"

"Carbon dating places it at over one hundred and fifty million years old. It predates any known civilization. We're not sure what it's made from. It's some kind of alloy we've never discovered before. But whatever it is, wherever it came from, it's nearly indestructible. After all those millennia, time has done little to blemish its surface. Until I can prove otherwise or something else like it is found, those hieroglyphs are perhaps the last of their kind, the final remnants of a language long dead—forgotten in the tides of the eons."

"Wow," Knight said. "That was deep, Commander. Very poetic. I take it your way with words is one more talent God saw fit to grace you with?"

Katherine gave a laugh. "I used to write poetry when I was a little girl, back on Serimar. In the afternoons, I'd go under the big elm tree in my grandmother's backyard and sit there for hours with a pen and paper. Most people don't like to write freehand anymore, but I've always liked doing things old school."

Knight stuck his hand into his jacket. He took out an envelope from his inside breast pocket and presented it to her. "Speaking of old school," he said, "This is for you."

Crease lines wrinkled Katherine's forehead. Paper envelopes were almost obsolete. Everything was digital. If someone took the time to actually write this by hand, it was important.

She took it and turned it over—and that's when she saw the seal it bore: a globe, flanked to the left by a fleet of warships and to the right by the spiral form of the Milky Way Galaxy crowned with a diadem of stars.

Her eyes widened.

She knew what that hallmark belonged to: High Command (HighCom), the ruling arm of the military to which both the marines and navy answered.

Now she knew she was in trouble.

HighCom was commanded by the highest ranking members from both the navy and marines and headed by the Chairmen—fifteen beings, one individual from each member race elected to be the voice of their entire species.

Cautiously, Katherine popped the seal and opened the envelope. Inside was a folded letter. She removed it, carefully unfolded the thick parchment, and read it.

Her mouth dropped open. Words escaped her, flew out of her like air from the lungs after a hard punch to the gut. She stood there, stunned.

A mistake she thought. *This has got to be a mistake.*

She glanced up at Knight as if looking for some kind of clarity—some kind of answer.

He didn't give it. He couldn't. He didn't know what was written on the parchment. His orders had simply been to deliver it.

All Knight could do was answer with a shrug.

Katherine averted her gaze, looking now out of the observation window. Her stare was fixed at what her life had consisted of for the past month: the Monolith.

This doesn't make any sense.

It didn't have to. In her mind, she told herself that sense or not, orders were orders. She was an officer in the navy. Her duty was to follow the direction given to her by her superiors, wherever they took her, and she had never let her personal feelings conflict with that. So why was *this* so hard? So *different*?

She loved what she did here. What was to become of it?

She pondered that in silence for a long while.

"Commander," Knight spoke up.

Katherine had to practically tear her gaze away from the window to look at him. She licked her lips. "Yes, sir?"

"The contents of that letter are time sensitive, I'm afraid. On my way here I was ordered to arrange transport to take you to the spaceport."

"Transport?" Katherine repeated. "Right. Um, when do I leave, sir?"

"Immediately. I suggest you get to your quarters and start packing. There's a car waiting for you in the lot outside. The driver will take you to the spaceport. Your shuttle leaves from there in an hour, so you had best not tarry."

"I suppose I shouldn't," she muttered.

"I don't know what that letter said," Knight said consolingly. "And it's not my job to. But chin up girl, yeah? Whatever Command has in mind for you, I imagine it'll be well worth your time. It was a pleasure to meet you, Commander Taylor. I hope one day our paths may cross again."

Katherine gave him the proper respects and left the observation room in deep thought.

In the sea of unanswered questions she struggled to swim through inside her mind, she tread desperately to stay afloat lest they swallow her up.

Despite the thousand and one questions she wanted answers to, there was one that rose above them all. It stabbed at her more than any other, pierced her like a cold, iron sword:

What was about to happen to her?

CHAPTER TWO

0344 hours, January 19, 2343
Sol System, planet Mars
OMI Archeological Excavation Facility 007125-22F
Codename: "Leonidas"

"Toothbrush, hairbrush, toothpaste, floss—crap. Where's my razor?"

Katherine rushed to the bathroom. The razor was resting atop the marble counter. How had she not seen that?

"Okay," she muttered and set the razor on the bed along with her other toiletries. They seemed to be all there. Was she forgetting something? She did a mental tally of the things she'd brought.

Her civvies were on the bed, neatly folded; her personal belongings gathered; uniform shoes in the bag—*crap!* That's what she'd forgotten—her *uniforms!*

She raced for the closet.

"God," she huffed.

Irritation was setting in. There was a lot to do, and in so little time. Why would they only give her an hour to pack, leave for the spaceport, and then expect her to catch her shuttle to Earth in time?

"Are you going somewhere?"

The voice made Katherine jump. She spun about and saw her assistant, Lieutenant Kanea Fjoder, standing in the doorway. Katherine had been so worried about getting packed that she hadn't even heard her come in. "Kanea." She put her hand on her forehead and sighed. "I was going to say goodbye, honestly I was."

"What do you mean you were going to say goodbye?" Like all Chixil did when they were perplexed, Kanea rapidly blinked her two sets of eyes. "Katherine, what's going on?"

Katherine glanced at the archaic human wristwatch on her arm. "Forty-five minutes," she whispered. She opened the closet door. "I've got to finish packing. I don't have long to explain. Get in here and shut the door if you want to hear it."

Kanea complied. She tapped the door's holographic display and sealed it shut. "I've never seen you in such a hurry. All-Maker, your face is flushed. What's going on?"

"I've been reassigned," Katherine said as she took her three uniforms off the rack. She laid them neatly on the bed and began to fold them.

"What?" Kanea stepped closer. "*Reassigned?* Why? Where?"

"The Captain that arrived this morning without notice, Knight, he gave me a letter from High Command. It was written by Lord Fleet Admiral Terrence Carr. Damn it. Where's my journal?"

Kanea's eyes widened. "Admiral Carr?" She repeated in disbelief. "What the stars did you do? Are you in trouble?"

Katherine snorted. "Kanea, I have no idea."

"Well, what did the letter say? Why are you being reassigned?"

Katherine opened the drawer on her nightstand. "Gotcha," she muttered and snatched her journal. "Admiral Carr has *requested*—such a lovely word for ordered—that I meet him at the Thames Naval Academy on Earth at oh-nine-hundred sharp. That's all I know. It's all the letter said."

"What do you think he wants?"

"I can't even imagine."

"You do know who Admiral Carr is, Katherine, don't you?"

Katherine looked at her and cocked her head in a "you think?" manner. "Of course I do. He's only one of the most famous people in the galaxy, Kanea. His face is all over the extranet. Who doesn't know him? I *do* get out *sometimes*, you know. Where's my journal?"

"In your hand, Katherine."

"Oh, thanks."

Kanea put a hand on her hip. "I'm not a human, and even I grew up admiring Carr. Stars, I had friends at the academy who *worshipped* him. Everyone did. The man's a legend. You heard what he did when the Rebels attacked Mars a few decades ago, right?"

"I may have. Refresh my memory. And hand me that mirror, please?"

Kanea passed the small folding mirror to her. "He was only a NCO at the time. He was the Tactical Officer aboard the frigate *Presnik*. Anyway, a large group of Rebels managed to board and hijack three Coalition frigates. Only the *Presnik* and two corvettes were near enough to respond immediately. The Rebels turned the corvettes into Swiss cheese and hit *Presnik* so hard she lost a third of her crew, including the Captain and XO. No one knows for certain why, but none of the other crew wanted to assume the mantle of command, so Carr stepped up to the plate. Imagine, a *junior lieutenant* taking command of an entire ship! Carr outmaneuvered the Rebel ships and destroyed all three of them. He sure did earn all the medals and the promotion he got afterwards."

"You know, I think I do remember one of my professors giving us a lecture about that when I was a cadet at Le Ferro Academy," Katherine said.

"You should," Kanea replied. "It's in the history books. I've seen Carr in more vids than I can count. Have you ever noticed he never smiles, though? In all the vids I've seen, I don't think I've seen him smile once."

Katherine took a small box off her nightstand and checked to make sure her most prized possession was in there—a pendant, in the form of an angel, with diamonds studding the wings, small emeralds for eyes, and a halo of pure gold. It carried more value to her than all the jewels and currency in the universe. It had been given to her by her grandmother after she graduated from the Academy. Her grandmother had passed four years ago.

"You're either really lucky Carr wants to see you, or really, *really* screwed."

"Thanks for the confidence boost, Kanea," Katherine said. She huffed. "Okay, that's it." She zipped up her duffle and looked at her assistant. "That's everything."

"Are you coming back?"

Katherine shrugged her shoulders. "I hope so. If not, I want you to know you've been a lot of help these past few weeks. You've been more than an assistant, Kanea. You've been my friend, and I appreciate that. Thank you."

Kanea assumed attention and snapped off a firm salute. "Take care of yourself, Commander."

Katherine returned her salute with a smile. "Same to you, Lieutenant."

They parted ways at the door. Kanea went in the direction of the mess; Katherine slung her duffle over her shoulder and started down the hallway toward the security checkpoint.

She remembered reading an article on Admiral Carr a while back. He was bestowed with the UGC's highest and most prestigious military award, the Galactic Star.

It was an achievement few living people could hold claim to. In her life, she'd only ever heard of it being awarded posthumously. Yet Admiral Carr had received it while alive. Twice.

From what she knew, he and Vakari Chairman Hurundus Fercon were the only living recipients who wore the Star on their chests.

Well, if this all goes south, at least I get to say I met him.

She passed an Ura scientist as she rounded a bend in the hallway.

He stood to attention. "Ma'am."

She nodded.

The Ura were an odd race. They resembled the greys of ancient human myth—tall, slender, lanky aliens with large, bulging eyes and skinny necks that barely looked like they could support their ovular heads. Three long, skinny digits at the end of each hand were adept at surgical and medical procedures.

Katherine soon arrived at the facility's security checkpoint—a slim corridor with a titanium door at the other end. The guard sitting in the security booth off to the right could operate the door with the touch of a button.

"Commander Taylor …" The guard's gruff, tri-vocaled Vakari voice drifted in over the speakers. "Good morning. Going out, ma'am?"

"I am, Corporal."

"Right. Stand by."

The red light over the door turned green. It slid open, parting at a vertical seam. She stepped outside and worked her way down a winding stone pathway that led away from the entrance to Leonidas down a small, grassy knoll.

The sound of chirping birds made her smile. Sometimes she forgot how pleasant it was to be outdoors. Like she'd done a million times before, she made a mental note to not get so engrossed in her work and to take more time to enjoy the little things in life. The birds were singing happily, nesting high in the evergreen trees that lined the perimeter of the inner courtyard.

Katherine presented her ID to the MP guarding the inner checkpoint—a six-meter high polycrete wall, looped across the top with a row of archaic, but effective, razor wire. Two watchtowers overlooked the thick steel gate. They were manned by MP snipers who were stationed round the clock. In skilled hands, the Seraph sniper rifles they carried could hit a target over three kilometers distant. Their 16.5mm rounds could punch through any type of body armor in existence.

She was admitted through the checkpoint and made her way to the parking lot.

A human male in navy dress uniform leaned against a car. When he saw her, he straightened his posture and waved to get her attention.

It was safe to assume that was her ride.

She worked her way through a rainbow assortment of parked cars and shuttles toward him. As she neared, she spied the single gold stripe of a junior lieutenant on his sleeve. He had a cigarette in his hand and took one last long, deep drag of putrid smoke before he snuffed it out on the hood of the vehicle.

Katherine wrinkled her nose. *How charming.*

"Ma'am," he said and saluted. "I'll be your ride to the space port this morning. Allow me." He opened the passenger-side door for her.

She slid into the seat.

"It's about a twenty minute ride to the Arganorus spaceport." He took his place behind the wheel. He flipped the ignition switch on, put the car in gear, and stepped on the acceleration.

Katherine looked out of the window at Leonidas as it shrunk in the distance. She thought of Kanea Fjoder. She'd make a good assistant to whatever egghead HighCom was going to bring in to replace her. Katherine sighed. She'd miss Kaena. But most of all, she'd miss the Monolith.

Would she ever see it again?

CHAPTER THREE

0850 hours, January 19, 2343
Sol System, planet Earth
Thames Naval Academy
London, England

"Please welcome Lord Fleet Admiral Terrence Carr to the stage," Fleet Admiral Kastanie Vorstov said into the mic.

Every cadet arose and stood to solid attention. The audience behind them got to its feet and applauded thunderously. They hooted and hollered as Terrence Carr walked up the steps and began the all-too-long march across the stage.

He could hear the snaps of the cameras and see the flashes go off in his peripheral vision as he walked across the stage. The applause was nearly earsplitting. There were cheers. *They weren't a quarter this excited for any of the previous guests of honor.* He approached the podium center stage.

Vorstov stood aside and saluted. She smiled.

She's the one who should be giving this speech, not me. Carr returned her salute. *Kastanie deserves to be giving this speech. This applause should be for her.*

Admiral Vorstov extended her hand. "It's good to see you again, sir."

Sir. Six years ago we were the same rank. Then they decided I was the better candidate for Councilor. She has twice the integrity I do. Carr gripped her hand. "Likewise, Admiral," he replied.

"Try not to look into the lights, Terrence," she whispered. "Damn things are blinding."

"Thanks for the heads up."

Vorstov took a step back and snapped off a final honorary salute. She pivoted on her heel and walked off the stage. Carr took his place behind the podium. He gripped both sides of the wooden edges and waited for the commotion to die down.

It went on.

And on.

And on.

He sighed wearily and held up his hand to quiet the crowd. His gesture stifled them—but only after a few dozen more photographs. Finally, the audience sat down.

"Thank you." He heard his own voice thundering through the auditorium's speakers. It sounded strangely unfamiliar. "Today, we are here to honor these fine men and women, these newly ordained soldiers, as they take the next step on their way to becoming officers in the United Galactic Coalition's military.

"Leadership isn't just about *commanding*. It's about setting an example to your fellow soldiers, taking responsibility, and upholding the UGC's laws and customs to their highest standards. As a soldier, you will be the protectors of the Coalition and all her worlds and colonies. But as a leader, your actions will reflect what those worlds and colonies stand for—freedom, equality for all races, and the principle that if we work hard enough, we can achieve anything. To be a part of the UGC is to be free, to be equal. But in order to do that, we must work hard, and we must always be prepared to give the ultimate sacrifice—our lives—in defense of the Coalition and everything she stands for. A leader displays this in the way he or she lives his or her life, in his or her everyday actions. Leaders show those under their command to never falter in the face of those who would seek to do us harm, prey on the weak and the innocent, or take away from us our *freedom*.

"As you now take the next step on your way to becoming that person, that beacon of the Coalition's pride, that *leader*, remember these words: Freedom ... Unity ... and Honor.

"Thank you."

The audience erupted into a thunderous tirade of applause and cheer.

As they honored him with a standing ovation, Carr turned and walked off the stage. His new objective was to get out of sight as fast as he could. The media would swarm him if they got the chance; beg him to give an interview and tell him how great and terrific he was—how he was the shining example of everything the UGC stood for.

There are over fifty other Lord Fleet Admirals and Lord Generals they could say that to. And most of them actually deserve it.

Carr pulled up his sleeve and checked the spring and gear watch on his wrist—a relic from an age long passed. 0900. His special guest would be arriving any second.

He took a left at the T-junction and started for the lobby. He wanted to be there to greet her.

Commander Katherine Taylor was nothing short of a genius. When he'd read her file, it had surprised even him.

She was fluent in eight languages, seven human and one alien—*Firum*—the primary Vakari tongue, and she could read and understand seven other alien languages. Taylor came from a modest background. After primary school she was accepted into the UGC's most prestigious—and most expensive—school: Le Ferro Naval Academy on planet Svarok. She'd graduated valedictorian with degrees in several areas, including zeno-morphology, zeno-archeology, chemistry, and theoretical physics—with a doctorate in each of them.

During her short but distinguished six year military career, she had been involved in some pretty clandestine projects for OMI—among them projects involving experimental nano-technology, sending scouting probes out beyond the bounds of explored space, and she had even presented OMI with new ways to improve mass accelerator technology.

As far as Carr was concerned, Katherine Taylor was the most intelligent woman in the galaxy. And he wasn't the only one who thought so.

There were a dozen military departments that wanted to get their hands on her.

Up until recently, she had been stationed on Mars at the Monolith site, where her zeno-morphology, chemistry, and zeno-archeology skills were being put to the test. But she was too valuable an asset for that. Carr needed her for something else, something so much bigger and astronomically more important.

There was a sudden rumble in his jacket's inside breast pocket. Carr stopped. He reached in and pulled out a small, black tablet—a Telecom pad, a device that served the denizens of the Milky Way as a main communication outlet. It could be used to talk, video chat, or send messages to any other uplink in the network.

For security reasons, Carr's tablet was locked so that messages could only be accessed when he entered a coded word and his thumb was placed on the screen to verify his fingerprint. He followed the protocol and a notification snapped up on screen: there was an unread message in his inbox. He tapped the icon at the bottom of the screen. The message opened.

It read:

UGCHC EXECUTIVE DIRECTIVE 009-4210241AA

CLASSIFIED (BETA-FIVE)

>AUTOMATED TRANSMISSION FROM UGC HIGH COMMAND SECTION ZERO FOLLOWS:

To: Lord Fleet Admiral Carr, Terrence J. _ Service No. 6775439-900TC UGCHC

Priority: ALPHA

To all Councilors,

An emergency assembly is being convened. All Councilors off world are to report to Katana immediately. Transportation will be provided at the spaceport nearest your location. You

have until 1900 on the 20 of January. All those not present by then will have to join Council Session via hologram.

This is an ENCLAVE-level emergency.

>AUTOMATED TRANSMISSION FROM UGC HIGH COMMAND SECTION ZERO ENDS

Carr creased his brow.

Only under the absolute worst circumstances imaginable would an Enclave emergency be declared.

This changed everything. Emergency assemblies were rarely called; in fact, during his lifetime there had only been one instance of an Enclave-level emergency. It was when Rebels had set off a nuclear weapon in the middle of a city—and six million people died.

He hoped nothing like that had happened again, but with the threat of galactic civil war looming over the horizon, shining brighter than any star in the night sky, it was highly possible something like that had happened … or maybe something worse.

Carr deleted the message per protocol and tucked the pad back into his jacket. He continued on to the lobby—albeit with a spring in his step.

Commander Taylor would have to be briefed and brought up to speed. This wasn't what Carr had originally planned for her, but his orders were clear, so she was just going to have to tag along to Katana with him. It was a long journey from Earth, so at least there would be plenty of time for him to explain everything to her: why she had been pulled from the Monolith, for what purpose he needed her, and what her knowledge of zeno-archeology might unlock.

He stepped into the lobby. The seal of the academy was elegantly constructed in a colorful mosaic of tiny gemstones in the middle of the floor. He spied a woman in navy dress admiring a picture hanging on the wall—Commander Katherine Taylor.

She turned her head and looked his way.

Carr almost stopped dead in his tracks.

How?

How is it she looks so much like Lena? He couldn't stop his eyes from glazing over at Lena's memory. Especially not when that memory was so deeply embedded in someone else's likeness—Katherine's nose, those deep, blue eyes, the complexion of her skin, the way she wore her dark brown hair. But he quickly checked it, suppressed it, and it subsided.

He was far enough away from the commander that she didn't notice.

She snapped rigidly to attention. "Sir," she said. "Commander Katherine Taylor reporting for duty."

"At ease, Commander," Carr said. "I'm Lord Fleet Admiral Terrence Carr. It's a pleasure to finally meet you." He extended his hand to her.

It took her a second to shake it. She looked surprised at his gesture at first, then firmly grasped his hand. "It is an *incredible* honor to meet you, sir," she said and grinned.

God, she even has her smile. Carr ignored the mental picture flashing in his mind. If he didn't … "The honor's mine, Commander," he said. "You have quite a CSD. I've looked through thousands of potential candidates, but when I saw your dossier, I knew you were the one."

"Candidates, sir?"

"Yeah. I'll explain everything to you on the way to the spaceport."

Katherine furrowed her brow. "Um, the spaceport, sir?"

He nodded. "Yeah, I'll explain that one too. Do you have your things ready to go?"

"Yes, sir. I checked my bag in with security at the front gate."

"Good," Carr said. "Then we'll pick it up on the way out."

Katherine looked confused, as confused as he had ever seen someone, but, to her credit, she simply nodded her head. She knew better than to question orders. Carr admired that. "I'm ready when you are, sir."

Carr led the way. Katherine trailed close behind him as they left the lobby through the huge front doors, strolled through the gardens, and into the security checkpoint near the front gate. She gathered her single duffel and they continued onward to the parking lot.

A midnight black shuttle with "UGC" painted in big white letters on the door was waiting for them. It was an unmanned craft, programed to take the quickest route to the spaceport, automated like most of the other shuttles in the galaxy. The doors opened and Carr climbed into the driver's seat. Katherine settled in next to him. They buckled in as the doors hissed shut and the shuttle rumbled to life. The holographic control suite flickered into existence on the dashboard and a moment later, the shuttle lifted up vertically and shot out of the lot. At first chance, it worked its way into a lane of shuttles flying high above the streets.

Finally, he was able to focus his attention on the commander.

"I'd like to get straight to it," Carr said to her. "I'm sure you're wondering exactly why I had you pulled from the Monolith Project."

"Yes, sir," she replied. "It's kind of been on my mind."

Carr gazed at her a fraction of a second too long. He quickly cleared his throat and continued on. "Several months ago," he began, "Archeologists came across a network of alien structures buried hundreds of kilometers beneath planet Tyram. As the excavation continued, the archeologists eventually discovered a massive underground cavern—and found an entire alien city inside, perfectly intact, like it had been built yesterday. Over the next few months, six other sites were found, one of them the Monolith on Mars. All are roughly the same age as the Monolith, about a hundred and fifty million years old. They were considered the most significant finds in galactic history … until we found something else."

Carr saw the expression on Katherine's face. Anticipation glowed in her eyes like red-hot embers. It seemed like the seatbelt was the only thing keeping her in place. To say he had piqued her interest would have been a *colossal* understatement.

"Inside of the structure called the Spire on planet Atlantis, scientists discovered something hidden in its lowest chamber: a crystal. From what we can tell, this is an actual working piece of alien technology. A few days ago, the crystal was moved up from the site to a research facility codenamed 'Tilarus.' Unfortunately, the scientists haven't been able to make any progress. They have no idea where to even begin. This is why you were pulled from the Monolith, Katherine: I need you to figure out just what this thing is.

"Your knowledge of zeno-linguistics, zeno-morphology, and archeology exceeds anyone I've ever read about. You've got the commendations to prove that. I need someone like that. I need the best; someone to spearhead this thing, not just the research into the crystal, but this project as a whole. You're reassigned to High Command as the project's head scientist. You will report directly to me. I'll also be able to grant you a beta-five level security clearance. You will have all the funding you'll ever need, as well as all the resources HighCom has at its disposal. Effective immediately."

Katherine's mouth hung ajar. The mix of emotions dancing across her face conveyed excitement, disbelief, and curiosity. There was eagerness, too. However, there was also caution.

Carr knew he was asking a lot of her.

She looked hard at him before speaking, peering deeply into his ice-blue eyes.

"Admiral," Katherine said. "Sir, I don't know that I'm as good as you think I am, but I promise I will give this everything I've got. I would consider it an *honor* to work by your side, sir."

Carr couldn't prevent it. For once, he didn't want to stifle the tiny smile that graced his lips. "The honor is mine, Commander Taylor. Welcome to High Command."

Katherine gave another of her beautiful smiles. She had a mouthful of perfectly straight, pearly-white teeth. "Would you mind if I asked a few questions, sir?" she asked.

"By all means, Commander."

Katherine had several questions about the other sites, the Spire in particular. He couldn't remember all the details, but he tried to recall what he could.

Poor thing. Her mouth moved a mile a minute and it didn't stop until the shuttle rolled to a stop at the Halcyon Tower.

Halcyon was a massive installation thousands of kilometers high that served as a conduit between the ground and the Orbital Docking Station (ODS) *Finae* in high geosynchronous orbit around Earth. There were three other Conduit Towers around the planet.

Inside an hour, Carr and Katherine arrived at *Finae.*

The station was four kilometers in diameter, making it the largest in the Sol system. She could hold hundreds of ships—freighters, leisure craft, shuttles, and even light capital ships like corvettes and frigates.

Among the forty-six warships and shuttles connected to the station's many umbilicals was the *Spirit's Walk,* a military executive shuttle.

The *Spirit* had had another task before High Command rerouted its flight path. Now its purpose was to ferry Carr and Katherine to planet Katana.

They passed through the shuttle's decontamination chambers and were welcomed by the Captain. He escorted them to their private VIP quarters.

Before they parted company, Carr said to Katherine, "I've got some things I need to take care of, but you should try and get a few hours' rest. You look tired. Later, I'll transfer a few data files to your telecom pad for you to get started with. Let me know if you need anything."

"I will, sir," she replied. "Thank you."

As he settled into the ridiculously lavish VIP room, Carr felt his jacket pocket rumble again. He pulled out his telecom pad to see that he had received a message from Chairman Hurundus Fercon.

It was coded under the highest security classification that existed—beta-five. Carr entered his unique passcode and the message snapped up onscreen. As he read it, ice water trickled into his stomach and his blood ran cold. The very hair on his neck stood on end.

The Chairmen had been right to elevate the military into a state of emergency.

The Tilarus facility on Atlantis, the research outpost studying the alien crystal, had been attacked ... and neither it nor the several dozen marine guards stationed there were responding.

CHAPTER FOUR

There was a river, a beautiful, clear-blue river, meandering through a lush green, tree-covered valley and disappearing off into the horizon. She sat alone upon a moss-covered mound, surrounded by the brightest, prettiest flowers she'd ever beheld. There was a taste of fresh strawberries in her mouth. A refreshing breeze sallied in from the east, blowing through her hair and fluttering the dark red ribbons on her pigtails. She knew she was home, sitting on a riverbank near her grandmother's house, on the planet Serimar. All was as she remembered it: quiet, tranquil, sunny. As she looked to the sky, trying to pick out an animal silhouetted in the clouds, she heard a loud screech erupt from somewhere behind her. She turned around, scanning the countryside, searching for the source …

Katherine opened her eyes.

The alarm clock on the nightstand beside her shrieked loudly.

"Damn," she sighed. So much for her perfect dream. She reached over and almost hit the sleep button before she saw what time it was: 1745. She could scarcely believe it. She'd slept for over ten hours.

Katherine exhaled deeply and sat up. She rested her back against the bunk's headboard. She was more tired than she'd realized—or cared to realize. Her work was her fuel. That, together with coffee, aided in a joint effort to keep her going.

At the moment, she felt strangely out of place. This much sleep at one time was something she'd been unfamiliar with for a while.

It baffled her. How could she have slept?

After the bombshell the Admiral had dumped in her lap back on Earth, she felt so awake and excited—her heart thumped away, her pulse quickened. Her mind raced, thinking about the vast amount of work that would need to be done, and all that she and the galaxy could learn from this crystal and the other ruins. After several hours of examining the data Carr had sent her, going to the mess to grab a meal, and then working some more, she'd had the biggest crash of her life. She hardly re-membered crawling into bed and going to sleep … and she sure hadn't expected to stay that way for ten hours.

Perhaps it had all been too much on her body.

Katherine briefly considered dozing back off. Another three hours sounded nice. She could probably use it. There simply wasn't time right now, though. Carr had called earlier and said he wanted to see her at 1800.

She rubbed at her tired eyes and yawned.

These quarters were incredible. God, she wished she were important enough to be given luxury like this. This executive shuttle was nicer than most high-end apartments. She yawned again, stretched, and then whipped the sheets off her body and swung her legs over the side of the bunk.

Katherine stretched her back until it answered her with a satisfying crack.

She stood erect and walked across the lavishly furnished cabin, passing a beautifully scrolled oak desk on her way to her private bathroom. After a refreshing shower, she wrapped a soft, silky-smooth towel around her body and opened the door to the armoire. Its hinges creaked.

Her uniform hung on a rack, ribbons still perfectly centered above the left breast, and jacket and trousers devoid of any wrinkles even after nearly two days' wear. She removed the towel and threw it on the bed. As she pulled on her undergarments, she began to think of Carr.

Before resting, she'd done a little curious snooping.

Admiral Carr had enlisted right out of school at age seventeen, and had been commissioned as a junior lieutenant five years later after participating in the successful Deimos, Lagrange, and Hepton Campaigns against the Rebels.

As he ascended through the ranks, he went on to win every major UGC award and citation for bravery, valor, and honor, and remained to this day the Coalition's most decorated officer in service. He was the center of media attention his entire career and was universally considered a hero—a shining example of all humanity strove to achieve. His climb from enlisted to the highest-ranking officer in the navy was a UGC legend.

Katherine spent several hours watching dozens of news vids about Carr from all over the extranet. However, early in his career, something had changed the admiral and not for the better.

He never smiled again. He never laughed again. He rarely showed any emotion—period. Even after all these decades, Carr's face still bore that same mask of grim resolve. For a man in his sixties, Carr was remarkably fit for his age and didn't look a day over fifty. Yet, he always appeared so tired, so world-weary, so stressed. There were dark circles under his eyes, creases around his mouth from the always present tight draw of his lips, his eyebrows furrowed as if in constant contemplation.

As respected as he was, as such an inspirational figure to so many, Katherine had never seen someone appear so unhappy in all her life.

She'd heard from a few sources that his wife had left him—taking their daughter with her. The rumor was that she hated the fame and couldn't take living in the spotlight anymore. It might have been true. It was just one of the many rumors circulating among the extranet and senior officers in the fleet. Whatever it was that had actually happened to him was a mystery, but Carr had never been the same since.

He seemed kind, though, genuinely kind. There was a warmth about his voice—soothing, calming—an almost fatherly tone.

He's a curious soul for sure, Katherine thought as she finished brushing her hair.

She gave her uniform a quick inspection in the mirror before grabbing her cap, tucking it under her arm, and leaving her room. She marched through the *Spirit's* winding corridors—making this left and that right purely from the memory of having passed through this way only once before. Her sharp memory served her well here. Though only a hundred meters long, it would be easy to get lost inside this ship. She arrived at the bulkhead to Carr's room. She rapped firmly on the metal three times.

"Enter," she heard Carr say from the other side.

She tapped the door's central holographic display and it opened.

Carr was reading something on the computer terminal at his desk. His dress jacket was hung over the back of the chair and the sleeves of his white shirt were rolled up to his elbows. It looked like he hadn't slept since she had last seen him. He appeared exhausted but stood when she entered.

Before Katherine could salute, he held up his hand and said, "At ease, Commander." He gestured to a chair. "Please, sit." As she nestled down in a seat, he asked, "Did you get any rest?"

"Yes, sir," she replied. "Did you? You look tired."

"Unfortunately, sleep wasn't part of the benefits I received once I took this job. Glad you were able to get some, though. You're going to need to be awake and attentive for this Council Assembly we're attending."

Katherine quizzically cocked an eyebrow. "Um … *we,* sir?"

"Yes," Carr said. "We." He leaned back in his chair. "Before I met you at the academy, an order went our across the Coalition, recalling all Councilors to Katana for an emergency meeting. The situation was classified as Enclave level. It's not something that happens every day. They're keeping details battened down tight. All I know right now is contact with the Tilarus Facility on Atlantis has been lost."

"That's where the crystal is, right?"

Carr nodded. "Yes."

"Is it the Rebels?"

Carr shook his head. "No. The entire Council wouldn't have been recalled like this if it had been, and definitely not under the pretense of an Enclave-level emergency. This is something else. And as for the 'we,' I've spoken with Chairman Fercon and requested you be allowed to attend the Assembly. As the new head of the research effort into the Artifacts Project, and given the reason this session was called to order, I feel shutting you out isn't going to help speed things along. In fact, I'm sure you'll be of some help."

"Admiral," Katherine began, "I—"

The overhead coms snapped on and a voice said, "Admiral Carr, sir? We've arrived. There's a shuttle waiting for you in the hangar bay."

"Understood," Carr said.

The channel snapped off.

"Ask me anything you'd like on the way," Carr said and grabbed his jacket. "How long do you need to pack your things?"

"I never took most of them out of my duffle bag, sir," Katherine replied.

"Excellent. Go grab it and meet me in the lift."

"Yes, sir."

She hurried back to her room. She gathered her toiletries and stuffed them into the duffel. She zipped it up and made for the lift where Carr was waiting for her beside the elevator door with his hands clasped behind his back.

Katherine could swear he appeared to perk up when she appeared around the corner, but, concluding it was her imagination, she dismissed the thought.

"Have you ever been to Katana?" Carr asked her on the way down.

She shifted her weight to take some of the duffel's pressure off her right shoulder. "No, sir. But it was on my bucket list."

The lift jolted to a stop. The doors parted for them and they stepped into the shuttle's hangar. It was small and cramped, with only a single transport craft docked on the far side. By the craft's airlock, three armed marines were ready to accompany her and Carr down to Katana's surface.

It didn't take long for them all to board and get strapped in. The transport's engines rumbled to life and she lifted vertically off the deck. The pilot tapped the aft thrusters and the tiny craft tore out of the hangar with surprising speed.

Katherine leaned forward in her seat and looked up the aisle into the cockpit. Through the canopy, she got her first glimpse of the UGC's capital planet.

Cream-colored clouds swirled high in Katana's skies. Great swaths of green jungle covered each great continent. The largest of the continents—Palador—easily dwarfed the others in size. Lakes hundreds of kilometers wide provided water and hydroelectric power to dozens of sprawling megacities. Mountains carpeted in rich shades of green and brown that were twice the size of anything on Earth towered above the ground. Glistening emerald seas ripe with islands and hundreds of kilometers of archipelagos encompassed all major landmasses. The oceans surrounding it were teeming with exotic marine life: Opular Fish, Fintoctopi, and massive striped Sunwhales three times as large as the biggest marine mammal on Earth.

Incoming and outgoing traffic was innumerable—thousands of vessels crisscrossed lanes in open space. Thirty massive ODSs held hundreds of freighters, warships, and private and leisure craft, while Vakarus Station, the most gargantuan orbital docking installation in existence, berthed another six hundred ships. There were thirty-five refit-and-repair stations orbiting the planet, each so large the mightiest ships in the galaxy—the Elysium-class Dreadnaughts—were able to dock with them, and twenty-seven shipyards where numerous warship hulls were under construction.

Katana was protected by the First Coalition Fleet, a home fleet of five hundred and seventy starships ranging in size from corvettes to mighty dreadnaughts. Five hundred Omega-class Orbital Weapon Platforms (OWPs) drifted in high orbit above the planet. Each station was built around a colossal magnetic accelerator cannon that used electromagnetism to accelerate a four thousand ton ferrous projectile at terrifying speed.

Seventeen billion inhabitants called Katana home, including its natives, the Vakari—a race of militaristic, saurian beings. Over the centuries, they had transformed their home into the hub of all military activity in the UGC. Katana held the title of the most heavily populated planet in settled space.

The little shuttle shook when she entered the planet's red-tinted atmosphere. As they broke through the cloud cover, Katherine saw something that took her breath away.

A black stalk rose in the distance, growing inexorably larger as the shuttle approached. It was a line stretching from the ground high into the sky—a tower, vast, unimaginably tall. Its peak stabbed through the clouds and scraped the planet's lower atmosphere.

Katherine knew immediately what it was: UGC Headquarters— Zenith Tower, the nexus of the Coalition and all it stood for—an impregnable, forty kilometer-high bastion of black steel and stone. It was not only the heart of Katana, but also the heart of all the Milky Way.

She had never seen anything like it. She knew it existed of course, but to see it … it was a remarkable piece of architectural engineering. She gazed in amazement until it disappeared behind a row of buildings when their transport landed on a pad at one of the Tower's outlying facilities.

The bay lights above her changed from red to green. Katherine eagerly unbuckled her harness and slung her bag over her shoulder. The airlock cycled open. She followed Carr out and onto the pad.

The temperature on Katana was warm, tropical, and sunny.

Thousands of shuttles and transport craft zoomed a few kilometers overhead, and some only a few dozen meters. The hum of engines and smell of exhaust filled the air as transports and military dropships touched down to the left and right of their pad as far as the eye could see. The Tower had an enormous influx of traffic.

A lieutenant in navy dress strolled across the pad toward them. An ID card on his breast pocket identified him as a HighCom security officer. He had a K2 magnum holstered at his side.

"Lord Carr, Commander Taylor," he said and saluted. "Chairman Fercon has sent ahead an order that none of the Councilors are to be stopped by security. If you two would please follow me, we'll go straight to the Tower."

For some reason, Katherine was relieved when the security detail trailing her and Carr finally departed while they followed the lieutenant to a small shuttle-car. They jumped into a reserved lane of traffic and flew through every security checkpoint without stopping.

Zenith Tower's outlying buildings stretched out from the main tower like the spokes of a wheel. Though Katana's capital—Elima City—rested a few kilometers away to the northeast, the Tower complex was a city unto itself.

Soon, their shuttle slowed to a stop twenty meters from the Tower Gate in the Outer Courtyard, a paved stone yard enclosed by a twenty meter-high granite wall.

Katherine stepped out behind Carr. She craned her neck skyward for a look at Zenith Tower. It rose for several kilometers, but became shrouded in clouds the farther up she looked until it totally disappeared. A flight of native Swapbeak birds squawked as they passed high above.

"You'll have to leave your bag with me, ma'am," the lieutenant said to Katherine. "I'll make sure it gets back to you."

She complied and followed the Admiral on. They flashed their IDs to a pair of MPs at the security checkpoint and were admitted through the gate.

The Inner Courtyard spanned the entire eight kilometer base of Zenith Tower. Trees and flowers grew in abundance in perfectly pruned gardens spread at even intervals across its expanse. Everything about the Tower was huge, massive—the walk from the gates to the titanic twelve meter-high double doors was a thirty-meter march.

Happy birds warbled enthusiastically in the tops of the tall Blackwood trees.

Katherine was mesmerized by the staggering variety of beautiful, brightly colored flora: reds and greens, blues and yellows, purples, whites, and pinks. She'd always loved flowers. Seeing these reminded her of when she was a young girl picking wildflowers on the banks of the Telimad River outside the city back home on Serimar. She would come home with a huge bundle in her hand to give to her grandmother, who would place them in a large vase and proudly display them as the centerpiece on the dining table.

This place was almost *too* serene, like something out of a dream. Hopefully, there'd be no alarm clock to wake her up this time.

The guards on post by the entrance stood to arms as a collection of internal cogs and gears began to turn, and the huge, dull-golden colored double doors of Gate 033 swung silently wide open.

She followed Carr through and into the Tower Presidium.

And she thought the Courtyards were big.

The Presidium floor stretched one hundred meters on either side of her and was alive with tens of thousands of beings from all over the galaxy. Two hundred people sat at reception desks, and another few hundred marines stood on guard by the impenetrable wall of metal and weapon detectors and scanners of all types.

"Jesus," Katherine muttered under her breath.

Beings of all kinds, from all of the Coalition's fifteen member species to its various client races, worked here here day and night, sometimes for years on end.

She and Carr were directed through to the front of the crowd waiting by the security scanners. The MPs quickly hustled them through to the other side, much to the aggravation of some of the crowd.

Two marble staircases arose from this section of the Presidium and spiraled upward to the second floor. Katherine saw a man standing at the bottom of the east staircase. When she got in range, she spied the insignia on his uniform's collar and recognized him as Albert West, Lord General of the Marine Corps.

He was a bit older than Carr, perhaps late seventies. His grey and silver dress uniform was adorned with a full color spectrum of ribbons and medals.

As they shook hands, West clapped Carr on the shoulder.

"Nice to see you, Terrence," he said.

Carr nodded. "Likewise, Al."

Katherine stood to attention.

"At ease, Commander," West said. "We don't have time for formalities. You two are late. The session's about to begin. Come on." He turned and began the climb up the massive staircase. Carr beckoned Katherine ahead and brought up the rear. When they reached the top, they followed the hallway to an awaiting elevator. West pressed a button on the holographic panel, and the doors closed. The lift began its climb up three thousand three hundred and twenty one floors to the Sanctuary, the Council's assembly room.

The ride up took several minutes. Katherine listened in silence while West filled Carr in on what he had heard in the past few hours.

"Whatever it is," he said, "It's big. I mean *really* big. Fercon's put the military on full alert. Shipping lanes are being closed all across the galaxy. I don't like this, Terrence. Not one bit. I hate not having good intel on *any* situation, and the Chairmen are really keeping the lid on this tight."

Carr nodded his head in acknowledgment. His facial expression was still the same: lips tightly drawn, eyebrows furrowed, though his piercing blue eyes were locked on the elevator's doors in a distant, contemplative stare.

The elevator stopped; the doors opened.

Katherine tried to keep up with Carr and West's quick strides. She followed them past two fountains so grand the water actually ran like a waterfall from the walls and pooled into marble sinks two meters in diameter. The Sanctuary's furnishings were exquisite, unlike anything she'd ever seen before. She knew it was nothing new to Carr or West, not by a long shot considering how long they'd served on the Council, but she'd never seen anything so fancy in her life—paintings on the walls that would sell for millions of credits apiece, astronomically expensive Hermak carpeting, plush, lavishly upholstered furniture; the UGC had spared no expense.

The hallway ahead forked into two separate paths, but both wound their way around the Sanctuary in a circle until they converged into a single short corridor with massive double doors at the far end.

Carr and West gave their uniforms a last, quick check. With a curt nod, Carr prompted Katherine to do the same.

She made sure her nametag was precisely aligned, ribbons perfectly centered, black wool of her dress jacket free of lint. Satisfied with her appearance, she nodded.

Carr gave West a nod of his head, and West opened the door.

The Inner Sanctum was already full when Katherine stepped in behind Carr. Over three hundred pairs of eyes turned to gaze at them.

The room was dominated by two enormous, crescent-shaped tables, each facing the other so they encircled a large holographic display projector. The three hundred Councilors—top ranking officers from the marines and navy, executors, ambassadors, and scientists—were seated at the larger of the two tables; the smaller of the two sat atop a raised dais.

That one was reserved for the Chairmen.

So this was them. This was the committee that decided the fate of not just a planet, or a system, or even a sector, but the entire galaxy. These were the beings that made the UGC what it was. Most were military, but many weren't. These beings, representatives of each of the UGC's fifteen member species and its clients, made the decisions that shaped everyday galactic life.

Katherine took notice of six beings not present in corporeal form, but instead projected holographic images that floated a few centimeters above their seats. They had been too distant to have been recalled in such a short time.

West went left to find his seat. Katherine followed Carr round the table to two empty chairs near the bend. Once seated, she felt a little more comfortable since the room's attention was no longer focused on her.

She couldn't help but wonder what the other Councilors thought of a non-Council member being present for something as serious as an Enclave-level emergency. She mulled over the dozens of possibilities in her mind until she heard someone shout.

"Atten-*hut.*"

The room stood as one.

A small door at the back of the Sanctum opened. The Chairmen walked in—single file—one representative from each member race. They were the elected delegates that represented their people's voice in the galaxy.

Katherine remained at solid attention, daring only to take shallow breaths. She was in the presence of the highest, most important beings in the galaxy.

Human Chairman Samantha Neller took a seat to the left of Vakari Chairman Hurundus Fercon, who was seated in the middle and to the right of Tiberan Councilor P'Turi Omas.

Once settled, Fercon spoke, "You may be seated."

They sat in unison.

"Thank you all for coming on such short notice," Fercon said. "We don't have a lot of time, so I'm going to get straight to the point. At oh-seven-hundred hours on January nineteenth, an unidentified object was detected in the Argus system about two hundred thousand kilometers from planet Atlantis. A nearby cruiser on patrol, the *Memento Mori*, was ordered to investigate. After relaying a visual to FleetCom, the *Mori's* captain followed proper first-contact protocols. He brought his ship to battle stations and attempted to establish communication on a reserved frequency. No response was broadcast back. Exactly thirty-two seconds later, the *Mori* was struck with some kind of energy-based weapon, and exploded. She was lost with all four thousand two hundred hands."

Katherine was a bit unnerved.

That energy weapon must have been incomprehensibly powerful to destroy it in one blow.

Cruisers were huge ships. They boasted extreme firepower and carried a massive contingent of marines and ground vehicles. At over a kilometer long and armored with several meters of rock-hard battle plate, they could take on most anything and win.

Was it a rebel weapon ... or did it belong to something ... *else?*

"Spy drones in the area relayed feeds back to FleetCom HQ that showed this object moving toward planet Atlantis," Fercon continued. "There were noticeable cones of exhaust radiating from aft engine ports and running lights along its lateral lines that confirmed this isn't an *object* at all—it's a *ship*. It moved into orbit over Atlantis, in geosynchronous alignment with the Tilarus research facility. At oh-eight fifty, all communication with Tilarus ceased. We haven't heard a whisper since. There is a very, very small possibility this ship could belong to the Rebel Republic, but the logical, and much more likely possibility, is that we have just made contact with a previously undiscovered alien race."

A troubled murmur worked its way around the room.

Carr and Katherine shared an uneasy glance. They were both thinking the same thing.

The discovery of a new race seeking membership into the UGC, one willing to be peaceful, would cause stress enough. But the discovery of a new alien race that was *hostile* ... well, she couldn't think of anything worse. The Rebels were pushing hard. They'd found new leadership and with it, newfound fire and fanaticism in their cause. A war with another race would mean the UGC would be fighting on two fronts. It wasn't a scenario that would bode well for the UGC. Optimism could only go so far. If there were ever a time for this *not* to happen, it would be now.

"My people still hold true to the belief that there is no such thing as a *coincidence*," Chairman Omas offered. He put emphasis on that last word. "But whatever the motive for attack actually is, I can't dismiss the likelihood that the alien crystal discovered a few days ago in the Atmorus Mountains is somehow linked."

"We know nothing about it," Chairman Neller said, "This crystal—it could be some kind of key to an ancient weapon of mass destruction, or even a weapon itself. Or it might be nothing. Perhaps it's simply a pretty piece of rock, a jewelry piece for whatever race built it. Unfortunately, that isn't a risk we can take. Whatever it is, whoever these attackers are—Rebels or aliens—the UGC cannot afford to let that object fall into their hands. Its recovery is of paramount importance."

Though the alien threat needed to be dealt with, and quickly, Katherine found herself agreeing with Chairman Neller. The crystal's recovery was top priority. It had to be kept safe and studied. If these aliens had indeed attacked because they wanted it, it meant it was important.

"So we send in the marines," a Councilor offered.

There was a murmur of agreement among the Councilors.

"May I offer another option?"

Katherine was surprised to hear the voice had come from Carr. She turned and looked at him.

Fercon leaned forward and meshed his hands together, a smile on his face. "Of course, Admiral."

"We send in the Shadows," Carr said.

A few of the Councilors whispered among themselves.

Katherine furrowed her brow. She had no idea what a *Shadow* was, but the idea seemed to appease Chairmen Fercon and Omas, who leaned back in his chair and folded his huge arms across his chest. Chairman Neller, however, didn't look convinced.

Fercon slowly nodded his head. "I agree. Perhaps this is a job better left to the Shadows. Unfortunately, there isn't a whole lot of time to debate this. Every second spent doing so is another second the attackers gain. I ask that you all weigh the proposition and make your decision." He gave the Council a full three minutes to think, but it looked like most of them had already made their decision long before he said, "All right. All in favor, raise your hand."

There wasn't a second's pause. Three-fourths of the room raised their hands.

All of the Chairmen then turned their heads to look at Fercon, as if searching for his response. Chairman Neller rested her elbows on the table and raised her eyebrows in his direction. Katherine could tell Fercon carried far more political power, more authority, than the rest of the Chairmen. Though they were all considered equals, it was clear Fercon held the highest—yet unofficial—power.

"Then we are agreed," he replied. "We send in a team of Shadow Operatives to recover the crystal. We'll keep you all posted on the situation. I ask that you all remain in the Tower for the time being. The Council will convene again soon. Are there any questions?"

No one spoke.

Fercon stood. "This session is adjourned."

As the Chairmen arose from their seats to leave, everyone stood to respect. Fercon remained standing in front of his chair while the room emptied. Carr stayed in place as well, and Katherine was unsure of whether to leave or to stay. Then he turned to her and said, "I'll explain everything to you shortly. Just hang tight."

Fercon approached them. Katherine almost tripped over her chair trying to get to attention.

"A pleasure to meet you, Commander Taylor," Fercon said. "You've made quite an impression on Admiral Carr. Please, at ease." He looked at Carr and clasped his hands behind his back. With a smile, he said, "The Shadows. Quick thinking, Terrence."

"Like you didn't know," Carr said. "I could tell by the look on your face you knew I was going to propose using my Shadows."

"I wouldn't make a very good politician if I didn't know my own cabinet, now would I? I assume you already have the names of the Operatives you wish to send on the Op?"

"I do, sir," Carr said.

"Then let's hear it."

Katherine heard him say two names; one a human named Soren, and the other an Asgard named Lux.

"This is a high risk mission, for sure," Fercon said. "Who's leading the Op?"

"There's one man I know who'd be best to place in command of the team," Carr said. "He's got one of the most distinguished dossiers of any Shadow in service and just as many medals as you and I do. He's one of my top Operatives."

"I'm all ears, Terrence."

"I can't think of anyone better than Lieutenant Commander Kileeus Scales."

Section II:

A Taste of Things to Come

CHAPTER FIVE

2300 hours, January 20, 2343

Electus Borealis System, planet Tanto

Dai City, The Blackhole Nightclub

The target was close now. He could hear every word the man was saying.

"—and I told that son-of-a bitch he was either going to pay me, or I was going to blow his brains all over the cargo deck."

That got thunderous laughs and hoots from the thugs surrounding him.

Kileeus Scales took a seat at the bar three stools down from his target. He'd have to wait until the man left the nightclub; there were far too many people in here for him to risk a firefight.

Scales absorbed his surroundings, something he'd been trained to do until it was instinct.

First, he needed to find a way out. His eyes darted round the club. He spotted one emergency exit on the far end of the dance floor roughly fifteen meters from his position. The only other way out was the front entrance. There was also a single door in the far southeast corner, likely leading to a staircase.

A good deal of furniture was placed sporadically around the night club; chairs, overly upholstered sofas, tables—good cover should a gunfight erupt. But that was only as a last resort; only if things went badly.

There were close to seven hundred people in the club dancing and drinking. That would make a fair crowd to blend into should he have to double back after the assassination.

Scales had been tracking this human, Hans Greborovitch, for three weeks. He was well renowned for being a major black market trader and one of the biggest crime lords alive. Scales had chased his target all the way from the Prin system to planet Garng, on to the Yesarian Moons and the colonized Hades asteroid belt before finally trailing him to planet Tanto. It was odd that a criminal as notorious as he would choose Tanto as a resting place, as it was nearly bursting at the seams with UGC military activity. MPs and Gate Marshals kept a neat tally of every being leaving, entering, or set to arrive.

How Greborovitch managed to sneak past the security guards at the docks and evade capture was beyond Scales, but it was likely he'd paid someone off.

The man had more tendrils than a sea of orcanopithici, or as the human expression went, he had his fingers in a lot of pies. He had eyes and ears everywhere and an entire network of corrupted politicians and powerful beings from all walks of life. He was slippery, too. When Scales had first received orders to eliminate him due to his actions during the Mindir uprising, which included supplying the local Rebel faction with arms, he had had no idea that the pursuit would have taken him this far into the home sector.

Though pursuing Greborovitch around a few systems, doing some investigating, and staying hidden in the shadows was easy, he'd learned in decades past that a Shadow's mission was *never* as it appeared. There were always endless potential complications—snags—that could turn an outwardly monotonous situation into the worst possible scenario. There weren't many scenarios he couldn't take charge of and turn around, though, no matter how bad. He was sure about that. He'd never lost control of a mission in his life.

Except once. Only once.

That was so many years ago, though. He was so young then. He'd been careless. Foolish. Stupid, even. He had much more experience now, much more wisdom. Scales swore he'd never lose control of another mission again in his life.

Some would have called that oath arrogant. Perhaps they were right. But those that knew the Vakari psyche would say it was part of the natural Vakari way of thinking: an overconfident personality, the ability to keep cool under pressure—both were traits all members of the species carried.

The quills atop his head quivered as he shifted his weight.

Though far from the tallest individual of his race, Scales stood a fraction over two meters tall. A bundle of dark red quills growing from the crown of his very vague reptilian-like head to the base of his neck were tipped with a band of blue, giving a clear indication of his age. He wasn't considered middle-aged yet, at least, not by Vakari standards. His species lived long lives, on average past one hundred years. However, if counting standard Gregorian years, Scales was already in his fifties. He was more fit and in shape now, more attuned to the intense physical demands of being a Shadow than he had ever been before, and had already tucked nearly a lifetime of military and combat experience under his belt.

"What'll it be?" The Tiberan bartender's resonant voice interrupted Scales' thoughts.

The Shadow refocused his attention to the barman in a way that made it seem as though he was nothing more than another anonymous drinker lost in his own thoughts—Instead of a highly trained elite soldier. "Murandia," Scales said. "Neat." A modest liquor, nothing too expensive. It's nice, smooth taste would be a pleasant refreshment, though he didn't make a habit of drinking while on assignment.

"You got it, buddy."

As the bartender turned to remove the bottle of Murandia Special from the shelf, Scales cleared his throat and said, "You know, friend, make that a double."

The tender smiled in acknowledgement; well, the Tiberan equivalent of a smile, anyway, which was more like a click of his mandibles.

A sound tactical choice: if Scales paced his sipping, a double shot of liquor would give him the time he needed to wait for his target to make a move.

Perhaps.

Scales gave Greborovitch a quick side glance with his extraordinary peripheral vision. So far, he hadn't budged. He was still drinking like a fish with his henchmen.

The bartender slid a glassful of liquor across the bar to Scales. Slowly, he sipped it with the air of a man trying to drown-out his troubles.

Scales kept a mental tally of how many drinks his target knocked back: four … six … ten—before reaching almost two dozen. If he continued to drink like this, Scales wouldn't have to kill him; he'd drop dead from alcohol poisoning.

Greborovitch's bodyguards, if that's what such an undisciplined bunch could be called, were consuming as many alcoholic beverages as their employer. Fools, they shouldn't have been diluting their minds. They should have stayed aware of everything going on around them at all times in order to be ready for the unexpected.

And as they would find, the unexpected was only a few barstools away.

The bodyguard numbered six: two Tiberan, a human, two Asgards, and a Vakari.

Scales knew all the thugs by name except for the two Tiberan. This was the first time he'd seen them, though that wasn't a factor that was going to stop him from eliminating them if he had to.

Pacing himself, Scales sipped slowly until Greborovitch finally stood up and stretched.

"All right boys," he slurred. "I gotta take a piss." He picked up the coat draped over the back of his stool and, with the help of a member of his posse, shimmied into it. The bodyguards closed in around Greborovitch in a tight semi-circle and followed him to the restrooms at the other end of the building.

The target was on the move.

All of those weeks of pursuit and spying culminated in this moment: it was time to strike.

The bathroom, a perfect place for a kill: no witnesses, and the enclosed space would be to his benefit. Hand-to-hand combat had always been to his benefit.

He casually downed the rest of his drink and handed his credit chip to the bartender. The Tiberan scanned it, deducting what was owed for the alcohol. He handed it back to Scales and nodded his head in farewell.

Scales arose. He stretched and rubbed at his eyes to further embrace the tired, troubled Vakari he meant to portray. He turned and started for the restrooms, locking Greborovitch firmly in his sights. His eyes narrowed, his vision sharpened; the target zoomed in much closer—much like the enhanced image in a long-range sniper scope.

Scales gently pushed his way through the crowd of beings on the dance floor, not once losing sight of his target. His concentration was solid and impossible to break. The music in the club was so loud that its beat shook the teeth in his head. Excellent. If he should have to use his pistol, no one would notice the noise.

Greborovitch opened the door and disappeared into the bathroom. Both Tiberan bouncers stood watch on either side of the entrance with their arms folded across their chests. The protruding grips of their holstered pistols were meant to be clearly visible.

Scales neared the door. The larger of the two Tiberan—and that was saying a lot—eyed him suspiciously as he approached them.

In outward appearance, Scales didn't look like much of a threat. The clothes he wore were normal, but expensive. A pair of midnight-black, freshly polished Tikon dress shoes were complemented by dark form-fitting trousers and an equally black thermal shirt, over which was a tailored high-collared black Busharin coat trimmed with emerald colored fabric. The front of the coat was meant to be worn open, flaring out at the waist and hanging down in a split body-wide tail to Scales' calf.

But, as these two thugs were about to find out, looks could be *very* deceiving.

Scales analyzed the situation in the few seconds it took him to stroll up to the Tiberan.

There was no way he was getting into that bathroom while the two were still alive, so he'd have to eliminate them. Using his pistol wasn't an option, as that would compromise his element of surprise. The only way was a stealth assassination.

As Scales closed the last meter of distance between them, he reached inside his coat and rested his hands on the hilts of two hidden, quarter-meter Silven daggers strapped to the back of his belt.

With one fluid movement, Scales unsheathed the knives and lunged forward. In a lightning-quick blur of motion, the throats of both Tiberan were slit before they ever knew what was happening.

They clutched at their wounds, and fell backwards, slumped up against the wall. Blood poured from their deep gashes.

Scales flung the dark violet blood from the knives and quickly sheathed them. As he pulled the bathroom door open he turned and looked out at the club. No one had noticed yet, but he'd have to dispatch his target with great haste; two dead Tiberan were going to attract a lot of attention … and fast.

He entered the bathroom and closed the door behind him.

Greborovitch was relieving himself in one of the urine tubs along the far wall; the rest of his guard were either doing the same thing or washing their hands and faces.

The Asgard bodyguard, a being named Zush, jumped in surprise at the sight of Scales. "Hey!" he yelled, alerting the other bodyguards, "How the hell did you get in here?"

All of the beings in the room turned to face Scales, and none were more surprised than Greborovitch, who stopped midway through zipping up his trousers, an astonished expression frozen on his face. Though drunk, he sure wasn't dumb. He knew the two guards he left at the door wouldn't have let anyone in there alive.

Whatever bewildered feeling Greborovitch had quickly subsided. He smiled and spoke with his usual hint of arrogance. "Man," he said, nodding. "You must think you're big shit, killing two Tiberan like that, huh Vakari? Think you're some kind of badass?"

Scales eyed the thugs, who began taking offensive positions and reaching for their weapons. He readied himself for action.

"I'll tell you what," Greborovitch smirked, "Why don't you show my boys how badass you really are."

With that, the thugs attacked.

The closest bodyguard, a tall and lanky human, thrust a knife towards Scales' abdomen.

Scales sprang into motion. He sidestepped the attack with ease, grabbed the man's wrist and bent his arm backwards until he heard a loud *pop!* The knife fell from his grip. Scales snatched it from midair and sunk it into the back of the man's neck, severing his spinal column.

The thug went limp and fell to the floor with a *thump.*

The rest of the men leapt into action and went for Scales simultaneously.

Zush attempted to tackle him, but Scales stopped him by jabbing him in the throat with outstretched fingers and a hard left hook that knocked him sideways into the wall. His head left a sizable hole.

Scales dropped to the floor on his back, held up by his palms, and kicked his legs in a scissor-motion, sweeping the legs out from under Karrus, the Vakari thug. Before Karrus fell to the ground, Scales sprang backwards through the air, landing on his feet in time to counter a punch from Oran, the second Asgard.

Scales caught the being's punch with his palm and twisted his wrist until it broke. With the vaguely bird-like alien screaming in agony, Scales drew back his fist and smashed it into Oran's beak three rapid, bone-crushing times. The punches had so much force the beak splintered and Oran fell backwards, knocked unconscious, black blood squirting from punctured arteries like little mini fountains. By then, Karrus had recovered from his fall and thrust all of his bodyweight behind a punch. Scales blocked it with crossed forearms and countered with a blow to his mouth. Teeth flew free and skittered across the tiled floor, staggering him.

Scales turned round to see Zush wrench free a towel rack from the wall. He swung it at Scales like a cudgel, but the Shadow was too quick. Scales caught the metal bar in his palm and yanked it from Zush's grasp. He clobbered the Asgard in the head with it, killing him, the thick metal bar bending from the force of the blow. The sound of crunching bone could have been heard on the dance floor.

Taking advantage of the precious split second it took Scales to regain his stance, Karrus fumbled in his jacket and produced a K-2 pistol.

He leveled it and fired.

Scales sprang high into the air in a forward arch, dodging the bullet completely and landing behind Karrus. He quickly turned, but Scales knocked the gun from his hands before he could fire again. He connected a roundhouse kick with the side of Karrus' head and broke his neck.

Oran, though still in excruciating pain, managed to pick himself up off the floor. Putting all of his weight into a tackle, he lunged for Scales at full speed. The Shadow held back all but a tithe of his strength and whipped his leg upward into an arch in a lightning-fast motion. The toe of his boot smashed into the bottom of Oran's chin and sent him flipping head-over-heels before landing on the ground in a crumpled heap—dead. His black blood pooled on the white floor.

Scales spun to face Greborovitch.

The man was petrified in the same spot as when Scales had first walked into the bathroom. His face was twisted into a horrified grimace. Sweat beaded on his forehead and his hands shook as he stared wide-eyed—disbelievingly—at the bodies before his feet, bodies of the toughest men he could find.

He slowly brought his eyes up to meet Scales' gaze.

Scales smiled. "I guess your boys weren't as badass as they thought."

Though the fear on his face was evident, the arrogant bastard still had the nerve to taunt his assassin. He rummaged in his pocket and withdrew a large switchblade.

Scales cocked an eyebrow. This was almost humorous.

"You don't want any of me," the target said in a shaky voice. "I … I'll cut you up good, you hear me?" Greborovitch actually summoned the courage to lunge at him.

Scales' eyes narrowed. A cloud of dark purple began filling the yellow sclera of his eyes, like food coloring dropped into a glass of clear water. His retinas sharpened, and he shot his arm out in front of him, stopping Greborovitch in his tracks and lifting him a meter-and-a-half into the air. He appeared to be wrapped in a transparent field of energy. It glowed purple and encased him like a bubble. He couldn't move a muscle. He screamed in horror as the switchblade he carried slipped harmlessly from his grasp and fell to the floor.

"What are you!?" He screamed. "What's this black magic shit?"

Scales almost laughed.

When he'd used his X interface in the past, he'd heard it called many things, but never "black magic." That was a new one. It definitely wasn't black magic. It wasn't even regular magic. It was science.

Most Shadows possessed the ability of telekinesis. For those that qualified, upon their initiation into the program, Operatives were given an implant on the back of their brainstem. This microscopic chip, dubbed the "X interface" was able to gather unused energy in the brain and culminate it into psychic energy that allowed its user to pull, throw, or lift objects to and from great distances.

Greborovitch hovered in midair a split second longer before Scales flung his arm to the side and slammed him into the wall with bone-crushing force. He released his hold of his X interface and let Greborovitch plummet to the ground. He landed hard on his back. The purple bubble slowly dissipated from his broken body.

Scales walked near and stood over the man's body. His frightened eyes stared back at Scales. He was pathetic—defenseless—completely at the mercy of the assassin who stood looking down at him. Scales pulled a SIB-7 energy blaster from a holster at his side. He looked Greborovitch straight in the eyes for a full second before he squeezed the trigger. The pistol discharged a bolt of energy straight into the man's forehead.

Scales exhaled and lowered his gun.

It was done.

As he holstered the SIB, the gears in his mind began to turn. He had to find an exit. There was no way he could leave the way he had come in; his act would be witnessed by every being in the club. The last thing he needed was someone seeing him leaving the scene of a massacre.

Shadows did things like that in secret. That's why they were called Shadows.

There was no way of knowing exactly how long it would be until someone saw the two dead Tiberan at the door. Seconds, maybe. A minute. He didn't know, but he did realize that he needed to get out of there as soon as he could.

Scales searched the bathroom for an exit. He spotted a thin tin vent covering a duct in the ceiling. That was his ticket out. He moved across the room in a rapid stride, opened one of the stall doors, and stood on the toilet. The vent came free with little effort. He gripped both sides of the duct and hoisted himself up, pulling his entire body into the ceiling with his powerful biceps.

Mere moments later, the bathroom door opened, and in walked four members of the club's security force, pistols drawn.

"What the stars happened here?" one of them asked as he stood horrified at the sight of five bloodied corpses.

Scales heard their conversations continue while he made his way through the duct. As quickly as he could, he belly-crawled through the dusty, grimy shaft—following it until he came to the exit he'd hoped for: another grate, this one with beams of light shooting through its bars—shafts of light that were coming from the outside. He could hear the muffled sound of city life; his freedom lay just beyond those bars. This grate was thicker than the former, however. There was no way he was going to rip it off with sheer strength. That left one alternative.

Scales un-holstered his SIB, aimed, and fired at the grate's weakest points. The iron sagged and melted. After a few more shots, Scales was able to kick it out of his way. It clattered to the street below.

He jumped out of the duct, dropped three meters, and found himself in an alleyway beside The Black Hole. When he walked back round to the club's entrance, he overheard two men talking on the sidewalk.

"I'm telling you, man," one of them said. "This club is to die for."

Scales smiled to himself. He walked nearer the two men and said, "I actually just left. I found myself displeased."

"Why is that?" the other asked.

"Someone left a big mess in the bathroom."

With that, Scales, smiling at his dark humor, turned and walked away.

He started down a dimly lit street back to his apartment and disappeared into the shadows.

Fifteen minutes later, he approached the front door of his pad. During his time spent on Tanto, he had lived in one of the Shadow's many safehouses, one of the mundane looking apartments or condos that served as an Operative's base of operations. There were thousands in the galaxy with at least one on every major planet, moon, or colonized asteroid, depending on its size. Some planets were home to a dozen or more.

It was pitch black on Tanto by then. Its two moons had faded behind the Chexsena Mountains and the street's lights, though on, didn't provide the greatest illumination.

Scales was about to open the door when he stopped dead. It was already slightly ajar.

Someone was inside.

He immediately un-holstered his SIB and stepped into the house. He cleared his corners. There was no one in the hallway. Scales reached behind him. He shut the door and locked it quietly.

If someone was bold enough to break into a Shadow safehouse, then they were going to have to deal with the Shadow. There was no escaping.

He swept the ground floor room by room, but found nothing. Then, he had a curious revelation: the door wasn't forced open; it wasn't even damaged, so that meant no forced entry. Whoever was currently hiding in his house clearly had access to the Shadow safehouses; a safehouse couldn't be opened without confirmed verbal verification of a code word unique to that particular Shadow and confirmation of their voice patterns by High Command. A thief wouldn't have that ability. Even a Rebel counter-operative, a Snake, wouldn't be able to open the door. It was simply impossible to break into a Shadow Safehouse.

That left only one other possible explanation: there was another Shadow in Scales' house.

He didn't know how that was possible; there weren't any other Shadows on the entire planet.

Something wasn't right, and that was all the more reason not to let his guard down.

With one final glance around the foyer, Scales started up the stairs, treading softly, his footfalls noiseless. He reached the top stair and stepped onto the threshold of the second floor. His acute sense of hearing picked up the slightest of sounds; something that sounded like someone dropping a needle on a concrete floor. It came from behind the door at the end of the hall behind him. He spun round and brought his

SIB to bear. He gripped it tight. He walked the length of the corridor, took a deep breath—

—and the door opened to reveal a man standing there, holding a pistol of his own; both men had their weapons trained at the other's head.

Simultaneously they both dropped their guns.

Scales exhaled explosively in relief. "Goddamn it, Soren," he said frustratingly. "I almost blew your head off."

Soren, a fellow Shadow, stretched his lips into one of his trademark big, toothy, defiant smiles. "I could have shot you, too, you know."

Scales sighed. "What are you doing here? And why are you in your dress uniform?" He brushed past Soren and took a seat in a chair by the hearth. "I wasn't aware there were any Operatives on assignment in this system."

Soren took a seat adjacent to him on an expensive looking armchair. "There weren't," he said. "At least not until today."

Scales cocked his eyebrow in a silent question.

"The boss needs us." Soren sat back lazily in the chair and crossed his legs. "Got some beer, by any chance?"

"The boss needs us?" Scales repeated in question, ignoring Soren's request. "Who's us?"

"You, me, and Lux."

"For what?"

"You didn't get the message?"

Scales shook his head. "No," he regretfully admitted. "The last assignment I was on, this idiot pulled a knife and tried to stab me with it. He would have succeeded if my telecom pad hadn't cushioned the blow."

"You actually let him stab you?" Soren laughed. "Is the great Kileeus Scales starting to lose his touch?"

"No, there were six of them."

"So? You've fought more."

"Yes, but I didn't see the fifth or sixth man until they jumped down from the roof of a building."

Soren laughed. "You're getting old, Kileeus. Perhaps you should retire?"

"Soren," Scales said, trying to refocus the attention back on the matter at hand. "What did the Admiral say?"

"The message I got yesterday said that we were to make for the nearest spaceport, and that transportation would be waiting to take us to the Paracturus Sector."

"The Paracturus Sector?" Scales repeated. "What the hell for? Why way out there?"

Soren shook his head. "I don't know. The message didn't say, but I was told there would be a briefing once we arrived. The captain of the ship taking us is an old friend of ours."

"Penkala?"

Soren nodded his head. "The very same."

"Hmm," Scales muttered. "When do our orders say we leave?"

"Now. Penkala's ship has orders to leave from *Nerafis* Deep Docking Station at oh-four hundred tomorrow. That gives us a little under five hours. Are you ready?"

Scales stood. "I need to get a few things here first. What about Lux? Where's he? And how did you know you'd find me here?"

"I was nearby. I checked the Shadow Database and saw you were on Tanto. I know you too damn well—knew what safehouse you'd be using, so I thought I'd drop by. I honestly had no idea you were out, though. And I talked to Lux over telecom. He's on Hyperion Two. I assured him we'd beat him to *Nerafis.*"

Scales smiled. "No we won't." He arose and started for the bedroom. "When have we ever beaten Lux *anywhere?* I need to shower and change. Give me five minutes."

CHAPTER SIX

"Ten-*hut,*" Scales called as Captain Penkala walked through the bulkhead and into the briefing room.

He was a behemoth of a human, in his mid-sixties, standing around six-foot-nine and heavily muscled. He had a full head of pure white hair, greyed ages ago, and a long, discolored scar that ran from his left temple to the corner of his mouth. The blow to the face that gave him the blemish also blinded his left eye. He'd been a Shadow himself once, many decades ago, but had long since retired from active Shadow service. However, he and his ship still continued to serve, ferrying Operatives to and from high-risk missions.

"As you were," Captain Penkala said.

Scales, Lux, and Soren took their seats.

"It's good to see you again, Kileeus," Penkala said. "And you, Soren, Lux."

"And you, sir," Scales said.

"Likewise, Captain," Soren said.

Lux nodded respectfully.

The Captain cleared his throat. "Normally I'm not given the details of your missions, but this is a special case. This isn't one of your usual assignments." He handed each of the Shadows a holopad.

Scales took a minute to look it over. As he read, he narrowed his eyes in deep thought. He and his team would be up against an assumed alien threat. The word "alien" meant they had an enemy no one had encountered before. The prospect of a race of beings they had no intel on, nor knew what to expect from, troubled him deeply. He didn't like it.

"Sir," Scales asked, "HighCom believes these aliens are after this artifact?"

"Correct," Penkala replied. "So if they want it, it's got to be important. Your mission is to recover that crystal and wipe the facility's storage bank clean of all data, whatever the cost. HighCom considers these objectives an alpha priority."

"What about survivors?" Soren asked.

"All that matters is that artifact," Penkala answered. "Command considers the rescue of survivors as a secondary objective. You get in and get out, understood?"

"Yes, sir," they answered.

Scales didn't like that. The mission was important, he agreed. But if there were survivors there… he stopped himself. He'd cross that bridge when he got to it. No use in dwelling on it now.

"While you're on the ground," Penkala said, "a UGC battle group is going to distract the alien ship from orbit and draw its attention away from the Tilarus facility—giving you a smokescreen of sorts to slip in quickly and quietly. Scales, you're being given tactical command of the recovery op. Do whatever you need to do to complete your mission, understood?"

"Understood sir," Scales replied.

For all the unknowns in this mission, he felt a million times better that Soren and Lux would have his back in this. After three years apart on separate missions, designation "Knife Team" was back in action together.

"The Office of Requisition was kind enough to put a few field armories in the hold," Penkala said. "The three of you will have access to a good arsenal. With that, I'll conclude this briefing and give you time to plan. We're about four hours out from Atlantis. Let me know if you need anything."

The Shadows stood to attention as Penkala left the briefing room.

Scales analyzed his teammates. He knew Lux and Soren well. They were his two closest friends—and he was well aware of their abilities.

Lux had the sharpest eyes of anyone Scales had ever served with, and that was really saying something. He could shoot a target through the scope of a sniper rifle right between the eyes from four kilometers away.

Soren had remarkable knowledge of explosives and his expertise in electronics was unsurpassed. He was qualified to pilot almost *anything*—starships, dropships, interceptors—the list went on. Soren also had extensive weapons training.

Scales himself was a master of hand-to-hand combat, martial arts, and assassinations, and his accuracy with a firearm was surpassed by few. Though nowhere near the strongest or fastest of the Shadows, he was definitely the cleverest. He was also classified as an X2, the second most powerful grade of psychic users in the program.

Between the three of them, they'd be unstoppable. Their skills would have no weaknesses. Where one was frail, the other was strong. There'd be no task they couldn't accomplish as a team.

"Okay, boss," Soren said to Scales, "what's the plan?"

For hours, Scales, Soren, and Lux reviewed topographical data and schematics of the facility, and they watched the footage recorded from the time *Momento Mori* encountered the alien ship up to the time of its destruction. To Scales' regret, they couldn't pull up any footage from Tilarus' internal security cameras to actually see what the enemy looked like—if they were indeed aliens and not Rebels. From the available data, Scales didn't think it was the latter, but one never knew what to expect where they were concerned. They'd given the UGC some surprises before.

The Shadows finished formulating their battle plan by the time the lights in the briefing room flashed red once, twice, and a klaxon followed—signaling the Shadows that the *Autumn* was nearing its drop off point. They took the elevator down to the cargo deck and began to don their Venerator combat armor.

EPITAPH: REVEILLE

Venerator armor was unique from all other combat suits the UGC military produced. It was comprised of several different layers of special materials, most of which were developed specifically for the Shadow Program. The armor also came in a wide range of different variations tailored to suit any mission or an Operative's individual needs.

But armor only provided defensive protection. It was in offensive power that a Shadow truly excelled.

Scales removed a MAR-5 assault rifle from its rack. The MAR was the UGC's mainline workhorse weapon. It had a high rate of fire, was reasonably accurate for an assault rifle, and carried a thirty-two round magazine that was capable of firing a host of ten millimeter rounds, from Armor Piercing to shredder, to more exotic types.

His sidearm needed to fit the mission. He usually carried a SIB-7—one of the military's only energy-based weapons—but he decided against it. A SIB didn't have enough kick.

The plan was to go in heavy.

In favor, he chose a K-2 pistol, thinking its 12.7-millimeter slugs would provide firepower the SIB simply couldn't. He slid it into a holster on his thigh and sheathed a combat knife on the side of his boot.

Scales grabbed six extra clips each for his MAR and pistol. He slipped them into pouches on either side of his waist. Two frag grenades were held in place by magnetic strips on his right thigh.

OMI had provided two additional pieces of equipment for this mission. The first was a homing beacon. When activated, Captain Penkala would be able to home in on their position and extract them.

The second was a transparent, steel-glass cylinder meant for holding the crystal. It was magnetized so his armor could carry it.

He was ready. A quick look at Lux and Soren said they were, too.

Per their plan, Lux had the role of sniper, hefting a Seraph sniper rifle as his primary weapon.

Soren slid a clip into his MAR and cycled the bolt. The corridors were tight in Tilarus, so he elected to sling a X77 shotgun across his back for close-in work. Grenades and magazines lined his waist.

They double-checked all of their gear, taking care to make sure everything was in perfect working order. If, for some reason, even one piece of equipment malfunctioned on the battlefield, or even worse, in the middle of combat, the result could be fatal.

Scales' stomach suddenly lurched, which meant that the *Autumn* had just dropped out of FTL. The hold's iridescent tube lights went blue and flickered twice. The XO's voice came over the coms.

"Transition from FTL to sublight successful. We've begun our approach to Atlantis and are running dark. All crews: battle stations. I repeat, battle stations. Set Condition Alpha throughout the ship."

"Fancy a wager?" Soren asked.

Lux balanced the tip of a titanium-carbide combat knife on his finger. "What?"

"Fifty creds says I get the first kill."

Lux kept the knife perfectly balanced for a second longer, then his hand jumped. The knife arched high into the air, the blade gleaming in the light. In one fluid motion Lux plucked it mid-fall, twirled it between his three digits, and sheathed it in place on his chest. He looked at Soren. "You're on."

Soren smiled. "Now we're talking." He turned to Scales. "What about you? Fifty creds?"

Scales shook his head. "No. I still owe Lux a hundred creds from last time."

"Jesus, man," Soren said. "That was three years ago. How do you even remember that?"

"I do," Lux calmly piped in.

"Well of course *you* do," Soren said. "You're an Asgard. You guys remember like … every time you've ever done *anything.*"

"What can I say," Lux said flatly. He shrugged. "It's a gift."

Scales heard the elevator doors hiss as they opened, and the men looked over to see Captain Penkala step into the hold.

"The battle group has arrived," he told them. "They're about to distract the ship and give us our smokescreen. Two kilometers out is the closest I can get you. Any closer and we risk being seen. Activate your beacon once you've got the crystal in your possession and we'll pick you up. Good luck, Knife Team."

Scales, Soren, and Lux snatched their helmets from the tables and pulled them over their heads. The airtight pressure seals locked. Their

HUDs (Heads Up Display) came to life—team biomonitors, a smart-link to their weapons, a compass, a motion sensor, and FOF tags were displayed on the inside of their helmet's visors.

The bay doors opened with a rush of cool air. Knife Team inched closer to the edge of the ramp.

Scales peered over and saw white, snowy terrain thirty meters below them. He exhaled slowly and closed his eyes. He cleared his mind of all thoughts, worries, and doubts. The mission objective—and the safety of his team—was the only thing he needed to be concerned with right now.

He opened his eyes.

The light above them pinged green.

"Shadows," Scales said. "Execute."

Knife Team jumped out of the moving prowler, freefalling nearly a hundred feet before landing on the hard ground below. Their armor's physics threshold cushioned the blow to little more than a stomp. Scales stood erect and watched the *Autumn* zoom overhead, arch high into the atmosphere, and disappear in the clouds.

He shouldered his MAR-5.

"We're on our own now, guys," he said. "Stay alert."

Two green acknowledgement lights, representing Soren and Lux, winked on his helmet's HUD.

A hilly landscape, blanketed by a thin carpet of white snow and dotted with leafless trees and a vast variety of plants, stretched out before them. Tufts of dead, light brown grasses poked through the snow, scattered in bunches as far as the eye could see in all directions. The ground leveled out some kilometers away, eventually flattening out and rolling to a halt at the roots of a mountain range, where the Tilarus facility—and the crystal—were waiting.

Scales held up his hand. With two fingers, he motioned his team forward.

CHAPTER SEVEN

Motes of amber lights flickered to life, warmed to gold, and spun clockwise, collecting in a tight circle and culminating into a bright strobe of white light. The *Brandenburg* materialized into normal space and slowed to sublight speed as she emerged from an FTL jump.

She was followed closely by three frigates, *Light from High Heaven*, *Emerald Eyes*, and the *Pyongyang*.

"Exit from FTL successful. Drive cores are hot," Lieutenant Lushe said from engineering.

The hum from the ship's FTL drive could be heard as it cooled.

"All weapons systems online," Lieutenant Terrik reported from weapons.

"Coms online," Lieutenant Verran said.

"Navigations online," Lieutenant Mor called.

"We're green across the board, Captain," Lieutenant Gaeda, the ship's tactical officer, reported.

Captain Bill Parsons gave his tactical officer a nod.

"Retract blast doors, Lieutenant Gaeda," Parsons said.

"Aye, sir."

The titanium blast plating protecting the bridge's wrap-around glass viewscreen pulled back to reveal an Earth-sized planet, boldly framed against a starry backdrop, spinning lazily on its axis.

Thousands of kilometers of rich emerald oceans glimmered as they reflected the light from the Argus system's G2V-type star. Fluffy white clouds glided gracefully with the wind, drifting silently over a green, snow patched continent.

From up here, Atlantis looked deceptively tranquil—still, quiet, calm.

But God knew what was going on down there. These attackers—be they aliens or Rebels—may very well have killed every last one of those poor souls at Tilarus.

"Rendezvous with the rest of the battle group has been successful," Gaeda reported. "They all report green across the board."

"Move us into battle formation Delta," Parsons ordered.

"Aye, aye," Lieutenant Mor replied.

The *Brandenburg*'s engines flared. She maneuvered into a wedge formation with the other ships, with her right at the tip.

On the observation window, a small white box framed an object sixty-five thousand kilometers in the distance.

"Lieutenant Gaeda," Parsons said as he stared intently at the screen. "Magnify."

"Aye."

The image enlarged and leapt forward on the main viewscreen for a closer look.

Aliens or not, this ship sure *looked* alien.

The prow of the ship—if indeed that's what it was—was shaped like a teardrop. Amidships, it was bloated and swollen, like it was ready to burst. A half-dozen bulbous lobes protruded from this grossly deformed-looking midsection, and dozens of craggy, sharply tapered spires shot out from its ventral hull. Its stern ended in such a way that it afforded the ship the appearance of some kind of wildly alien cuttlefish.

Side charts appeared next to the image and relative data scrolled across them. Spectroscopes attempted to read and then analyze the ship's proportion of elements, then the words *"Error—Elements Unknown"* appeared overtop the graph.

Wherever this thing had come from, it was massive—six kilometers from stem to stern.

That was the size of the largest ship in the UGC arsenal, the Elysium-class dreadnaught. An entire fleet of warships couldn't withstand the punishment even a single Elysium dreadnaught could give.

Parsons' battle group only numbered four—his destroyer plus three light frigates. If this ship possessed the firepower of an Elysium dread-naught—and why wouldn't it—would four ships be enough?

As a commander, it was his job to weigh in every factor, every odd—and that included the likelihood of success.

Defeat … death … they were sobering thoughts—ones that dangled dangerously close to becoming a reality—and ones that would keep him on his toes, keep him alert and focused on winning—on surviving. He was going to do what he did best—lead. Lead and win.

Parsons turned to his coms officer. "Lieutenant Verran, try to hail it one last time."

"Aye, aye," she replied.

Parsons tapped his foot nervously on the deck as he watched ten seconds tick off the holoclock bolted above the prow viewscreen.

"Unable to establish communication of any kind, Captain," Verran said. She was a green officer, and young. Her lack of experience made it difficult for her to conceal the distress that seeped into her voice.

Parsons exhaled slowly. He'd reserved a grain of hope—just a grain—that perhaps this altercation could have been resolved peacefully without the loss of lives, but if those bastards wanted a fight, he'd gladly give them one. "Patch us through to Command."

"Aye, sir. Buoy located, uplink established."

The weathered face of Fleet Admiral Roger Tang, director of Fleet Command, snapped up on the main holographic display screen in front of Parsons. Parsons straightened his posture.

"Talk to me, Captain," Tang said.

Parsons clasped his hands behind his back. "We have arrived sir," he said. "Target is in sight. Our attempts at communication have been unsuccessful, as predicted. Battle Group Prometheus reports all green. We're ready, holding station approximately sixty-five thousand kilometers out. Request permission to engage."

The Admiral nodded. "Permission granted. You have a green light to engage. I repeat, green light to engage. Execute Operation: Nightshade."

Parsons nodded. "Acknowledged, sir. We will engage. Operation: Nightshade to commence."

"Captain … good luck. I'll be standing by on the priority channel. Let me know the minute that thing is a pile of floating scrap. Admiral Tang out." His image faded. The screen cut to black.

Parsons locked his gaze with the alien ship on his viewscreen. His eyes were slits.

Though apprehensive, years of careful training prevented Parsons from showing the slightest trace of it. He had to maintain a calm demeanor; set a good example. It was his job as a commander. In battle, soldiers looked to their leaders for guidance. If he displayed calm, showed them he was in control and confident, they would feel that way, too.

But the truth was. He was just as nervous as his crew was.

"Lieutenant Gaeda," he called. "Sound General Quarters. Set Condition Alpha throughout the ship."

"Aye, sir," Gaeda replied.

The overhead lights in the CIC flickered three times. Warning klaxons sounded all throughout the destroyer to alert the crew to their combat stations.

"Guns," Parsons said. "Disengage all weapon locks. Begin charging Aegis capacitors to one hundred percent. Warm up all offensive railguns. Prime Rapture missile pods oh-one through ten and get me a firing solution. Standby to engage on my order."

"Aye, sir," Terrik replied. His nimble Uran fingers danced across the keypad as he rapidly typed in commands.

"Helm," Parson continued, "heading zero-three-one, inclination one-seven point seven-four. Engines to two-thirds power. Divert the other third to the Aegis capacitors."

"Aye, aye, sir," Lieutenant Mor replied. "Heading zero-three-one. Inclination one-seven point seven-four."

The *Brandenburg* set out on her new course and nosed slightly "up," aligning herself with the enemy ship.

"Echelon is right beyond us Captain," Verran reported. "They report they're combat ready. Battle group is standing by and is waiting for you to make the first strike before engaging."

"Weapon locks disengaged, sir," Terrik called from his station. "Aegis cannon charged and ready to fire." He tapped the screen in front of him. "Railgun systems are hot. Missiles armed and crews standing by. Aegis and Rapture firing solutions plotted."

Parsons would open up with his ship's main cannon, the Aegis, first.

Ship-mounted Aegis cannons functioned as the primary offensive weapon on UGC warships. They operated on the same magnetic acceleration principles orbital Omegas did, though Aegis cannons were scaled much smaller in size. Their size, however, did not diminish their power. When fully charged, they could fire three hundred ton ferrous-tungsten rounds to a speed of over two-thousand kilometers per second every four seconds. The impact from just one round expelled enough kinetic energy to surpass any nuclear explosion.

Heavy destroyers like the *Brandenburg* were graced with having a much larger version than other vessels. She could fire a round twice as heavy, though she took three times as long to recharge. It was both a blessing and a curse. It required a destroyer's commander to time his shots perfectly in battle.

Parsons smiled inwardly—it was also what made destroyer captains so damn good. "Lieutenant Terrik," he said over his shoulder. "Fire Aegis."

"Aye, sir. Aegis firing."

The lights in the *Brandenburg*'s CIC dimmed as the Aegis cannon coughed. The firing sequence sent a boom reverberating along the length of the destroyer's hull.

The round flew across the abyss of space—a slug of super-heated metal blazing red-hot across the blackness.

Parsons held his breath and waited for the round to hit as he gazed at the enlarged image of the ship on the screen in front of him. He could hear his heart pounding. He counted the seconds to impact.

It struck.

"Direct hit," Terrik reported.

The Aegis round smashed into the starboard side of the alien ship's hull.

A plume of fire and grey smoke sprayed into space as the super-dense round punctured the armor plating and tore through the interior of the ship.

The vessel was knocked sideways into an erratic spin, but only briefly. As its captain regained control, RCS thrusters fired corrective bursts and the spinning slowed until it eventually stopped.

That's when Parsons saw it.

The Aegis round had left a small, jagged, red-ringed hole in the ship's starboard armor, amidships. It was leaking ribbons of red plasma that vented into space. There were cracks in its armor near the area of impact. They too belched plasma.

Parsons heart fluttered. He blinked.

He'd made *barely* a dent. A *dent*.

It was clear to him now these were no Rebels—they were indeed aliens.

Their armor plating was exponentially more powerful, more durable than anything the UGC possessed. Even the largest ship in the Coalition's fleet would have suffered serious damage from a single destroyer's Aegis round.

"Okay," he muttered. "Let's see how many you can stand before I crack you wide open. Terrik: ready another Aegis round."

"Aye, aye."

Parsons knew nothing about this armor, what it could endure, or what it was even made from. However, he *was* confident that *nothing* could withstand any sustained barrage from an Aegis cannon for long.

He may not have caused much damage, but he'd certainly gotten their attention.

The alien vessel slowly came about—turned to face the battle group. Motes of brilliant crimson light flickered into existence on the ship's bow and gathered into a circle, slowly becoming bright enough to pass for a star twinkling in the distance.

"Thermal sensors are registering a major heat spike, Captain," Lieutenant Gaeda warned.

The bright sphere of energy on the alien ship's hull became so intense the ship itself seemed to disappear in an aura of red light … then there was a blinding flash.

A fine red beam tore across the emptiness of space and closed the distance to its target in an instant.

The beam hit the *Emerald Eyes* on her bow. It bisected her.

Parsons' heart leapt into his throat. He watched the two sections of the frigate drift silently apart. Strobes of light flashed and flared as explosions and decompressions ejected debris and hundreds of bodies into dead space.

"Okay," he muttered. "The game's on, you son-of-a-bitch. Lieutenant Mor, break formation. Move us ahead on course zero-zero-one by two-seven-niner. Engines all ahead full."

"Aye, sir," he replied. "Answering all ahead full."

"Verran, tell the battle group to break formation and fire at will."

"Aye aye, Captain."

"Terrik, fire all primed missiles."

"Aye, missiles away."

The crew heard the muffled *thump, thump* of missiles leaving their tubes. The exhaust from a barrage of over one hundred missiles left streaks against the darkness.

They slithered toward their target.

Lieutenant Terrik sat straighter. "Impact in three … two …" he licked his lips, " …one."

Fire splashed across the front of the alien vessel's hull. The missiles tore deep into its armor.

The *Pyongyang* and *Light from High Heaven* answered with a salvo of their own payload of missiles.

However, before the new wave of Raptures could cover half the distance, the alien ship fired a hail of point-defense lasers that vaporized two-thirds of their number.

The rest hit. Explosions erupted with violent effect.

The frigates followed up with a steady stream of Aegis rounds.

"Prime Rapture pods eleven through twenty-five," Parsons ordered. "Plot a firing solution. Aegis status?"

"Aegis at ninety-seven percent, Captain," Terrik answered. "Ninety-eight, ninety-nine … one hundred percent. Aegis ready to fire."

"Give it to them."

"Firing, aye."

The *Brandenburg*'s lights winked and she shuttered. Another heavy round flew true and punched through the ship's prow.

A massive explosion bellowed outward from the new hole, swelled, then quickly died in the vacuum. The ship listed to port, her crumpled nose bleeding red plasma, and was soon obscured in a haze of ionized metal and debris.

"Make sure they don't get up again," Parsons bellowed. "Fire missiles."

"Missiles away!"

The other captains had the same idea. The frigates spit an additional Aegis round apiece, then followed up with another volley of Raptures. They fell in line right behind the *Brandenburg*'s.

This final knockout barrage of more than four hundred high-explosive missiles impacted the alien ship's hull.

Through the haze, faint balls of fire strobed.

"Gaeda," Parsons called over his shoulder. He didn't dare take his eyes off the screen. "Scan for activity of any kind."

"Initiating deep scan," Gaeda said.

Ten seconds elapsed.

"Nothing, sir. I'm not registering any activity from the enemy ship. No lights or energy of any kind detected." He looked up from his station, a smile on his face. "Target destroyed, Captain."

The crew let out a cheer.

Parsons allowed himself a tiny smile.

"Patch me through to the *Heaven* and *Pyongyang*," he said.

"Aye, aye—"

"Sir!" Lushe interrupted. "Our scanners are going haywire!"

The CIC's lights flickered. Every screen and monitor flickered once, twice, then washed over with static and went dead.

"Captain!" Lushe shouted and pointed to the main viewscreen.

Parsons turned right as the curtain of haze swirled, and out of it the alien ship plowed through, two orbs of light charging on the tip of its prow.

Parsons' jaw dropped in disbelief.

"… No."

A pair of crimson beams lanced forth; they scythed into the bows of both the *Heaven* and *Pyongyang*. They were swallowed in a veil of fire.

"Get us out of here, Lieutenant Mor!" Parsons shouted.

But there wasn't time.

All Parsons could do was watch as the alien ship's weapons began recycling for another charge. Dual globes of crimson glowed ever brighter and intense with each millisecond; two hellish orbs, burning with rage and fury, growing angrier and angrier, until finally they were like the eyes of the Devil himself.

He exhaled.

The last things he ever saw were the balls of dazzling red light culminate into twin lances of powerful, utterly deadly energy.

The *Brandenburg*, along with its captain and the rest of its eight hundred crew members, was vaporized.

CHAPTER EIGHT

The com crackled to life.

"Knife-three to Knife-One," Lux said. "No hostiles detected. The area ahead is clear. No movement. The facility looks dark."

"Acknowledged, Knife-three," Scales replied. "Keep your eyes open. Let me know if anything changes."

"Roger that."

Scales knelt, hidden from sight, in a cluster of thick, dark-colored trees.

The branches on the tops of the leafless trees rustled with a frigid breeze that blew in from the west. It reminded him how lucky he was to be kept warm by his armor's thermal undersuit.

"Knife-two," he said over the com, "how's the road looking?"

Soren held position at the base of a small bridge spanning an icy stream. The long dirt road to Tilarus lay beyond.

"Clear as far as I can see," Soren's sly voice replied. "The only obstruction is a crashed rover. From where I am, I can still hear the engine sputtering. Looks like someone was here not too long ago."

"Understood," Scales said. "Move across the bridge into position behind the rock cairn and try to hail the facility on UGC emergency bandwidth Lonely Oak. I'm on my way. Knife-One out."

Scales stood up and sprinted as fast as he could out from the cover of the trees. He ran across the flat frozen field. The snow crunched beneath his boots with every step. As he crossed the wide bridge, he took careful notice of what appeared to be bloodstains—he couldn't tell from which race the blood had come.

"Knife-One," Lux broke in. "I've got movement. Two hundred meters from the entrance of Tilarus."

Scales ducked into cover behind a mass of boulders next to Soren. "Roger, Knife-three," he said. "Identify, over?"

"Negative, Knife-One. Target disappeared like a damned ghost. Nothing registers on thermal or infrared."

"Damn it," Scales mumbled. "Acknowledged. Stay sharp. We're moving to the facility garage. Wait until we're forty meters out, then follow. Acknowledge?"

"Aye, aye."

Scales gripped his MAR tight and turned his head to Soren.

"I'll take the left side of the road," he said. "You take right. Stagger ten meters behind."

"Got it."

"Move."

Scales and Soren broke cover—Scales went left round the rocks, Soren right. They made for the vehicle garage to the portside of the facility, their weapons shouldered. With Lux at their backs, Scales felt pretty safe—all things considered. As they ran, he scanned the surroundings high and low for any contacts. Whatever Lux had seen through his scope was gone, at least as far as Scales could see. There was no sign of it. However, he didn't let his guard down.

By the time Lux caught up with them, snow had begun to fall again and the wind had picked up considerably. Swirls of snow whipped around their boots.

Soren once again tried to signal the facility on the emergency channel. He waited a few heartbeats, then looked at Scales, and shook his head; no response.

Knife Team proceeded to the objective. They began their climb up a series of switchback ramps. The entrance bulkhead to Tilarus loomed imposingly beyond, shielding whatever lay behind with thick titanium.

Halfway up the second ramp, the toe of Scales' boot kicked something. It skittered away with a metallic cling. Then he saw it: hundreds of spent shell casings, calibers of all sizes, littered the ground.

"God," Soren said in surprise. "There must be over a thousand rounds here. The marine garrison put up a hell of a fight. Wait—" He pointed to something ahead. "What's *that?*"

Scales followed his finger. He saw red translucent liquid spattered everywhere. It was splashed and smeared across the walls like paint on a canvas. The ground was slick with it. Puddles of it led on, upward, all the way to the door at the top.

"Unknown," Lux reported. "Scanners say it doesn't match anything in the database."

"This just keeps getting better," Soren muttered.

"Stay frosty," Scales advised.

When they reached the top, the Shadows found a nasty and startling surprise—one that even Scales hadn't anticipated. The entrance bulkhead had been completely destroyed. The metal was bent and twisted inward, as if bashed in by some great exertion of force. That, or it had been blown open with one hell of an explosive charge.

Whatever happened, it wasn't a door that would open on a whim; it was half-meter thick titanium blast-plate.

The corridor ahead was almost completely black. The Shadows flipped their under-barrel flashlights on and stepped into the facility.

Red lights flickered overhead. Many were broken, sparking, and some even dangled, held in place only by their wires. The Shadows' heavy boots chomped down on broken glass. Bullet holes and strange score marks pocked the walls on either side.

Scales ran his hand over one of the score marks. It was still hot.

"Are those plasma burns?" Soren asked.

Scales shook his head. "I don't know. Definitely energy weapons' scoring, though. Keep alert, guys."

Their destination was the labs, a series of complexes that descended ever-deeper underground.

They pressed on, slowly, purposefully, ever alert, anticipating anything, painfully aware that something could leap out of the shadows at them, anytime, anywhere. In this perpetual darkness, anything could be hiding.

Scales pulled up the layout of the facility on the upper right corner of his HUD.

The seconds ticked away, the minutes went on.

So, too, did Knife Team. The Shadows kept their senses on the highest alert. With every step through the labyrinth of rooms and halls they navigated their way among, they expected something to jump out of the darkness and strike them down, but as time passed, and the rooms they came across were devoid of any signs of life, the absence of an enemy only increased the uneasy feeling in Scales' stomach. After what had seemed like an eternity, they found themselves in the lab antechamber.

This was perhaps the most dangerous leg of the mission. Absolutely anything could be shielded, waiting to pounce, behind the two-meter long bulkhead, locked tight on the far side of the room.

Scales clenched his jaw. It was too quiet here; too still. The telltale signs of battle all around them—shell casings, broken glass, bullet-hole riddled walls—screamed that the marines here had fought and fought hard. Yet, there wasn't a single body. Why hadn't they met any opposition? And what happened to all of the people stationed here?

There were too many questions without answers, too much mystery to a mission that he and his team had barely begun. If there was one thing Scales had learned after nearly thirty-four years of service, it was this: in these situations, things could go to *Dishnaku*, and go there fast.

They needed to move quickly.

The antechamber's floor was slick with more of the odd, red liquid. Lux knelt down and worked a bit of the stuff between his thumb and index finger. "It's cold," he said. "Really cold. Almost feels like ship coolant."

Scales crouched on his haunches and felt the liquid. It was quite sticky, and exactly how Lux had described it: cold. Freezing.

Scales opened his mouth to comment, but something caught Lux's attention and his head snapped toward the lab bulkhead with an eagle's quickness.

The lab bulkhead hissed, creaked, and began to open.

"Contacts!" Scales bellowed.

Scales and his team braced their MARs tight against their shoulders as they scrambled into cover.

Scales steadied his aim, ready to engage the new threat. He rested his finger a hair away from the trigger.

Seven armored UGC Marines shuffled out of the darkness. They leveled their guns at the Shadows. Their faces were filled with a fright Scales had never seen before.

"Drop your weapons!" Scales yelled. "Drop them now!"

For a moment, both parties remained still. Their weapons were trained on one another, each with the impulse to open fire immediately. Scales was tempted to fire on them, but he didn't. These marines weren't the enemy; they had to be the detachment stationed here. He wouldn't let his guard down, though. The FOF tags displayed on his HUD registered them as friendlies. However, at the moment, they still posed a threat to him and his team. Frightened, battle-weary soldiers could act with rash, and often foolish, actions.

"This is Lieutenant Commander Kileeus Scales. Drop your weapons *now* or we *will* open fire. That's an order!"

"Stand down!" A man's voice yelled from the darkness behind the marines.

Looking greatly relieved, they all dropped their aim.

A Tomlyn stepped out from behind his men and walked toward Scales. He gripped a shotgun white-knuckled tight in his partially furred hands.

The Shadows still had their weapons trained on him. To expect anything was part of their creed.

"Forgive me, sir," the Tomlyn said. "We thought you were *them.*"

The canine-like being snapped off a lazy salute. Scales spotted the stripes on his armor's shoulder, and gave the order to Soren and Lux to lower their guns. Scales studied the Sergeant closely.

He wore a battered suit of combat armor and his grimy and bloodied face was covered in cuts and nicks. The fur around his short snout was singed. His left shoulder pauldron was cracked and dented. This man was a mess. Judging by the way he looked under the eyes, he hadn't slept in days. His marines didn't look any better.

"Are you in command?" Scales asked.

"Yes, sir," he replied. "Or, I am now, at least. Sergeant Arykas Ventrol."

"Sergeant, what happened here?" Scales asked gently. He'd learned from experience that in dire situations, the calm, reassuring voice of an officer could do wonders for morale.

"What happened here?" Ventrol repeated. "Um, we were attacked, sir."

"By *what?*"

Ventrol stared at him in disbelief. "You mean you haven't seen any of them yet?" He let out a nervous laugh. "We need to get inside, sir. Now. This is the only room they haven't been able to penetrate. You'll see them soon enough. They'll come back." He turned and walked back into the labs. "They always do."

Soren and Lux exchanged a glance, and then looked at Scales, who jerked his head for them to follow. The Shadows followed Ventrol through the bulkhead and into a large foyer. The marines sealed the bulkhead behind them. Laboratories were arranged to the left and right of the foyer, five on each side; their titanium doors were sealed shut. On the room's opposite end, a locked door similar to the entrance bulkhead led deeper into the facility, down beneath Atlantis' crust.

The marines weren't the only people that had taken refuge in the room.

To his surprise, Scales found it populated by twenty-one people: what was left of Tilarus' scientists. They were safe. Physically, most were relatively unharmed. Only a handful had superficial wounds, but mentally, they all looked as battered and exhausted as Ventrol and his marines did. These people had been through some kind of nightmare Scales had not the mind to imagine. There were makeshift bedding and boxes of supplies scattered all across the floor. The air was humid and thick with the smell of sweat and staleness. Everyone looked absolutely terrified.

Scales needed answers. Now.

Ventrol plopped down hard on a lab stool and propped his shotgun against some crates. He took a long gulp of water from his canteen and poured what was left on his head. With a grunt of satisfaction, he massaged his neck with his hand.

"Ventrol," Scales said, "I'm on a mission to recover the alien artifact the science team found. Do you know where it is?"

He sighed. "Oh, that thing. Damn. And I thought you guys were the rescue party. Before the attack, the science team locked the crystal up tight in the C labs, six levels down in the bunker. As far as I know, it's still there."

Scales breathed a sigh of relief. At least the crystal was safe. "Sergeant, I need to know what happened here."

"I don't even know where to begin, Commander," Ventrol said.

Scales knelt down next to him so the two were eye level. With a *hiss* the airtight seal on his helmet released. He slowly removed it from his head so that Ventrol could see his face. "Start from the beginning."

CHAPTER NINE

0845 hours, January 21, 2343
Argus System, planet Atlantis
OMI research facility 0574A-115
Codename: "Tilarus"

"The beginning," Ventrol repeated with a nod. "Right." He shifted his weight. "Well, almost two days ago the Major gets this message from one of the eggheads that some kind of ship appeared near the planet and destroyed one of our cruisers. About fifteen minutes later, our long-range coms and primary power cut out. Then, we started getting reports of unknown enemy contacts outside the facility. I was in the mess hall when I heard gunfire. I knew that we were being invaded, but I *still* don't know who was invading us. I don't know what they are. They don't look like anything I've ever seen. They're huge—at least three meters tall and more muscular than the biggest Tiberan you ever saw. They managed to breach the facility within minutes. We didn't stand a chance. We fought, but they pushed us back deeper and deeper. By that time, what was left of the science team was gathered in here, so we fell back and sealed the door."

This is what Scales expected. He was oddly alarmed, but he didn't feel surprised. They were told an alien threat would almost certainly be encountered. But now he had a new mission, a personal one: he was not going to leave these people here. The recovery op hadn't changed; he was going to complete his mission objectives—but he was going to make sure these people were coming back onboard the *Autumn* with him. They deserved at least that much. Shadows weren't just operatives; they were the protectors of the galaxy.

"Where's your CO?" Scales asked. "Where's the Major? Did he die?"

Ventrol closed his eyes and shuddered. Something about that question made him feel uneasy. Scales knew he'd somehow struck a nerve. Ventrol squirmed in his seat. "They … took him, sir. They took him." His face twisted into a grimace, like it physically hurt him to think about it. His eyes were alight with a burning fear.

Scales narrowed his eyes, "What do you mean they took him?"

"When they attacked us, some of my men emptied entire clips into their bodies and they didn't even blink. They just kept coming. Our dead or wounded that we couldn't get to in time were dragged away, some still kicking and screaming. The bastards just took them. We don't know what happened to them. Their transponders stopped working shortly after we sealed the door. Did you see any dead people outside?"

"No," Scales said apologetically.

"Before we could get everyone into the bunker," Ventrol continued, "The Major took a hit to the back from some kind of beam weapon. It burned right through his armor. He was a little ways down the hall, about six meters from me. When he fell, I turned to run and get him, but they snatched him up. We heard his screams until the door closed. As for the aliens, we managed to kill at least seven of them … and they took their own, too. They dragged them away like they were nothing more than sacks or bags of garbage."

Scales sighed.

Now things were complicated. This terrible situation had escalated even more. Not only were there now civilians to protect, but the enemy was also taking prisoners, though for what purpose was unclear. To torture for information? For bargaining chips? For eating? He didn't know. There was one thing for certain: he needed to get himself, his team, and these people out of here as fast as he possibly could.

"When you opened the door," Scales said. "What did you mean by, 'They'll come back. They always do.'?"

"We'd been holed up in here for nine hours when we thought of trying to contact the surface somehow. Our scanners indicated there were no signs of life. They were wrong. They don't appear on thermal or infrared. Six of my men went out to the coms room, but the aliens came back. That battle had a similar effect, and they took them. Four more tried to see if they could get down to the garage and grab one of the APCs so we could all get as far away from here as we could … they took them, too. They took ten more of my men. After that, we waited in here for the rescue team. We've been hearing movement outside for almost a full day. They've been trying to find a way to get at us, but this seems to be the only room they can't get into. I guess the door's too thick, however we're not going to be getting out that way, either."

Scales locked gazes with Ventrol. "Sergeant, you did well. You kept these people safe. Be proud of that. My team and I will take it from here."

Ventrol nodded. "Yes, sir." He didn't seem so sure.

"Tell your marines to get these people up and ready to move out."

"You're taking us with you?" Ventrol asked with surprise.

"Well, I'm sure as hell not leaving you here."

Ventrol raised his eyebrows. "Ah-ooh to that, sir."

"Can you take me to the crystal?"

"Sure thing." The Sergeant stood and grabbed his shotgun. "It's in the lowest level of the labs, about fifty meters down, past the rear blast doors." He called four of his marines over. "I want everyone ready to leave by the time the commander and I return, understood?"

"Yes, Sergeant," they cried in unison.

Scales turned to Soren. "Start wiping the data. I want it gone by the time I come back."

"Roger that."

Lux was dressing the wound one of the marines—a young Borean corporal—had sustained to his brachium. He sterilized it and began wrapping it in self-healing bio-bandages.

"Lux," Scales said with a quick glance around the foyer. "When you're finished, help these marines get everyone on their feet."

"You got it."

Scales put his helmet back on. It sealed. He unslung his MAR and turned to Ventrol. "Lead on, Sergeant."

"Aye, sir." Ventrol tapped a few keys on the holopanel next to the C labs bulkhead. It opened with a hiss.

Scales followed him down a gradually declining corridor. They went deeper and deeper under the ground. Overhead lights snapped on along the way to guide them down into the darkness ahead.

"I don't suppose you have any idea what this thing is, do you?" Ventrol asked.

"I have no idea," Scales replied. "All I was told was to retrieve it. We'll let the eggheads try and figure that one out."

"I'm sure they'll have a goddamn field day with it."

The hallway came to an abrupt halt before a titanium door.

Scales leveled his MAR at the door and nodded.

Ventrol entered his access code, and the doors drew apart at the middle and slid back into the wall. Scales found himself looking into total blackness. Ventrol flipped his barrel light on.

"The lab has its own set of power generators," he said while they traveled down the length of the hall. "We had no idea how long we'd be down here, so we turned off all non-essential systems to save power."

"Is there any other way in here besides this door?" Scales asked.

"No. We're fifty meters underground. The walls are encased in three meters of polycrete and titanium on three sides. There's no way those things could get in here unless they brought one hell of a digging machine, and I kind of think we'd have heard that from the foyer." They stopped before yet another blast door. "This is the last one."

"They really wanted this place secure," Scales said.

"Yeah," Ventrol replied. "I used to think it was ridiculous, but now I'm thankful for all these obnoxious thick doors." He opened it.

Scales stepped through first and swept the room clear. It was then he noticed a small orb of white light flashing in the distance. "What is that?" he asked.

Ventrol hit a switch and the lights in the room flickered on and showed Scales exactly what that orb of light was.

The crystal lay before him on a slab of smooth granite.

He approached it cautiously. For all he knew, the thing could leap out and grab him. When he got up to the slab, he knelt down to take a closer look.

The crystal was sharply tapered on either end and had a bluish-purple, smooth pearlescent surface that radiated a pulsating blue glow surrounding it in an aura of mystery. A tiny orb of internal light continuously flashed silver. Yellow motes of light collected around the core with each strobe.

"Pretty little thing, isn't it?" Ventrol asked.

Seeing it, Scales was unsure how fragile it might be. "Can I pick it up?"

"Yes, sir. That thing is as hard as tetriite. Maybe harder."

Scales reached around and removed the small transportation cylinder from his back. He wrapped his fingers around the crystal.

Odd. It was strangely warm.

It made him feel uneasy.

He gently placed it in the storage container and sealed the air-tight lid. He held it up to his eyes and twirled the cylinder in his hands; inspecting it.

His com crackled.

"Scales, we've got a situation," Lux said. "You need to get up here. Now."

He and Ventrol double-timed it back to the lab foyer. Soren was there to greet them at the door.

"They're here," he said. "They're back—just like Ventrol said."

"Damn it," Ventrol bellowed.

"Did you get the data wiped?" Scales asked.

Soren answered with a curt nod. "Affirmative."

There was an eruption of noise outside the room, a cacophonous melody of screeches played at a dozen different pitches all at once. Something clattered against the foyer's bulkhead. They heard a buzz; felt a rumble. Then there was the sound of metal scraping against metal, grinding, chewing. The noise droned on and on.

Scales knew what was happening.

"They're trying to cut through the goddamn door," Ventrol said in disbelief. He called his marines up to the front.

They didn't have much time.

Scales surveyed the room.

Scared beyond belief, the scientists were all huddled up next to one another in the farthest corner by the C-labs bulkhead. Most were in tears, trembling with an indescribable fear. The marines began taking defensive positions behind some overturned desks and tables, ready to fight to the last.

Scales admired that, he really did. But as much as he hated to admit it, these men—these soldiers, scientists—were a liability to him right now. There were going to be casualties if they stayed and fought. That was something that would be out of his control if he allowed it. He needed complete control of this situation if he was going to get everyone out of here safely.

Ventrol started pumping his shotgun full of fresh shells. "What now, sir?"

"Ventrol," Scales said. His voice was calm, but full of authority. "I want you and your men to get every single civilian out of this foyer and into cover behind the C-lab bulkhead. Then, you're going to follow them and seal it behind you."

Ventrol paused. "We're not going to fight?"

"No. You've done your duty—all of your men have. I said I was going to get you all out of here, but in order to do that I need you to do exactly as I say. My team and I will deal with whatever is on the other side of that door. No matter what happens out here, no matter what you hear, you do not open that door until you hear from me. Do you understand?"

"Sir." Ventrol nodded regretfully. "Yes, sir."

"Good. Now get to it. We're running out of time."

"Yes, sir!"

Sergeant Ventrol gave the order and his men snapped to. They began hustling the scientists into the C-labs corridor with lightning quickness.

"What's the plan, Scales?" Lux asked.

"We lock and load," he replied, "and show those bastards what a dose of Shadow tastes like. Get into cover."

Behind the door, the buzzing and grinding was getting louder. It wouldn't be long now. Small dents started to appear in the metal.

The Shadows scattered and took cover behind the room's load-bearing columns. Their weapons were shouldered, trained at the door; Knife Team waited for the inevitable.

"The civvies are cleared, Commander," Ventrol shouted.

"Get your ass behind that door and remember what I told you," Scales said.

"Aye, sir." He ordered his men behind the bulkhead. They disappeared into the darkness. Before he stepped through, Ventrol turned and said, "See you soon, Commander."

Scales nodded.

The bulkhead rumbled and started to close. It sealed with a resonating bang.

The Shadows were alone and Scales felt more in control.

"Make them wish they'd stayed on the other side of that door," he said to his team.

Lux and Soren's acknowledgment lights winked on his HUD.

The noises coming from whatever hellish machine was breaching the bulkhead became ear shatteringly loud, worse than the barrage of a thousand artillery guns all firing at once. It thundered yet louder and louder—a deafening shrill that was piercing even through Scales' helmet's audio filters.

Bang.

Silence.

Scales exhaled slowly. He tightened his grip.

The room quaked.

He steadied his aim.

An explosion sent the meter-thick solid titanium bulkhead skidding across the floor as if it were cardboard. It lodged itself deep into the back wall.

Scales, Soren, and Lux finally got their first glimpse of *them.*

A bipedal being stepped through the door—tall, over three meters in height, with a sick brown, mottled hide. Plates of a gunmetal-grey armor protected its chest, shoulders, forearms, and torso from the waist down. Exposed wires and long, transparent tubes filled with a rushing red liquid wove themselves in and out of different parts of its body. On the left side of its chest was a small device, consisting of two concentric rings revolving around a flashing crimson core. Atop a broad, sinewy neck was an ugly, bald head set with two large, red eyes. Dark, fleshy appendages hung down from the back of its skull. Its upper and lower jaw was enclosed by two sets of fang-lined mandibles.

It sniffed the air as it scanned the room, remaining unaware of the hidden Shadows.

Scales lined up the creature in his sights. He exhaled slowly. His trigger finger twitched and his MAR coughed a three round burst that caught the alien in its chest—center mass.

It stumbled back and trumpeted a multi-vocal roar. The red translucent liquid Soren had found in puddles oozed from the wounds. It must have been blood. The tubes running from behind its shoulders into its chest fed the substance through the creature like blood through veins.

Lux and Soren followed up with a series of short bursts.

The bullets peppered its hide. Streams of red blood spilled from dozens of holes. But it didn't go down, nor did it appear to be affected at all. If anything, the rounds just seemed to make it angry.

The alien bellowed a low, guttural growl; and then leveled the weapon it clutched in its right six-digit hand.

The tip warmed to red; crimson grains of light collected along its firing channel. It spit a beam of red energy that cut into the pillar that Scales hid behind.

But the Shadow was too quick.

Scales sprung out from behind the pillar just as the beam vaporized it and sent debris shooting off in every direction. He dove and fired a hail of rounds from his MAR.

Then four more of the creatures stepped in behind their buddy, and Scales knew they were in for a tough fight.

As he came out of his roll and prepared to right himself to spray the creature with the rest of his clip, Scales had an epiphany.

That little mechanism on its chest … what if he were to hit it with a few rounds? Would the creature go down?

Time to find out.

Scales came up crouched on one knee. He shouldered his MAR tight, aimed very carefully; his target was small. He relaxed, exhaled, and fired. A five round burst struck the circle dead center.

The alien bellowed. It staggered backwards and fell to the ground in a heap.

Bingo.

Lux and Soren popped around their pillars. They opened up with a spray of full automatic fire. Ten-millimeter rounds hammered into the second alien's chest, too many for its armor to handle. It cracked and dented, oozing liquid. Rounds severed the tubes on its shoulders, spilling more of its blood, and shredded its flesh. It finally went down with a thud.

The Shadows darted around the room, running from cover to cover, dodging energy bolts and returning fire of their own.

Scales fired his MAR until the ammo counter read 00 and it rattled empty. He slipped back behind cover, released the mag, slapped a fresh clip home, and swat-turned behind the next pillar. A beam of energy shattered the one he had stood behind mere moments before.

He primed a grenade.

"Grenade out!"

He lobbed it into the center of the aliens. They looked down at it, not sure what it was. One of them stooped down and picked it up.

It detonated, obliterating the creature and its buddy. Scales, Soren, and Lux concentrated their fire on the last hostile.

Scales sighted down and sent a three-round burst into its chest-ring.

It went down immediately.

Their clips were depleted.

"Try to aim for that thing on their chests," Scales said over the coms. He swapped his clip. "Seems to be an instant kill."

Soren cycled the bolt on his MAR. "Goddamn, those things are tough."

"Ammo check," Scales said. "How are we doing?"

"We probably can't last another round like that," Lux said. "Especially if there's more this time."

"Agreed." Scales felt to make sure the crystal container was undamaged. "I think it's time for us to get out of here."

He opened a com link to Ventrol's microbead. "Ventrol, this is Scales. It's all clear. Open that door and let's get out of here."

Ventrol's voice crackled in his ear. "Roger that, Commander."

The bulkhead eased open. Everyone spilled out into the foyer.

"Lux, Soren," Scales said. "Scout on ahead and make sure the coast is clear. I'll help Ventrol with the civilians. As soon as you get outside, radio me so we can start to move. Go."

Lux and Soren acknowledged Scales' order with a nod. They stepped carefully over the bodies of the aliens and slunk back into the darkness.

"Let's get ready to move, ladies and gentlemen," Scales called. "Ventrol, civilians in the middle. You and I are on point. The remainder of your men will bring up the rear."

"Understood, sir." He turned. "All right, you heard the commander. Marines, cover the rear of the column, science team, you guys are in the middle. Keep tight and move fast. Those things are going to come back eventually. We need to be gone the next time they do. Move it."

Scales thought he heard the faint crackle of gunfire. He opened a link to Soren and Lux.

"Knife Team, report contacts."

"Just two," Lux's voice came in. "Waiting at the entrance. They're down and out. Path is clear, come on out."

"Solid copy, Lux." Then, to everyone, Scales said, "Guys, let's move."

"Don't let your guard down, marines," Ventrol warned. "This isn't over yet."

Scales remembered the path he'd taken on the way in. This left, that right, this hallway, that room. He and Ventrol lead the way through the pitch-black hallways and winding corridors. They stayed as alert as they'd ever been.

Scales allowed himself a sigh of relief when he saw the daylight shining through the front door.

They stepped out into the sunlight.

Scales reached down for his belt and flipped the homing beacon on.

"Got it," he said over the coms to Soren and Lux. "Beacon is on."

Suddenly, his com exploded with static.

"—amn it, Scales, do you read me?"

It was a familiar voice.

"Scales here, sir," he replied. "I read you, Captain Penkala. We have the crystal in our possession as well as the survivors. Request *immediate* evac, over."

"I'm on my way. Get out into the open. ETA four minutes."

"Solid copy, sir."

Scales, Lux, Soren, the marines, and the civilians moved out into the open field. Exactly four minutes later, the *Autumn* appeared in the sky, and Scales made sure all the civilians and marines were well into the belly of the ship before he and his team boarded.

When the cargo elevator came back up, Scales found Penkala waiting to greet them. He didn't look pleased. His face was grim as he stood with his hands clasped tightly behind his back.

"Damn fine work, Scales," he said. "Damn fine. Unfortunately, we'll have to pop the champagne and celebrate later. We've got a big problem. That ship suddenly jumped out-system twenty minutes ago. We didn't know why until High Command informed us they received word that another crystal was discovered on Arcturus Septum a short time ago. We assume that's where they're headed. Your orders are to go in and perform another recovery op. But it isn't going to be as easy this time, Scales. Arcturus Septum is a major population center. When those aliens attack, and there's no reason to assume they won't, there's going to be complete chaos. Get what rest you can and get ready for round two. We're seventy-two hours out."

Scales popped the seal on his helmet. He took it off and tucked it in the crook of his arm.

"We'll be ready, sir."

"I hope so." Penkala turned on his heel and marched off toward the bridge, "because a whole new war just started."

VEHICLE: MDGM

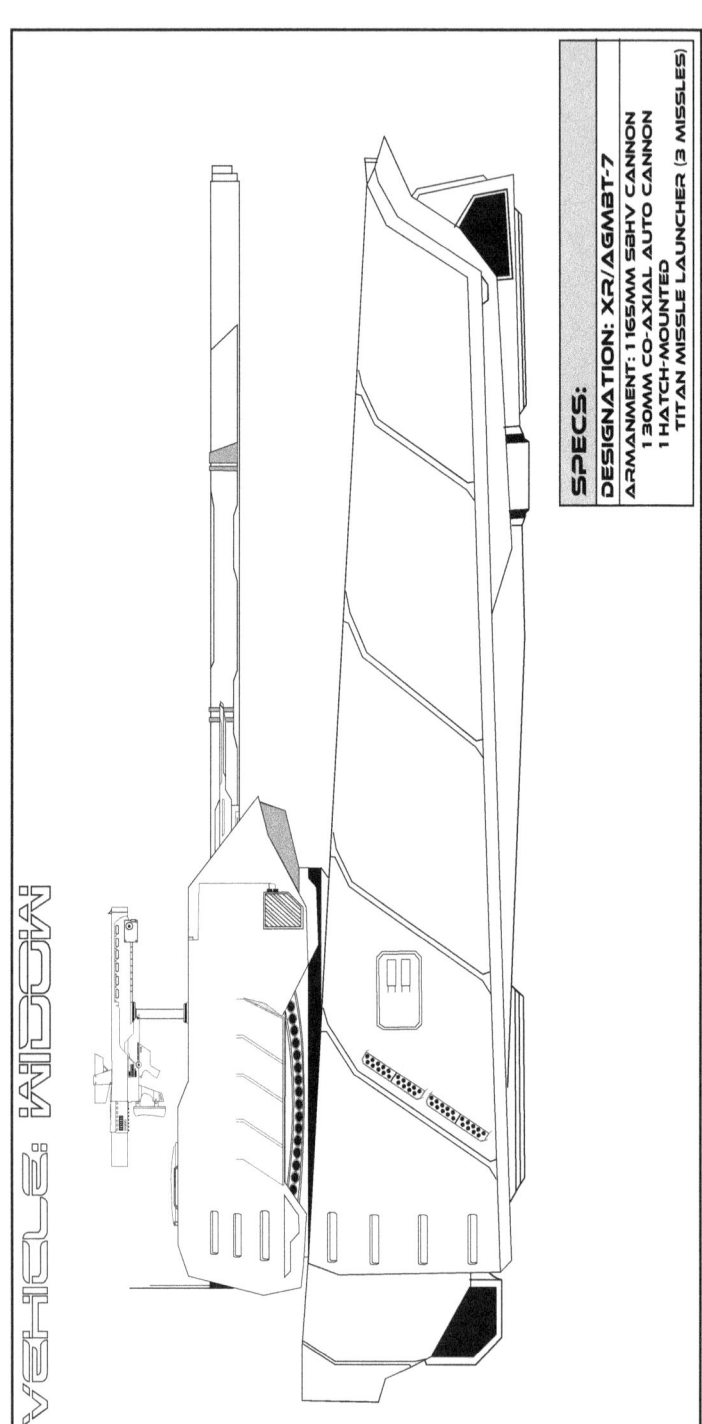

SPECS:

DESIGNATION: XR/AGMBT-7

ARMANMENT: 1 165MM S3HV CANNON
1 30MM CO-AXIAL AUTO CANNON
1 HATCH-MOUNTED
TITAN MISSLE LAUNCHER (3 MISSLES)

Section III:

The Siege of Arcturus Septum

CHAPTER TEN

0920 hours, January 24, 2343

*Delta Sagittaurii System, aboard UGC Cruiser **Argent Sky***

On patrol near Arcturus Septum

Seventy-two hours later

The ship's warning klaxon blared.

Roy Locke jumped in surprise.

The executive officer's harsh Tiberan voice came in over the speakers. "This is the XO. General quarters: all hands to battle stations. Repeat, all hands to battle stations. Condition Alpha. Seal all pressure doors. This is not a drill. Lancer squadrons Alpha through Constellation to the ready. Lieutenant Locke report to Captain Lyl in the briefing room at once."

The coms snapped off.

"Great," Roy muttered.

He leapt out of his bunk and got dressed as fast as he could. He cursed to himself; he was supposed to be off duty for the next two cycles, but something told him his next shift had started early.

When he stepped off the lift in his grey duty uniform and walked onto the busy command deck, enlisted and officers alike, carrying charts and datapads, brushed past him. A fire team of armored marines jogged down the corridor. He stood aside for a pair of pilots rushing for the lift.

Things were busy, although typical for a call to battle stations. He wondered if they had encountered a Rebel patrol.

That seemed unlikely in such a heavily defended system like Delta Sagittaurii. Although, Roy had to admit the bastards were getting bolder as of late. It wouldn't be outside the bounds of reality to think they might have actually decided to attack this system.

Another fire team of marines double-timed it past him.

Two marines stood guard at the briefing room door, MAR-5 assault rifles cradled in their arms. They stood at arms when Roy approached.

"Head on in, sir," one of the guards said. "Captain Patterson and Captain Lyl are already inside."

Roy raised his eyebrows. "Captain Patterson and Captain Lyl?"

Then this was serious. Usually, Roy reported to Lyl, as Lyl was in command of the *Argent Sky*'s marine garrison, but if Patterson was there, something wasn't quite right.

"What's going on?"

"I don't know, sir," the guard replied.

The bulkhead parted and Roy stepped inside.

Two lieutenants, part of Patterson's bridge crew, no doubt, were standing near her with datapads in their hands. Data scrolled rapidly across their screens. Captain Lyl was talking with one of his officers. Through the overhead coms a mess of mixed static and radio chatter was coming through.

"*—break off, now. First Echelon, form up to provide coordinated fire on the lead ship. Second Echelon, defend the orbital guns from boarders.*"

"*—said now, damn it. Lieutenant Yulan, charge our Aegis capacitors and get me a firing solution for all forward Rapture missile pods.*"

"*—can't hold out much longer. Our weapons' systems are disabled and I have fires on all decks. I understand, Admiral, but drive core output is down to thirty-six percent.*"

Roy stood to attention while he waited. He listened to the coms intently. Whatever was happening, it sounded like a full-scale invasion.

Captain Patterson had her hand pressed tightly to her ear, listening in on a headset.

"Aye, aye, sir," she said in her raspy voice. "We're on our way. Affirmative. Aye, sir. I'll assemble the ground team. ETA to rendezvous point is thirty minutes. *Argent Sky* out." She handed the headset to one of the lieutenants, and said, "Send our coordinates to FleetCom HQ and tell them we're making best speed."

The lieutenant nodded. "Aye, aye, ma'am."

She sighed heavily and rubbed her chin. She then took notice of Roy standing behind her. "Ah, Lieutenant Locke. At ease. Step over here. I want you to see something."

Roy followed her over to Captain Lyl. The officer he was conversing with snapped a salute and hurried away with an armful of datapads.

"Sesyl," she said. "Hand me that datapad, please?"

"Yes, ma'am." Lyl handed over the small holographic pad he held.

Patterson thrust it at Roy. "Read this quickly," she croaked. "We're short on time."

It read:

INCOMING

UGC FLEET COMMAND FLEET-WIDE BROADCAST

From: Fleet Admiral Tang, Roger. L. _Service No. 0045195-660RT UGC FC / Commanding Officer of Fleet Command Head Quarters

To: ALL UGC warships in Pandora, Amphilla Fross, Delta Sagittaurii, and Vermillion Systems

Unknown enemy hostiles have engaged our forces at planet ARCTURUS SEPTUM. All UGC warships in aforementioned systems are hereby ordered to immediately terminate all operations and form up at Coordinates 0015-6629 Constellation-Alpha-Nova for immediate offensive action. Ground teams are requested for deployment to combat enemy presence on surface. ALL ships, FLEET-WIDE, are to be brought to FULL COMBAT READINESS and await further orders. FLEETCON is now elevated to BLACK.

This is an ENCLAVE-LEVEL emergency.

>END TRANSMISSION

Roy cocked his eyebrow. He looked up. *"Unknown?"*

"Correct," Patterson replied. "A new race, from what I've been told. They arrived in-system five minutes ago and attacked with no prior warning. Some of their smaller vessels even made it down to the surface and started deploying troops into every major city on Arcturus Septum. The battlenet is awash with so much chatter that we can't discern any more information beyond that."

"No demands?" Roy asked.

"None that I've been informed of."

"They must have some fleet for Command to recall ships from four systems," he said incredulously.

"They only number between twenty and thirty, but the problem is they're pretty damn tough. Reports say their ships are capable of withstanding more than three Aegis rounds."

The situation had really changed, and not for the better. Hell, he would have actually *preferred* Rebels. A new race meant he'd have virtually no intel on them, and, as a marine, he knew poor intel led to bad outcomes.

"What do you need me to do, ma'am?" he asked as he handed the pad off to Lyl.

Patterson put her hands on her hips. "I know you're rostered off for the next two cycles, Locke, but this changes things. Captain Lyl, if you please."

"Ma'am." Lyl stepped forward. "FleetCom is requesting each ship send available combat teams down to the planet's surface. I want you to head down to the barracks and suit up because you're going down. I'm placing you in full tactical command of the ground teams. Your objective is to rendezvous with friendly forces and help assist in the evacuation of Elysium City."

"Why pick me, sir?" Roy asked. "First Lieutenant Torrcan is—"

"Torrcan doesn't have the combat medals you do, marine. You wondered why you weren't drummed out of the service after striking a superior officer? That's why. Now get your ass down to the armory, grab your gear, and meet Lieutenant Torrcan by the motor pool."

Roy saluted. "Yes, sir."

As he hustled for the barracks, he smiled. This was his chance to get back into the saddle after all these weeks. This was his chance to get back into *combat*. It's what marines did. What they were *born* to do: fight.

During his court-martial, they'd found him guilty of assault. He was demoted, busted down from first lieutenant to second for punching that stupid Vakari major in the face during a bar fight. Fortunately for him, they'd both been off duty; otherwise, he'd have been given a hefty jail sentence, and that wouldn't have even been the worst of it.

Instead, they'd given him indefinite ship duty. Marines were supposed to be rotated on eight-week cycles—he'd been on the *Sky* for fifteen weeks.

It was irritating, but at least now he was finally ready to get back into the thick of the action.

As the lift descended through the decks of the cruiser, Roy ran his fingers through his cropped, light brown hair and sighed. He was ready for this.

When he arrived at the barracks, hundreds of marines were suiting up and preparing for battle. The immensely wide, high-ceilinged room served as the marine's assembly and staging area aboard the *Sky*.

Dozens of Angel dropships hung suspended in place by large magnetic docking clamps in overhead compartments that honeycombed the starboard wall. Their crazy navy pilots were anxious to disembark. Widow grav-tanks, Ranger Light Combat Vehicles (LCVs), APCs, and dozens of other combat vehicles and VTOL aircraft were being prepped to go aground with the marines and provide them with a heavy boost in firepower.

Roy hustled across the floor to the armory at the far end of the bay. He opened his locker and placed his duty uniform on the rack.

Marine Battle Dress Uniforms (BDUs) consisted of an under layer of black, formfitting woven-polymer fatigues worn underneath a light ballistic vest that extended to the elbows and the groin area. Over this, Roy strapped on the gunmetal grey body armor—a composite titanium and carbite plating overlaid with a thin layer of tetriite battle-plate and coated in ablative stealth paint. It afforded exceptional defense against ballistic weaponry. The upper torso and waist sported several utility and tactical pouches, as well as numerous clips, and the armor plating itself was inlaid with magnetic strips for the purpose of attaching additional weapons and gear.

Roy was an experienced marine. He'd had a lot of practice suiting up since enlisting eight years ago. It only took him a few minutes to put everything on. He laced up his boots, then grabbed a standard-issue helmet from the locker shelf and closed the door. He tucked the helmet under his arm.

The next stop was Munitions Distribution.

Each marine had a personal weapons rack that held all the weapons they would use in the field. Roy submitted to a retinal scan at the entrance to the enormous munitions storage room. A moment later the scan passed. He was admitted as the impenetrable steel bulkhead parted at the seams.

He found the rack with *"—2LT. Locke, Roy. J—"* stenciled above it. He inserted his keycard into the security panel. The red light on the panel turned green. There was a metallic ping and his locker opened.

He set his helmet down on the counter and snatched a MAR-5 off the rack. Marine standard-issue, but he frowned—perhaps it wasn't the best weapon for this mission. He put it back and grabbed a Razor Carbine in its place. He shouldered it and looked through the sight. It had a smaller clip size than a MAR did, but carried the same 10mm rounds. As a carbine, the Razor was also significantly smaller and more lightweight. It was just as durable as a MAR, too. Satisfied, he slung it.

Roy liked to travel light. He'd learned that speed and maneuverability lent an enormous boost to combat efficiency, perhaps even as much as firepower did, if not more.

He picked up a combat knife. He twirled it between his fingers and then balanced it across his index finger. The weight of the tungsten-carbide blade was evened out by a solid diamond-shaped pommel. He sheathed it and holstered a K-2 sidearm. He slipped several extra magazines and four HE fragmentation grenades into his utility pouches, along with a smoke canister and a long-range night-vision scope for his carbine.

He slung his rucksack over his shoulder. It contained a kit every Marine needed to survive on the field: water, rations, batteries, and the like. Roy carefully double checked to make sure his trauma kit had everything it was supposed to: bandages, medical tape, disinfectant powder, painkilling capsules, surgical tools, and a canister of biodine, a brown, foul-smelling, wound-sealing analgesic and blood coagulant. It was designed to expand to fill the space of a wound, and, as Roy had seen during his last tour … hold insides together.

He stuffed his helmet back under his arm. As he strolled out of Munitions, he heard someone yell his name.

"Locke!"

He looked up and saw it was Torrcan.

"Shit," Roy muttered under his breath.

Torrcan was going to be absolutely furious that Lyl had elected to have Roy lead the ground team instead of him.

He had a cup of steaming coffee in one hand and a datapad in the other. He casually took a sip of his coffee as Roy stood to attention before him.

"Sir," Roy said, "reporting for duty."

"As you were," Torrcan said irritably. "You better give me one hundred percent down there, Locke. Don't fuck this up. And if I hear about you striking a superior officer again, I'll put my foot so far up your ass, you'll taste it. Now fall in. I've got to make this briefing quick."

He got a promotion two weeks ago and already he's got a big head. If he thinks he can keep talking to me like that, the next superior asshole I strike will be him.

Roy didn't let his ire get the best of him. He wasn't going to give Torrcan the satisfaction of seeing him angry. "Yes, sir," he said dramatically.

Torrcan shot him a glare, then looked away and shook his head. He made for a raised dais.

Arrayed before it was the assembled ground-team—four hundred and sixty marines. Roy took position to the right of the dais and stood at parade rest. The marines all snapped to attention and saluted when Torrcan stepped onto the stage.

Roy surveyed them. They all looked eager, more than ready for action. They'd caught the scent of battle and were ready to pursue. But each man still thought they'd be fighting Rebels. That aliens had appeared hadn't entered anyone's wildest thoughts. That revelation would certainly change a few attitudes.

"At ease, marines," Torrcan said. "Listen up. At oh-nine fifteen, FleetCom received a distress call from Arcturus Septum Command that the planet had fallen under attack by an unknown enemy."

A murmur thick with confusion and alarm made its rounds among the marines. Listening, Roy stood in silence.

"That's right," he continued. "Unknown. Command says they're a hostile, as-of-yet unidentified alien race. We've been called in to assist in the evacuation of Elysium City. Second Lieutenant Locke has tactical command of the ground team. He'll be leading the mission and you'll report directly to him. Now go kick some alien ass! Show them what a mistake it was to mess with the marines. Get to your assigned squads, all of you. Be ready for combat! ETA to drop-off, twenty-six minutes. Dismissed!"

The marines echoed a battle cry of "*Ah-ooh!*"

Roy left for his assigned team—Python Squad. It was comprised of veterans, men and women of every combat-able race that had fought the Rebels across the galaxy, some for more than two decades. They were a tight-knit squad, and Roy wouldn't want to go into battle with anyone else.

A woman's voice filtered in through the speakers. "All squads, report to designated dropships." It was followed by Captain Lyl. His unmistakable, fast-talking Ura voice boomed over the ship-wide com.

"This is Captain Lyl. You all know what to do. Whatever the hell those alien creatures are, they're sure going to know what a mistake it was to pick a fight with us. I want you to crush them under your boots with so much force that the very surface of the planet cracks! We're marines, Goddamn it, so let's show them how we fight. First in!"

"*Last out!*" the ground team thundered in unison.

"Damn right. Now get some, marines."

Roy led Python Squad across the deck to their designated dropship. This was going to be different than fighting the Rebels. He knew nothing about these aliens, had no intel on the situation; he was going into a warzone almost completely ignorant of what was waiting for him and his men. But this he *did* know: Rebels, aliens; he was ready for this. Roy allowed himself a smile as he started up the Angel's troop bay ramp.

Angels were the UGC's mainline troop transport and were capable of both all-atmospheric and space flight. They could lay down an impressive amount of supporting fire on the battlefield, and their transport-pod bellies had the capacity for thirty fully armored marines. Their graceful looking, backward-sweeping wings and their reputation for pulling soldiers out of hot zones contributed to their nicknames.

Roy took his place in the port jump seat row and rested his carbine across his lap. He was a little nervous—not scared, just the usual pre-mission jitters. He wondered what these aliens were going to look like. Could they be even uglier than the ones he had to see every day?

The Angel's pilot began her preflight checks. The ramp closed. Roy felt his seat vibrate and heard the Angel's engines warm up. There was a jolt as the docking clamp glided backwards, spun ninety degrees, then guided the dropship into the launch bay. There was a sharp murmur of air as the interior of the troop bay sealed.

Roy could hear his squad mates: deep, steadying breaths, the shifting of armor, the scraping of plate across assault rifle.

The *Argent Sky's* aft hangar bay doors opened. The atmosphere vented with a deafening hiss.

"Execute!" Captain Lyl barked over the com.

The clamp released its grip. The Angel dropped violently out of the bottom of the cruiser and plunged into the black abyss. Her thrusters fired up, corrected her pitch, and then the engines flared and carried her into formation with the others. The dropship shuddered hard as she entered Arcturus Septum's atmosphere.

There was a bang. Roy felt the vibration reverberate along the dropship's hull.

"Hang on, marines!" the pilot yelled.

The trembling grew more intense—far more so than it should have been this early in the game.

Suddenly, the Angel banked hard to port, then starboard; she dove.

Roy's stomach lurched.

The overhead lights in the bay flickered and went out.

The Angel shook so violently it rattled the teeth in Roy's head.

Something wasn't right. Roy tried to steady his breathing and remember that the pilot was in complete—

Bang!

There was an explosion. Something tore through the transport pod's starboard hull. Shards of titanium ripped through the bay, cutting and dicing several members of Roy's squad. He felt the spray of blood on the side of his face.

"*Shit!*" He heard the pilot say. "We're hit!"

The cockpit's glass canopy cracked and shattered. Glass and debris were sucked through and into the sky. The pilot screamed and slumped over in her seat.

Roy's heart rate skyrocketed. His breathing became erratic.

The engines sputtered, flared … then died.

The marines still alive began to scream. Others went limp in their harnesses.

Roy's own vision began to darken; the gees were becoming too much to handle.

Through the canopy, he watched them scythe through the clouds as they dropped out of the sky faster and faster. A cyclone of frigid air rushed through the cabin. It stung like a thousand knives as it whipped against his face and took his breath away.

When they finally penetrated the cloud cover, Roy saw the ground below growing inexorably closer, knew it was over, and heard an ear shattering *smash*.

Everything went black.

CHAPTER ELEVEN

0920 hours, January 24, 2343

Delta Sagittaurii System, planet Arcturus Septum

Delphine Military Base, Delphine City

Casey Keller slowly exhaled, allowing the music to take her over—to block out the world around her. At peace, she lay motionless—letting the music wash away all her stresses and worries. She was in her own tranquil realm.

She wasn't rostered in for her next cycle until oh-eight-hundred on the twenty-seventh. That left her close to three more days' down time, and all she was in the mood to do was read and listen to music.

Penny would probably try to get her to go out into the city tonight. Maybe she'd consider it later, but for now at least, she wanted to take advantage of the precious private time she she rarely got enough of.

With her duty uniform hung neatly in her locker, Casey stretched out lazily on the top rack of a double-tiered bunk in comfortable civilian clothes: a light blue, sleeveless shirt, brown pants, and a pair of combat boots.

"Well?"

Casey jumped and opened her eyes. A tall, slim, blonde haired woman was standing next to her bunk.

Casey removed one of her earbuds. "Well what?" she asked.

Staff Chief Penelope Redfield folded her arms across her chest. "You know what," she said and smiled. "The date, Casey! How was the date?"

Casey rolled her eyes. "You interrupted my rock music to ask me that?"

"I'm guessing by your tone it didn't go well."

Sighing, Casey sat up and rested her back against the headboard. "Well," she said, "I left base shortly after the evening briefing and met Mark in town near the markets. He took me to a lovely French restaurant for dinner. We talked, and after our meal we had dessert and some wine. It was actually pretty romantic up until the point when we were leaving and he decided to put his hand on my butt."

Penny grimaced. "Damn. What did you do?"

"I didn't feel like spending the rest of the night in jail, so instead I decided to say exactly what I thought of guys like him in French and left. Even though he didn't understand a word I said, I think he got the message."

"Damn," Penny sighed. She leaned forward and rested her arms on the bunk "See, this is why you need me to set the dates up for you."

Casey snorted. "No, thank you. Not after what happened last time. No."

"What do you mean?" Penny asked. "He was *cute!*"

"Penny ... he was forty-eight years old."

"So?"

"I'm twenty-one."

"When it comes to love, age—"

"He had four kids," Casey reminded her calmly. "With four different women."

"Well," Penny countered, confounded, "You need to get out more. Mark is like—What?—Only the second guy you've actually had ask you out on a date face to face since you got here, right? If you got out more and met more guys, I wouldn't always have to set up dates for you. As your best friend, it's kind of my job. Hell, go out tonight. Come with me, Till, and Vexus to the bar tonight. Maybe you'll meet a guy there you like."

Casey shook her head. "Thanks, really. But I think I'm done dating for a while."

"Why?"

"Need a break, I guess."

"Or maybe you need to get laid."

Casey responded with a glare. Her her drawn lips said it all.

Penny raised her hands in front of her defensively and backed up. "Just saying, is all. But maybe if you did, just once, you wouldn't be so uptight about everything."

Casey jammed her earbuds back into her ears. "What? Sorry, I can't hear you."

Penny shook her head, Knowing this was a battle she wasn't going to win—especially not with Casey—she left.

Casey breathed deeply, closed her eyes, and resumed her rock music meditation.

At a fraction under five-foot seven, Casey was by far the shortest person on base. A few of the Tiberan liked to make jabs at her, but she knew it was all in good fun. It didn't bother her. Casey knew she stood out among the other humans stationed at Delphine Base. She had shoulder-length, fiery-red hair and green eyes—both of which were rare features to find on a human nowadays. Her skin had a slightly pale complexion to it, but the sun didn't burn her anymore like it used to when she was a little girl.

She barely heard the shrill that came in over the coms. She killed her volume in time to hear the base commander, General Delany, say:

"Lieutenants Anderson, Pionim, and Suzwanus: report to the CIC at once."

Curious. She knew for a fact Anderson was off duty. But it was probably nothing important. She thumbed the holographic play icon on her datapad and resumed her song—nodding her head to the beat.

Military life wasn't what she had thought it would be. When she joined the navy, she'd had this idea she'd experience the idyllic romance of serving on a ship in deep space, end up falling in love with a strong, brave, yet sensitive man who loved risking his life in defense of the

Coalition and all it stood for—like in so many of the gooey romantic love vids she enjoyed watching.

Unfortunately, the military turned out to be everything but. After school, she was accepted into the *Académie Militaire des Officiers* in Paris. In five months, she'd never received a ship posting; instead, they had stuck her here on Arcturus Septum right after she graduated from the academy.

She hoped the rest of her term wouldn't be so dull.

The coms shrilled again, heralding another message, and Casey again paused her music. This time, General Delany called a long string of officers to stations.

Just as she began to wonder if anything was actually wrong, the whole room shook with a violent tremor. Startled, Casey sat up and removed her earbuds.

Delany's voice boomed over the coms. His usual calm tone was replaced by his command-mode voice.

"This is General Delany. All units to arms. I repeat, to arms. Delta Protocol is now in effect. I repeat, initiate Delta Protocol procedures. All officers to CIC at once. Any off-duty personnel are hereby returned to active duty. This is not a drill."

"What the hell?" she muttered.

Casey tucked her pad into her pants pocket and hurriedly swung her legs over the edge of the bunk.

A massive quake threw her out of bed and onto the cold, hard metal floor.

Crack!

Glass broke.

Shards of splintered glass and ceiling rained down onto her body.

She covered her head with her hands as best she could.

She didn't know how much time had lapsed—a few moments, several minutes—but she slowly opened her eyes and rapidly blinked. Her vision was blurry, black dots swarmed about like carrion birds circling around a carcass. She tasted the familiar coppery-ting of blood in her mouth. There was a dull throbbing pain in her head. Vertigo washed over her when she tried to stand. She grabbed onto the bunk for support. In a half-daze, she stumbled out into the hallway where a stampede of blurry figures ran by her toward the exit.

She was knocked to the ground by the crowd. Then there was a blinding flash of light, a thunderous quake so violent that it rattled the brain in her skull, and all Casey saw was blackness.

Consciousness flooded back into her body several minutes later, and her nose picked up the smell of smoke and gunpowder. The ground raced rapidly by below her; she bounced up and down. It was then that she realized she was draped over someone's shoulder.

She tried to ask him what in the world was going on, but she couldn't get the words out. All she could do was mumble incoherent, slurred babble.

There was a soft popping noise, a so-familiar repetition she knew she'd heard before, but couldn't quite place. Voices were muffled. Everything sounded as if she were underwater.

But soon, the soft popping became all-too-clear: the unmistakable crackles of automatic weapons' fire. The muffled voices morphed into curse-laden screams of desperation, fear, and pain.

She saw blurry figures running around her—then the flash of muzzles. Her vision returned home temporarily, and she lifted her head up to look around.

What she saw frightened her.

The base was in a state of sheer, unbridled chaos. People were firing weapons, explosions were detonating in the distance, and she could hear the roars of engines as fighter and interceptor craft raced overhead.

Marines took cover behind anything they could find: hill-sized chunks of polycrete, overturned vehicles, burning buildings. Shell casings littered the ground. Their fire was concentrated on targets she couldn't yet see. She craned her neck as high as she could manage, but it seemed everything past twelve meters was obscured in a haze of black smoke and dust.

Whoever's shoulder she was on carried her to the armory, where Staff Sergeant Tillium was motioning violently for everyone to fall back into the building.

Her vision began to blur again.

"Here, take her," the man carrying her said. She was passed off to a pair of navy corpsmen. Casey tried to get a look at the man—her rescuer, her savior—but he turned away and quickly ran out the door.

Then everything went black again. The darkness once again enveloped her.

"You're going to be ok, ma'am," she heard one of the corpsmen, a Borean woman, tell her. "Hang in there."

When she came to, she found herself in a long, dim corridor, propped up against the wall. Numerous other injured soldiers lined the hall like dominoes. Some groaned in pain. Others cried.

"Lieutenant Keller," someone said.

She snapped her gaze back front and center to see a Tomlyn medic crouched in front of her. His face was close to hers.

"I'm Corporal S'varan. Follow my light, please." He proceeded to conduct a series of field tests on her, and was satisfied to find no indications of a concussion. He examined her cheek and the long, deep gash she wasn't even aware she had. He dressed it.

"This is going to sting a bit, ma'am." S'varan sterilized her wound. "There are still tiny fragments of glass embedded in your skin. I'll have to get them out before I can seal it up."

Casey was still in a bit of a daze. Or maybe it was more shock now that she could actually think about what the hell had just happened.

What the hell *did* just happen?

"S'varan," she whispered weakly, "what's going on?"

"Try not to talk, Lieutenant," he said. "The base has been attacked. That's all I know."

"Attacked?"

"I said try not to talk."

Her thoughts were a jumble. It was hard to concentrate. Then, it slammed into her. Her eyes widened and she gasped: *"Penny!"*

Where was she? Had she made it to the armory? Was she even alive? Casey struggled to move. The urge to find her best friend burned within her like fire.

"Lieutenant," S'varan's voice was calming, but authoritative. "You need to hold still while I do this. Don't make me call for help. Please. We're swamped enough as it is."

She cursed him, but reluctantly complied. She didn't even feel him remove each shard of glass with a pair of tweezers. All she could think about was Penny—if she was alive, and if so, where she was.

"Ok, ma'am," S'varan said. "You're all patched up. But stay here and try not to exert yourself."

The very few medics were becoming overwhelmed. Injured soldiers were filling the hall in droves. Two people raced past her. They were carrying a bloodied and bruised woman between them. Casey could make out the features: the blonde hair, fair skin, slender figure.

"Penny!"

She scrambled upright and ran after them. They propped Penny up against the wall. Blood dribbled from her nose.

Casey sat down beside her. She stroked Penny's bloodstained hair. "Pen ..."

"Shit, Lieutenant," a familiar voice said from behind. "I thought I told you to stay put, damn it." S'varan crouched next to her and opened his medical kit. "I thought I made myself clear."

Casey's temper flared. "Shut up and help her, damn it!"

S'varan wisely said nothing and began wrapping Penny's head in gauze. She had received several lacerations to her forehead and face, some large, some small. Blood ran from her ears. Casey saw a deep gash on her forearm through a shredded sleeve.

"How is she?" Casey asked after several grueling minutes.

"She's unconscious," S'varan replied tersely while stitching her arm wound. "Her arm's cut pretty deep. I won't know if she has a concussion until she wakes up. To be honest though, she's almost one-hundred percent compared to some of the others." He finished the stitch. "She should be fine. Stay with her and get me as soon as she wakes up. And listen to me this time."

When he left, Casey put her head in her hands and sobbed.

"Uhhhn."

Startled, Casey looked up to see Penny's blue eyes staring right at her.

"So," Penny said hoarsely and licked her blood-encrusted lips, "How was *your* morning?"

The smile on Casey's face couldn't have been bigger. She laughed in relief; her cries of pain had now become tears of mirth. She sniffed. "S'varan?" she called over her shoulder. "Corporal S'varan? Get over here!" She flung her arms around Penny's neck and squeezed her tight. "God," she said, "I thought I'd lost you."

"Chief Redfield," S'varan said, "I hate to break up an emotional moment, but there's a lot of people a hell of a lot worse off than you are, so let go of Lieutenant Keller and let me get to it."

"Oh, S'varan," Penny muttered, "you're always so polite with the ladies."

Casey reluctantly sat back to let him conduct his tests, but kept a strong grip on Penny's hand.

"Well," S'varan said at length, "besides a very mild concussion, you're fine. Take these." S'varan dropped some pills into Penny's outstretched hand. "They'll help with the headache. If you can manage, eat something and drink as much water as you can."

"Will you go to the hotdog stand down the street for me?" Penny asked.

Someone started yelling S'varan's name; it sounded urgent. He gathered up his med kit and hurried away.

Penny sighed. "God," she grumbled. "I really need a drink."

"Yeah," Casey huffed. She patted Penny's hand. "Two for me, please."

"What the hell is going on?" Penny asked.

"I don't know."

They sat in silence, listening to the horror that lurked outside the walls of the armory: crackles of gunfire, explosions, screams. There was a battle raging out there, one being fought with bullets and grenades, tanks and aircraft.

But inside the armory, Casey was caught in the midst of another battle. The medics were fighting a frantic battle against death and infection—trying to save as many as they could … and they were losing. A lot of people had grievous—and many mortal—injuries: missing limbs, internal bleeding, brain-swelling, the list went on. The medics and corpsmen were doing their best, but they lacked the proper tools for surgical and serious medical procedures. Most of their equipment had been left behind. Improvisation was serving as the only wall separating life from death—and it was under heavy siege.

"Soldiers. Listen up."

The voice caught Casey's and Penny's attention. They turned toward the direction of the voice and saw General Delany standing on top of a crate. His face was smeared with blood and soot. His silver and grey dress uniform was a mess.

"Arcturus Septum has been attacked," he said. "I don't know how many casualties we've taken … hundreds, a thousand maybe. For now, we have to assume we're all that's left. We cannot stay here. These walls are thick, but a few concentrated explosions will crack this armory open like a tin can. More importantly, we've got wounded that need to be evacuated. There's an entrance to the sewers in the lowest sub-basement. The tunnels run for kilometers. If we follow them, they'll take us right to Delphine City. From there, we'll evac our wounded and regroup at the marine rally point.

"A lot of our friends are still out there fighting. But we won't do them any good staying here, not until we get out there and into the fight with them. This entire base is connected by tunnels and passageways, so who knows, we may even meet up with them at the rally point. Now gear up, and get ready to move out. The sooner we get our wounded to medevac, the better." Delany took a quick look around. "Who's next in command? Step forward."

Casey looked around the room. Her gaze flittered from face to face, joining the others in the search for the next highest-ranking officer. She knew all of the officers on base, but none of them were here. More people were missing than she thought.

"I guess that's you, Casey," Penny mumbled and nudged her.

It took a moment to register in her mind; to hit home. When it finally did, Casey's eyes widened in grim realization. She was next in command? *Her?* She'd never been in command before! Not in a live fire situation like this, at least. Not when it mattered. Not when her mistakes could cost people their *lives.*

She cursed to herself.

With reluctance, she slowly stood. "Um … I am, sir." She took one last hopeful look around. Yep. It was her. "I, uh … I think."

Delany stepped down off the crate. He motioned for her to come closer.

"Casey," Delany said, "We're going to split into two teams, Sword and Shield. Sword will recon ahead and make sure the path is safe—, make sure that those things aren't down in those tunnels. Shield will help transport and defend the wounded. I want you to lead Sword. I'll stay behind to lead Shield and make sure everyone gets out."

All the color drained from her face. "Permission to speak freely, General?" Casey asked.

"Yes, of course."

She lowered her voice so only he would hear. "We're in the middle of a battle right now. I don't have any combat experience, sir. I have no idea what to do. I've only ever fired my weapon on the range."

"And from what I remember in your file," Delany said, "you were a damn good shot. How many people can hit a moving target with a rifle dead center at five hundred meters? You registered as a class two marksman, am I right?"

Casey rubbed the back of her neck nervously. "That was different, sir. No one was shooting at me then."

Delany fixed her with his blue-eyed "I have faith in you" stare. He was placing a lot of trust in her. She wasn't quite sure if that was an honor … or a burden.

There was nothing she could do about it now. She was an officer. This was her job. It's what she had trained for, and she knew going in that something like this might have happened one day— but she thought she'd have had a better chance at winning the lottery instead. "I'll uh … I'll do my best, sir," she ceded with a sigh.

"I know you will," Delany whispered to her. He placed a reassuring hand on her shoulder. "You can handle it. I wouldn't have asked you if I didn't think so. I want you to pick a squad of seven. The rest will stay back with me. Now go and get your gear. We need to move out soon."

She saluted. "Sir, yes, sir."

"And Casey?"

"Sir?"

"I'm glad to see you're okay."

"Thank you, sir. You, too."

Staff Sergeant Rendonus Tillium had begun distributing weapons, gear, and what little body armor he was able to salvage from the armory's north wing. Its roof had collapsed, and arms and armor were coming up short.

Casey picked up a MAR-5 assault rifle lying atop a crate. It wouldn't be anywhere near as accurate as the marksmen rifles she'd used before, but it could certainly lay down an impressive field of fire. It also had the reputation to afford its user surprising precision if fired in short, quick bursts.

Casey looked down the sight, slapped a clip into the receiver, and cycled the bolt. She thumbed the safety on. She grabbed two extra clips, a frag grenade, a fiber optic probe, and a K-2 sidearm. Tillium also handed her a TACTICOM pad, a dual-functioning wrist-mounted device that displayed three-dimensional holographic maps and acted as a short-range motion sensor.

Medical kits were in very short supply. Only five had made it out of the supply rooms. What remaining medical equipment there was belonged to the six combat medics, and after treating almost everyone, they were running dangerously low on supplies.

Casey needed to act fast. Moving the wounded out was becoming a time-sensitive task.

Her selection for a squad was limited. Thirty-five people, including her, had made it into the armory, and only twenty-one were fit for combat. Most would have to stay back and help move the wounded. She would have been short one more, as Corporal S'varan said Penny needed to sit it out and take the medevac dropship when it came, however, after a heated argument, and Penny threatening to punch him out, the Corporal—wisely—cleared her for combat.

Casey inwardly smiled. Her deep admiration for Penny's determination went farther than words could describe. There was no way she was going to be kept from this fight; those creatures had made a fatal mistake: they'd ticked her off, and now she was going to make them regret it.

Though hers and Penny's personalities were as different as night and day—Casey's shy, relatively quiet, introverted character, and Penny's loud, sarcastic, foul-mouthed and hot-headed demeanor—she was

Casey's best friend, and Casey knew that she could count on her for anything.

She needed teammates like that, teammates she knew she could depend on. That made Penny and Tillium natural first choices for squad mates. They'd both seen combat before, and they were very proficient at it. She would need a medic, just in case something happened, so S'varan was chosen among the other five.

Delany was hunched over a three-dimensional holographic map overlaid on top of an empty munitions crate surrounded by a few of the NCOs when Casey approached. "We're ready, sir." She said. Then under her breath, she added, "I think."

"Excellent," Delany motioned to the map. "This is a layout of the sewer systems. It'll be a two kilometer hike, but if we cut into this junction here—" He pointed to a junction highlighted in blue. "We'll bypass about six floodgates, and emerge here." He rested his finger on another section of sewer, this one highlighted in green. "From there, it's a little under a kilometer's walk until we reach this manhole, from which we'll emerge about a half-kilometer from this location." He indicated a blinking blue triangle. "The word is that this is the marine rally point. We want to avoid these areas." He traced a set of lines highlighted in red. "Here, here, and here. The water there is too deep for us to traverse in. I've already relayed the information to your TACTICOM pad.

"You're my eyes on this, Casey. I want you to keep in constant radio contact. If you have any concerns, or detect even the slightest movement from anything bigger than a rat, I want to know. Any questions?"

Yeah, she thought, *a billion of them.* She bit her bottom lip and shook her head. "No, sir." *None that would help, anyway.*

"Remember your combat training and you'll do fine. When you get to the first junction, radio in the 'all clear,' and we'll follow right behind you. Understand?"

"Understood, sir. I won't let you down."

Delany gave her a tiny smile. "I know you won't. Now get to it, Lieutenant. Clock's running."

Penny and Tillium were checking their gear when Casey approached.

"The elevators are shot," Tillium said and slapped a clip into his MAR. "We'll have to take the stairs. It's thirty flights down to sub-level seven."

Penny huffed heavily. "Son of a bitch," she muttered.

"You sure you're feeling okay, Chief?" Tillium asked Penny. "We can have all the fun without you, if you'd rather stay behind."

"What, and miss the chance for some payback?" Penny cycled the bolt on her MAR. "Hell no."

Casey gave the order to move out.

They hustled down the hall toward the stairwell. Even as they went farther and farther underground, they could still hear the faint signs of the battle raging above. An occasional dull thump would send dust falling from the ceiling.

The tension made Casey grip her MAR tighter, but she continued on.

"Hey, Till," Penny called. "Five hundred credits say I get the first kill."

Tillium snorted. "Deal. But if I get it, drinks are on you for a week, and I get to choose the place."

"Fine."

They pressed on in silence. As they went deeper, the cold, dark corridors become yet darker somehow; the stillness grew stiller, the cold air colder.

It was unsettling.

Casey felt like a different person; MAR in her hand, grenade in her pocket, as ready as she could ever be to stare combat dead in the eyes. This mundane day she'd planned to do nothing but lie in bed had sure made one hell of a one-eighty degree turn.

This would be her trial by fire.

CHAPTER TWELVE

1130 hours, January 24, 2343

Delta Sagittaurii System, planet Arcturus Septum

Angel 043 crash site, Location: Unknown

Roy gasped.

His eyes fluttered open. Life flooded back into his body. He blinked rapidly, vision blurred, and for a moment had trouble remembering where and who he was. But as his blotchy vision cleared and his eyes adjusted to the dim light, the nightmare surrounding him slowly came into focus.

The walls of the troop bay were smeared with the blood of his squad mates—their mangled bodies strewn all about, broken on impact when the dropship crashed on the planet's surface.

Was he the only one who made it?

Instinctively he wiggled his fingers and toes; no paralysis—and he still *had* fingers and toes.

That was a good sign.

He grunted in pain as he rolled on his stomach. He licked his lips. The bitter, coppery taste of blood made him spit, and he coughed until he gagged.

There was no way of telling how long he'd been out—it could have been minutes, hours, days— but the distant staccato of gunfire meant there was still a battle going on out there.

As he struggled to his feet, sharp pains tore through his abdomen. Black dots flecked his vision and vertigo forced him back down to his knees. He took a few deep, ragged breaths, trying to fight through the pain. He wondered if there was any internal damage. Roy reached for his thigh, expecting to find his trauma kit, but discovered it was gone. It had been ripped away during impact.

He cursed. *Doesn't that just figure. The one time I need the son of a bitch …*

His whole body throbbed. There wasn't anything he could do about it, though, at least not now.

He grimaced in pain as he took a quick look around. He smelled smoke and could feel the heat from a fire. There was a hissing noise below the deck—hydraulic fluid, maybe … or leaking fuel waiting to ignite. He needed to get out of this burning wreck. Fast.

Struggling to stand, Roy leaned against the hull for support. The dizziness returned, but then passed. He stumbled around the destroyed bay, checking the pulses of his fallen teammates, hoping that maybe, just maybe, some of them were still alive. They weren't. It was just him.

Roy closed his eyes. He wanted to feel sorrow, anger, but he didn't allow himself to. He couldn't right now. This was neither the time nor place to mourn. A fierce battle was raging out there, and with the internal damage he may have sustained, he needed to find a medic.

The crumpled mass of titanium that used to be the rear bay doors was impenetrable. He'd never get out that way. He searched for another way out. The emergency port and starboard hatches were twisted and smashed. He could try and get out through the cockpit's canopy, but no … the cockpit bulkhead was a ruin.

Then he noticed it—a jagged hole in the ceiling. Water dribbled down and had already made a good-sized pool on the deck. The hole was just large enough for his body to squeeze through, but it was going to be an agonizing task. Roy took a quick last look around, and that's when he spied his Razor under one of the seats. His helmet and rucksack were nowhere in sight.

He could have scavenged a rucksack from one of his fallen squad mates, but he'd never make it through the hole with that on his back. And truth be told, he wasn't sure he had the strength to heave it through. However ... he could manage a helmet.

He quickly disregarded the thought—the bay was filling with a roil of choking black smoke. He'd make do without one.

He slung his rifle and stood on one of the starboard-side seats. He exhaled, steeled himself, and leaped forward.

He grabbed the rim of the hole. The sharp metal edges bit deep into the palm of his hands, drawing blood. With a bellow of painful exertion, he managed to hoist his body up and out onto the drop ship's hull.

Rain fell from the sky in sheets. Words couldn't describe how good the cool spring rain felt beating against his face.

His mouth felt dry—like it'd been swabbed with cotton. He opened it and tried to catch a few drops of water on his parched tongue.

It was the most refreshing thing he'd ever tasted.

Roy slid down off the hull and finally planted the soles of his boots firmly on the earth. However, the pain in his lower abdomen had nearly overtaken him. His breath came in sharp, ragged gasps. He braced himself against the Angel's hull. He let the pain run its course. After what seemed like forever, it finally subsided to a dull throb.

Roy let out heavy sigh of relief. He felt light-headed and dizzy. Thirsty. Exhausted. But he needed to press on, push forward, and, most importantly, find out where he was.

He limped carefully over the pieces of wreckage. Once he was out into the open, he did a quick scan of his surroundings.

His bird had crashed in a field of green, waist-high grass, leaving a wide three hundred meter skid across the earth. To the north, towering pillars of smoke bellowed high into the sky. Distant explosions boomed over the horizon like muffled thunder, an unbroken repetition of dull thumps that sent the ground beneath his feet trembling ceaselessly. Sporadic crackles of gunfire echoed in the wind.

There had to be some marines nearby, or at least someone that would pick up a transmission. His helmet carried all his long-range com gear. Without it, Roy would have to rely on the short-range microbead intercom in his ear canal. He jammed a finger into his ear until he heard the com click.

"This is Lieutenant Roy Locke to any UGC forces in the area," he said weakly. "Respond, over." All he got in response was static. He waited a few heartbeats before speaking again. "I repeat, this is Lieutenant Locke to any UGC forces in the area. Please respond, over."

Nothing.

"Shit," he mumbled.

A rustle in the grass to his right grabbed his attention.

He unslung his Razor and went to investigate. He hadn't taken four steps when he felt the very earth around him shudder. He heard a whirring sound behind him and wheeled about, Razor shouldered. In the sky, a large, black object grew closer, rapidly approaching him. He immediately threw himself prone.

He tried to remain still and ignore the extreme pain throbbing through his abdomen as a black shadow surrounded him in darkness.

An alien craft passed overhead.

It was twenty meters long, brisling with six long, sleek objects that pulsed with strobes of deep crimson light. The ship's dark, mottled hull was covered with chitinous spurs, bearing more resemblance to the hide of a crocodile than to a metallic surface. The ship's engines emitted a deep, resonating rumble.

Roy lay perfectly still, performing a series of mental exercises designed to take his mind off the pain. Concentrating, he closed his eyes. Then, the rumble tapered off and he opened them. The shadow of the alien craft was gone.

Carefully, he got to his knees and watched the ship cruise slowly away.

It went fifty meters before something struck its port side. The projectile caused an explosion to blossom across its hull. Roy ducked instinctively, and only when he spotted a faint exhaust trail did he realize someone had fired a missile.

The craft stopped and hovered. All six guns swiveled round on ball joints, searching for a target—and the ship started to come about when three more missiles slammed into its starboard side. The force of the impact rocked the ship from side to side. Roy heard a string of internal detonations. A chain of explosions burst through the hull, swelled, and finally engulfed the ship. It slammed nose-first into the ground.

The force of impact caused the ground to buckle beneath his feet. It knocked him on his back. After a moment of fighting to stay conscious through the pain, Roy found the strength to stand and leaned on a piece of the Angel's engines for support.

Seven marines popped up from over the top of the tall grass like a pack of prairie dogs. Four of them hefted Titan Missile Launchers on their shoulders.

"Hey!" Roy yelled.

"We hear you, sir!" one called back.

The marines waded through the grass toward him, an assortment of beings—three humans, a Vakari, two Asgard, and a Tomlyn medic.

"Nice fireworks show," Roy said.

His eyelids fluttered and he fainted.

When he came to, Roy was lying on his back, looking up at the weathered face of a scruffy looking human marine. He caught the red chevrons of staff sergeant on the man's pauldron.

"Hang in there, sir," the Staff Sergeant said. "Evac's on its way. How are you feeling?"

Roy licked his blood-encrusted lips. "Like shit."

"As well you should," someone said at his left.

Roy turned his head.

Sitting on his haunches next to him, the Tomlyn medic was smoking a cigarette. "You've got a lacerated liver and four cracked ribs, but how you walked out of that crash with nothing more is beyond me. Someone's really watching out for you up there. I pumped you with some painkillers and a double dose of biodine. It'll start healing your liver and set and mend the ribs."

"Thanks, Doc." With the staf sergeant's help, Roy was able to sit up.

"Staff Sergeant Alec Lister." He offered Roy his canteen. "Two-Twelve ASG. Gamma Squad."

Roy took it graciously and swallowed a few big gulps. "Thanks." He wiped his mouth with the back of his hand. "Second Lieutenant Roy Locke. Nice job with the ambush."

Lister grinned. "Glad you were able to get a front row seat."

Roy rubbed the back of his neck as his ears picked up a familiar—and welcomed—sound: the whine of an Angel dropship's engines. The whine quickly grew into a howl as the ship neared. It landed a dozen meters from their position. The gust from its engines sent the tall grass into a fit.

"Come on, sir," Lister said. "Hopefully this ride will go a little better than your last one."

With help from Lister and the Tomlyn medic, Roy stood up. He limped up the ramp into the Angel's troop bay. The cramped, close walls conjured up a bad memory—blood smeared walls and the twisted, broken bodies of his men. He shook it off and took a seat near the middle of the bay. The rest of the men piled in. Lister was the last to board. He parked himself next to Roy.

"ETA to base about two minutes," the pilot said over the com.

Lister fished around in his utility pouches and pulled out a cigarette. He lit it and puffed thoughtfully before offering the pack to Roy, who shook his head. "No thanks. Give me a situation report, Staff Sergeant. Thing's didn't look good from that field, at least not to me."

"They're not," Lister replied. "The attack took us completely by surprise. It all happened so fast. By the time word came down from Command we were being attacked, hundreds of enemy dropships had already deployed ground troops into every major city on the planet. You should have seen the news vids, El-tee. Civilians were getting cut down in the streets, buildings were on fire, falling, and our boys were taking an ass whipping. We couldn't have been any less prepared for this. My company was called in to defend the FOB at Ryhs Airfield. When Command picked up your dropship's distress beacon, our CO—Major Firan—ordered me and my team to look for survivors. I guess that enemy gunship had the same idea."

"Distress beacon?" Roy asked.

"Yes, sir. I guess your pilot managed to activate it before the crash."

"Staff Sergeant," the overhead com crackled with the co-pilot's voice. "I tried to raise the FOB, but there's nothing on the link but static. We—oh shit. *Shit!* Staff Sergeant, Lieutenant, you better get up here. *Now!*"

The two men jumped up and made for the cockpit.

Lister stepped through the door first, and the cigarette dropped from his mouth. "Oh, my God."

As Roy stepped in behind him, his eyes widened at what he witnessed out of the canopy window.

Three alien ships—each a hundred meters in length—hovered over Ryhs Airfield. Lances of red energy leapt from the underside of their hulls, sending firestorms across wide swaths of land.

The Forward Operating Base was getting pulverized.

"What do we do now?" the pilot asked.

Without breaking his gaze, Lister replied, "Up for a little payback, El-tee?"

Roy nodded. "Hell yes. I owe these bastards one."

"Bring us in as close as you can, and then set us down," Lister told the pilot. "They're not going to take that base."

The pilot looked at him as if he were crazy. "What the hell are the eight of you going to do against *that?*" He gestured towards the window.

"Whatever we can," Lister said. "Now quit bitching and find a place to park this bird."

The staff sergeant debriefed his men in the bay. "Marines," he yelled to be heard over the hum of the Angel's engines. "Hell's going to be one lonely place if we don't fill it with every one of those alien sons-a-bitches first. Let's give them something to remember!"

"Ah-ooh!" they cried out in unison.

"Our primary objective should be to get to HQ, sir." Lister slapped a fresh clip into his MAR. "Are you sure you're okay to do this?"

"I'm fine," Roy said. "There's no way I'm going to miss this. I owe those assholes some serious payback." The biodine in Roy's system had set his ribs. He was still in a bit of pain, but he could handle it. Nothing was going to keep him from this.

The lights in the cabin flashed red. With a hiss, the bay doors opened. A rush of air surged through the bay. The Angel descended rapidly until it hung a few meters off the ground. The flashing red lights pinged green.

"Touchdown!" the pilot said over the com.

"Go, go, *go!*" Lister yelled.

The marines jumped out of the troop bay and hit the ground running. They'd landed five hundred meters outside the base. The endless *pop, pop, pop* of automatic weapons fire and deafening blasts filled the air. Shell casings skittered and crunched under Roy's boots. Smoldering, glassy craters pocked the road all around them.

They raced through the gates. The guardhouses on either side had been blown completely apart; their debris littered the road.

Fires burned. Columns of smoke reached into the sky. Bodies were scattered everywhere.

Twenty meters ahead, a squad of marines took shelter behind a quartet of portable battle shields, blind-firing wildly at adversaries Roy couldn't yet see. One of them—a staff sergeant—spotted them coming and motioned violently.

Roy skidded behind the cover of the shield. Lister and the others followed in quick succession.

"Lister," the Staff Sergeant panted, "welcome back to base. You're late, as usual."

"Shut it, Silva. Is Major Firan alive?"

"As far as I know. Command bunker was the first thing to get hit, but most of the staff made it out. They hit the com tower, too."

"What's the plan, Staff Sergeant?" Roy asked.

"We have to get to the CIC and activate the anti-air cannons," Silva replied. "Our fighters can't launch without some covering fire."

Something thumped across the face of the shield with enough force to put two dozen tiny dents into the six centimeters of titanium battle-plate.

"Echo squad's supposed to meet us there," Silva continued, "But those bastards have them pinned down, too. They're over there, in the mess hall. I don't know how much longer they can last. Those things just won't go down."

Roy raised his body up slowly, poking his head up just enough so that he was eye-level with the top of the shield.

He got his first glimpse of the attackers.

They were huge, ugly things. Wires and tubes snaked in and out of their bodies. Their upper limbs were thick, unnaturally muscled, and their legs were equally massive.

When their weapons flashed, they coughed forth a cacophony of red, teardrop shaped liquid, lances of crimson energy, and needle-fine red beams.

A short twenty-five meters ahead, over twenty were advancing towards Echo squad's position in the mess. Echo's gunfire was sporadic. They weren't concentrating their fire on only a few targets at a time. Instead, each member of the twelve-man squad seemed to have a different target. It was proving to be a poor tactic. They should have known better; they were panicking. They weren't going to last much longer.

Roy scanned the area in search of anything to give them an edge. A second later he found it.

A Widow grav tank lay partially propped against an obstacle, its cannon pointed up to the sky.

That was it. That was their edge.

Roy sank back down behind cover. "I've got a plan," he said, "but it's risky."

"It beats the hell out of staying here," Lister said. "What have you got, El-tee?"

More energy bolts splashed across the front of the shield. One of them punched through the titanium, whooshing past Roy's face and singeing his cheek. Molten steel dripped from the searing hot, red-ringed hole. The surface of the shield heated up several degrees in temperature.

"I'm going to jump into that Widow and fire up the fore thruster engines," he told them. "That should generate enough lift to kick her off that chunk of polycrete and upright, then I'll use the cannon to blast them out of our way. The only problem is you're going to have lay down covering fire for me while I get there."

"Sounds like a plan to me, El-tee." Lister said. "Just say the word."

"All our weapons seem to do is piss them off," Silva interjected. "What the hell do you suggest?"

"Lister," Roy said, "how many missiles do the Titans have left?"

"One round apiece, sir."

"Good," Roy nodded. "That should distract them long enough for me to get to the Widow."

"We better do it quick," Silva said. "Echo's running out of time."

Another series of alien energy weapons splashed across the plate.

"Get ready to empty those Titans," Lister yelled to his men. He shouldered his MAR. "Ready when you are, El-tee. Good luck."

Roy eased his way to edge of the shield. He peeked out again to check and make sure he had a clear run. There were no obstructions in the way. It was going to be a hell of a dash, though. If those things spotted him, he'd be dead in an instant.

His grip on the Razor tightened. Roy stood up, inched forward, and readied himself to run. He took a deep breath—and broke for the Widow as fast as he could.

"Fire!" Lister yelled, then Roy heard the unmistakable thumps of the missiles leaving their tubes. They shrilled over his head, trailing exhaust.

The ground shook moments later when the missiles struck their targets. Red liquid and chunks of thick brown flesh rained down onto the asphalt. Several of the aliens had been blown to smithereens. The rest wheeled around toward Lister and Silva and opened fire. The distraction gave Echo squad a few precious seconds to reform, and soon the aliens were caught in a crossfire.

They were doing a good job of managing it, though.

Roy was almost to the Widow.

A bolt of energy hit the ground near his left foot, splashing thick, searing hot liquid onto his leg. His greaves sizzled and bubbled, and the heat coming through his armor plating blistered his leg. He hollered in pain, but he kept going. When he reached the tank, he tucked and rolled; slammed his back up against the safety of its heavily armored hull.

Energy weapons scorched the road in front of him, leaving deep, sizzling scoring marks.

He opened the tank's hatch and hoisted himself into the cockpit.

The tank was at an angle, so it took some degree of effort to strap himself into the pitched seat. With that done, he took a few seconds to orient himself with the controls. He pushed the ignition button and felt the tank shake as its engines warmed up.

A warning klaxon blared in the cabin, an automated alarm that meant the tank was no longer level with the ground. Roy flipped it off.

His fingers danced over the keyboard; he locked in a selection of operational controls. After making sure the 165mm smoothbore main cannon was fully functional, he transferred all of the engines' power into the forward propulsion thrusters. His finger hovered over the booster ignition.

"Here we go," he mumbled and jabbed the button.

The Widow's engines had so much force that the momentum threw Roy backward. He thought his neck was going to snap. The tank righted itself, and he quickly attempted to distribute the propulsion engines' thrust evenly. The tank pitched port, then starboard. It finally leveled out.

Roy punched in targeting data and spun the tank's cannon fifty degrees port so that it faced the aliens.

Seeing this new threat, most of them had now concentrated their fire on him, giving teams Sierra, Gamma, and Echo some respite. However, their weapons had no effect on the Widow tank's thick armor plating. They simply pinged harmlessly off the titanium surface.

Roy grinned. "Payback is one big bitch."

The Widow's cannon fired.

The area became obscured in a thick cloud of smoke. A hail of debris and concrete was still raining down when the smoke cleared, revealing the grisly, charred remains of the aliens. Sierra, Gamma, and Echo squads emerged from cover and made their way to the Widow.

Roy climbed out of the hatch and stepped down off the tank. "Not so tough now, are you, you sons-a-bitches?" He kicked a hunk of flesh.

"Shit, El-tee," Lister said, "you made that look easy."

Roy gauged up the marines assembled before him. He was the ranking officer here. That was protocol. But chain of command aside, he'd proven himself to these marines that he was capable on the battlefield.

His original mission didn't matter right now. He was cut off from command, and didn't even know how far away from Elysium City he'd crashed. He needed to do what he could, and right now, this moment, was what mattered. These Marines had risked their necks to save him—it was time to return the favor. They had to get to the CIC and activate the AA batteries—and it was his job to make sure they did.

Roy unslung and shouldered his Razor. "Marines … let's go give our flyboys their window."

CHAPTER THIRTEEN

"I thought 'being in the shit' was a figure of speech," Penny quipped as she and the rest of Sword team trudged through knee-deep sewage.

"*Shiala,*" Tillium swore in his native Vakari tongue. "It stinks down here."

"*Quiet,*" Casey hissed and held up her fist, signaling her team to stop. She crouched low. "Penny," she whispered, "come here."

As quietly as she could, Penny slogged through the muck. She thumbed off the safety on her MAR.

"What is it?" she whispered.

Casey pressed her finger to her lips. The noise came again; a faint, distant sloshing sound, followed by low, guttural growls. She thumbed her own safety off and brought her MAR to bear.

Penny turned and gave a series of hand signals to Sword team. They fanned out and took defensive positions with their guns shouldered and ready to fire.

The growling continued. Whatever was sloshing around in the sewage was coming fast. It was dark ahead. Casey thought of flipping on the MAR's under-barrel flashlight, but chided herself and quickly decided against it. It would have been a poor tactical choice because they had the jump on whatever was moving their way.

"It's close," Penny whispered. "Very close."

Searching for any sign of movement, Casey focused on the darkness ahead. Her heart stopped when two pairs of big, yellow eyes suddenly appeared—staring right at her. The creature lunged forth out of the abyss. Snarling, it leapt for her, its mouth full of razor sharp teeth.

She and Penny opened fire.

Their muzzle flashes lit up the sewer tunnel like day. The creature's lifeless body splashed down on its side a meter away. Dozens of bullet holes had punctured its body. Rivulets of dark red blood oozed from every one of them.

"It's a darzok." Penny sighed in relief as she checked the creature's body. "It's just a fucking darzok."

"That sure as hell doesn't count as the first kill," Tillium said. "That's just an animal."

"We'll sort that out later, Till," Penny said.

Casey was still crouched on one knee, MAR shouldered. She realized she'd been holding her breath. Exhaling slowing, she tried to steady her nerves as she lowered her MAR.

Penny placed a steadying hand on her shoulder. "You okay, Casey?"

She nodded. "Fine," she whispered and licked her lips. "Let's keep moving. I want complete silence. Hand signals only."

When they reached the first junction, Casey opened a com link to Delany.

"Shield, this is Sword. We've reached the first junction. It's safe to come in behind us, but be weary of darzoks. We ran into one down here. How copy?"

"This is Shield," Delany's voice crackled in over the com. "Solid copy. Good work, Lieutenant. We're right behind you. Proceed to the next checkpoint and standby for further orders. Shield out."

Casey tapped her TATICOM pad. A three-dimensional map of the sewers flickered to life a centimeter above her wrist. "It's another eight hundred meters to the RV," she told her team. "The sewer forks fifty meters ahead into two paths. Penny, Till, and I will take the north. S'varan, you and your team take east. When you come to the first junction, hang a left. We'll meet up at the RV. Understood?"

S'varan nodded. "Understood, ma'am."

"Good. Let's move out."

The teams split.

Penny took point. Their voyage through the foul-smelling sludge resumed. The sewage slowed their speed considerably, and strange noises caused them to halt and listen several times along the way.

Fortunately, both teams were left unhindered by any more darzoks, or any other kind of wild animal.

S'varan and his team reached the rendezvous point shortly after Casey, Penny, and Till.

A rusty metal ladder clung to the side of the wall. It reached up from the sewer water, serving as the conduit that connected to their target manhole covering seven meters above.

Casey opened a com channel to Delany. "Shield, Sword. We've arrived safely at the RV, sir. No sign of anymore darzoks. Awaiting orders, over."

There was a brief moment of static before Delany's voice came in loud and clear. "Shield, here. Copy that, Lieutenant. You are to hold position and wait for us to arrive. In the meantime, send some eyes up through the top of that manhole and get me a visual. Delany, out."

Casey reached into her pants pocket and pulled free the fiber optic probe. She uncoiled it and plugged the end of it to her TACTICOM pad; the probe's images would be relayed right in front of her. She slung her MAR and began to climb the ladder. When she reached the top, she snaked the probe up through a small slit in the manhole.

A tiny screen snapped up on her wrist. The image was that of a dark street, littered with crashed shuttles and ground vehicles. As Casey rotated the probe one hundred and eighty degrees, she saw a massive hulk of something laying adjacent to the probe. It was so large that it blocked out the rest of her field of vision.

Was it the body of a person? Some kind of animal?

She squinted, thinking hard, and was still trying to deduce what it could be when it started to move—and that's when she realized it was a foot … the foot of some kind of beast.

No. Not a beast … it was an alien.

It was one of them.

She couldn't see any more of the creature. It was so large and heavy she could hear its footfalls thumping the ground even beneath a meter of concrete. She could also hear what sounded like at least one more walking around up there.

Casey withdrew the probe and tucked it back into her pocket. She grabbed both sides of the ladder, slid all the way down, and splashed into the water below.

"How are we looking, Casey?" Penny asked.

"We've got a problem." She unslung her MAR. "A big one. Those things are right above us."

Penny shook her head and swore.

Casey took a steadying breath—she knew what had to be done. The hunk of metal that was her MAR felt suddenly very, very cold.

She raised Delany once again.

"Shield, Sword. Come in, over."

There were a few moments of silence, but Delany's calm voice came in seconds later. She could hear his team sloshing through the water in the background. "This is Shield. What's the situation above, Lieutenant?"

"General, we've got contacts above us. I counted at least two, but there's a strong possibility there could be more. We—" she paused, almost not believing what she was about to say "—we're going to need them out of the way before we can move our wounded up through that narrow hole. I … request permission to engage."

"Shit," Delany muttered. He was silent a few moments. "Permission granted. Keep steady, Casey, and give the bastards our regards. Radio in when you've finished cleaning house. Shield out."

"Listen up," Casey said to her team. "We have contacts sitting right above us, and we need to clear them out before we can move our wounded out of here. There's at least two of those things up there, but expect more. We're going to move to the next manhole and emerge a block away. That should let us keep the element of surprise. We're going to split into two teams. Katana will move in from the north and draw their fire; Saber will flank them from the south. We'll snare them in a pincer. Penny, Till, and I are Katana. S'varan, you've got Saber. Understood?"

"Yes, ma'am," her team replied.

When Sword reached the next manhole, Casey once again climbed the ladder and cautiously slid the probe topside. Like she'd hoped, there wasn't any sign of movement. The street was empty. She retracted the probe, wound it back up, and gave Penny the all-clear signal, who in turn relayed it to the team. Casey carefully raised the manhole-cover with the barrel of her gun— just enough so she could see out and double check.

Though not protocol, Casey insisted on being the first one out. This was her plan. If there was company, she wanted to be the one in trouble, not her teammates. It wasn't the kind of thinking that was familiar to her. She found herself surprised. Maybe she was starting to get the hang of leadership after all.

A quick look around and it was confirmed; they were alone.

She slid the manhole-cover backwards; heard it crunch against the asphalt. She slowly climbed out, MAR held tightly in her left hand, ready to open fire. She scanned the area and found she had emerged in a dirty, narrow alleyway, wedged between two rows of buildings that stood half a kilometer high.

This area of Arcturus Septum was locked in an almost permanent springtime climate, but today the air had a sharp chill to it, and a cold, hard rain fell from the sky. It all sent a shiver running down the whole length of her spine.

God, combat was miserable business.

She swept the area a full three hundred and sixty degrees before giving her team the go-ahead.

Her hands shook—tension, cold … trepidation.

After her last teammate was out, she and Penny slid the manhole-cover back into place.

"Okay," Casey whispered, "you know the drill. S'varan, wait until we draw their fire, then hit them from behind."

"Understood, ma'am," he said with a nod of his head.

"Good luck."

The teams separated.

Casey, Penny, and Till moved down the alleyway at a run. Penny was on point, Till covered the rear. They were wary not to step in any puddles; silence was key, a weapon just as keen and deadly as their assault rifles.

They reached the end of the row; the street in front of them was littered with cars and shuttles. Some had been crushed by falling debris from the buildings above; others were intact, simply abandoned. The first and second-story windows of the buildings Casey could see ahead were shattered.

They halted. Penny and Till split. Each took positions against the last buildings on opposite sides of the row—the main street was right in front of them.

Casey crouched a few meters behind. She scanned the tops of the buildings for any sign of enemy activity, particularly snipers.

Penny and Till popped round their corners and swept the street for hostile enemy forces. Penny raised her offhand and gave Casey the thumbs up. Casey then moved forward and patted Till on the back. He spun about. Penny motioned them forward with two outstretched fingers.

Single file, Katana kept low—Penny on point—while they made their way up the street. For cover, they kept their bodies as close to the buildings on their left-hand side as they could manage.

All Casey could think about was whether she'd survive this, whether she'd make a bad call, a bad decision that would lead to the death of them all. Was she cut out for this? Was she cut out to be a leader?

She was uncertain if she was the best person to be leading these men, although it did bring her consolation to know Penny was with her. Like her, Penny was a crack shot, but she was also a marine, and had the proper training for front-line combat. This wasn't going to be her first firefight.

Casey also had Till. He had served in the Marine Corps longer than both she and Penny had been alive, and had come out unscathed from every battle he'd ever fought. He was also a friend.

Casey hoped that her inexperience wouldn't get in the way of the operation. She'd take a bullet for Penny or Till in a heartbeat, but what she didn't want was for them to focus on protecting her and let their personal feelings toward her distract them from what needed to be done.

She felt hypocritical. But wasn't it the duty of every leader to protect those under his or her charge, yet scold them for risking their safety in her defense? Wasn't it her duty to risk her life in defense of her men? Her teammates? Her friends?

Military protocol or not, she would be damned if she'd let anything happen to Penny. Or Till. Or anyone else on her team. She'd lost enough people today.

Three hundred meters down the stretch was an intersection, and to the left, the enemy lay waiting.

The intersection was choked up with a labyrinth of vehicles, and Casey knew the advantage it brought was twofold: it would provide an extreme amount of cover, and prevent the enemy from retreating once Saber showed up.

Casey whispered, "Stop." They halted and pressed their backs up against the wall of a café, six meters from the street corner. Casey motioned for them to come in closer.

Penny shook off a shiver. "They sure fucked this part of the city up."

"All right," Casey said in a whisper. She brought out the fiber optic probe and inserted the end into her TACTICOM pad. "Let's see how many there actually are." She slung her MAR and dropped prone. She crawled until she was a meter away from the corner of the café. She bent the end of the probe and eased it round the corner.

Casey's heart dropped far into the depths of her feet. Her assumption had proven to be correct. There were more than two—there were *six*!

The aliens were gigantic, easily three meters tall.

She wasn't a scientist, but the creatures had many features that alluded to a partial synthetic composition. They also had flesh, or at least what appeared to be flesh, and a small ring on their chests that pulsed with red light.

So were they a hybrid of machine *and* organic? Synthetic technology was just now dawning for the UGC, but to mix organic matter with machines was something she didn't think was possible.

She retracted the probe, coiled it, and eased back to Penny and Till. "Remember how I said there may have been more than two?"

Penny and Till nodded.

"I was right. There are six. And they're taller than a damn Tiberan, and twice as wide."

Till shifted his weight and sighed. "This should be fun. What do you want to do, Casey?"

"Saber should be in position," she whispered. "I hope. So we just have to draw their attention long enough for S'varan to come in from behind and finish them. We'll use that mess of vehicles as cover." She pointed to the cars with her MAR. "How many grenades do we have?"

Tillium patted his utility vest. "I've got two."

"And I've got one, so that makes three. What about you, Pen?"

"Two," she said.

"Okay," Casey said. "So five grenades and our assault weapons. We all have extra mags. If we need to, and something tells me we might, we'll pool our reserves."

She exhaled deeply and let the back of her head rest against the brick wall. Her breathing was ragged. Her heart felt as if it was going to burst from her chest. She'd never been so nervous in her life.

"Casey," Penny's calm voice soothed her. She placed a hand on her shoulder. "You're going to do fine. Till and I have got your back. We're a team, remember?"

"We're with you, Casey," Till said. "You've gotten us this far. We're with you the rest of the way."

Casey answered with a weak smile and nodded. "Okay. Thank you." She took a steadying breath. "Right. Let's get into cover and start the parade."

Penny and Till shouldered their MARs.

"We're ready when you are," Penny said.

"Move!"

They broke for the vehicles at a low run and slid into cover behind a cargo truck. There was a huge titanium cargo container resting on its bed.

Casey stuck her head out to get a view of the aliens. She felt the slightest splash of confidence begin to wash over her previous doubts and fears. They had the element of surprise *and* the advantage of a flanking maneuver. Her feeling of assurance shattered into a million fragments when two more of the aliens walked out of the nearest building— dragging four civilians between them.

"*Merde!*" Casey hissed and sank back down.

"What?" Penny asked. "What's wrong?"

"Two more of them just walked out of the bakery, and they've got prisoners. Civilians. Four of them."

"God *damn* it," Penny said through clenched teeth. "Is this going to get any better?"

Till poked his head round the corner. "We need to do something fast."

"Get ready to lob those grenades as soon as the civvies get clear." Casey stood up and shouldered her MAR; pressed the stock tight against her shoulder. Her hope was that a well-placed burst would distract the aliens, make them forget about their prisoners long enough for the civilians to run clear, and get out of the line of fire.

She didn't hope. She prayed to God.

Casey sighted up the closest alien, aimed for the odd mechanism on its chest, steadied her breathing—and squeezed the trigger.

A four-round burst caught the chest-ring dead center. A jet of red liquid fountained outward. The creature howled, went rigid, and crumpled to the ground.

The others turned and began to fire into the thick of the vehicles, but they couldn't yet see their assailants. As Casey had so hoped, they momentarily lost interest in their civilian prisoners and dropped them to the ground.

The civilians seized the opportunity and scrambled as fast as they could down the street in the opposite direction.

Penny and Till lobbed their grenades.

They detonated in a gout of fire and smoke, blowing two of the aliens apart and sending a hail of chunks of flesh and red gore raining down onto the street.

Penny and Till followed up with a barrage of full automatic fire.

A firestorm of rounds slammed into the aliens' body armor, too many for it to handle. They punched through the plating and punctured the areas that weren't covered; the bullets tore into flesh and severed cords.

Another dropped dead.

Alien weapons' fire thumped and sizzled as it hit the cars and shuttles in front of their position. Rounds dented the thick titanium cargo container, and some even punched through it. A lance of searing hot energy scythed into the truck—straight through the container. It missed Penny's head by mere centimeters. It was so hot she bellowed a cry of pain, but she kept firing.

Casey was tempted to open up with full automatic fire, but kept firing in short, controlled bursts until her MAR clacked dry.

"I'm out!" she screamed and ducked down low. She ejected the spent magazine, slapped a fresh one home, cycled the bolt, and popped back up. She had an alien in her sights—she focused hard, steadied her breath—but the sound of gunfire erupting behind the creatures broke her concentration.

Saber had arrived.

The aliens began to back slowly into the bakery, concentrating a majority of their fire on Saber.

One of S'varan's marines was cut down by energy beams; she was sheared completely in half.

"Advance!" Casey yelled over the sound of gunfire to Penny and Till.

They broke cover and started for the front row of vehicles, shell casings streaming from their guns in torrents as they ran. Saber was really putting the pressure on the aliens, keeping the mainstream of the attention on them. Another marine was struck with energy weapons. He fell.

The aliens had shrugged off a barrage of rounds like they were nothing, but after a grenade took out two more and blew the legs off a third, the concentrated fire from both Katana and Saber finally brought down the last three in a relentless firestorm of ten-millimeter rounds.

And then, it was over.

The air was still and quiet, thick with the smell of gunpowder and smoke.

"Make sure they're all dead," Casey said. "I don't want any more surprises."

They moved from body to body, putting four rounds into each one: two through the head, two through the chest-ring.

The alien without legs was still alive when Penny approached it. It snapped its mandibles at her and uttered a low growl. Red liquid bubbled and frothed from its mouth. She planted her foot in its chest and raised her assault rifle.

It seemed to laugh.

"Foolish creature," it gurgled. The sound of its deep, resonate voice unnerved her. "You cannot kill us."

"Oh no?" Penny said. "Fucking watch me." She emptied the remainder of her clip into its head, spattering it to a pulp. "You all sure look dead to me."

Casey raggedly exhaled. Her hands were shaking. She was sweating. Her heart was pounding in her throat. But she had done it, and she was alive. She surveyed her squad. Saber had taken two casualties. She turned to Penny. "Well," she said panting. "That was different."

Penny didn't have time to reply.

A creature—this one almost a full meter taller than its friends—jumped down from the roof of the bakery, a two meter-long sword in its hand.

Before Private Walker knew what was happening, the alien thrust the sword through his back—impaling him. The alien flung him into the side of the building with a bone-crushing smack. Petty Officer Yilez managed to squeeze off two rounds before it picked him up by his head and threw him into Penny and Till, sending them all flying. It sideswiped S'varan with its fist—knocking him to the ground.

Then it made a beeline for Casey.

She didn't even have time to raise her MAR. All she could manage was to squeeze off a quarter clip from the hip. The bullets ripped into the alien's head, but it didn't stop coming. Then she saw the sword scything for her in a downward cleaving motion.

Time slowed down.

Casey threw herself to the ground and watched the sword slice the air she had occupied only moments before. It hit the ground with so much force the asphalt cracked. Her MAR skidded across the ground and stopped four meters away.

The alien would take a second to recover—maybe two—so it was either get up and make a run for the MAR now, or get sliced in half.

She chose the former.

Casey scrambled up from the ground and sprinted toward the assault rifle. It was three meters away, then two—it was almost within her grasp, but she stumbled, lost her balance, and fell hard on her stomach. The impact knocked the wind right out of her.

She gasped for air, rolled on her back.

The big alien was standing over her.

It raised its sword high to strike one final blow.

Its head exploded.

Bits of hard material and translucent red gore splashed all over Casey's body. The alien's sword dropped harmlessly from its grasp and its body fell forward. The ground quaked beneath it.

Standing in its place was General Delany, palls of smoke curling from the barrel of the shotgun in his hands.

Casey, her mouth agape, let out a cry of both disbelief and reprieve, and fell backward onto the asphalt. She laughed. "I owe you one, sir." She panted. "A big one."

Delany stood over her and offered his hand.

She took it and he helped her to her feet. She saw Penny helping Till up from the ground. They both looked unharmed. S'varan was a bit dazed, but he was otherwise fine. The others, however, were dead.

S'varan went and fetched the civilians that had almost run head-long into Saber team during the fight from their hiding spot. When they arrived, they offered to assist in helping move the wounded up the ladder and out of the sewers.

When everyone was topside, Penny radioed for evac.

Casey stood next to Delany as the two somberly watched the medics lay blankets over the bodies of the four soldiers that had been lost ... lost under *her* watch.

"You did well, Casey." Delany said. "And I mean it. But there are always casualties in war. You can't blame yourself for it. You just have to accept it and go on."

"Does it always feel this way?"

"Not to everyone," he said, "but it does to me."

"General, sir?" Penny approached. "Bird's on its way. ETA three minutes."

"Very good, Chief," Delany said. "Pop some smoke, and make sure the civvies and our wounded are ready for dust off as soon as they arrive. Lieutenant, go with her."

They saluted. "Sir, yes, sir." They said in unison.

"You're never going to believe who one of those civvies is," Penny said to Casey as they made their way toward the ruined building sheltering the wounded soldiers.

"Who?"

"Sarah Finoc."

"That really terrible reporter on TGN? The one that gets punched out like twice a week?"

Penny laughed. "Yep. And damn, speak of the devil, here she comes."

Sarah Finoc was practically standing in front of them when Casey looked up.

"Lieutenant," she said and held out her hand. "Sarah Finoc. Trans Galactic News. Thank you for saving my ... *our* ... asses back there."

Casey shook her hand. "You're welcome. How did you end up as hostages?"

A grim expression came over Finoc's face. "I was doing a story on the attack when my entire crew and I were ambushed by those things. When I woke up, my editor and I were the only two left. I don't know how those other people got there, or what those things did to the rest of my crew."

"Well, you're safe now," Casey said consolingly. She didn't want to ask any more questions. This woman had been through enough. "Evac is on its way to take you to the nearest planetary evacuation zone."

"Thank you, again, Lieutenant, and to you, Chief," She looked at Penny and nodded. "Maybe you guys could give me an exclusive after this mess is all cleared up."

"God," Casey whispered as Finoc walked away. "Poor thing. And to think I actually laugh every time someone slugs her."

"Casey," Penny turned to her. "You did a hell of a job back there, and I mean it. I'm proud of you."

Casey smiled. "Thank you, Pen. I couldn't have done it without you."

"Yes, you could have," she replied. "Not as fashionably, of course," she said playfully, "but you could have. Now let's go see who's ready to get the hell out of here, shall we?"

Casey and Penny helped the medics prep the wounded for evac. When the Angel dropship arrived, everyone helped in loading the injured soldiers into the troop bay. Delany gave them a quick pep talk then took his place next to Casey. They watched the dropship lift off.

"So what's next, sir?" Casey asked.

"I need to get ahold of command," Delany said. "Let them know—"

An earsplitting eruption of thunder cut Delany off mid-sentence, and some kind of projectile struck the portside of the Angel. The soldiers dove to the asphalt as it—and every soul aboard—exploded. Six alien gunships flew in over the tops of the buildings, blasting up bits of asphalt as they unleashed a barrage from their weapons.

Delany grabbed Casey's arm and hoisted her to her feet. "The Telecom Tower!" he screamed to be heard over the sounds of battle. "Run!"

Casey and Delany bolted across the street as fast as they were able. Bolts of alien energy-weapons' fire tore up the concrete around them; several people had already been mowed down by the time Casey and Delany reached the Telecom Tower's steps. Penny, Till, and three others were already at the top of the steps, firing their MARs at the alien dropships. Casey looked behind her to see them unloading dozens of alien foot soldiers.

"Get inside!" Till yelled.

He and Penny were the last to step through the lobby doors. When they closed, Penny smashed the keypad with the butt of her assault rifle. The doors' locking mechanism jammed, barring the aliens from entry—at least conventionally. However, it also sealed everyone inside.

They regrouped in the lobby and took the stairs up to the highest floor. Once in the rear-most office, they barricaded the doors with desks, tables, and chairs.

"*Fuck!*" a corporal yelled as he kicked a chair. "Now what are we supposed to do?"

"Shut it, marine!" Till snapped. "Get ahold of yourself. And that goes for all of you. We're not out of the game yet."

Casey looked around the room. She counted fourteen heads. *Fourteen* of them had made it in.

Panting heavily, Delany had his hands on his knees. "Till, get on the horn and relay our coordinates. Hopefully someone will respond."

"On it, sir."

"Chief," Delany called for Penny.

"Sir?"

"Take an inventory on our weapons and ammo."

"Yes, sir."

Delany was in his sixties. The run up a hundred flights of stairs had really taken its toll on him.

Casey touched his shoulder. "Sir," she whispered. "Are you okay?"

"Yeah," his voice was shaky. Not from fear, but from exertion. "I'll be fine."

Penny finished tallying their equipment. Casey wished her report to Delany were better. There were enough weapons to go around, but ammo was scarce.

"We're really going to have to make every shot count when those things come through that door," Penny told him. "After that … the only thing left is hand-to-hand, and, for some reason, I'm not feeling good about that for us."

"Maybe someone will respond to our distress call before it comes to that," Delany said. "I am the Deputy Chief of Arcturus Septum Command. Let's hope that counts for something today."

Casey crouched down behind an overturned desk and rested the barrel of her MAR on its surface. She leveled it at the door. Penny took position next to her.

"I cannot believe that just actually *fucking* happened," she whispered to Casey low enough so that only she would hear. "Everyone aboard that goddamn Angel ... God," her voice trailed off.

"I know," Casey replied.

For a long while, they all listened to the noises many floors below—glass was breaking, doors thumped as they were kicked down. The aliens were searching for them.

A marine wiped sweat from his forehead with the back of his palm. "How long before they get in here?"

Casey shook her head. "Not long."

CHAPTER FOURTEEN

1205 hours, January 24, 2343

Delta Sagittaurii System, planet Arcturus Septum

Ryhs Airfield FOB

"Lieutenant Locke," a voice came in over the com. "This is Major Firan. The CIC is under heavy enemy assault. Delta and Lima squads are doing their best, but they won't hold out much longer. What's your ETA?"

Roy jammed a finger in his ear. "Almost there, sir. ETA about three minutes. Do we know the strength of the enemy?"

"Last report put their number around fifteen. Take them out and activate the air defense cannons so my fighters can launch. Do it soon, son. We're running out of time. Keep me posted. I'll be on priority channel six. Firan out."

Dull explosions continued to thump the ground beneath Roy's boots. The air was thick with the smell of smoke and fumes. Screams and echoes of gunfire were all around him.

The monsoon-like rain pelted Sierra, Gamma, and Echo squads without mercy, and it showed no signs of yielding any time soon; it penetrated their fatigues, soaking the marines right down to the bone while they ran toward the furious battle raging at the CIC. The long stretch of road before them was cracked and pitted with smoking craters. The buildings on either side didn't look much better. Many had suffered serious structural damage.

Roy and his marines had been able to scavenge extra magazines and Titan missiles from a small armory along the way. They'd need them once they got to the objective.

They were close.

The CIC was just around the next turn. It served as the control center for the entire base defense system, and if the enemy took it, there would be no hope for an effective counter-attack.

When they rounded the corner, Roy gauged the situation.

More than a dozen aliens had Lima and Delta squads pinned down tight, blasting them with salvos of crackling beams and bolts of angry red energy. The marines took cover behind a wall of battle shields; periodically, they tried to answer with gunfire of their own.

Scores of bodies from both sides littered the road. The aliens had taken significant casualties, though they were steadily advancing toward the marine blockade.

With a series of hand motions, Roy told Echo and Sierra to double back and wheel left, which would bring them into a flanking maneuver. He then split Gamma into two fire teams.

"Open up with those Titan missiles on my signal." Roy told them. He held up three fingers and counted down … three … two … one. He made a fist. "Fire!"

Two sets of missiles thumped as they left their tubes. They streaked forward and punched into the thick of the alien foot soldiers. A shower of limbs and red gore fell to the ground, giving Lima and Delta squads a much-needed window. They popped up from behind cover and concentrated their fire, spraying the aliens with hundreds of rounds.

Roy and his men charged forward, emptying their clips, just as Echo and Sierra emerged from behind to join in the relentless assault.

The aliens didn't panic. Either they weren't afraid of death, or they didn't care. Their movements were executed decisively and purposefully. They took time to line up shots and paid for it dearly, though they took out a number of marines before finally succumbing to the maelstrom of gunfire.

Once the last alien stopped moving, Roy ordered the teams to cease fire.

There was no need to check the creatures' bodies; most had been spattered and shredded into a mess of blood, pulpy flesh, and something else.

Echo was now down to half-strength. Sierra and Gamma had taken four casualties each. Delta and Lima together totaled nine men.

It was hard to swallow, but right now they had to cut their losses and activate those AA cannons. The base's survival—and the survival of hundreds more—depended upon it.

"Silva," Roy called. "You and the rest of the squads hold the line."

"Roger, sir."

"Lister, you and Gamma on me. We've got to get those AA guns online."

"With you, El-tee."

Roy and Gamma stepped through the double doors of CIC.

The interior of the building was a mess, strewn with the bodies of dead navy techs. Roy and his marines wove their way through a labyrinth of overturned desks, tables, and fallen debris to the ops room in the back of the structure. Lister and two others checked the dead bodies in the hopes that maybe someone was still alive—they weren't.

Roy frowned. *So many lives.*

The ops room had suffered considerable damage. Several light fixtures dangled from the ceiling by their wires, spitting showers of sparks, and a fallen steel beam had flattened an entire row of coms stations. He picked his way to the back of the room, where he found the fire control station against the far wall. To his relief, it looked unharmed.

Roy slung his Razor.

He furiously typed in a series of commands on the station's keypad. On the screen above him, a readout of the anti-air guns appeared. Only thirty-six of the original hundred were functional.

He hoped that number would be sufficient enough to buy the fighters enough time to launch.

The guns were calibrated. Roy jabbed the execute key.

Nothing happened.

An error message flashed onscreen. He attempted a second time—retyped the commands more carefully, pressed execute again ... nothing.

"Damn it," he muttered through clenched teeth. He looked over his shoulder. "Lister, I need a tech. Now."

The Staff Sergeant sent Corporal Lurren forth.

"Something's wrong," Roy told him. "The AA guns won't activate. For some reason, the signal isn't getting through."

Lurren crouched down and removed a panel from the side of the station. He felt his way through the tangled mess of wires and cables.

A few seconds later he looked at Roy and said, "Sir, the main uplink circuits are fried. The station can't send a signal through to the AA guns unless I repair it."

"Well isn't there a backup station somewhere?"

"There is, sir," he said and pointed. "Two actually. But they're both underneath that slab of polycrete."

"Great," Roy said under his breath. "How long will it take you to fix it?"

"At least fifteen minutes, sir," Lurren said.

Roy opened a com channel and patched it through to priority channel six. "Major Firan? This is Lieutenant Locke. Come in, over."

There was static, then he heard: "Firan here. I read you, Lieutenant. What's your situation? Why haven't those AA guns fired yet?"

"Sir, the station is damaged. We are attempting to repair it, but it's going to take some time. We're moving as fast as we can."

"Hold on, Locke," Firan said.

Roy heard him talking to someone, and then he came back and said, "Lieutenant, whatever you're going to do, you had better do it quick. You've got a large enemy force inbound, estimated at least thirty strong."

Roy's hands clenched into fists. "Jesus, we can't catch a break," he muttered under his breath. "What's their ETA, sir?"

"ETA four minutes. All squads are currently engaged with enemy forces. I cannot send you any reinforcements. You're on your own. Hold that CIC at all costs, do you understand me?"

"Yes, sir," Roy said. "I understand."

"Glad to hear it, Locke. Give those creatures everything you've got. Good luck. As soon as those AA guns come online I'll scramble the fighters. Firan out."

Roy turned to Lister. "Lister, we've got over two dozen of those things coming our way. We need to hold this position until Lurren can complete his repairs. Go outside and get everyone ready."

Lister nodded. "Sir, yes, sir." He promptly left.

"Lurren," Roy said to the young corporal. He knelt down next to him. "We'll buy you all the time we can, but you've got to move fast. Once you make your repairs you activate those guns ASAP."

"Understood, sir."

Roy made his way outside where he found the squads checking their equipment, swapping magazines, and pulling the battle shields into a tight semi-circle around the CIC's entrance.

Staff Sergeant Silva had taken a quick inventory of their remaining ammunition and explosives. The numbers were fair, but they wouldn't have the ability to last for an extended duration—especially not after the firepower it took to put just one of those aliens down.

Gamma squad's medic insisted on pumping Roy full of more stims and painkillers to boost his ebbing strength. He would have refused, but battlefield fatigue and the physical trauma resulting from the crash were taking its toll. He popped a handful of pills and downed them with a swig of water.

"I'm getting movement on radar," Silva reported. "Enemy forces three hundred meters and closing fast."

"All right," Roy yelled. "We hold this position and smear whatever comes our way. I want short, controlled bursts. Concentrate your fire on their chests. That seems to be the quickest way to bring them down."

The marines quickly scrambled and took defensive positions behind the battle shields, weapons shouldered and ready to open up.

"Two hundred meters," Silva said.

"One fifty ..."

"One twenty-five ..."

"As soon as they come in range, let them have it," Roy ordered. "Remember, short, controlled bursts."

"One hundred meters."

"Ready those Titans and fire on my order," Roy ordered. "Empty both tubes."

"Enemy forces twenty-five meters and holding."

All eyes were glued to a curtain of smoke and dust that hung ahead twenty meters distant. It clung to the road and obscured what lay beyond, providing an advantageous smokescreen for the enemy.

Roy heard the scuffle of footsteps, and the enemy emerged from the haze.

"Missiles, *mark!*"

The Titans thumped, sent three sets of missiles whooshing forth. They impacted the ground in front of the aliens and consumed them in a cloud of smoke and fire. There was hardly a second's pause before the next wave of four burst through the smoke at a run.

The marines opened up.

A storm of hundreds of rounds peppered the aliens' mottled hides and tore their bodies to ribbons. They stumbled and fell, only to be bounded over by a dozen more. Their weapons discharged, spitting forth streams of crimson beams and bolts of red energy that slammed into the fore of the battle shields—and half-a-dozen unlucky marines.

Roy ducked behind cover and heard a succession of energy blasts thump across the face of his shield. He popped up, sighted his carbine on the nearest alien's chest, and squeezed the trigger three times. A trio of four-round bursts found their mark. The ring flickered and sparked, and the creature fell.

He sighted another alien and emptied the rest of his clip into its head. The bullets ripped into its flesh and sprayed the road and its nearby friends with crimson gore.

It fell forward, dead.

Roy dropped back down behind cover, ejected his spent clip, and slapped a fresh one into the receiver.

Before he had the chance to come back up, two aliens broke through the line and vaulted over the top of the battle shields.

Long, semi-transparent crimson blades materialized from a slit on their wrists. They crackled with an unnatural energy. The aliens stabbed and slashed, took out seven marines in less than five seconds. One man's head was lopped clean off his shoulders. His heavy Tiberan body crumpled to the ground.

Roy saw Silva squeeze off a round from his shotgun, blasting the blade-arm of the first alien completely off. Howling in rage, translucent red blood squirting from its shredded nub like a fountain, it spun to face him. Silva promptly answered its roar with another blast to the chest, putting it down.

He spun to face the second alien. But before he had the time to pump another round into the chamber, he was impaled by one of the meter-long blades through the abdomen.

The alien lifted his body from the ground, brought him in close to its face, and roared in victory.

Silva's last act was shoving his shotgun under the creature's chin and pulling the trigger.

Its head exploded and the blade dissipated.

Silva fell on his back, his eyes staring blankly up at the sky. Blood dribbled from the corner of his mouth.

Losing Silva sparked a pang of rising anger in Roy. "Keep your fields of fire tight!" he yelled to his men. "Don't let any more of them through!"

He pulsed the Razor's trigger until his clip ran dry, ducked down, swapped his clip, and primed two grenades. "Frag out!" He sent them over the top, heard them detonate, and took a second to open a com channel to Lurren.

"Corporal," he panted. "What's the status? How much longer?"

"Almost done, sir," came the reply. "Just a few more minutes!"

"Hurry up, goddamn it!" Roy growled. "It's getting ugly out here!" He cut the link.

"Lieutenant!"

That was Lister's voice.

Roy looked up and saw him pointing out toward the road. He arose to witness two of the largest beings he had ever seen coming straight for the blockade.

They were a full meter taller than any of the others, and one a quarter-meter taller than its companion. In their hands they each carried a two meter-long, grey metal blade.

Roy and the remaining marines gave them everything they had.

Countless rounds hammered into them, spilling rivers of red blood, but it didn't faze them. The beings broke into a sprint, their long strides covering the several-meter distance in seconds.

Then they leapt over the barrier of battle shields.

One man was crushed under the weight of a gigantic, three-toed foot. Lister was sideswiped with a fist that sent him reeling end over end over the barrier. His MAR was knocked from his grasp. He landed hard on the road.

The larger of the two spun round to face Roy.

It lunged.

Roy took a bracing stance and met its charge by slamming the butt of his Razor into its jaw as hard as he could. He heard a sickening crunching sound. The creature staggered backward; strings of green slime ran from its mouth.

In the millisecond it took the creature to recover, Roy leveled his carbine and fired.

His ten-millimeter shredder rounds hit their mark.

The creature bellowed a deep, guttural growl and swung its sword.

Roy threw himself sideways out of the way and saw the half-meter wide blade crash into the battle shield he had stood in front of seconds before. The titanium battle plate crumbled like foil under the weight of the blade.

Roy rolled upright, crouched on one knee, and again fired his weapon.

The alien snarled. It ran forward and plowed into Roy's body full force.

Stars exploded across his vision—and then, blackness. When he came to, he was lying about five meters away from the barrier; the alien had sent him flying. Still dazed, Roy tried to locate his Razor, but he couldn't. Black dots flecking his already blurred vision, he struggled to stand, and saw the figure of a dark, tall being approach.

His attacker wrapped a massive four-fingered hand around his throat and lifted him upwards, bringing him close to its face.

It opened its mandibles and roared—drenching Roy's face with green slime. Its breath smelled like death, and Roy soon began to lose the sensation in his legs.

He had to do something and fast. The loss of oxygen was causing his senses to taper off slowly, and the sound of the ongoing battle began to dim until it was little more than a dull whisper.

His hands free, he fumbled for his utility vest and pulled out a grenade.

The alien looked at him with what would have passed for amusement.

Roy unsheathed his combat knife and thrust it through the thing's outstretched arm as hard as he could. As it howled in pain, Roy pulled the pin on the grenade and stuffed it into the creature's mouth. It released its grip and began wildly clawing at its maw. Roy fell, mustered all of his strength, and scrambled to get as far away as he could. He hadn't gone far when he heard a muffled thump and felt ice-cold liquid shower his body.

He stumbled, lost his balance, and fell.

It took several moments for him to catch his breath and recompose himself. His strength was almost completely gone, the energy to keep going was fueled now only by adrenaline. He stood up and walked over to get a look at the body of the alien. Its head had been blown off at the shoulders. He casually removed his combat knife from its arm and flung the blood off of it.

He turned and saw the chaos in front of the CIC.

Most of his men were down; dead or wounded—he didn't know.

One of the huge aliens—those juggernauts—was still alive, swiping Roy's men left and right. Lister and two other marines were fighting it in a similar duck-and-fire fashion as he had been, but they wouldn't hold out much longer.

Roy sprang into motion. Full speed, he sprinted for the Juggernaut almost before thinking about it, the only weapon in hand his combat knife.

He leapt over the shields and onto the Juggernaut's back. Trying to shake him off, the alien shook violently left and right, then forward. Roy held on with all his might. When the alien stopped moving for an instant, Roy jumped up on its shoulders, reached forward, and buried his knife into its chest-ring.

The creature went rigid; Roy slipped and fell backwards onto the hard road. He rolled out of the way in time to avoid being crushed by the Juggernaut's falling body.

"Lieutenant!" Lister called in surprise. "Holy *shit!* Are you okay?"

"Regroup," Roy said weakly. "We need to regroup."

"Copy that, sir," Lister said and offered his hand.

Roy accepted it and Lister helped him to his feet. Roy stooped and picked up a discarded MAR-5. He and Lister reformed with the remaining marines behind the shields. They pulled the bodies of the dead and wounded behind cover and took the brief respite to scavenge as much ammo and spare equipment as they could.

A final wave of aliens—numbering well over two-dozen, plus three more of the Juggernauts—began to steadily advance. Their weapons spit an unrelenting barrage of deadly energy.

The marines opened up with their final salvo. This was to be their last stand.

Roy bellowed in anger as he squeezed the trigger—unleashed a hellstorm of full-auto fire.

An alien went down.

He swapped his magazine and opened up again.

Another crumpled under his barrage.

Roy ejected his spent clip. He grabbed for his ammo pouch. He pulled free his last magazine.

He slid it into the receiver and cycled the bolt.

"Lieutenant," Lurren's voice broke in over the com. "Repairs are complete! Activating AA defenses now! Standby!"

It couldn't have come any sooner.

"Hold this position!" Roy yelled over the roar of gunfire. "Give them all you've got! Do *not* let one more through!"

"Got it!" Lurren cried. "AA guns online!"

The anti-air cannons came to life.

They blossomed up from the ground like flowers, spun to face the enemy assault ships, and opened fire. Their twin-barreled autocannons spit 25x115mm high-explosive shells by the thousands, providing a screen of covering fire long enough for the Lancers to finally get in the air.

"Keep the fire on them," Roy shouted to be heard over the deafening sound of gunfire. "Make them pay for every last inch!"

The hail of bullets continued, but the marines' effort to keep this last wave of aliens at bay was ebbing. The creatures numbered too many. In no time, they were nearly on top of the CIC barricade.

In his mind, Roy acknowledged that this was the end. He was oddly comfortable with it. He'd given it all he had. It was all he could have asked for—all any marine could ask for.

Then the coms burst with static, and through it a voice thundered in Roy's ear, "This is Lancer Wing Two-Alpha. Take cover!"

A pair of Lancer fighters flew overhead. Their assault cannons flashed, raking the road in front of Roy's position with a firestorm of gunfire. Their 50mm rounds blew the advancing aliens to pieces.

Roy and his marines let out a cry of victory.

He allowed himself a smile of relief.

"Thanks Two-Alpha," he said over the coms. "You're some damn guardian angels, you know that?"

"No problem, sir," came the reply. "That's the least we could do. Try to stay out of trouble. Two-Alpha out."

The marines watched as the autocannons continued their assault. Lancer fighters and a squadron of Raptor Interceptors swarmed around the three alien assault ships like wasps, stinging hard. Chains of fire erupted across their hulls. They listed; the combined fire from both autocannons and fighters too much to handle, and they were finally engulfed in fire.

The earth trembled when they crashed.

"Lieutenant Locke," a familiar voice said over the com. "Lieutenant Locke, this is Major Firan. Come in, over."

Roy touched his ear. "This is Locke. I read you, Major. Mission accomplished, sir."

"Good job, son. Damn good. I'm sending some squads to relieve you and your men. Medics are on their way, too. Get checked over and hydrate. We'll talk soon."

"Acknowledged, sir," Roy said. "Locke out."

Lister checked Silva's neck for pulse.

He knew he was dead, but there was no harm in it.

Roy knelt down next to Silva. His pale eyes were staring blankly up at the sky. Roy closed them with his fingers, and he and Lister sat for a moment in silence.

"We'll make damn sure they all died for something. That Silva died for something," Roy whispered. "Not just for the base, but for the whole planet. When we wipe those alien bastards off this rock, we'll make sure they leave knowing what a mistake it was to fuck with the Corps."

Lister nodded. "Ah-ooh to that, sir."

Roy heard the hum of an Angel dropship's engines in the distance. He watched the two specks quickly grow into full size. They touched down twenty meters downwind. Their bay doors opened and disgorged several squads of combat-ready marines and several medics that thundered down the ramps and spilled out into the open. They were accompanied by a fleet of rangers and two Widow tanks.

It was a welcome sight.

The surviving soldiers from the CIC battle were being tended to. Crates of food rations were being cracked open and distributed. Dozens of marines carried sheet-covered stretchers into the loading bays of the Angels.

Roy sent Lister over to the queue of soldiers waiting to be seen by the field medics stationed at a makeshift command center. Behind them were plastic-covered cubicles. They were filled with stretchers and crammed with medical equipment of all types. Some were spattered with blotches of blood—red, blue, purple; the spectrum continued.

Roy let the medics check him over. The biodine that Gamma's medic had pumped him with was doing its job. Satisfied, they sent him on his way.

"Take it easy," one of them said. "Biodine clamps onto bones like concrete, but you get hit like you did earlier too many more times and it *will* come lose."

"I'll keep that in mind, Doc." Roy said.

His com crackled.

"Lieutenant Locke, Firan. I need you to report to the command bunker right away."

"Roger, sir," Roy replied. "I'm on my way."

He climbed into a waiting Ranger transport. When he arrived, he saw the command bunker had sustained pretty heavy damage. He stepped over hunks of debris as he made his way in. Two MPs stood guard on either side of the entrance. They stood at arms as he passed.

Inside, techs and logistics officers were rushing this way and that; two dozen were hunched over screens, monitors, terminals, and holographic layouts. A tactical display table dominated the center of the room. Huddled around it were six men. One of them was an Eka bearing the insignia of a major.

Firan looked up as Roy approached. He said something to the people around the table and walked over to greet him.

Roy snapped to attention and saluted. "Lieutenant Locke reporting as ordered, sir."

Firan returned his salute with a six-digit hand. "Come over here." The cartilaginous horns sweeping backward off his head quivered slightly as he spoke. "I want to show you something."

Roy followed him to the tactical display table.

"Bring up Delphine City," Firan said to an officer over his shoulder. "Grid oh-four-nine by six-twelve."

"Yes, sir."

The table's surface warmed to an electric blue. It took only a moment for the table's internal light projectors to stitch together a city, complete with holographic buildings, skyscrapers, blinking red dots, and—hovering ominously over the city's streets like a pestilence—the painfully familiar silhouettes of more of the alien ships Roy had just helped to destroy.

"This is Delphine City," Firan said, "One of the planet's largest population centers. It—and the nearby Delphine Military Base—fell under attack approximately five minutes after the initial assault. It doesn't look like Delphine Base had the same amount of luck we did. By all accounts, the base has virtually been destroyed. However, some people managed to make it out, including the Deputy Chief of Arcturus Septum Command, General Arnold Delany. A short while ago, we picked up an SOS transmission from him requesting aid. He and a handful of other soldiers from Delphine Base are holed up inside the Telecom building here." Firan pointed to a building blinking green. "They've been broadcasting for hours, but we've only just got our long-range coms back up. The general is a high-value target. As the closest surviving base within a hundred kilometers, I've been ordered to send a few squads to get him out of there ASAP. Are you up for another assignment?"

Roy nodded. "Yes, sir. I still have one hell of a bone to pick with those things."

"Good to hear," Firan said. "You're the most experienced officer I have left, so I'm putting you in command of Fifth Platoon." He pointed to the flashing red dots. "Now, these represent enemy strongpoints. Avoid them as best you can. Your top priority is getting General Delany out of there—whatever the cost. Anything else is a secondary objective. Am I clear?"

"Crystal, sir."

"I've uploaded the data on known enemy deployment locations to your COMM database. I have two Angels already being fueled to take you and Gamma, Sierra, and Tango there. Luckily, our armory is still relatively intact. Take whatever you need to get the job done. Dustoff is in twenty minutes at CIC. Dismissed."

Roy saluted, spun on his heel, and left. As he walked through the gate, he smiled inwardly.

Another mission. Another objective. But most importantly, another chance to cream the enemy. What he'd told Firan was true—he had a lot of payback to give them. And they were damn well going to know it by the time he was done.

SECTION IV:

THE BETA CRYSTAL

CHAPTER FIFTEEN

1335 hours, January 24, 2343
Delta Sagittaurii System, planet Arcturus Septum
Delphine City

Through the high-powered scope of his Seraph SRX7AM-S3 sniper rifle, Neravar Lux observed several columns of aliens marching through the streets of Delphine City. Five kilometers to the northeast, a small fleet of dropships were unloading scores more.

Thirty were clustered around the Telecom Tower, standing guard.

There was no sure way of knowing how many more were inside.

Scales and Soren had taken positions in buildings on opposite sides of the office tower that Lux was using as a sniper perch.

"Knife-One," Lux said over the com. "I count approximately thirty targets standing around the Telecom building. Could be double that inside."

"Acknowledged, Lux," Scales replied. "What's the enemy's strength in a seven hundred meter radius?"

"The greatest number of enemy forces is concentrated almost four kilometers to the east. Looks like a few patrol columns between here and Telecom, but nothing we shouldn't be able to evade."

"Acknowledged," Scales said. "Flag those areas then pack it up and get down here on the double."

"On my way."

The com link terminated.

Scales brought up the city's layout on his HUD.

Lux had marked the areas occupied by enemy troops in red. Scales wanted to avoid as much enemy contact as possible. Too much attention could alert the aliens to the Shadows' presence, and reel in half the city's occupation force into the resulting firefight. He and his team were good, but Scales didn't like those odds.

Their original mission to recover the crystal had encountered a slight snag. The site where it was being kept had been locked down since the attack started, and only a member of Arturus Septum Command could lift it. Unfortunately, there was only one man left alive who had that power, and he was stuck in the Telecom Tower.

The flashing red beacons representing enemy patrols followed set paths on Scales' HUD, mirroring their real-time routes. He studied the map carefully. In less than a minute, he'd formulated a plan.

If he and his team timed it right, they could sneak past the first patrol using a back alley and slip into the Telecom building's rear loading dock door before the second patrol passed. That would get them in.

However, getting out was going to require quite a bit more thought.

And there wasn't a whole lot of time for that.

Reports said Delany and his men had been holed up in the tower for over two hours. Scales had no idea why the enemy hadn't gone inside in force yet. It was odd, but he would take whatever he could get. He was grateful they hadn't, no matter what the reason. If captured, Delany represented a significant security breach. He possessed knowledge of sensitive and top-secret information that could compromise a lot of UGC worlds, colonies, secret military installations—and countless people.

"Scales," Soren said over the com. "I'm picking up two inbound targets, five clicks out and closing fast. Radar's flagging them as UGC Angels. The number of IFF transponders I'm seeing indicates thirty-six marines are aboard."

Scales cursed under his breath. If he didn't stop those marines from engaging, they were going to ruin his element of surprise. They'd go in guns blazing and attract the attention of every alien in the city.

However …

He mused over the situation for a second, considered how useful the marines could prove in his plan. The exit strategy he hadn't yet thought up was starting to grow a bit brighter. Almost before he realized it, he'd already put a plan in motion.

"Guess they're here for Delany, too," Lux quipped over the open channel.

"Scales, Angels holding position six hundred meters southwest, position umbra-delta-alpha one-one-four," Soren reported. "Let's hope those aliens didn't hear those engines over the sounds of the storm."

Scales had to alert the marines not to engage, and he had to do it fast. The thought of sending out a general transmission flashed in his mind, but he quickly realized it was too risky a move to broadcast on an unencrypted channel.

He hurriedly brought the transponders up on his HUD, located the highest-ranking officer—*Second Lieutenant Locke, R*—and patched his link through to the marine. "This is Commander Kileeus Scales to Lieutenant Locke. Do not engage the enemy. I repeat, do not engage the enemy. You are to hold position and await further orders. How copy?"

Static and white noise popped in his ear for a full seven seconds before the lieutenant responded. "Solid copy, Commander," the marine—a male—said. "I have orders to rescue a high priority target from the Telecom Tower, sir. It's urgent that my team and I get there ASAP."

"I acknowledge, Lieutenant," Scales replied. "My team and I have the same orders. But this is going to be a pretty one-sided fight if we don't coordinate our efforts. I'm sending coordinates for an RV point, six hundred meters due north, position kinet-terra-constellation two-five-niner. You are to report there immediately for a briefing. Do you copy?"

He heard the lieutenant sigh. "I copy, sir. But with all due respect, we need to move quickly. The general is running out of time and we—"

"Just do it, Lieutenant," Scales cut in. "That's an order."

There was a pause, and then Locke said, "Yes, sir. On our way."

Scales cut the channel and opened a squad-wide link to his team.

"Lux, Soren—change of plan. Marine reinforcements are on their way. Pack it up and come to me on the double. Triple if you can manage."

"Yes, sir," Lux and Soren said almost simultaneously.

Within seconds, the Shadows met up and started the short dash to the RV, a large, five-story apartment building twenty meters from their position.

They got into cover and waited for the marines to show up.

Scales hoped they'd make it quick. The lieutenant was right; the general was running short on time.

"This is supposed to be a stealth op," Soren muttered to Scales over the coms. "Marines don't have the reputation for being the most discrete bunch around. They're only going to get in our way."

"Hey," Lux said in protest.

"Oh c'mon, Lux," Soren countered. "You've been in the Shadows for twelve years."

"Doesn't mean I stopped being a marine, sailor-boy."

"You hearing this, Scales? The *raptor* just actually called me sailor-boy. If it wasn't for us *sailor-boys* flying you around, you *ground-apes* would never get your asses anywhere."

"At least we marines can get shit done."

"Yeah, but you're so damn loud, everyone knows where, when, what, and how when you do."

"Look in the mirror, Soren."

"We need help on this, Soren," Scales piped in. "There's no way we can do this on our own."

"So I take it you have a plan?"

"Yes."

"You wanna share?"

"Not right now."

"Oh, balls, you're never any fun."

Scales picked up movement on his radar. His IFF tagged them as friendlies. "Lux, watch our six. Alert me at the first sign of enemy movement within three hundred meters."

"Aye."

"Soren, on me."

The two Shadows emerged from cover to greet the marines.

Scales couldn't help but think of how alien they must have looked to the soldiers in their sleek, black, full-body combat armor. Only a handful of people outside of the Shadow Organization had ever even heard of the elite warriors, and fewer still had seen them fully armored—and lived to tell about it.

The marines filed into the apartment complex's courtyard. With a flurry of hand signals from the lieutenant, two fire teams broke off from the group and took defensive positions in the surrounding buildings.

When Scales and Soren emerged from the shadows, four marines raised their weapons, unsure exactly which side these tall, strangely clad figures were on. The others took a defensive posture, and tightened the grip on their weapons.

With his superior Vakari eyes, Scales saw a few inch their fingers closer to their triggers. "Stand down," he bellowed before the situation turned sour.

"Drop them, guys," the lieutenant said. The marines lowered their weapons—slowly—but still remained in stance, uncertain.

Scales approved. That kind of alertness in a situation like this meant these men had been trained well.

"Sir," the lieutenant stepped forward to meet Scales and Soren. He snapped a crisp salute. "Second Lieutenant Roy Locke. I'm in temporary command of Fifth Platoon. Sorry for the edginess. It's been a long day."

Scales returned his salute. "Lieutenant Commander Kileeus Scales. No apology needed. We're dangerously short on time and we need to do this fast, so I need you and your men to listen up."

"All ears, sir."

"My team and I are under orders from High Command to extract General Delany. We had devised a plan to slip in undetected, but I'm afraid getting him out is going to be the problem. That's where you and your men are going to come in. Have you had any previous engagements with our guests?"

"Yes, sir," Locke replied. "We all have."

"Then you know how difficult this is going to be," Scales said. "My men and I are going to draw the enemy away from the Telecom building, giving you and your platoon the chance to sweep in, get

Delany, and get him out. We're not sure how many of those things are inside, but it shouldn't be more than you and your men can handle. However, there are several hundred of those things within running distance. Once we draw them out, you're going to have to move fast. We can't hold off a force that large for long."

With something akin to disbelief in his eyes, the lieutenant stared at him. "Sir, if you don't mind me asking, how many of you are there?"

"Three."

"Commander, I don't mean any disrespect, but there's no way in hell the three of you can hold off a force that size for any extended duration. It'll take us at least fifteen minutes to sweep in, get to the top, and back out again. You're going to be overrun in seconds."

"Leave that to us, Lieutenant," Scales said sternly. "You just concentrate on your job."

"Commander … that is the worst plan I've ever heard. It's suicidal, for you as well as for us. Once they overwhelm you, they're going to double back to the Telecom Tower and swarm us before we can even get to the middle floor—provided you even last that long. My men and I have engaged them before, which is why I know there is no way in the whole damn galaxy the thirty-six of us can survive against a force that big. We'll all be dead long before we can reach the general."

"Lieutenant Locke, my men and I are Special Forces," Scales said in a firm tone. "So when I tell you we can hold them off long enough for you to complete your mission, I mean it. I understand your concerns, but I am giving you a direct order. If you're incapable of following it, I'll place someone else in charge. Either way, Delany's out of time, so you need to make your decision now. Can I count on you?"

Locke stared at him. His lips were a razor-thin line. "Yes, sir," he finally said after a long few seconds. Frustration laced his voice.

"Good," Scales said.

He understood where Locke was coming from, as well as the way his plan sounded, and Locke's concern for the wellbeing of his men. But this was a desperate situation. There wasn't time to sit down and draw up another plan. It was the best he had. And he was confident he, Lux, and Soren could hold the aliens off … for a short time.

Scales tapped the screen on his forearm-mounted TACTICOM

pad. A holographic display of Delphine City shimmered to life, overlaid with two pulsing routes—one blue, one green—with the green leading to the Telecom Tower.

"You will follow this route," Scales said, motioning to the green route with an outstretched finger. "Hold position here," he indicated a flashing red triangle, "until I give you confirmation that the enemy is too distracted with us to notice you crawl right up their ass. Do you understand?"

"Yes, sir."

"Excellent." Scales tapped his wrist and Delphine City disappeared. "I've relayed the plan to your command interface. Now we need to move. Get your men ready, Lieutenant. It's time to get the general the hell out of that tower."

CHAPTER SIXTEEN

1350 hours, January 24, 2343

Delta Sagittaurii system, planet Arcturus Septum

Delphine City

The rain that pelted the streets of Delphine City fell in sheets, shelling Roy and his marines with a relentless barrage of liquid artillery as they hustled through the city's backstreets.

This weather was almost as screwed up as the commander's plan.

Scales was crazy. No, not crazy. The man was fucking nuts. How could an officer as high ranking as he think that foolish, suicidal strategy of his was going to work?

Had the circumstances been different, and *hundreds* of aliens weren't going to be drawn into a firefight against three people, Roy would have given Scales credit—and respect—for risking his life and the lives of his teammates to give Fifth Platoon a short window of time to get the general to safety.

This was different. It wasn't heroism—the odds couldn't have been any less in their favor— it was suicide. Roy didn't care if he and his team were Special Forces or not. No matter how good they were, they weren't *that* good.

They weren't *invincible.*

And Roy and the rest of Fifth Platoon were going to pay the price unless he went in, rescued Delany, and got out as fast as he possibly could.

Speed would be their greatest ally here. It was their best—and possibly only—weapon that would see them through this alive.

"Lieutenant," the commander said over the com. "I relayed a rendezvous point to your interface. You and your men are to meet my team there once you have Delany. How copy?"

"Solid copy, sir," Roy said.

The channel clicked off.

Roy huffed in amusement. *I'll at least humor the poor son-of-a-bitch. He'll never live long enough to actually meet us there. We might not live long enough to get there.*

Fifth hustled through the back alleys, painfully aware that an alien could be around the next corner. Fortunately, they reached their destination, a small back alley two hundred and seventy meters from the Telecom Tower, unhindered. Roy held up his fist and gave a series of hand signals. The squads stopped and fanned out. Once the commander gave the order, they were going to make for the building's rear and enter through the loading dock doors.

At least that was the plan. And hopefully one that would go unnoticed—and unimpeded.

But, as Roy had learned over the course of his eight years of service, things never went according to plan.

A Talon Battle Rifle in his hands, he crouched down behind a dumpster. He opened a link to Scales. "Commander, this is Locke. Fifth Platoon in position. I say again, we're in position, over."

"Acknowledged, Lieutenant. Like I said, once we start the show, you're going to have to move fast. Good luck. Scales out." The channel snapped off.

Roy sighed. "Crazy son-of-a-bitch," he mumbled.

Ten slow seconds went by.

He shifted his feet to even out some of his rucksack's weight. At least he'd had time to grab some decent kit before he'd left Ryhs Airfield.

Twenty seconds ticked away.

He tightened his grip on his Talon. His patience were wearing thin. They were being rapidly replaced by frustration.

Thirty seconds.

Then he heard it—crackles of automatic weapons fire erupted down the street; an explosion. The battle had started, and so, too, had the clock.

Roy caught the sounds of strange barks and grunts, then the pattering of heavy feet as the aliens ran toward the firefight. He heard the roar of engines and saw two gunships rumble overhead.

He shook his head slowly.

This is so fucked.

A few seconds later, the com crackled to life, and Commander Scales said, "Execute! I repeat, execute now!" His voice was almost completely drowned out by gunfire.

"Acknowledged, Commander. Executing now." Roy turned to his team and motioned them forward. "Go, go, go!"

The marines burst out of the dark alley and through the backstreets at a low run. Roy could hear the furious assault the commander and his team were spitting out; the explosions and gunfire were unyielding.

He wasn't lying about their skills; that three-man team was putting up a fight damn near equivalent to a few squads of marines.

Roy just hoped it would last long enough.

A flash of lightning lit up the darkened sky, and Roy caught sight of the Telecom Tower in the distance. Its peak loomed high above the city streets.

One hundred seventy-five meters from the tower's docks, at the head of the column, Sergeant Mabalo held up her fist, bringing the squads to a halt. The marines fanned out and took cover.

Fireteams Pelo and Flame wheeled around to watch their six.

Roy opened a link to Mabalo.

"What is it, Sergeant?"

"I see two hostiles, standing guard by the cargo docks, but I'm not sure if they have any friends. Standby."

Roy waited twenty grueling seconds before Mabalo came back.

"Confirmed, sir. Just two. How do you want to do this?"

"All squads hold position," Roy said over the squad-wide com channel. "Be as quiet as you can. I'm coming to you, Sergeant Mabalo."

Roy made his way up to the head of the column, where Mabalo and two others lay prone. Another flash of lightning streaked across the sky, allowing Roy a glimpse of the all-too familiar silhouettes of two massive, shadowy figures.

Mabalo was looking through a pair of night-vision binoculars when Roy dropped down onto his belly beside her.

"Good eyes, Sergeant," he said. "Mind if I take a look?"

She passed the binoculars.

Roy put them up to his eyes and summed up the situation. He passed the binoculars back, crawled backwards, and then got to his knees. He motioned for Corporals Corra and Murad—both highly skilled snipers—to come front and center.

"There are two hostiles blocking our way into the building," Roy whispered to them. "I want them taken out. Take roost on either side of the alley and target the glowing ring on their chests. That should bring them down. Use the fire escapes to get to the roofs. Go."

Both nodded in silent acknowledgement. Roy watched the two Asgards sling their rifles and disappear back down the alley as the darkness swallowed them up.

Lister crouch-walked his way over to Roy.

"How many of them are there?"

"Two," he whispered. "I sent Corra and Murad to take them out. Tell Corporal Guarus to find the tower's floor plan and relay it to Sergeant Mabalo. I want her to know where every entrance, exit, stairwell, elevator, and fire escape is located."

"On it, El-tee."

Corra's voice filtered into Roy's ear.

"Sniper one in position."

"Sniper two in position," Murad said almost immediately after.

"Standby, Lieutenant," Corra said.

"Hand me the binoculars," Roy whispered to Mabalo.

Through the scopes he watched the aliens.

Suddenly they stiffened and appeared to sniff the air as if something had caught their attention. They abruptly turned toward the alleyway—

exposing their chests—and a split second later Roy heard twin reports of thunder, though these hadn't come from the sky.

The aliens went down hard, their chests blown apart by the Seraph rifles' 16.5mm armor piercing rounds.

"Target's neutralized, sir," Murad reported.

"Good work, marines," Roy said. "Stay roosted and keep an eye open. Make sure the coast stays clear, and alert me if anything changes."

"Roger, sir."

Roy passed the binoculars back to Mabalo.

"Sergeant," Roy whispered. "We clear?"

She scanned the area carefully with her acute Asgard eyesight and nodded. "Clear, sir."

"Right. Marines, let's move!"

They double-timed it. Their heavy combat boots thudded down hard against the wet asphalt. They splashed through puddles and pools of rainwater. The marines emerged into the tower's back lot. As Roy stepped over one of the aliens' dead bodies, he heard Lister mutter, "Ugly bastards," and follow up with a prompt kick to the thing's head.

The lot was teeming with abandoned loading equipment, cargo containers, and forklifts.

Some of the machines were still powered on. Something hit Roy—something that he hadn't thought of before. There were no bodies. Not one, neither here nor in any other part of Delphine City he'd come through.

He couldn't determine if that was good or bad.

The marines made their way up a loading ramp. At the top were four garage doors and a maintenance door.

Opening the garage doors would have attracted too much attention, but the maintenance door was the perfect entrance.

Unfortunately, Roy found it locked. It was a thick steel door, far too heavy for their assault rifles to penetrate with any real effect. However, a controlled explosive charge would do the trick.

"Lister," Roy said over the coms. "I need this door open."

Lister sent a demolitions expert who examined the door, made a few calculations, and took a small block of Comp-5 out of his pack. He pulled off the protective strip covering the adhesive tape and planted the shaped-charge a few centimeters above the holographic panel. He motioned for everyone to stand clear.

There was a muffled *bang*, a flash of white light. The charge had done its job.

Mabalo and Tango squad took point.

The tower's interior was pitch black. The only light was the occasional flash of lightning filtering in through the windows. The rain rattled against the glass, an ominous, shapeless beat that made Roy clench his jaw. Rivulets of water slid down the glass, blurring everything outside. If there were any contacts out there, a visual check wasn't going to be of any use.

The marines flipped their barrel lights on and pressed onward.

Sergeant Mabalo led them through a maintenance access way and into the Telecom Tower's lobby. The expensive, richly embroidered Vesuvian carpets were covered in soot, dust, and fallen bits of ceiling. The once proud, lively lobby looked as if a tornado had passed straight through.

Fifth took cover behind anything they could: overturned tables, sofas, plush armchairs, and a fallen pillar that nearly stretched the length of the room.

Roy, Lister, and Sergeant Mabalo took refuge inside the almost fully enclosed reception desk.

A single staircase rose to meet a second floor balcony at the lobby's far end. Off to the balcony's left, a stairwell led to the third floor.

Roy was weary of the balcony. It overlooked the entire room and left them exposed to an assault from above. If that happened, the results would be catastrophic. He needed to get his men out of the lobby and move on as quickly as he could.

Various corridors branched off to the north, no doubt leading to the many elevators, security rooms, and stairs. That left the marines at another disadvantage. The enemy could spill in from all sides.

"Mabalo," Roy whispered. "Where's the general?"

She clicked a button on her helmet, and the tiny holoscreen over her left eye expanded, wrapping around her field of vision. "I'm picking up multiple heat sigs on the top floor." Her eyes moved rapidly from side to side while she scanned loads of information scrolling across the optical screen. "As for our new alien friends—nothing. I'm not seeing one sign that they're even here."

"You say it like it's a bad thing," Lister muttered.

"It may be," Roy countered. "Those things might not show up on thermal. That would only give them the jump on us, and we're pretty damn vulnerable here. Mabalo, find us the quickest route to the top and let's get this over with."

"Roger that, sir." Mabalo was silent a minute, then said, "Sir, the general and his squad—they're moving! Looks like their breaking into a run. What the hell are they—"

Mabalo never got to finish her sentence.

A beam of energy lanced through the air and blew her head apart, showering Roy and Lister with blood, bits of bone, and grey matter. Before her lifeless body hit the floor, six alien soldiers shuffled out from the third floor stairwell and onto the balcony, just as Roy had feared.

He cursed in anger as a bolt of searing hot energy hit the ground in front of him. It melted the carpet and fused it to the polycrete underneath.

"Open fire!" Roy shouldered his Talon and fired up at the balcony with a spray of full automatic fire—hoping to get lucky and catch one of the things in its vulnerable spots.

Fifth Platoon opened up.

The lobby quickly became saturated with the smell of gunpowder and smoke. A haze filled the air.

The aliens' energy weapons were burning right through the wooden reception desk. Roy knew he and Lister had to get into solid cover or they would eat them up in no time. The thick marble pillar looked like it could hold its own. Most of his marines were already sheltered or moving behind it. He tapped Lister on the shoulder and they vaulted over the desk and sprinted for their lives. The rest of the teams provided a screen of covering fire. Roy mantled over the top of the pillar and braced his back against the marble. Lister jumped down right next to him.

Roy checked his Talon's ammo counter. It was down to half. Bolts of energy slammed into the wall in front of him, showering the marines with molten debris. Roy turned, popped up, and fired a stream of rounds.

The bullets caught the target alien in the head. Blood sprayed from its wounds, and the thing slumped forward and tumbled off the balcony to the floor below.

Roy ducked down and swapped his mag. He flipped his battle rifle's selective fire mode to burst.

Corporal Tempem squeezed the trigger on his M34 Grenade Launcher and sent a 40mm grenade soaring up toward the balcony. It exploded in a cloud of fire and smoke. The volley of energy weapons ceased, and Roy gave the order to hold fire. When the smoke cleared, he found chunks of alien blown all over the place.

But the momentary feelings of reprieve were stifled when another squad of creatures filed onto the balcony, taking the place of their fallen brothers.

Both sides traded a storm of fire.

"Son of a *bitch!*" Roy growled. "Keep on them, marines!"

"Can't we catch just *one fucking break?*" Lister bellowed as he sprayed the balcony with a sustained burst of automatic fire.

Tempem poked his head up from the pillar and was about to level the playing field with another 40mm grenade when a particle beam burned through most of his head.

Roy sighted down on the alien farthest to the right and squeezed off two four-round bursts.

The alien moved—it was a clean miss.

Roy cursed and fired again.

This batch got through and tore into its chest-ring. It stiffened and fell backwards.

When he ducked down to reload, Roy saw Tempem's grenade launcher laying a few feet from his dead body. In one motion, he lurched forward and snatched it up. He cocked open the hinge-action chamber and double-checked that a grenade was loaded and ready to go. It was. He snapped it closed and shouldered it tight.

As he popped up from cover and prepared to fire, a storm of gunfire suddenly cut down the alien nearest the third floor stairwell.

Roy realized the bullets had come from the stairwell, and not from his marines.

Half the aliens rounded to face their new assailants. The other half concentrated on Fifth.

Roy sent a grenade soaring up to the balcony above. It blew two of the creatures apart and sent four more tumbling to the ground below.

The marines didn't give them the chance to get back up. They emptied their clips into the aliens' bodies. The rounds pulped their hides and released rivers of gore.

The remaining three creatures on the balcony were sliced to pieces by an unrelenting stream of automatic fire from the unexpected allies somewhere near the third floor stairwell.

The fighting stopped.

All was still, silent.

Roy exhaled deeply.

He waited, listening.

"Clear up," a male voice called.

Roy licked his lips. "Clear down," he said with a sigh of relief.

An assortment of seven soldiers—both marine and navy—strode onto the balcony. They were holding a variety of assault weapons and clad in a disharmony of dented armor, dirty fatigues, and bloodstained civvies.

One of the men wore a grey and silver marine dress uniform. Roy spotted the glint from the gold stars on his collar. Now he knew exactly who had come to his aid; it was General Delany and his men.

"So," the general called down. "I take it you have a plan to get us out of here?"

Roy stood. "Yes, sir." He patched a link through to Scales. "Commander, we have the general and are making for the RV. Repeat, we have General Delany. Get out of there."

There was silence.

The channel washed over with static and white noise.

Roy swore. He had no idea if the commander was still alive. It was unlikely, but he couldn't wait. They had to get out now.

Fifth led Delany and his battle-weary mix of soldiers out of the tower through the loading docks.

When they emerged back into the lot, Roy could scarcely believe the sounds of an ongoing firefight still echoing in the distance. He didn't know how it was possible that the commander and his men were still alive and kicking. But he didn't want to think about it. It didn't matter. Delany was his priority. The RV was his objective. The only thing he needed to focus on was getting the general there unharmed. Once he did, he'd figure out what to do about evac.

It wasn't long before they reached Scales' RV coordinates, the courtyard of an apartment complex six kilometers from the tower.

General Delany and his team walked through the doors and into the lobby.

Then … the firefight stopped.

That was it.

The commander and his men had finally been overtaken.

Roy breathed a sigh of regret. He chided his naivety—he'd really started to believe that Scales was going to pull through. He posted Murad and Corra as lookouts on top of two adjacent apartment buildings.

Now he needed to figure out how to get Delany out. Immediate evac wasn't an option. The city was still too hot for a bird to touch down inside. They'd need to get out of the city and into the open.

Roy started for the apartment complex's interior. Everyone, himself included, was exhausted. However, they had to be more alert now than ever. Danger was still present, and until they were safely out of the hot zone, Roy was going to make sure his marines were on their toes.

He stepped through the apartment's automatic doors and found Delany standing with his back to him in the lobby. He was conversing with one of his soldiers—a woman—when Roy approached.

She stood about five-foot-seven and had a trim, curvy figure with long legs. Her fiery-red hair was pinned into a loose up-do. She was a mess. The dirty civilian clothes she wore were grimy and splashed with familiar red gore. But it didn't matter. Neither dirt nor grime did anything to spoil her gorgeous features. She was beautiful. Absolutely stunning.

Roy waited until she finished talking before he stood to attention and saluted. "Sir," he said.

Delany turned about. "At ease, son. Nice job back there."

"Yeah," the redhead said to Roy, "nice job. What took you guys so long? We lost seven people waiting for someone to come."

Delany turned to her. "Casey ..."

"It's fine, sir." Roy looked at the woman and narrowed his eyes. Her beauty had just taken a dive. "Casey, is it?"

"Yes. Casey Keller. *Junior Lieutenant* Casey Keller."

"So you're an officer, then?"

"Were the words *Junior Lieutenant* not obvious enough for you?"

Ire welled up inside of Roy. Who the hell did this woman think she was? "If I had to guess," he said, "I'd bet you're an academy type, correct?"

Casey shot him a cross glare. "What the hell does that matter?"

"Well," Roy said as calmly as he could manage. It took all of his effort to keep his anger in check and not lose it right then and there. "If you had enlisted and actually *earned* your rank by experiencing battle first hand, experiencing exactly what it means to be an officer instead of sitting in a classroom and hearing about it, you would know that during a situation like this, things can get a little *hectic. Princess.*"

She stepped forward. Her eyes were slits. "You know where you can stick your *first-hand battle experience?*"

"Enough!" Delany said. "Both of you lock it down. We're all tired and strung out, but arguing with each other isn't going to do us a damn bit of good. Casey, this planet is under attack. You should be grateful Lieutenant Locke arrived when he did. And you, Locke, take it easy on her. She's been through a lot today, and it's only her first rodeo. She lost a lot of friends and isn't taking it too well. And she's earned her rank just as much as anyone else here has."

Roy and Casey held their glares for a few moments longer, and then Casey curled her lip and shook her head. She spun around and walked away to cool off. After several steps she stopped and put her hands on her hips and huffed.

Roy couldn't help but take notice of her near perfect figure. When he realized he was staring, he tore himself away and focused his eyes back on Delany.

The general regarded him with a cocked eyebrow. "Now," Delany said, "I speak for all my men, including Casey, when I say thank you for getting us the hell out of that tower."

"Actually," Roy said, "I think my men and I owe you the thanks. Those aliens had the superior position. I'm not sure we would have lasted much longer in that lobby. Are you injured, sir?"

"No," Delany replied. "Everyone's fine. We're just tired. We fended those things off for hours. They wouldn't come in force, only a few at a time. Four or five, maybe. We probably killed fifty of the bastards before you came."

"Hmm," Roy said. "That's … odd."

"Actually," Delany said, "I don't find it odd at all. They knew they had us. I think they wanted to wear us down, wear down our ammo, our spirits. Fighting these things … it's not like fighting the Rebels. We're dealing with a very different kind of enemy here. Those aliens don't fear us. They don't fear death, either, and they want us to know it. Inside that tower, as they sent wave after wave, they showed us they don't stop … and they *never* give up. They know how deadly a weapon psychological warfare can really be."

Delany exhaled heavily. He rubbed at his scruffy chin. "Anyway," he continued, "when we picked up Marine IFF transponders on the scanners, it was actually Lieutenant Keller here who suggested we break cover and make a run for it. So, thank her."

Roy looked at her and raised his eyebrows. He was curiously impressed. He hadn't expected to hear that. "Wow," he said. "That was a pretty good call, princess."

Casey spun around. There was a hellish gleam in her eyes. "Princess?" she repeated. "What the *hell* is that supposed to mean?"

Roy opened his mouth to speak, but Casey stifled him. She held up her hand. "You know what? I don't even want to hear it." She waved at him in a dismissive manner.

"General, sir," she said to Delany as she brushed a lock of fiery red hair from her face, "I strongly recommend we radio for evac and get you out of here before any more of those alien things turn up."

"Negative, Lieutenant," a voice said from behind.

Startled, Roy, Delany, and Casey turned about to see the armored figure of Commander Scales standing in the doorway. His black armor was streaked red with alien blood.

Casey and Delany had looks indicative of shock. Roy's mouth dropped open. "No fucking way," he muttered under his breath. "Commander, sir!" He snapped an honorary salute. "You are the toughest …" his voice trailed off. For once, Roy was at a loss. "Oh, my *God.*"

Scales nodded. "Nice to see you too, Lieutenant." He saluted Delany. "General, sir. Lieutenant Commander Kileeus Scales."

Delany stared in silence. His eyes flickered up and down the commander's body. With furrowed brows, he licked his lips. "At ease, Commander."

"Commander," Casey said to Scales. "What did you mean by negative? You *are* here to get the general off the planet, right?"

Scales sighed. To help alleviate some of the tension, he popped the airtight seal on his helmet and removed it. "Yes, but only after I've completed my mission, Lieutenant," he answered.

"What mission?" Roy cut in. Lines creased his forehead. He folded his arms across his chest.

"My team and I are under orders from HighCom to perform a priority alpha extraction from the Rencorrus facility," Scales explained. "In order to do that we need someone with the proper clearance to lift the lockdown."

"So they did lock it down." Delany rubbed at his chin again. "But Commanding-General Frulnar is—"

"He's dead, sir," Scales said.

Delany closed his eyes and sighed. "Damn it," he whispered in grief. After a few heartbeats, he opened his eyes and said, "I guess I'm next in line."

"Correct, sir."

"General," Casey interjected. "You're the highest ranking officer left on the planet. We have to get you out of here."

"Casey, Lieutenant Locke," Delany said, "Could you give the commander and me some time alone?"

Casey started to object, but then her mouth snapped shut. Fuming, she stormed past Roy and went outside into the rain.

Shaking his head, Roy left the commander and Delany alone in the lobby. *That girl's got one hell of a stick up her ass.* Roy wearily massaged his eyes with his index finger and thumb. He needed to sit down. He'd been at this for hours with no rest. His stomach gurgled. No food, either. And he could drink a river dry.

He took his rucksack off his shoulders and dug for his canteen. Sipping it, he roamed the apartment's halls. He found Lister resting comfortably on a sofa in the east lounge. His rifle was resting across his lap and he had his feet propped up on the coffee table.

Lister acknowledged him with a nod. "El-tee."

Roy took his rucksack off and plopped down hard on the couch.

It felt like such a relief. He ran his fingers through his hair, drew in a long, slow breath, and then let it out while he leaned back against the cushion and put his feet up on the coffee table. "Damn," he muttered. "You might have to yank me up off this couch, Lister."

"I was going to tell you the same," Lister chuckled. "You look troubled, sir, if you don't mind me saying. Well, more so than you have been today, at least. Is there anything you'd like to get off your chest?"

He debriefed him on what the commander had said to Delany.

"He needs him to lift a lockdown?" Lister mused over it a moment. "What did they lock down?"

"I don't know. Someplace called Rencorrus or something."

"Never heard of it."

"Yeah, me neither. Probably classified."

"Yeah," Lister agreed. "Well, classified or not, I hate being a pawn in some damn chess game."

"Yep," Roy sighed. "But that's HighCom for you."

Lister drummed his fingers against his MAR. "What now?"

Roy shrugged. "I don't know. But I'm going to sit here for as long as I can."

One of the members of the commander's team, a human male—lean, tall—stuck his head in the door.

"Lieutenant Locke, Staff Sergeant Lister," he said, "The general wants to see you."

Roy and Lister swapped a quick glance.

"I guess relaxation time's over," Lister muttered.

He and Roy grunted as they pushed themselves up off the couch. Lister's knees cracked when he stood upright.

Roy slung his rucksack over one shoulder and followed the human—one Lieutenant Soren—through the halls and back into the lobby.

"Sir," Roy piped in as they walked, "If you don't mind me asking, how did you and your team manage to hold your own against those aliens for so long?"

"We had to," Soren said matter-of-factly.

Roy rolled his eyes. He had wanted a more in-depth answer than that, but he decided not to press the issue. It really wasn't his biggest concern right now.

Several people were already present in the lobby.

Delany and Scales had gathered Casey, a Vakari Staff Sergeant named Tillium, a tall, slim blonde Staff Chief named Penelope Redfield, and the third, mysterious member of Scales' team, an Asgard called Lux.

Roy, Lister, and Soren completed the council of ranking NCOs and officers. They took their place in the semi-circle gathered before Scales and the general.

"I've been in contact with Command," Scales began. "I requested they give me permission to fill you in on our mission. My team and I are good, but after the events of today, it's now clear to me that trying to do this alone isn't an option anymore. I need your help.

"We were dispatched to recover an alien artifact found in a ruin deep within the Teckstuck Mountains, at a site designated as Rencorrus. Intelligence believes that these aliens have attacked Arcturus Septum in order to find it, which means that whatever this thing actually is, it's important. HighCom has designated its retrieval as priority alpha."

"Commander," Chief Redfield spoke up. "If I may?"

"Go ahead, Chief."

"Why all the secrecy? If this thing is so important, why wouldn't HighCom have sent in every available marine battalion they could?"

"Well, as I understand it," Scales explained, "HighCom wanted to keep this as quiet as they could. Our mission was supposed to be simple: get in, grab the artifact, and get out without drawing any attention from either ally or foe. That way, there would be less of a chance those aliens would discover its location. A massive movement of troops would have been too suspicious. But those things have made this a lot harder than it was supposed to be. Their occupation is planet-wide, and, as I'm sure you're aware, nothing's going according to plan today."

"And you need the general to lift what lockdown, exactly?" Tillium asked.

"The Rencorrus site was only made known to the upper echelons of Command," Scales said. "That circle included both the chief and deputy chief of Arcturus Septum Command. When the aliens attacked, High Command was able to lock the entrance to Rencorrus down. Only those people made aware of its existence have the codes to lift that lockdown. But the only two people on this planet who possess them are Commanding-General Frolnar and General Delany. Unfortunately, Commanding-General Frolnar is dead."

"Where are our reinforcements?" Casey asked.

"The princess has a point," Roy added. "Why hasn't FleetCom sent in a fleet to wipe those things out of the sky? That is the navy's job, after all, isn't it?"

"Command sent word that two hundred and forty-six warships are on their way from neighboring systems," Scales replied coolly. Obviously the navy comment had failed to get to him. "They're set to arrive in two days."

Everyone but Delany sighed in dismay. He remained silent, as Scales had revealed this information to him during their private meeting. However, telling by the look on his face, Roy imagined he was feeling the same hopelessness as everyone else.

"Might as well be two years," Lister mumbled under his breath.

"We have to play the cards we've been dealt," Scales said. "It's not the most ideal situation, but it is the truth. There are already a few platoons of marines stationed at Rencorrus for security. A small team will head into the mountain with me and the general to get the artifact. The rest will have to hold that position until we succeed."

Casey lowered her gaze to the floor. Delany rubbed at his chin. Roy folded his arms across his chest. Penny shook her head.

It was a disturbing prospect, holding position against those things for… how long? Hours? It wasn't something Roy was looking forward to, or something he wanted for his men. However, the commander was right; if the recovery team had any chance of success, they would need everyone else to prevent the aliens from following after them. As Scales had said before, it wasn't the most ideal situation, but it was, though however unsettling, the truth.

Scales scratched the top of his head. "Listen, guys." He toned down the stern command voice Roy had heard from him since they met. This time his tone had a more calming manner to it. It was full of understanding. Scales did connect with them, was totally aware of the grim reality they faced. "I know you've all been through hell today. Lux, Soren, and I haven't slept in three days. But we can't afford to falter now—this is our last push. This is what the battle for Arcturus Septum was for. And if we complete our mission, if we get that crystal and get it safely into space—this battle ends. Those aliens have a purpose for being here—this is it. We take away that purpose, and we take away their will to fight."

Scales looked at their faces in silence, taking the time to lock gazes with everyone arrayed before him. He let the measure of his words sink in before he tapped his forearm. His TACTICOM conjured up a holographic topographical map of the area for everyone to see.

"The Rencorrus site is forty kilometers north of here," he said. "With all the enemy activity, it would be far too great a risk to call for transport. We'll have to hump the distance on foot as quickly as we can. It would be to our benefit to cut through Arigonne Forest. That way we're not as vulnerable to enemy air support. From there, it's almost a straight shot northeast to the site. Command has sent in a resupply package for us here." He jabbed a finger at a blinking blue beacon. "Grid four-eight-four by two-oh-six. Twenty kilometers from target.

"General Delany is still the ranking officer here, but my orders give me full tactical command of this mission. That being said, General, is there anything you'd like to add, sir?"

"I think you've put everything in place, Commander," Delany replied.

"All right," Scales said. "This briefing is concluded. Go gather your gear and your squads and prepare to move out. We don't stop until nightfall. Dismissed."

CHAPTER SEVENTEEN

0500 hours, January 25, 2343
Delta Sagittaurii System, planet Arcturus Septum
Arigonne Forest, roughly 20 kilometers from OMI Site 099876-711X
Designation: "Rencorrus"

Casey shifted her weight on the cold, hard forest floor.

She sat on a small canvas at the foot of a one hundred fifty meter-tall Imperial Redwood tree, reluctantly chewing on bits of her meal ration. The package's content description claimed it was a nice blend of human food—potatoes, chicken in gravy, green beans—but all it looked like was sludge, and it didn't taste much better. But she was so exhausted, so incredibly sore, and so hungry she honestly didn't care. It was the first meal she'd had in over twelve hours, and she'd need every last bit of it to keep up her strength.

At least it was laced with heavy nutrient and vitamin supplements.

Casey washed the last bite down with a swig of water from her canteen.

A slight gust of wind rustled the branches of the treetops high overhead. A shiver ran down the length of her spine, and she clutched the thin military-issue blanket draped over her shoulders, pulling it tighter. The rain had tapered off during the night—something she was thankful for. The damp forest floor was now cloaked in a thick blanket of fog. Occasional, gentle breezes would send wisps of it swirling about her ankles. The early morning air was sharp and cold.

She'd never felt so uncomfortable in her life. Earlier she'd gotten the opportunity to rinse her face and neck clean of all its dirt and grime in a small pond, but her damp, filthy clothes were freezing and she was chilled to the bone. Her tussled red hair hung down, brushing against her shoulders. There were cuts and nicks all over her body.

She needed a shower, a hot meal, and a week's worth of sleep.

The commander had sent a team to recover the resupply package that Command had dropped off. Once they returned, they'd all be on their feet again on a nonstop march to the Rencorrus Site.

Casey didn't know how much she had left in her. The last several hours had taken everything she had, every last ounce of her will, skill, and endurance. She had to keep going, though. She didn't come this far to stop now. If the commander was right and this was indeed the deciding battle for Arcturus Septum, she'd see it through to the end. There was no alternative. Her life depended on it, as did the lives of everyone else.

She glanced up and studied the makeshift campsite.

Sleeping away as if nothing had happened at all, Penny was curled up under another of the huge Imperial Redwood trees six meters away. Tillium and four other marines were sitting in a circle playing Cordum, a Vakari card game analogous to poker. General Delany was reviewing a plan of some sort with Commander Scales. The Asgard named Lux had fieldstripped his MAR and was cleaning the various bits and pieces with a wire brush. More than once she'd caught Lieutenant Locke stealing glances at her, but he appeared pretty preoccupied chatting with Staff Sergeant Lister.

The commander had sent everyone else to recover the package. They weren't expected to be back until 0545.

Casey leaned back and rested her head against the redwood's hard, knotted bole.

There were birds chirping merrily somewhere above, nested cozily in the thick canopy. The crisp air, though cold, was refreshing to breathe in, and smelled faintly of juniper and sage.

Nature was oblivious to what was happening on this planet. Or maybe it didn't care. Maybe it refused to yield to all the wanton death and destruction the aliens had decided this world was due for.

Under other circumstances, Casey may have considered sitting in the middle of the forest under a tree listening to the sounds of nature, a calming and pleasant experience.

But the threat of death lingering overhead like a malevolent rain cloud was sobering, and it kept her aware that they could all die at any moment.

She didn't even know she'd nodded off until she heard twigs crunching. She opened her eyes to see Lieutenant Locke standing over her. He had a blanket rolled up and tucked under his arm. "Thought you looked a bit cold," he said and patted the bundle.

She shook off a shiver. "Thanks."

Roy looked around and regarded the forest with a crinkled brow.

"I'd bet those instructors back at the academy never told you that you might actually have to sleep in a forest someday, did they?"

With a derisive smile, Casey shook her head. "You're really hung up on the whole academy thing, aren't you? I wonder why. Are you afraid we actually come out making better soldiers than someone who enlists? Or is this just your way of flirting?"

Roy chuckled. "You would think that. No, I was just trying to look out for a fellow soldier. Did they not teach you to do that at the academy? It's called camaraderie, princess."

Casey could barely hold her ire in check. Her temper flared. "Why do you keep calling me that?" She growled.

"Because you act like there's some pole jammed up your ass," Roy shot back. "And your attitude? That's exactly what all the richy rich girls like you acted like back home where I came from. That's what they thought they were—princesses."

She retorted with a laugh. "So you think I'm some stuck-up rich kid?"

"I think that's exactly what you are. An only child to some obscenely wealthy parents used to getting whatever the hell she wants."

Casey gave him a dagger-sharp glare. "You don't know anything about me," she said coldly.

"What? Are you telling me I'm wrong?"

She swallowed, hoping to down some of the anger boiling within her. She exhaled deeply. It took all she had to force a smile. "I appreciate your *camaraderie*, Lieutenant Locke, but I'm fine, thank you. You can leave the blanket here or take it with you. Better yet … how about you shove it up your ass?" She tilted her head. "It's up to you."

For a second, he was silent. Then he raised his eyebrows and smiled, and he dropped the wadded-up blanket. He turned to leave. "I'd tell you the same thing," he said over his shoulder. "But that pole probably takes up all the room."

"Jerk," she whispered under her breath as he walked away. She admitted she found him somewhat handsome in looks. At six-foot-three, he was broad-shouldered and muscular, and had pretty brown eyes and close-cropped brown hair.

But she curled her lip in disdain.

Locke's looks were satisfactory, but his character? No. He was an ass; arrogant, opinionated, and judgmental. *And why the hell would he assume I have richy rich parents?*

Casey snorted to herself. She leaned back against the tree and closed her eyes. "That couldn't be farther from the truth," she grumbled. She looked at the folded blanket laying a meter away. "Oh, what the hell?" She grabbed it, doubled it up over the first blanket, and pulled it tight round her shoulders. She leaned back against the tree, found the most comfortable position she could, and closed her eyes.

"Casey," someone said gently some time later. "Wake up."

Casey opened her eyes.

Penny was crouched next to her. "Come on, the commander wants us for another briefing."

Casey ran her hands through her hair. "I was having the loveliest dream," she said. "I was sitting in a cold, damp forest on some planet I'd never heard of until a few months ago. Aliens were attacking and I was so far past the point of exhaustion I thought I was going to drop."

Penny managed a smile. "Funny, I was dreaming the same thing." She patted Casey on the shoulder and stood. "Come on, you."

Casey snatched the blanket from her shoulders. As she arose, she yawned and reached her arms skyward for a stretch. Her back made a loud, satisfying *crack.*

"I'd kill for a shower," Casey commented as she followed Penny across the campsite. She shivered and rubbed her arms for warmth.

"Yeah," Penny said. "Me, too. And hell, mine wouldn't even have to be hot. I'd settle for cold."

"What's the longest you've ever been in the field without a shower?"

"Two weeks," Penny replied.

"No razor, then?"

"Combat knife," she said. "But it's a lot easier to cut yourself that way."

Casey subtly felt her underarm. "I'm good for now," she said. "Thank God I shaved yesterday. But if we're out here too much longer, you'll have to teach me that trick."

"It's harder than you might think."

The commander had a holographic map displayed from his TACTICOM resting on a stump. Casey saw Till, Locke, Lister, Lux, Soren, and Delany already gathered round him. Till and Lister made room for her and Penny as they found their place in the circle.

"Word just came in over the coms that enemy forces are being pushed back," Scales reported. "Slowly, but steadily."

"Well that's good news," Till said.

"Maybe now we can call in some birds to fly us to Rencorrus," Roy said.

"No," Scales countered. "Any kind of transport is still too risky, especially with the general in tow. We're walking the rest of the way on foot like we planned." Scales turned to Soren. "What gifts did OMI leave us under the Christmas tree?"

"A nice assortment of small arms, mainly assault weapons, and plenty of ammo. There were also three crates of grenades, two Titan launchers with four missiles apiece, and two ADE turrets with a thousand rounds each. There are rations and equipment, too."

"I'll take it," Scales said. "Okay, our path is here." He motioned to a blinking red path that snaked through the forest. "This is the most direct route to Rencorrus. Taking it allows us to bypass the foothills and the

Ripstron River. No more breaks—we're going straight to the site. Make final preparations to move out. Assemble your squads and grab some of our new gear, but don't load yourselves down. The ADE turrets are heavy enough. It's already going to take extra time to heft them, and I want us to travel as light as we can. Lux, I want a five-man bodyguard around the general at all times." He met Delany's eyes. "You're too valuable an asset, sir."

"Very well," Delany said.

"Let's get it done, guys."

It took less than ten minutes for everyone to pack up the campsite. Lieutenant Soren and two others began to distribute the new gear.

Delany must have told Soren Casey was an excellent marksman, because when she approached, he said, "Here, Keller," and handed her a Talon Battle Rifle. "That should give you a hell of a lot more accuracy than a MAR. It does have a smaller clip, however, but it makes up for it in stopping power. It fires eleven-point five-millimeter rounds in four round bursts. And take these." He gave her four clips. "They're shredder rounds. They tear through flesh like paper. Now go grab yourself a sidearm. There's grenades in that crate over there, too."

"Thank you, sir." Casey slung her rifle over her shoulder.

A marine allocating sidearms passed her a K2.

There were dozens of grenades—plenty for everyone. If the previous battles had been any indication, they would need them. Casey clipped two to her belt.

Under the lee of an enormous boulder off near the campsite's perimeter, Penny was stuffing extra equipment and some explosives the commander had given her to carry into a small sack. She pointed at the Talon. "New toy?"

"Yep," Casey replied. She unslung the rifle and shouldered it for the first time. She ejected the clip and checked that it was full. She was satisfied with its weight; it was even lighter than a MAR-5. The long barrel and full clip of ammunition balanced each other out nicely. There was a digital ammo counter displayed on a small blue holographic screen under the barrel shroud. She looked through the scope, made a few adjustments. "Nice."

"Casey," Penny came in close. "Listen, you've been one of the best friends I've ever had. I wanted you to know that. Just in case … well, you know, just in case."

"I know," Casey said and smiled. "You, too, Pen. But we'll be fine. And when this is all over, when we're back to hot food and soft, warm sheets, the first round is on me."

"That sounds like a plan," Penny said. "I'm holding you to that. God, I could use a drink now, though."

"Yeah," Casey muttered. "You said it."

"Do you think this thing will be worth it?" Penny asked as Casey buckled her pistol's holster belt round her waist.

"What thing?"

"Whatever the hell those scientists found. That crystal. Do you think it'll be worth all this? All this fighting … all this death?"

"It'd better be. Because all this … the price we've all had to pay, all those thousands of dead soldiers and civilians, seems too much for anything. But who knows …" She slung her Talon. "Maybe it'll be made of chocolate. Then we'll have a real reward waiting for us."

Penny chuckled. "If it is made of chocolate," she said. "I get the bigger half."

"Hey, I'm the ranking officer," Casey protested playfully. "I do."

A few minutes later, the mixed assortment of forty marines and sailors moved out of the relative safety of their campsite and started the march through Arigonne Forest. Scales sent Lieutenants Soren and Lux up ahead to scout out the area around Rencorrus.

With Penny and Till acting as Squad Leaders, Casey had been placed in command of Alpha and Constellation Squads. Lieutenant Locke was given charge of Tango, Gamma, and Sierra.

They'd hiked six kilometers when the first pale light of morning began to filter down from the canopy high overhead. Rays of gray light cut across their path as they trekked across the wet, dew-soaked earth.

The sky quickly turned overcast and the sun was swallowed up with clouds, the weather denying them much of the precious sunlight Casey so longed for. Just when she thought how thankful she was that it wasn't raining, the first few raindrops dripped from leaves high above, quickened their pace, and soon became a downpour.

All she had left to offer the weather was a tired, weary sigh.

No one spoke a word as they journeyed through Arigonne Forest. Maybe it was because everyone was exhausted. Either that or no one had anything to say. What could they say? Everyone Casey was with had been through complete, utter hell for the past twenty hours, and it was a battle that was still far from over.

Plus, if what Command believed was true, if the aliens were after the artifact, what would stop them from mounting another crusade to recover it after it was moved? Would anywhere truly be safe?

She didn't know. She needed to focus on the current situation—the here and now. All she wanted to do was concentrate on putting one foot in front of the other.

For a long while, Casey listened to the patter of raindrops hitting the thick leaves. It was both deafening and entrancing—more so than she realized. When she finally snapped out of it, she'd found the platoon had reached the edge of the forest.

Scales held up his fist.

They halted.

Casey could glimpse small strips of rolling grasslands through the gaps in between the thick, dark tree trunks.

"Everything looks clear, Commander," Lux said over the coms. "We're in the green."

"Right," Scales replied. "All squads proceed to the objective."

It was a twelve-kilometer march across a treeless, relatively flat grassy plain. In the distance, a range of rich, green, tree-covered mountains grew ever closer, rising seventeen-hundred meters above the plain. Their crested peaks were crowned with wisps of grey fog.

When they at last arrived at the Rencorrus Site, Casey discovered it was far from the sparsely defended zone she'd pictured.

Two Widow tanks, a small motor pool of several different variations of Rangers, and two full platoons of marines were stationed around the area. They milled about, tending to and putting up defensive emplacements. Behind a perimeter of battle shields were ten Automatic Defensive Emplacement (ADE) turrets; auto-acquiring 15mm autocannons, and two anti-air Hades Missile launchers.

A female Borean Lieutenant ran across the field to greet them. "Commander," she said to Scales, "General Delany, sir. You couldn't have gotten here sooner. Word just came in from Command: those aliens are coming. They've got ground forces, armor, and air support. They'll be here in less than thirty minutes."

"They finally found it," Delany said.

"Then we don't have much time." Scales turned to face the platoon. His helmet's amplified speakers projected his voice so that everyone could hear.

"This is it, ladies and gentlemen. This is the grand finale. Those aliens came to Arcturus Septum looking for the artifact. It's our job to show them how bad a mistake that was. We're going to cream the bastards so hard, splatter their bodies so far across this plain that they'll wish they'd never set their ugly feet on this rock to begin with. Get dug in and make sure your boots are laced up tight, because we're about to kick those sorry sons-of-bitches back to whatever hellhole they slithered out of."

There was a thunderous echo of hoots, applause, and battlecries.

Casey even joined in with them.

The commander had riled them up. He'd gotten them prepared for this one last, final fight. "Soren, Lux," he said, "You two have command of the defense. Chief Redfield, Tillium, Lister, Lieutenant Keller, and Locke, you're all on me. We're going to go into the site and claim our prize. Now get to it, marines! Hustle!"

They all scrambled to their tasks.

"General, sir," Scales said and motioned for Delany. "Over here, please."

Scales led the way down a small dell and through a thirty-meter-wide pool of waist-deep water. It was fed from a waterfall that spilled down from the foggy peaks of the mountains over a kilometer above, tumbling down countless craggy outcroppings of rocks to the pool below.

Casey had no idea where Scales was taking them. There was nothing beyond the waterfall but a solid stone wall. Unless they were going to be hiking up to the top, she didn't see any other visible route to the facility. She stepped into the water and worked her way in until it lapped at her waist. It was so cold. Scales was in front, then disappeared behind the waterfall. One by one, the falls swallowed them up. It was then Casey realized that the ruin must have been *behind* the waterfall.

Its creators had chosen a clever device that shielded its existence from any unwanted eyes.

Her feet were numb by the time she stepped into the falls. It soaked her; she stumbled twice as the silt beneath her feet shifted. Eventually, she found her way through and was helped up onto a small ledge at the base of the mountain wall by Penny.

A huge, dull gray rectangular door made of solid titanium had been welded over the entrance to the site to keep unwanted visitors out. Protruding from the side of the wall was a small holographic security panel. It was blinking red.

"General, sir," Scales said. "If you could please enter your codes to lift the lockdown."

"Of course." Delany stepped up to the pad. He typed in a flurry of numbers and letters on the holo keypad, and leaned in close and said: "DARKESTBEFORETHEDAWN".

The blinking red panel turned green.

"Authorization codes verified," a disembodied A.I.'s voice said. "Lockdown lifted."

The massive titanium door hissed, rumbled, and parted at a seam that Casey hadn't seen before. The two sides of the door slid into the mountain, and the soldiers stood before an opening in the rock.

Carved into the very stone of the mountains was a black archway, thirty meters tall and ten wide. Strange hieroglyphic symbols dotted the archway and disappeared down the hallway that led into the darkness.

"Thank you, sir," Scales said. "Let's proceed."

Delany fell in line behind Scales and Till. Casey followed closely behind him. For some reason, she didn't want to bring up the rear.

As they journeyed into the mountain, the glyphs on the walls warmed to red, then bright orange, then finally white, bathing the section of corridor they walked down with bright light, following them farther and farther into the mountain complex, silent sentinels guiding them through the darkness. Behind them, the lit glyphs faded and the darkness once again reigned.

Casey ran her fingers against the wall. It was glass-smooth. The glyphs appeared to part of the rock itself, or some kind of technology embedded deep within. "Commander," she said. "How old is this place?"

"Over a hundred and fifty million years," Scales replied. "According to Command."

Lister let out a low whistle.

"God," Casey said. "It looks like it was built yesterday."

The corridor sloped in a gradual decline as they descended deeper and deeper.

"Commander," Lux's voice crackled over the coms. "Enemy sighted. They're here."

"Roger that, Lux," Scales said. "Good luck. Give them the hell they deserve."

"Affirmative, sir." Then, to someone else, Lux yelled, "open fire!"

The mountain shook and the ground vibrated. Dust fell from the ceiling, and there were muffled crackles of gunfire and explosions that Casey could barely pick up.

The battle had begun.

The group pressed on in silence.

For an hour they walked deeper into the mountain cavern until the hallway's floor evened out and the corridor opened up into a chamber.

The ceiling was over a hundred meters high and the room itself stretched fifty meters from end to end, but the chamber looked as if it was just another passage, albeit an unbelievably massive one.

Casey was astounded.

How big were the things that built this place?

The floor before them was crystal clear to the point where Casey feared it might not actually be there and she would plunge into the black abyss below. When she stepped onto it for the first time, golden bands of light rippled out from under her feet like ripples in a puddle of water. The same phenomenon elicited some surprised comments and a few curses from Lister and Till.

The group was again guided by the strange glyphs lining the walls on either side, lighting their path through the darkness, though their illumination was several times brighter than before.

Distant, barely audible thumps and thuds were the only testament to the intense battle raging on the surface above, but they tapered off as the group went ever deeper until there was only stillness and silence.

An hour ticked by.

Then two.

Three.

A massive quake rocked the whole cavern.

Casey lost her balance and fell.

"Lux, Soren, report," Scales said over the com as Till helped Casey to her feet.

"—those tanks. *Shit*. Where the hell did they come from? Sergeant Kenval, empty your titans on those tanks, now!" The voice was Soren's. It was strained and hoarse. "Scales, Soren here. They've breached the first perimeter. That explosion you heard was them blasting their way into the mountain. Their gunships are deploying troops directly into the site now, and we're out of AA missiles. They're coming for you. We've lost almost a hundred men. Turrets A, C, F, G, and J are down. Widow two-four has been destroyed. We're giving them all we've got, Scales, but this is a heavy fight. We only have the strength to last a few more rounds. Hurry it up."

"Acknowledged, Adam," Scales said. "Hang in there. We're almost there."

The channel terminated.

"Guys," Scales said over his shoulder. "Hustle up."

They jogged double-time through the ruins, the golden ripples under their feet becoming more intense and rapid as their boots hit the floor.

At last, the corridor they were in opened up into a final chamber, this one so incredibly high and wide it was impossible for Casey to calculate its size.

In the middle, four daises rose, suspended in the air above one another by nothing. At the top was a pedestal, and floating in the air a meter above it—the crystal.

Scales called a halt and slung his MAR.

He walked up the platforms, onto the final dais, and was about to snatch the crystal when the coms erupted into static and white noise, then Soren's nearly drowned out voice broke in.

"Scales, they've breached our final perimeter. I'm sorry. There's too many. Even for us. You need to find a way out of there *right now!*"

The channel washed over with static.

"Soren," Scales bellowed. "Soren, are you there?"

Static.

"Soren!"

"I'm here," Soren broke in. His voice was shaky and weak. Gunfire crackled. Explosions rumbled like thunderclaps. "I've been hit. We're down to twenty men. Lux is down, Scales. He's not moving. Our scanners are picking up hundreds of inbound targets. Looks like every alien on this goddamn planet is inbound. I can buy you another ten minutes, but you'd better find a way out right now."

There was a deep, gravely horn-like sound—earsplitting and terrifying.

People started screaming. There was an explosion. The cavern shook in response …

The channel went dead.

Everyone exchanged troubled glances.

The commander stood atop the final dais, hands balled into fists at his side. Whatever emotion he was showing behind his helmeted face was a mystery, but Casey imagined it was one of pain.

If he felt anything like she had when she lost men under her command, he had to have been holding back tears.

Scales plucked the crystal out of the air and tucked it into a hardened case on his right thigh. He casually walked down from the platforms and unslung his MAR.

"The schematics Intelligence has on this facility say there's an alternate route we can use as an exit," he told them. His voice was flat. "We'll emerge on the other side of the mountains. If we move now, hopefully we'll—"

Scales never finished his sentence.

A bolt of red energy struck him in the chest and sent him flying backwards. He landed in a heap four meters away.

A clutch of aliens burst into the room from the far hallway.

"Take cover!" Till screeched.

Everyone unslung their weapons and scrambled to take shelter behind the limited cover of the room's center platform. Beams and bolts of energy soared over their heads. Locke and General Delany dragged Scales' motionless body into cover behind the daises. Penny, Till, and Lister opened fire.

"God*damn,"* Lister yelled. "Those things got here *fast!"*

"Locke!" Casey screamed over. "Is the commander okay?"

Roy removed the Vakari's helmet. Blue blood ran from his nose and the corners of his mouth.

"He barely has a pulse," Roy yelled over the sound of gunfire. "He won't make it out of here. And neither will we if we don't move now!"

"We can't just leave him," Casey yelled back in protest. She thumbed her Talon's safety off.

A ball of crackling red energy landed twelve meters in front of them. It detonated in a flash of angry red fire and crimson lightning.

Casey felt the heat from the blast wash over her. It took her breath away. She gasped for air as fragments of stone showered her. Globules of molten rock sizzled as they hit the ground all around her.

"You want to carry him on your back, princess?" Roy shot back.

She looked up as he braced his back against the platform's hard metal surface.

"Because that son-of-a-bitch is really heavy," Roy said.

"Will both of you zip it!" Till shouted. "Just shoot!"

Casey growled in frustration. She squeezed her Talon's grip white-knuckle tight and peeked round the corner.

Those things were in a bunch, shooting, slowly advancing. Lances of energy leapt from their weapons.

Casey shouldered up. The chamber was dim, but she could see well enough to sight down one of the aliens and fire a four-round burst into its chest, putting it down.

"Fire in the hole!" Lister yelled and lobbed a grenade up and over.

It detonated and blew four of the creatures apart.

The others didn't so much as flinch. They kept coming, shooting.

Casey sighted down on another, squeezed the trigger, and sent a burst of 11.5mm rounds into the thing's head. The bullets blew its head to pulp and the creature fell.

"I'm out!" Penny yelled and ducked down into cover to swap out her mags.

Casey took deep breaths, trying to slow the rapid beating of her own heart, letting only that sound in so that it drowned out all the other noises of combat. She steadied her shaking hands and took her time in picking targets and putting them down. Ten seconds later, four more had fallen.

Still the horde advanced, slowly, steadily inching toward the daises.

Her Talon clacked empty and Casey slid down. She ejected the spent clip, slapped a fresh one home, cycled the bolt, and popped up to fire again.

The enemy spilled out of the corridor en masse, as if their numbers had no end. They fell in droves of twos, threes, and fours.

Till fired his MAR until it was dry, but instead of feeding it another clip, he unslung the M34 grenade launcher across his back. He cocked it open, inserted a grenade into the chamber, snapped it shut, and sent a high-explosive round in the enemy's wake. The resulting explosion took out five of them and sent another half-dozen flying. Before they could arise, Penny and Delany made sure they'd never get up again.

Casey was down to her last shredder clip. As she expended its last four-round burst, she released it from the receiver and exchanged it with an AP clip with one fluid motion.

Maybe she was finally starting to get good at this.

Hundreds of spent shell casings lay all around the central platform when the enemy's numbers finally faltered.

Till, Delany, and Casey put down the last few stragglers.

"Holy *shit*," Penny said. "Jesus, don't those bastards ever give up?"

Casey inserted another clip into her Talon.

"Maybe you can ask them, Chief," Lister said. "I'm picking up a large enemy force inbound to our location. The radar is off the fucking charts. We've got ten minutes."

"We can't do this again," Delany panted. "We need to get the hell out of here now."

"Roger that, sir," Roy said.

"What do we do about the commander?" Casey asked.

"Till," Delany said. "Check his pulse."

Till knelt down next to Scales' lifeless body. He pressed his fingers to his neck.

"It's weak, sir," Till said. "He's not going to make it much longer."

Roy shook his head. "We couldn't get the poor bastard out even if we tried. That is, unless they taught princess here to fireman carry four-hundred pound Vakari at the academy."

"Locke," Casey said, "I swear to God I'm going to—"

"That's enough!" Delany bellowed. "Both of you shut up. Till, grab the crystal from the commander's body and let's—"

That horrifying, ear-shattering horn-like sound they'd heard earlier resonated throughout the cavernous chamber.

There was a *bang!* and the room shook so fiercely Casey was flung sideways.

Everything turned to darkness.

There was no sound. There was only the smell of smoke, gunpowder, and the taste of blood.

She felt something warm trickling down the side of her face.

"Get up," she heard someone say.

The voice was female. It sounded so close, yet at the same time, so distant, as if miles away.

"Get up now, goddamn it."

Why did she have to get up? She was so tired, she didn't think she could.

The blackness started to clear. She saw the outline of someone standing over her. One at a time, she was able to pick out the outline's features: blonde hair, pale skin, blue eyes, ears, a mouth.

Her nose caught the faintest whiff of familiar lily-scented perfume ... and then, as if at the flip of a switch, her vision and hearing both came back into focus, and she found herself staring right into Penny's eyes.

Casey reached up to brush her hair out of her eyes, but her hand touched something wet and sticky. Only when she brought it back down did she see it was blood.

Her blood.

"Casey, goddamn it!" Penny yelled and shook her violently. "Are you okay!?"

"I ... I think so," she muttered. "W ... what happened?"

She looked around blinking, trying to get her bearings. She spied a body sticking out from underneath a slab of fallen rock to her left. It wore a tattered marine dress uniform. It took a moment for her to register that it was Delany.

Her eyes brimmed with tears.

Penny grabbed Casey's head in her hands. Casey tore her gaze away from the general's body and refocused on Penny.

"Casey, listen to me," Penny said. "We've got to go, and we have to go right now. So get your ass up off the floor and *move* it!" She dragged Casey to her feet.

A searing hot pain tore through Casey's right arm and shot up into her shoulder. She looked down and saw the bone in her arm sticking right up out of the skin.

"Till!" Penny called as she looped Casey's arm around her neck. "Help me!"

"What happened?" Casey asked as she was carried off between them.

"The roof collapsed," Till replied. "It killed Lister and Delany. Locke's alive. He's up ahead."

"What about the crystal?"

"Locke has it," Till said.

Roy appeared out of the darkness. A stream of blood ran down the left side of his face, both his nostrils, and his ears. His face was mottled with dirt and dust.

"Lieutenant," Penny said, "take her. I've got to go back and get my pack. I think I dropped it. It's got the explosives in it."

"I've got her," Roy said as Penny handed her off.

"Hang in there, girl," Penny whispered in Casey's ear. She ran off back toward the daises.

"Penny!" Till yelled. "Look out!"

Casey didn't know what happened next, but she, Locke, and Till were blown several meters forward. Casey landed hard and the bones in her arm crunched. She screamed through the most intense wave of pain she'd ever felt. She fought to stay conscious. Black dots flecked her vision, but she wasn't ready to give up.

Not yet.

She tried to slow her ragged breathing, gritted her teeth against the pain, and when her vision cleared she found herself laying on her back in front of a slab of onyx.

She heard someone shouting curse words and snapped her head in the general direction. Lieutenant Locke was dragging Till's body behind a fallen chunk of ceiling.

"How is he?" Casey yelled over.

"He's dead," Roy replied.

Casey clenched her teeth and bellowed in anger.

"Casey, can you walk?"

"Yeah, I ... I think so."

"What the hell is that? *Shit.* It's one of those big bastards, those Juggernauts. It's coming right for us. I'll hold it off as long as I can. Get out of here."

"I'm not leaving you behind!"

"Just do it, goddamn it!"

Casey growled in frustration, anger, and anguish, and struggled to stand.

She spotted a trail of blood.

She followed it with her eyes and saw the figure of a woman propped up against the far wall, lying right next to the corridor that led out of the chamber. *"Penny!"*

Casey heard the whine of energy weapons' fire sizzle over her head. She sank down beneath the cover of the fallen chunk of onyx.

"Hold on, Penny," she shouted. "Stay down!"

"I've got two clips left, Casey," Roy yelled. "Those things run fast. You need to go."

He lobbed two grenades over the top and promptly followed with a stream of automatic fire from his MAR.

No.

She'd lost enough people today. Her good hand dipped to her thigh holster, and she pulled free her K2.

She was not going to lose her best friend.

She stood up and pointed her pistol into the Juggernaut's direction. She fired into its wake.

She didn't know how injured Penny was, but if she could just hold on a bit longer …

Roy looked at her with something akin to disbelief, but he quickly snapped out of it and resumed firing his MAR.

The Juggernaut sprinted toward them with terrifying speed. Roy and Casey's combined fire wasn't enough to even slow it down. It jumped over the rock Casey was behind, turned, and swung its sword. She screamed, threw herself to the ground, and rolled out of the way.

"C'mon, you ugly fuck!" she heard Roy yell as he fired his assault rifle. "Over here!"

His ruse to get the creature's attention worked. It immediately lost interest in her and rushed toward him. It met Roy with a flying kick that sent him sprawling to the ground in a heap.

She scrambled to pick up her weapon, but she wasn't quick enough. The pain in her arm was inhibiting her ability to maneuver properly. Her vision was now only a narrow tunnel.

The creature stood over Roy and raised its sword. He put his hands over his head.

Casey cried out to him.

It was over.

A purple shimmer surround Roy's frame.

Right before the blow struck, the alien's sword glanced off the surface of a purple bubble encompassing his body.

Four meters away, Scales stood with his arm stretched out before him. The tail of the bubble seemed to emanate from his very fingertips.

The alien looked unsure what to do. In the short time it took the creature to recover and think about charging this new foe, Scales shot his other arm forth and hit the creature full force with a powerful blow of pure energy. It connected with a sickening wet smack! and the creature flew backwards.

It didn't get back up.

Scales rushed over to Roy.

"Lieutenant," he said hoarsely, "can you move?"

"Yes, sir." Roy grunted. "I've got the crystal, too."

Scales helped him stand and they both hustled over to Casey.

Roy took her outstretched hand and pulled her to her feet.

Scales picked up a discarded MAR and shouldered it.

Casey took off in the direction of Penny. She clutched her injured arm tightly to her chest.

Casey dropped to her knees when she reached her. "Oh, Penny."

Penny smiled. Blood seeped from the corners of her mouth and she clutched at a smoking hole in her armor.

Casey peeled back her hand to reveal burnt, charred skin and bits of underlying bone.

"Come on," she said to Roy and Scales over her shoulder. "Let's get her up. We've got to help her."

"Casey," Penny said softly and shrugged her arm off. "I'm not going anywhere. I don't think I can even walk."

"Yes you can!" Casey bellowed through tears and clenched teeth. "Now like you said, get your ass off the *fucking* floor and move it!"

Penny laughed. She looked at Scales and patted the sack lying across her lap. Scales and Roy knelt down next to her. "Commander," she said. "I've got eight bricks of Comp-5 Command left in my bag. I'll detonate them once you get clear and hopefully buy you some time."

"What?!" Casey shrieked. "Are you crazy! *No!* You're coming with us, and that's final!"

"Commander," Roy said to Scales and pointed across the cavern's expanse.

A sea of aliens swarmed through the entrance.

"Casey," Penny said gently and clutched her hand. "You have been the best friend I've ever had. But I'm dying. You need to let me go. Please. Get yourself out of here. I want to do this."

Leaving streaks, tears ran down Casey's dirty cheeks. She squeezed Penny's hand tighter. "I'm not going to let you," she whispered

"Yes you are. Go, Casey." She looked up at Roy. "Lieutenant Locke, get her the hell out of these caves."

Roy nodded. "You got it, Chief. C'mon, Casey." He gently pulled her away and to her feet.

She wanted to fight him, struggle, but she couldn't. She didn't have an ounce of strength left.

She looked at Penny one last time, and then let Roy sling her arm over his shoulder and guide her down the corridor into the darkness. "Good-bye," she whispered.

Scales placed a hand on Penny's shoulder and gave it a squeeze. "You've done well, Chief. I'm proud of you and so is she."

"Thank you, sir," she said through tears. "Take care of her for me."

"I will. It's been an honor, Penny."

"Likewise, sir."

Scales limped down the corridor and hastened his pace until he caught up with Roy and Casey.

There was a roll of thunder as Penny detonated her explosives.

A wave of heat washed over them. A plume of dust and smoke engulfed the narrow tunnel.

Casey began to cry.

Roy put his other arm around her and squeezed. "It's okay, Casey," he whispered. "It's going to be okay."

Soon, they could see a light at the end of the stone hallway.

It grew larger and larger until finally they emerged into the golden sunlight. Casey looked up at the clear sky and closed her eyes.

"Call for evac," Scales said to Roy as he set Casey down by a tree. "Use the UGC priority channel."

Roy answered with a curt nod of his head. "On it, sir. Are you okay?"

Scales nodded. "Yeah," he smiled. "I think I need to sit down a minute and rest."

He fell to the ground unconscious.

WEAPON: K-2 MAGNUM

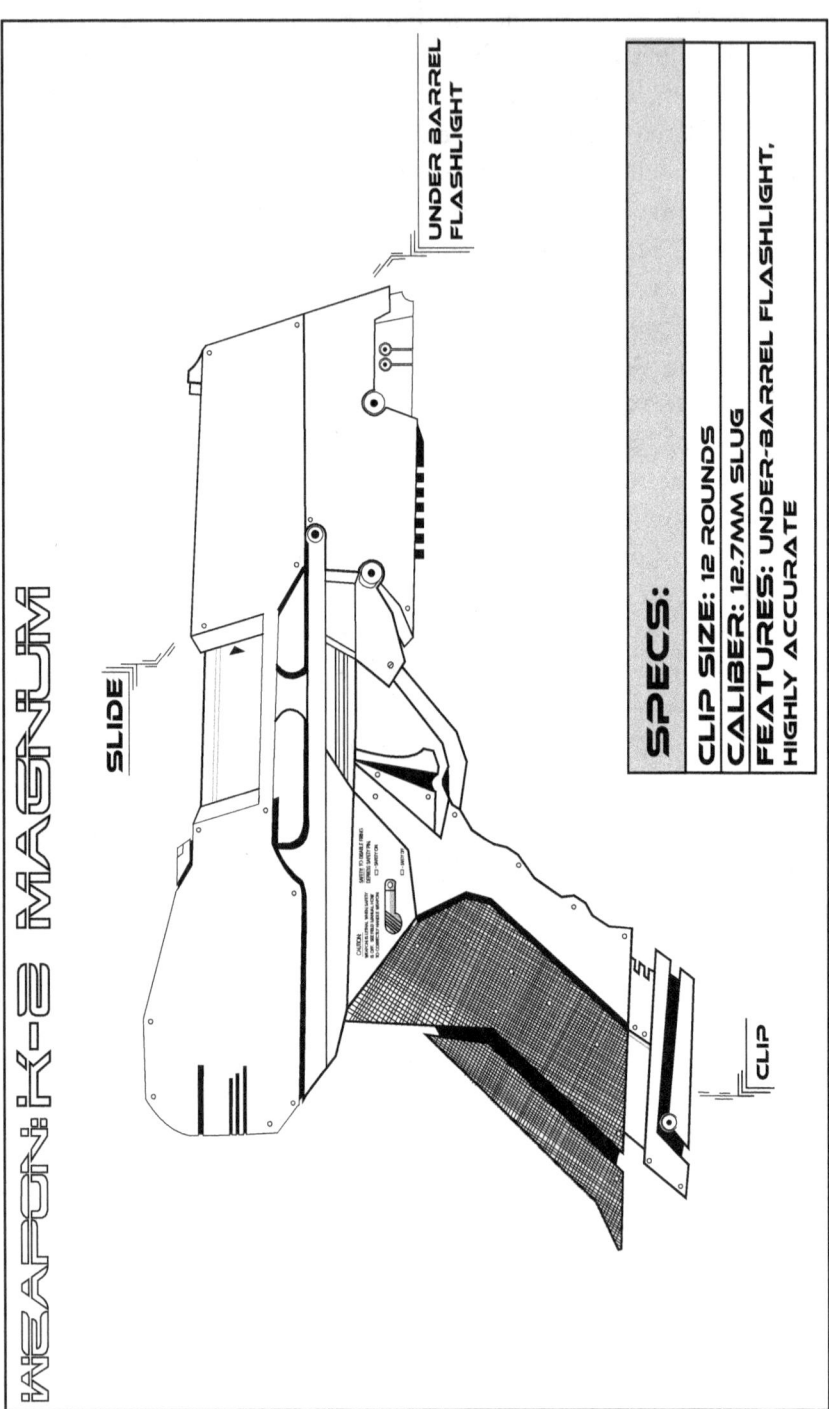

SLIDE

UNDER BARREL
FLASHLIGHT

CLIP

SPECS:

CLIP SIZE: 12 ROUNDS

CALIBER: 12.7MM SLUG

FEATURES: UNDER-BARREL FLASHLIGHT, HIGHLY ACCURATE

SECTION V:

NOVA TEAM

CHAPTER EIGHTEEN

Behind his archaic human desk, Terrence Carr took a sip of coffee from the mug grasped in his left hand as he skimmed through page after page of reports pertaining to the battle that had taken place on Arcturus Septum near the end of January.

Even after three months, the bad news kept rolling in.

He didn't know precise numbers, not yet, but he'd been told the military had sustained huge losses.

Civilian casualties always hit him harder, though—and there were going to be more than enough of those.

He wouldn't know how many until Commander Taylor delivered the updated casualty list to him.

Speaking of which, he looked at the clock. She was a bit overdue.

Both the Alpha and Beta Crystals were being kept safely on heavily fortified worlds, locked deep inside underground military installations and protected by thousands of marines, far away from any populated worlds and devoid of any civilian inhabitants.

At any given time, the navy had twelve massive battle groups stationed around each world. They would be ready to respond to any threat in an instant. Each battle group was headed by two *Elysium*-Class Dreadnaughts—the most powerful warships in the galaxy.

Carr and the other Councilors made damn sure there would be no mistakes this time around. Not after what those men and women went through on Atlantis and Arcturus Septum. If the enemy attacked this time, the military would be ready to respond in full force.

But the question many were asking was: When would they strike?

The aliens hadn't been seen since Arcturus Septum. After the Beta Crystal was recovered, they immediately stopped their attack and their ships jumped out-system. Those that didn't make it to their ships were left behind. Abandoned.

It was something Carr had found hard to grasp.

What kind of race left its own to die?

And that's exactly what happened. It didn't take long for the marines to finish clearing them out of the cities.

Since then, the enemy had dropped completely off the grid.

Carr set his coffee mug on the table. He leaned back in his chair and rubbed at his tired eyes.

Maybe it was time to take a little break.

Though not officially expected to report to duty until 0600, in actuality he'd been on duty since 0600 yesterday. He had only left his office twice—and both times were because he'd needed to take a much needed, head-clearing shower.

Carr pushed back from his desk. The two rows of medals under his jacket's rainbow array of campaign ribbons clinked and jingled as he stood up. He took a deep breath while he stretched his aching back. He'd have to remember to get some muscle relaxers from the doctor on his next visit.

As much as he hated to admit it, he was getting a bit old.

Behind him, a wall-to-wall glass window served as a partition separating the inside of his office from a quaint balcony. The veranda rose a hundred meters above the ground, overlooking a small meadow two hundred meters in diameter. It was well manicured, dotted with trees, hills, benches, and an artificial pond. It was the closest thing that most of the beings that worked in the tower night and day got to the outside world.

He opened the sliding glass door and walked out onto it. A slight, refreshing artificial breeze blew across his face. He leaned forward and rested his arms on the stone railing.

This section was reserved for the offices of the executors, ambassadors, councilors, and Chairmen. They were arrayed in a huge ring that encompassed the artificial landscape. Each building towered several hundred meters high. Those that worked here could look down and admire the park's placidness whenever they pleased.

His office was a bit more lavish than he would have preferred. It was eleven meters across, paneled with oak, and for some reason, it always smelled of cinnamon. Rare paintings, framed commendations, his saber, and other trinkets covered the walls.

Like every other councilor, he'd been assigned a secretary. She worked at her own desk in a room outside his door. Among other things, she took his calls, made his appointments, and configured his daily schedule. As Lord Fleet Admiral of the Navy, he didn't get much say in what activities his day consisted of.

But it was just part of the job. He'd long ago relinquished control of his own life when he took a seat on the Council.

It was a step down from frontline service. He wanted to be in the field. However at his age, no longer could he cope with the extreme physical demands of life on the battlefield. That didn't stop him from missing it, though.

It was quite peaceful up on the balcony. The chirps and warbles of real birds resounded through the park. They gave further aid to the illusion of being outside, though the park's cleaning crew hated them with a fiery passion.

Carr heard the overhead coms buzz. He poked his head inside the door.

"Yes, Carmiya?"

"Sir, Commander Taylor is here to see you."

"Send her in, and tell her she doesn't have to get permission every time she wants to see me."

"I did that last time, sir, and the time before that, and the time before that. She still feels barging in is being rude, but I'll tell her again."

The door opened, and in walked Katherine. She had her service cap tucked under the crook of her arm. Her black dress uniform was crisp and freshly pressed—as if he'd expect to see it any other way.

She took so much care in the way she wore her uniform. There was never a wrinkle or a single thread out of place. She always walked with a clip in her step, head held high and shoulders back.

He admired that.

She clutched a thick folder to her chest. It was no doubt stuffed with casualty reports. She snapped to attention.

"Katherine, please," Carr said as he held up his hand. "At ease. Would you like to join me outside?"

"Of course, sir," Katherine said.

She walked out onto the balcony and stood next to Carr. Her straight-as-a-board posture didn't ease up any.

Carr clasped his hands behind his back.

"God," she said as she gazed out over the meadow. "It's so pretty out here. It's like you're actually outside. It seems to get lovelier every time I see it."

"We'll take a stroll through it one day soon," Carr said. "Katherine?"

"Sir?"

"Don't look so tense. Relax."

"Yes, sir."

"Now," he said. "What's the word on our casualties?"

"Oh, right." She opened the folder and snatched a piece of paper out of it. "The Atlantis Incident claimed five warships and their combined seven thousand seven hundred twelve crew members, thirty marines, and fifteen civilian scientists. Arcturus Septum is a bit more, um … severe. Current count puts it at forty-five warships and two hundred ten thousand marine and navy personnel. That includes all members of Arcturus Septum Command. Civilian casualty numbers are still coming in, but," she paused briefly, "their number is around five hundred thousand."

Carr said nothing. He averted his ice-blue eyes to somewhere out across the meadow.

"Unfortunately, sir," she continued, "New casualty reports come in every day. This number is the most solid I can give you right now. There are still fifty thousand people unaccounted for, however."

That caught his attention. The Admiral snapped his head round. "Fifty thousand?"

He'd read the eyewitness reports from both battles. The enemy had taken prisoners. There were accounts of the aliens carrying off dead or wounded people—both military and civilian. But fifty thousand of them? "That's nearly another quarter of what our military losses totaled."

Katherine nodded her head. "Yes, sir. I know. Um … right now, we assume they were taken prisoner, but we don't know for sure."

"Any news on where those creatures went?"

Katherine snapped the folder shut. "Nothing. Not one damn whisper. It's like they just vanished." When he didn't respond, she said, "Maybe we taught them a lesson."

"Somehow I doubt that." He gazed out across the meadow again.

Few things could top this. At least the worst news he'd hear today was over.

Katherine nervously shifted her weight.

He realized his comment had made her uneasy. "We'll worry about that later," he said. The poor girl was under enough stress. "What's the status on Project: *Reveille*?"

"Ah, yes," Katherine said. "Well last night I couldn't sleep—"

"Yes," Carr said, "that's one thing they tend to leave out of the job description." He waved his hand dismissively. "Sorry. I cut you off. Continue."

"Quite all right, sir. Anyway, while I was laying in bed, I began thinking of how we could improve the ship's structural integrity without sacrificing her speed by loading her down with extra armor."

"Interesting," Carr said. "I'd like to hear it."

Katherine cleared her throat and took another paper out of the folder. She had drawn on it a series of sketches, with one in particular circled multiple times with blue ink. She set the paper on the balcony's stone railing and pointed to the highlighted drawing.

"See, this here," she pointed. "These are cross-bracings. If these were incorporated into *Reveille*'s superstructure along with a series of internal tetriite frames built into a kind of honeycomb-like pattern, she would be able to withstand far greater damage. With this design, she could sustain massive damage to her hull and still remain operational. Now this is still theory, though. However, we could test it first."

Carr studied the drawing. "I think it's a great idea, Katherine."

"It would require a massive overhaul to integrate her with this design, though," she said. "We'd basically have to start all over again."

"It'll be worth it. This will improve her combat efficiency ten-fold. And for what we have planned for her, she's going to need all the extra boost she can get. I'll head down to Admiral Kront's office later this afternoon and have a little chat with him about it. I'd like you to be there."

Katherine nodded. "I will be, sir. Thank you."

"We need this sort of thinking," Carr said, "especially on a project as vital to us as *Reveille*. Now, I don't suppose you've had any thoughts on weapons?"

"I was hoping you'd ask that." Her lips stretched into a beautiful smile that displayed a mouthful of perfectly straight, pearly-white teeth. "With the right components, we could upgrade *Reveille*'s linear accelerator capacitors far beyond what their normal operational limit would be, thanks to the power output of the new—"

"Admiral?" Carmiya's voice came in through the overhead speakers.

"Sorry," Carr said to Katherine. "Yes, Carmiya?"

"Sir, you asked me to inform you of Commander Scales' medical status, and the doctor just buzzed to say he's woken up. If you'd like to go and see him, I could arrange transport."

"That would be great, Carmiya, thank you. I'd like to leave at once."

"Already on it, sir."

The speakers clicked off.

"I'm sorry to have to cut this short," Carr said. "I won't be long. We'll continue this when I get back. Perhaps even over some breakfast, if you'd like. My treat."

"I'd like that, sir," Katherine said. She then looked at the Admiral for a few brief seconds, looked at him in a way that seemed she was almost looking *into* him, searching, fixing him with that pretty blue gaze of hers. She flashed another of her beautiful smiles. "Thank you."

"Of course," Carr replied. He then did something he never did—he smiled back. "Now make yourself comfortable and let Carmiya know if you need anything."

"Aye, sir."

"Oh," he added as he turned to leave, "And before I forget, should you need coffee, don't let Carmiya make it. She isn't too good at it. Just go down to the café."

Katherine laughed. "Thanks."

"You're welcome." He turned and left.

There was a shuttle waiting outside the building for him when he walked out the doors. He put his cap on his head and climbed in.

The shuttle departed for Serphus Memorial Hospital. It was located six kilometers from Zenith Tower in one of the hundreds of outlying facilities, though all were still part of the Headquarters Complex.

During the nearly twenty five minute ride, Carr took the time to review the injuries Scales had suffered during the events on Arcturus Septum. He didn't like what he read.

The vehicle touched down on the hospital's landing pad.

"Lord Carr to see patient oh-one eleven two, please," he said once he arrived at the reception desk.

The receptionist looked up from her computer with wide eyes.

"Lord Carr, sir!" She jumped up and nearly knocked over her chair. "Of course, sir. I'll have someone escort you there right away."

Carr was shown to the patient's room by a very chatty nurse. He was none too relieved when they finally arrived. The woman was giving him a headache.

Waiting for him outside the door, Doctor Thergis Storum was scribbling notes on a datapad with his stylus. "Hello, Admiral," he said without looking up.

Carr nodded. "Doc."

Storum tucked the stylus into his breast pocket and looked up.

"What's his status, Thergis?"

The doctor cleared his throat. "He's been in a coma for the past three months," he explained. "Mentally, he appears fine, but I'll need to conduct some more tests. Physically, however, he could be better. He sustained second and third degree burns to forty percent of his body, mainly on the torso. It will take some time to heal, but the scarring should clear up after a few tissue treatments, and his body is responding well to skin grafts. When he was admitted, both of his livers had suffered serious contusions, as did his left kidney. The biodine is healing them, but it'll be a while yet. He also has six broken ribs and pulled tendons in his legs and arms. There are signs of some atrophy in his muscles. He's going to need extensive physical therapy. He'll be out of commission for at least another two weeks. Now he needs time to rest, but since it's you asking I'll let you in to see him, just make it quick, Terrence." The doctor opened the door.

Carr stepped into the room.

A battered and bruised Vakari was hooked up to half-a-dozen machines and IVs that surrounded his hospital bed.

"Like I said: make it quick." Storum shut the door behind him.

The Admiral sat down on a chair next to the bed.

Scales opened his eyes slightly. He turned his head toward Carr.

"Hello, Kileeus," Carr said.

Scales licked his lips. "Admiral, sir." His voice was weak. "It's good to see you."

"And you, Kileeus."

"To what do I owe this pleasure, sir?"

"I wanted to see how you were."

Scales grunted. "I've been worse. Really tired, though. More so than I've ever been."

"It's the pain meds," Carr said. "Did they give you the rundown on your injuries?"

"No, sir. Only that I was in a coma for three months."

"Well, you had severe burns on your torso, but Storum says your body is accepting the skin grafting nicely. However, there are other injuries that will take some time to recover from. You've got some internal damage, several broken ribs, and pulled tendons in your arms and legs. I can't imagine what you went through on Arcturus Septum. You really pushed yourself, Kileeus, and you did it. You completed your mission. I'm proud of you."

"Thank you, sir," Scales said. "That was some assignment. How are Lux and Soren? I'd like to see them as soon as I'm able."

Carr lowered his gaze.

"Kileeus," he said gently, "I'm sorry to tell you this. By the time reinforcements got to Rencorrus, none of the defenders were left. Most of them were dead, but ... Soren's and Lux's bodies weren't found among the remains."

Scales closed his eyes and released a pained sigh.

"I'm sorry, Kileeus, I really am. They were good soldiers, all of them, and that goes double for Lux and Soren. Triple. They were two of the best operatives in the service. Their sacrifices, their courage, and their conviction were testament to everything the Shadows stand for. They had unshakable devotion to see any task, any mission, and any assignment through to the end. That speaks volumes about their character."

"What happened to Lieutenant Keller and Lieutenant Locke?"

"I'm happy to tell you both are alive and well," Carr replied. "Keller is healing up nicely and has been in psychotherapy due to some of the trauma she experienced during the course of the battle. Locke has been in the hospital for some time, but he's going to be fine. He's actually only four floors down in the recovery wing. He'll be there until the doctors clear him for active duty, which shouldn't be too long."

For all the pain—mental and physical—Scales managed a smile. "I'm really glad to hear that. They're both damn good soldiers. Might I make a suggestion as to where their futures lie, sir?"

"Of course, Kileeus," Carr said. "But later. You need to rest now. I'll check back in with you in a few days and we'll discuss it once you get back on your feet. I'm glad to see you're okay, Kileeus. You're a hell of a soldier. Now rest. That's an order."

Scales touched his forehead. "Aye, sir."

Carr left the Shadow to rest.

As he traveled back to his office, Carr acknowledged how fortunate he was to be the Director of the Shadow Program and have Operatives like Scales under his command. Had it not been for him, the crystals would never have made it off Atlantis and Arcturus Septum, and this whole God awful mess, pain, and all those deaths would have been for nothing.

But it wasn't over.

No way.

This was only the beginning. Carr knew that. The aliens would strike again. This time, however, the UGC would be ready, and so would he. He'd have his Shadows ready to respond in full—with a few new tricks up their sleeve.

CHAPTER NINETEEN

Casey plucked a speck of fuzz off the sleeve of her uniform.

She checked herself over in the mirror one final time. She wanted to make sure her freshly pressed black navy dress uniform looked crisp. A pair of newly awarded golden overlapping rings adorned her collar.

She'd been promoted to a full Lieutenant. The gold slashes on her sleeves and epaulettes displayed her rank as well. There was an extra row of ribbons above the one she'd already had.

She sighed. Yes, everything seemed to be in order. It had to be. Today was a big day.

Casey had received a letter three days ago from Lord Fleet Admiral Terrence Carr, handwritten personally by him, congratulating her on her heroism on Arcturus Septum. He also said that he wanted to meet with her at 0700 today in the Tower's ceremony chambers for a special ceremony that he, for security reasons, couldn't go into. He had assured her it would be nothing like her debriefing to the Admiralty Board.

She shuddered at the thought.

After her recovery, she had been called in to give a full account of the events of Arcturus Septum. Somehow, Casey had managed to stand at stiff attention before a board of twenty fleet admirals and commanding-generals for hours. They must have asked her the same questions six times six different ways. When it was all said and done, they dismissed her and she was given a temporary apartment within the Tower.

She wasn't allowed to leave until they said so.

It was an extremely nerve-wracking experience—one she hoped she wouldn't have to go through again.

On top of that, she'd been put on leave under orders from the Council. She had been required to complete a full psych evaluation before they'd clear her to return to active duty.

She hated the thought at first. However, after a few sessions, she realized having someone to talk to, a shoulder to cry on, was helpful.

All her friends were dead.

Penny was dead.

Her face still haunted Casey's dreams every night. Penny had been her rock during her time in the military, and the best friend she'd ever had. When she was fresh out of the academy, Penny had been there to guide her and show her the lighter side to life.

Casey hated talking about it. She cried every time. But after a few sessions with the navy shrink, she realized that having someone willing to listen to her was helpful.

He offered ways for her to cope with her failure. That's what it was to her, or at least what it felt like. It was her failure that had cost Penny her life—though he had told her it was no such thing, that the trials and tribulations of combat were to blame for Penny's death, not her.

Casey wasn't sure if she believed him yet.

The aliens had cost so many so much. Her loss seemed like only a drop in the bucket compared to the big picture.

There were children out there that were never going to see their parents again. They'd be bounced around foster homes. Some would find nice homes, nice families willing to accept them as their own, but many wouldn't. They'd have to make their own way—or be forgotten.

She knew all too well what that was like. The thought of anyone having to go through what she had made her furious.

Enraged.

It was for that reason she'd signed on for another five-year term. Her shrink had advised against it, said she needed time, but she disagreed—those aliens had started something, and she was going to finish it. For Penny. For her friends. For all those kids. When and if those creatures ever returned, they were damn well going to know how much pain and suffering they'd caused.

Looking herself over in the mirror, Casey saw her newly awarded medals gleam radiantly in the light on her chest.

She'd been awarded the Gold Star and Purple Nova for her actions during the battle. They hung below her ribbons. They jingled every time she took a step, reminding her they were there—and making her wonder if she really deserved them.

The Purple Nova was awarded to any soldier wounded on the field of battle. It was military policy.

But the Gold Star? What had she done to actually earn a medal that prestigious? Fire a few rounds from a gun? Run a couple kilometers? No. It was because she had aided in the recovery of some crystal that was probably as useful to the UGC as she had been to her friends.

Casey shut her eyes.

She inhaled deeply, held her breath for a moment, and then released it. She did this a few times. It cleared her head. The shrink had told her not to let these thoughts consume her.

Maybe he was right. Maybe she was being a little hard on herself.

She pushed it all to the back of her mind. It wasn't the time to do this. There were other things that needed her attention right now, and she didn't want to meet Lord Terrence Carr with a flustered face and tear-brimmed eyes.

She cleared her throat and checked over her uniform one last time.

She grabbed her service cap from a claw hanger on the wall on her way out.

Her apartment was located in the luxurious housing quarter that VIP guests, Councilors, and top brass lived in day in and day out. Even though the section her apartment was located in was meant only to temporarily house visitors, it was still nicer than anything she could ever afford. For the thousandth time, she wondered if there was some way she could persuade the military to let her keep that apartment.

She stepped into the elevator and punched the button. It began to descend.

The elevator jolted slightly as its gears ground to a halt. The doors hissed opened and she walked out into the busy markets. Vendors sold food, novelties, books, and anything else she could have imagined. When they told her the Tower was its own little city, they weren't lying.

She was stunned when she'd first arrived here almost five months ago. She had heard of the Tower, of course. Everyone in the galaxy had. However, when she stepped off that ship and saw it for the first time—that black mass of steel and stone shooting upward into the sky like a spike of obsidian, disappearing into the clouds—it took her breath away.

She navigated her way through the endless alley of vendors that stretched a kilometer in either direction, and eventually found her way to one of the floor's many shuttle stations—a thirty-meter wide, high-ceilinged chamber with multiple pads for shuttles to dock on.

In the Tower, one- to five-man shuttles acted much the same as cabs had in the big city where she grew up. But unlike cabs, the shuttles didn't charge a fare. If they did, she figured a person could chew through a paycheck simply getting from one end of the Tower to the other.

Within minutes, she had hailed one and told the onboard computer her destination. The cab lifted off the ground vertically and shot forward. It merged into a lane of traffic. Fifteen minutes later, it touched down on a pad a hundred meters from the ceremony chambers.

It was all too easy to get lost in the Tower, so she had to follow the directions from a directory in order to properly find her way to the chambers.

This floor was devoid of any vendors. Instead, the ten-meter wide main corridor was lined with offices and other hallways that branched off and snaked their way as far as she could see. There were several thousand people walking about—creatures of almost all races—trying to meander their own ways through the tide of bodies to reach their destinations.

Casey found her way through the crowd, though not without being elbowed and shouldered a few times.

With eight minutes to spare, she was admitted through the main doors of the ceremony chambers and shown into the foyer. A security checkpoint awaited her, and she was carded and her ID confirmed with a retinal scan.

A little unnecessary, she thought. This was the most well-guarded, fortified installation in the galaxy. No unauthorized person could enter even if they wanted to, and they sure as heck wouldn't make it this far on the off chance they did.

But High Command was infamous for its security protocols, and they'd done nothing but increase them since the events of Arcturus Septum.

Once security confirmed her to be *"—Keller, Casey Jillian—"*, two MPs opened a set of doors for her and she was ushered into a waiting room.

It was dead silent except for a dull thrumming of the air circulation system. It felt somewhat unsettling. She settled down in one of the padded chairs and crossed her legs.

The anticipation was killing her. She made a mental list of all the possibilities that this ceremony could be and checked off each one as they grew more and more unlikely.

She paused.

This was High Command she was talking about.

"Unlikely" was the word on which they started each day.

"Casey?"

She jumped.

She hadn't even noticed that someone sat on a plush couch at the other end of the room. A man, he was wearing a Marine Corps dress uniform.

Casey recognized him immediately.

"Hello, Roy." Despite military regs, Casey gave him a big hug. She stepped back and looked him over from head to toe.

He was freshly shaven, hair all nice and trimmed. He had been promoted since she last saw him. He was now a first lieutenant. The brand new rank insignia on his collar gleamed in the light.

"You look nice," she said.

"Thank you." He tugged at his jacket's high collar. "You do, too. Maybe a little soft around the edges, though." He smiled.

Casey laughed. "It's all those doughnuts. The bakery down the street from my apartment is my new favorite hangout place. So, you're actually calling me Casey now, huh? No more princess?"

Roy's face took on a more solemn expression. The smirk faded. His deep brown eyes looked more serious than she'd ever seen them before. "No," he said.

She was surprised at his earnest tone.

"A princess would have turned tail and run back in that cave on Arcturus Septum. When I told you to go, you pulled out your pistol with a bone sticking up out of your arm. You were prepared to die there rather than let that thing get at Penny. I knew then I'd been wrong about you. I'm sorry."

Casey smiled and touched his arm.

"Thank you, Roy. I owe you an apology too. I was mean to you when you walked through the doors of that apartment building. You and your squad had done the impossible—you'd gotten us out of that tower. You'd rescued us. And then I asked what took you so long." She shook her head. "I remember being just so angry that I'd lost so many friends, and I was looking to place the blame on the first person I could. It made it easier, I guess, making it someone else's fault." She shrugged. "I'm a complicated person."

"I understand," he replied. "Believe me. I've had my fair share of those days, too. But that's over with now. So tell me, what exactly are you here for?"

"I got a letter from Lord Admiral Carr," she said. "He said that he wanted—"

"—you to attend a special ceremony, but because of security reasons he couldn't talk about it," Roy finished. "Yeah. I got that same letter."

"Hmm." She turned away. "Think it has to do with Arcturus Septum?"

He shook his head. "I can't think of any other reason."

"I can't imagine what they'd want with us now," Casey said. She flicked the medal on his chest. "That Red Star of Valor looks good on you."

"Thanks," he mumbled and glanced down at it. "Hardly seems like I deserve it, though."

"You do deserve it, Roy," she said. "If it hadn't been for you, I would have stayed behind and died in those caves. Sometimes I wonder if I should have, but … " she trailed off. "You saved my life. I owe you one."

"You don't owe me anything, Casey," Roy replied. "Marines don't leave people behind … especially people we care about …"

They locked eyes. He stared right into her emerald green eyes, and she right back into his deep brown.

She smiled.

"Roy … I—"

A set of double doors at the other end of the room opened. Roy and Casey broke their gaze as an MP stepped out.

"Sir," he said. "Ma'am. They're ready for you. This way, please."

Roy and Casey exchanged a glance.

He raised his eyebrows. "After you." He beckoned to the door.

The MP stood aside and they walked through the entranceway. He pointed them down a hallway, and then closed the doors behind them.

Two tall oak doors waited for them at the far end of the corridor. The walnut-paneled walls were loaded with famous paintings, which included Fleet Admiral Te's victory over the Asgards during the Unification War in 656 BCE, the signing of the UGC Articles of Foundation sixty years later, and portraits of past Chairmen and Councilors. Wall sconces splashed the walls with a golden glow.

"Have you ever met him?" Casey asked Roy as they traveled down the corridor.

"Who?"

"Lord Carr."

"Are you serious? Hell, no."

The oak doors creaked and started to open on their own.

Roy and Casey stepped into the threshold of the ceremony chamber.

It was a massive circular room—fifteen meters in diameter. The crenellated ceiling, painted with murals of past battles the UGC had fought and won, rose nine meters above their heads. It reminded Casey of Michelangelo's frescoes on the ceiling of the Sistine Chapel.

At the end of the room, fifteen beings sat at a long, several-meter-high table, dressed in very fancy—and expensive—clothes.

Casey's eyes widened when she realized who they were—the Chairmen. "Oh my God," she whispered.

In front of the table on a raised dais, Lord Fleet Admiral Terrence Carr stood with his hands clasped behind his back, and to his side, a Vakari in navy dress—it was Scales.

When they were a few steps away from the lip of the dais, Roy and Casey halted. In perfect synchronization, they both snapped smartly to attention and saluted.

Carr and Scales returned their salutes.

"At ease," Carr said.

They both assumed parade rest.

Casey needed to look straight ahead, find a point on the back wall to fix her stare, but she couldn't help herself. She let her eyes flicker from face to face before they finally came to rest on Admiral Carr.

He stepped forward.

"First Lieutenant Roy Locke," he said, "Lieutenant Casey Keller, it is an honor to finally meet you."

Casey didn't know what to say when he extended his hand to her. Speechless, she shook it. Roy was next.

"I'm sure you both remember Scales." Carr gestured to the Vakari, who then stepped forward himself and took his turn in shaking their hands.

"It's nice to see you both again," he whispered.

Casey smiled. "You, too, sir," she whispered back.

"You look good, Commander," Roy whispered.

Scales bowed, then backpedaled a few steps.

"The Battle of Arcturus Septum was quite an ordeal," Carr began. "It stands as a reminder that our civilization, for all of our technological engineering, our steadfast courage, and our cunning, is not invincible. The arrival of those aliens brings to light the fact that this galaxy is far vaster than we care to believe. Its wonders—and its mysteries—are so far beyond our comprehension that it seems as though we stumble in the darkness. Compared to the mysteries of the Milky Way, we are prehistoric creatures living in caves—awed by and completely ignorant of everything around us.

"We lost a lot of good people at Arcturus Septum. Friends. Comrades in arms. Family. Those creatures cost us a lot, but we showed them that through bravery and perseverance, through unity and honor, this civilization, our civilization, this conglomeration of races called the United Galactic Coalition, will prevail.

"I would like to congratulate you both on the great heroism and bravery you displayed during the course of those few days. Your actions helped stem the tide of the alien invasion. You helped recover the Beta Crystal and ultimately drive the enemy back. You both showed that you possess extreme potential in leadership and survival, that your beliefs in the mission you were given and your sense of duty is put far higher than your own personal thoughts, misgivings, and even your lives.

"Those qualities are never overlooked. Bravery, valor, and honor are the principles on which this Coalition was founded, and soldiers like you are its lifeblood.

"There are several Special Operations programs that would love to get their hands on either of you, but there is one branch that is elite even amongst the elite of the Special Forces.

"These are the Shadows. They are operatives skilled in the arts of stealth, combat, and intelligence gathering. Their numbers are small, but they form both our first offense and last defense. Shadows are agents of the Council, individuals that possess supreme abilities that make them stand out among their peers.

"Scales made it a point to address to the Council and myself the potential he sees in the two of you. He served with you during the battle, and you both have made quite a lasting impression on him—and trust me when I say this: Scales isn't a man who is easily impressed. Through your actions, your integrity, and your willingness to lay down your lives for the chance to win, however small it may have seemed, you proved to him that there was something different about you, something that set you out from the rank and file. So when he suggested you two be given the opportunity to join the Shadows and be put under his command, I took it under heavy advisement.

"As Director of the Shadow Program, I offer you the chance to join our ranks, to become the best soldiers and finest commandos the galaxy has ever seen. There is no training program associated with the Shadows. A person either has the abilities we look for, or not. Shadows are neither chosen nor recruited—you are simply born.

"Should you accept this offer, I would consider it a great triumph to the program. However, you are under no obligation to join. If you feel the need to decline, you will both be returned to active duty to a posting of your choice and continue to further your careers. There will be no penalties of any kind against you, except that what is said here today is classified above top secret.

"So, now is the time for you to consider what I told you, and to decide—yes or no. This is a decision you must make for yourself, a decision independent of what the other may chose. I'll give you all the time you need to think it over."

Casey and Roy shared a long, long glance.

It took Casey a while of silent contemplation to compute all the information Carr had just revealed, but she then realized her mind had already been made up from the start. She looked into Roy's eyes—so, too, had his.

As one, they turned back at Carr and simultaneously said, "I accept."

Pleased at their victory, Scales and Carr looked at each other.

A trace of a smile formed in the corners of Scales' mouth.

Carr directed a nod of respect toward Casey, then Roy, and then said: "Congratulations. Welcome to the Shadows."

CHAPTER TWENTY

I am a Shadow.
This is my Creed.
My life I give in servitude to the United Galactic Coalition.
I will carry out every assignment I am given,
Without pause, without hesitation.
I will follow my orders, wherever they take me,
Be that the farthest arm of the Milky Way,
Or the coldest depths of the void of Dark Space.
I serve as a protector of the United Galactic Coalition,
Her Worlds and Colonies,
The Articles of Foundation,
And the Citizens of the Galaxy.
With this Creed, I do now affirm and avow my service as a Shadow,
My life as soldier,
And my unquestionable loyalty to the United Galactic Coalition.
In Unity, Strength,
In War, Sacrifice,
And in Death, Honor.
I am a Shadow,
This is my Creed.

—The Shadow's Creed, Article 1

0745 hours, May 29, 2343
Electus Borealis System, planet Katana
UGC Headquarters Complex, Zenith Tower
986th floor, Briefing Amphitheater 023

S cales stepped off the lift and strolled through the busy, crowded corridors on his way to the amphitheater.

His rainbow of campaign ribbons and medals stood out boldly against the black of his jacket. Each and every one was a prestigious award for honor and valor: three Purple Novas; Gold and Silver Stars, Medal of Valor; Order of the Red Star, and many more. For anyone who saw him, they served as an unmistakable testament to the soldier he was.

He was proud of every single one of them.

He made it through a security checkpoint outside the amphitheater. Admiral Carr had called a meeting, set to start at 0800. As usual, HighCom's security protocols kept him from saying what it was about, but he told Scales he was assembling a team to aid him, Roy, and Casey on their next mission.

Scales had no idea what the hell that meant. Shadows normally operated alone or in small groups. He hadn't a clue who these people were, why they'd need to come with him, or even what his next mission was.

But he didn't care. He was anxious to get back into combat.

He was overjoyed by Casey's and Roy's acceptance into the Shadows. They both were so young, but they showed so much potential—the kind that the UGC would need in the coming days. Asking Admiral Carr to give them the opportunity to join the Shadows was one of the best decisions he'd made in a long time.

Carr had said that he had something special in mind for the three of them, but what that was, again, remained a mystery.

It was an odd thing to have seen so much of the Admiral lately. During the last three months, Scales had seen more of Carr than he had in years. Not that that was a bad thing, though. Scales was honored by Carr's presence.

Carr was a human. There were those who had doubts about humans and their military capabilities even still, but there wasn't a soul alive in the entire Milky Way, be they Coalition or Rebel, Client or Independent, that could deny that Terrence Carr was, without a doubt, the best damn soldier of the age, and the brightest star in the sky of humanity. He stood for everything humans had fought so hard to achieve over the last two hundred fifty years. Even though the Vakari were the most militarily bred race in the galaxy, Carr was six times the soldier he was.

Standing guard on either side of the huge double doors leading into the amphitheater were two MPs armed with MAR-5 assault rifles. They wore full suits of marine combat armor.

When he approached, they stood at arms. The MP on the left, a marine Corporal, said, "Hello, sir. I need to see your ID before I can let you in."

Scales complied and gave the man his holocard.

The marine scanned it on a little handheld device. It blipped once confirmation had come through. "Sorry, sir. You know how paranoid HighCom can be. Head on in."

Scales gave a respectful nod of his head and stepped through the doors.

The amphitheater was a spherical room with a high-vaulted ceiling and crimson-cushioned chairs stacked up seven levels, ringing its perimeter. It could have held seven hundred people easily. A group of soldiers, Scales estimated around two hundred, were already present. Most wore navy service dress, although many wore the greys and silvers of the marines.

"Ten-hut," someone shouted.

The room rose as one and stood to attention.

"As you were," he said. He walked up the stairs.

In their dress uniforms, Roy and Casey remained standing.

"It's nice to see you again, sir," Casey said and smiled.

"It's nice to see you, Casey." Scales replied. "And you, Roy."

"Always a pleasure, Commander." Roy grasped Scales' hand in a firm handshake.

It was a human gesture, but Scales had grown accustomed to it over the course of his career.

"Who the hell are all these people?" Scales asked under his breath.

Before either could respond, someone yelled, "Admiral on deck."

The room snapped to attention as one. When everyone saw Admiral Carr stride in, they stood straighter. A very attractive young woman followed closely behind him.

Tall and trim, she wore a black navy dress uniform, and the gold bands on her sleeves and epaulettes denoted her as a commander. She had three vibrantly colored rows of ribbons on her chest. Her dark brown hair was pulled back into a small ponytail.

Both she and Admiral Carr took position on the center dais.

Admiral Carr said, "As ease, ladies and gentlemen. Take a seat."

Scales settled into a seat in between Casey and Roy.

"I'm Lord Fleet Admiral Carr." He gestured toward the woman. "And this is Commander Katherine Taylor. We have a lot to cover this morning, so I'd like to get started. Commander, if you please?"

"Yes, sir," Commander Taylor said with a curt nod.

She tapped a small holographic control pad on the brass railing lining the dais. The lights dimmed.

A holographic representation of an object Scales was all-too familiar with hovered in the center of the room. It was the alien ship he'd first seen orbiting Atlantis.

Something about it vaguely resembled that of a cuttlefish.

Its hull had a mottled texture. There were several long, sharply tapered spires protruding from its belly. Its surface was ribbed like the tail of an alligator. The ship's prow was teardrop shaped, and its midsection was bloated and fat. Numerous lobes swelled away from it like sores on a disease-ridden body.

"Good morning," Commander Taylor said. "The object you see before you is a vessel belonging to the alien race that attacked us earlier this year. This particular ship was first seen at planet Atlantis on January sixteenth at 0430 hours. Later, it and thirty-two other similar warships emerged from FTL near Arcturus Septum's satellite Choras at oh-nine-hundred fifteen hours on January twenty-first. The following is what was transmitted from the destroyer *Brandenburg* during its assault on the alien ship over Atlantis."

The holographic image of the alien ship shrunk, and three UGC frigates and a heavy destroyer snapped up a meter in front of it. The battle played out. The alien ship took a hit from the destroyer's Aegis cannon, until it fired weapons of its own. It made short work of one of the frigates before it shot needle-fine red beams at incoming Rapture missiles.

When Scales saw this, it made his blood run cold. He had no idea the battle above Atlantis had gone this badly.

After a few more hits, the alien ship proceeded to obliterate the entire battle group.

Scales lowered his gaze. Those soldiers had given their lives so that he, Soren, and Lux could complete their mission. He resolved to make their sacrifice mean something—make it worth it.

"Reverse and play back thirty point six to thirty five point three," Taylor said.

The video rewound itself and replayed the feed of the alien ship firing its weapons. The beam that shot forth from its prow glowed red. The image paused as the crimson lance reached across the expanse of space to strike the frigate *Emerald Eyes*.

"We have gathered that this ship possesses a type of magnetohydrodynamic weapons system that we presume uses electromagnetism to fire streams of molten metal at nearly the speed of light. The ship also uses smaller versions as a form of point defense. As you may know, metals in a molten state do not possess any of the magnetic properties they have as solids. To our knowledge, there is no way they can be accelerated by a magnetic field, no matter the strength. Needless to say, this kind of technology is far beyond our comprehension.

"These weapons are so powerful that they cut through the hull armor of a cruiser with no problem. However, our weapons didn't seem to have that sort of luck on its hull. A single Aegis round was practically ineffective. It got through, but did minimal damage. Though sustained fire from multiple Aegis cannons will eventually destroy the ship, its armor is astronomically stronger than the battle plate we use on our warships.

"The battle at Arcturus Septum had a similar outcome—though on a much larger scale. We were able to take out twelve of their thirty-two ships. However, we lost three times as many."

She tapped the panel, and the battle faded.

"The UGC has many scenarios and protocols that are to be strictly followed in the event of first contact with another species. Our galaxy is vast. The chances of other forms of intelligent life existing other than the few dozen races we know of are an almost certainty. We had hoped that contact with another race would be a peaceful experience. That couldn't have been farther from the truth.

"We know virtually nothing about these beings," she said, almost with compunction. "The only bodies that were recovered from the battles were either in pieces or so mutilated that nothing useful could be gleaned from them. We're not sure if these creatures are factually organic or not, though from what we can tell they appear to be a hybrid species of synthetic-organics. Nothing is known of their origins, or where they went after they disappeared from the Delta Sagittaurii system. We do know what they call themselves, though. These creatures are able to communicate, but most of the time they are unwilling to do so. There were several reports of them speaking with marines on the ground. In every instance, regardless of the race of the individual to which they were talking, these aliens were able to communicate in that species' native language. There was one instance in which a human marine's helmet was able to record the exchange via helmcam. The creature spoke to the man in clear, flawless English. Play the feed."

The speakers exploded with static. There was an unceasing report of gunfire and explosions. People screamed in pain. Anguish. Fear. Officers and NCOs barked curse-laden orders in frantic tones.

The battle faded into focus on screens decorating the railings of each tier of seats.

Marines fired their weapons. They were gunned down. They were flung into the air by red-tinged explosions. The living took cover behind anything they could find.

The marine recording the feed was thrown into the air by an explosion. The sky whirred round overhead until he landed hard and the feed cut out for a second. There were loud thumps as one of the creatures approached him. The picture faded back to show it standing over him. It clicked its mandibles.

"What the fuck are you?" the marine asked.

"We are the Vanguard," it said.

The creature leveled its weapon and fired.

The sound of the alien's voice sent a chill down Scales' spine. It was artificial and organic, strangely calm, unfathomably deep and gravely, like stones grinding atop one another.

Scales narrowed his eyes.

The enemy finally had a name: the Vanguard.

Taylor tapped the holopad once again, and the hologram of the alien soldier snapped up and hovered over the room.

Scales almost jumped up, sprinted forward, and tackled the image. This close to the enemy, decades of battlefield experience gave him the urge to grab the first weapon he could find and start shooting. Though only a picture, at this proximity to the enemy, it felt like a very real threat. He had to tell himself it was only an image composed of light. Through his peripheral vision, he saw Roy and Casey visibly tense up.

The Vanguard were huge beings, but the holographic image was greatly enlarged. Glaring at them all in defiance, it towered an imposing seven meters high, looming above the room.

"This is an image of the first of the two types of foot soldiers that were present during the battles," Taylor said. "Intelligence calls them 'Centurions.' They are every bit as strong as the armor on their ships. Reports say they were capable of withstanding a full clip from a MAR. However, they do have a proverbial 'Achilles Heel.' This glowing ring on their chests there? It acts as a sort of brain that, when shot or severely damaged, sends a kill response to their bodies. This little device seemed to be our saving grace, if you will, during these engagements. We still don't fully know what it is. However, it is a feature that is also shared by their larger brethren."

The picture of the Centurion faded. In its place, the massive, hulking mass of one of the colossal aliens, wielding a two-meter long sword, appeared.

"This is a Juggernaut," Taylor said. "It stands a full two meters taller than the Centurions—and is twice as strong. That's a very frightening prospect, considering what it takes to put a Centurion down. The Juggernauts were first encountered on Arcturus Septum. Their real role in the Vanguard military is not yet known, but they seemed to be used as elite shock troops during the battle. Like Centurions, Juggernauts have tubes slithering in and out of their body that pump a translucent red liquid through it. If I would guess, I'd say it was blood. However, analysis has come back inconclusive. It doesn't possess any properties associated with the kind of blood we're familiar with and it's as cold as ice to the touch. Right now, it's as alien to us as the Vanguard themselves."

She stabbed a button with her outstretched pointer finger and the image flickered once, then disappeared.

"We still do not fully understand the reason the Vanguard attacked us," she said. "However, the running theory is that it was due to the discovery of the Alpha and Beta Crystals. We haven't learned a wealth of information from them, but we don't believe they're of Vanguard origin. The crystals appear to have been created by another race, though how they tie in with the Vanguard is a complete mystery. I believe it's safe to assume that the crystals are far better off in our possession than in theirs—whatever they are.

"Shortly after the Beta Crystal's recovery, the Vanguard fled the Delta Sagittaurii system. We haven't heard from them since. As I said earlier, we have no idea where they went.

"We have every reason to assume the Vanguard will return, however. To think they won't, especially after the effort they put into getting the crystals in the first place, would be highly naïve... and naivety is a mistake we can no longer afford. Knowledge is power, and with that knowledge, this time, we have the upper hand. We have time to prepare ... and we have a secret weapon."

The assembled group looked to one another with raised eyebrows. A murmur worked its way through their rank. Scales, Casey, and Roy swapped glances, but otherwise remained silent.

Commander Taylor typed in a series of commands, and the hologram of a ship hovered above the amphitheater, slowly spinning clockwise.

"This is the *Reveille*," she informed them. "She is the first of her kind—a prototype cross between a corvette and a frigate called a Glaive.

"She has been outfitted with several state-of-the-art weapons, as well as many other features at the precipice of the Coalition's technological innovation. One of them is her armor.

"The hulks of Vanguard warships destroyed during the battle for Arcturus Septum were recovered and studied. In addition to two separate layers of tetriite battle plate, totaling fifty centimeters, the *Reveille* also possesses an overlaying of eight centimeters of Vanguard ship armor. We call it Adamantium. In ancient human mythology, Adamantium was the hardest substance in the known universe. It's a pretty fitting name, as this alloy is over four times as strong as tetriite, making it the hardest metallic substance known. As an added bonus, it's also half as light. Not being weighed down by too much tetriite allows *Reveille* to be fast, quicker than even a corvette, but with the added layer of Adamantium, she can take hits that would normally disable a cruiser. To further help bolster the ship's durability, the *Reveille* was constructed with cross-bracings and an interior honeycomb structure that affords her the ability to sustain massive damage, yet still function at one hundred percent efficiency.

"The *Reveille* is easily the fastest ship in the fleet in sub-light travel. But she has an upgraded FTL drive, too, which allows her captain to execute jumps far more precise than those of any other ship.

"In her two hangar bays, she carries a small wing of Lancer fighters, Angel dropships, and even a motor pool for bolstering offensive power during ground engagements, as well as crew considerations for three-hundred and fifty people.

"This ship is our first, direct response to the Vanguard threat."

Admiral Carr stepped forward. "You were all asked here today because you have been selected to be her first crew," he said. "Your service records, as well as your performances, say you are the best soldiers the navy and Marine Corps has to offer.

"But a ship, as they say, is only as good as her commander, and the captain of the Coalition's most advanced ship had to be in keeping with the standards of her highly skilled crew.

"Lieutenant Commander Kileeus Scales, you are hereby given command of the *Reveille* and her crew. Congratulations. I can think of no commander more fitting than you. I know she'll be in good hands."

For the first time in decades, Scales was at a complete loss as to what to say.

What could he say? He'd just been given command of his own warship. He'd long ago given up the aspiration of commanding a starship once he joined the Shadows. Yet here it was. Life had presented him with the opportunity.

No. He rescinded that. *Admiral Carr* had presented him with the opportunity.

He stood. "Admiral, sir?"

Carr clasped his hands behind his back. "Yes, Commander?"

Scales licked his lips. "Thank you for this *incredible* opportunity, sir," he said. "I'm honored."

Carr stared straight at him. His ice-blue eyes were fixated on him. "You've earned it, Commander," he said. "But the *Reveille* isn't your only responsibility now. The Council has long wished to put together a small band of Shadow Operatives that have the ability to move around the galaxy under their own power, an elite strike team that has full autonomy over any situation, any mission, and any assignment they're given. Commander Scales, as you, Lieutenant Keller, and First Lieutenant Locke already have a base of operations, we thought we'd start with you. You are now the three-man Shadow strike team codenamed *Nova Team*. It's your job to strike hard and fast behind enemy lines, be they Rebel, Vanguard, or some other threat entirely. You are still a part of the military, and still have to answer to the hierarchy of command, but that hierarchy is now almost exclusively restricted to the Council. You will report directly to us. As the Shadows are the right hand of the Council, *Nova Team* is the blade with which we chose to strike."

A slight smile touched Scales' lips and tugged at the corners of his mouth. He wanted to beam with pride. This was the highest honor the Coalition could bestow. But he was a soldier, and a Vakari at that. He quickly stifled the smile. Scales stood to attention and snapped off a firm, crisp salute.

Casey and Roy arose from their seats and joined him.

"We are honored, Admiral," Scales said. "We will not disappoint the Council … or *you*, sir."

"I don't doubt it, Commander." Carr returned their salutes. "You never have." Though Carr was a hard man to read, Scales detected admiration in the old man's stare. "With that, ladies and gentlemen, this briefing is concluded."

"Atten-*shun!*" Scales called.

The room of soldiers saluted the Admiral and Commander Taylor.

As Taylor marched off the dais, Carr said, "There's a briefing packet waiting for you in your quarters aboard the *Reveille*, Commander. It will provide the details for *Nova Team*'s first mission. On behalf of the entire Council, I wish you luck, soldiers. Dismissed."

Chapter Twenty-One

1032 hours, May 29, 2343

Electus Borealis System, planet Katana

*Aboard UGC shuttle pod **Vixen***

*En route to **UGC Glaive Reveille**, docked at Gamma Station Three*

"What does that mean, exactly?" Casey asked. She tapped her foot nervously on the shuttle's deck. She sat in a padded seat across from Roy and Scales.

Outside the viewport, the red skies of Katana slowly gave way to blackness as the shuttle broke through the atmosphere. Countless tiny stars twinkled in the distance. One of Katana's grey, bumpy moons, Dishnok, looked like it could fit in the palm of her hand.

"What does what mean?" Roy asked.

"Full autonomy," she said. "That we don't answer to anyone but the Council?"

"It means that we have complete tactical command of any mission we're given," Scales answered. "And that the Council is the only hierarchy we have to take orders from."

"Okay," Roy said, "say we're on a mission, and a five-star general tells us that we have to do something for him. Does that mean we can tell him to screw off?"

"Not quite," Scales said. "However, if his orders interfere with our overall mission, then we are within our right to assert our command. Doesn't mean we can tell him to go to hell, though. Superiors are still superiors, Roy. All Admiral Carr meant was that anything the Council tells us to do takes precedence over anything else."

"Well, that's no fun," Roy muttered.

"Are you okay, sir?" Casey asked. "That's the first thing you've said since we boarded."

"Yes," Scales replied. "I'm fine. Anxious. I've done a hell of a lot in my career, but I've never been in command of a ship before—my own, at that."

"I think you'll do fine, sir," Roy said. "You sure kick the crap out of every other job you do. Why should this be any different?"

"Thanks for the confidence boost, but commanding a ship is a lot harder than it seems."

"Any idea what our first mission together is going to be?" Casey asked.

"I have no idea," Scales admitted. "As soon as I read the packet, I'll call you two for a briefing. Hey … feel that? We're slowing down. We must be getting ready to dock with the *Reveille*. Fancy a look?"

They unbuckled their harnesses and went down the aisle toward the cockpit. Out of the glass canopy, Scales, Casey, and Roy finally got their first glimpse of their base of operations: the *Reveille*.

She was a beautiful ship. She was two hundred fifty meters long from bow to stern. There were countless viewports along her port and starboard side hull. She was sleek, fast looking, and painted black with a crimson stripe running horizontally along the length of her hull.

Scales admired the view. "Wow," he said in a low breathless tone.

The pilot tapped his display. The shuttle's thrusters flared and she moved in closer. Scales spotted several round grey ports on the portside hull—missile pods. As they drifted yet closer, Scales spied two pod-like devices protruding from the *Reveille*'s mid ships.

If they were some of the advanced weapons Taylor had mentioned, their functionality was a mystery to even him—and he'd familiarized himself with almost every weapon out there.

The amber-colored overhead lights strobed three times.

"I hate to ruin your fun," the pilot said, "but you guys might want to take a seat and strap in." Scales, Casey, and Roy complied.

There was a slight bump, then a lurch in their stomachs as the shuttle decelerated. The shuttle entered the belly of the ship. A moment later, the cabin pressurized with the interior atmosphere.

"Atmosphere is stable," the pilot said. He flipped some switches on his control console. "Dock successful. You're good to go."

Nova Team gathered their duffle bags stored under their seats. The cabin door hissed opened and a ramp extended.

Scales took a deep breath.

Casey and Roy stood aside. "Your ship, sir," she said and gestured to the bulkhead. "Lead the way."

Scales nodded. His footfalls echoing against the titanium, he made his way down the shuttle's extended stairs. He stepped off the last step and planted his feet firmly onto the *Reveille*'s flight deck.

Casey followed next, and then Roy.

Waiting to greet them were all three hundred members of the crew.

"Ten-hut." The crew snapped to attention and held a firm salute. There were humans, Asgards, Vakari, Tiberan, Tomlyns, Ura, Eka, Chixil, Boreans, and more. Every race capable of serving in front-line military duty was present.

Scales surveyed the crew. The sight of them was emboldening. They stood boldly together, united, ready to face whatever challenges the galaxy would throw at them.

"At ease, ladies and gentlemen." Scales gave them a salute of his own. In one motion, they assumed parade rest.

A human in navy dress stepped forward out of the crowd. He was around six foot three with greying brown hair and hazel eyes. His hair was precisely regulation length and parted to the right. "Commander, sir." He saluted smartly. "It's an honor to meet you. I'm Lieutenant Jack Hurley, your XO."

Scales saluted. "The pleasure is mine, Lieutenant." He extended his hand. "I'd like to depart as soon as possible. How soon before we're ready?"

"We're finishing final preparations now, sir. Ship is in final shake-down cycle."

"Excellent," Scales said.

"Shall I give you three the tour?" Hurley asked.

Scales nodded and looked back at Roy and Casey. They were as anxious to see the interior of the ship as he was. "Lead the way."

"Aye aye, sir." Hurley turned to the assembled crew. "Are you going to stand there all damn day? Get back to your duties. Double time it!"

The crew quickly dispersed.

"If the crew doesn't hate the XO," Hurley said to Scales, "then he's not doing his job. This way, sir."

Scales, Casey, and Roy followed Hurley through the halls and corridors of the *Reveille* and listened earnestly while he gave them the rundown.

"Everything about this ship is state of the art," Hurley said as they passed through a G deck corridor. In lieu of the titanium bracings, beams, and exposed bolts prevalent on other ships in the Coalition, the *Reveille*'s walls were plated with a layer of smooth, gunmetal grey titanium. A white stripe ran down the length of the halls indicating to the crew that this was G deck. Each deck was coded with a colored, luminescent stripe that would provide the crew with a sense of direction in the event of a blackout. "We have been given every scrap of new and upgraded equipment in existence, fresh off the line. Even our weapons have been given a complete overhaul."

"Give me the rundown on them," Scales said.

"We're armed to the teeth, Commander," Hurley said. "For point-defense against single ships and boarding craft, we have twenty fifty-millimeter batteries, each mounting four rail turrets apiece, with overlapping fields of fire on all vectors. Two massive eight-hundred millimeter Helix batteries with coordinated fire from eight Kestrel batteries and sixteen Rapier batteries can handle most close-in ship-to-ship engagements. If they're not enough, we have been given four prototype plasma cannons. When their magnetic field capacitors are fully charged, they are able to fire a bolt of plasma with each cycle. Their energy recycles every thirty seconds."

Scales raised his eyebrows.

Energy weapons on that scale were still in the development phase, or so he had thought. The UGC had long ago perfected small arms energy weapons, but the power levels required to operate starship-mounted plasma weaponry must have been astronomical. He was anxious to see them in action.

They stepped into a lift. Hurley punched the holographic button labeled 'F deck,' and they started to ascend.

"For long-range assault," he continued, "there are thirty Rapture missile pods mounted at various points along our hull, as well as fifty Sword pods, totaling three thousand five hundred missiles in all. For heavy ordinance, we have ten Hyperion torpedo silos and three Arkus tactical nuclear warheads, standard sixty-megaton yield.

Now, our main weapon is something special. It's called a Maelstrom cannon. It's a magnetic accelerator cannon the size of a frigate-mounted Aegis. However, the Maelstrom fires a one hundred ton round as opposed to the standard three hundred. Magnetic field recyclers and booster capacitors, coupled with our improved drive core, afford it enough energy to fire at full power every two seconds."

Scales mouthed, "Damn."

The lift jolted to a halt. When the doors glided open, the four of them strolled out into a massive room, the ceiling twenty meters high. It was ringed with a complex network of grated catwalks all built around a central sphere. The sphere itself stood fifteen meters above the deck and shimmered with blue energy. It emitted a thrum so deep Scales felt his teeth vibrate. Crackles of white light periodically leapt from its surface, though they dissipated harmlessly a few meters from their point of origin. There was an electric ting in the air. Scales could feel it in the roots of his quills.

Hurley beckoned to the sphere. "This is the new mark ten drive core. We're the first ship in the fleet to be outfitted with one. The mark ten can not only bolster our linear accelerator weapons, but can also put out four hundred fifty percent the power of a mark nine. That means this ship is capable of reaching speeds during sub-light that can surpass the fastest ship in the Coalition fleet. We were also graced with an auxiliary drive core, so when the primary is in cool down, our auxiliary kicks in. Needless to say, this ship is never going to lose power.

"Now speaking of power, the *Reveille* also has features similar to that of a prowler. The outer hull is layered with stealth ablative plating, which hides us from radar and sensors, and when our drive core operates below forty percent power, we are as dark as interstellar space. That effectively makes us invisible out here.

"Commander Taylor pretty much summed up our armor and hull's abilities to withstand a beating, so I don't think I need to elaborate on that further. Now on to our cargo."

Scales, Roy, and Casey followed Hurley back into the lift. During the ride, he explained how the *Reveille* was stocked with enough food and provisions to last the crew five years, ten if they all went to half-rations, and yet longer still if all non-essential personnel were put into cryo "sleep in the chambers housed on D deck. The lift deposited them at their destination.

Scales stepped onto a deck filled with pristine military vehicles. Several deckhands were tending to a Ranger. One of them rolled a tire across the deck to a pair of awaiting crew members, who grabbed it and inserted it on the back left axel. The men went to work tightening the lug bolts, their drills screeching. A woman in bright yellow coveralls passed a crate full of high-caliber rounds up to a man standing in the Ranger's back gun platform. He opened the box and took out a bandolier packed full of ammunition. He handed some of the heavy 'bullet-snake's' weight off to his partner, and together they loaded the Ranger's rear cannon. On the port and starboard-side walls, the two dozen cubby-holed garages and refit-and-repair facilities would maintain, fix-up, and put any vehicles damaged in combat back on the line at a staggering rate.

"We carry ten Ranger LCVs," Hurley said as Roy, Scales, and Casey trotted behind him through the rows of assault vehicles and tanks, "four Arvok APCs, two Widow tanks, and two Wyvern Utility VTOLs, as well as thirty marines that are capable of going aground during an engagement. We also carry a wing of eight Lancer fighters and four Angel dropships, all with full flight crew."

The quartet halted before some kind of vehicle. It was akin to some cross between a tank and an APC, over ten meters long and four tall, and had six massive wheels in place of treads or anti-gravity plates. Its design was sleek, its features trim and streamlined.

With the assault vehicle serving as his backdrop, Hurley turned about to face them, his hands clasped behind his back. "R and D has included something special in our motor pool, a new toy I think you'll find quite useful. It's called a Stalker. It's basically a mobile battle-field CIC with a small living quarters for three. This thing is like the *Reveille*: top of the line. She was designed for surveillance, to observe the enemy from afar, and creep right up their ass without them even knowing it. To help conceal her presence, the Stalker has been outfitted with photo-reactive plating, rendering her almost invisible. These plates mimic the surrounding environment perfectly, helping to blend the Stalker in like a chameleon. She's quick and quiet, too." He turned to face it. "Her primary function is stealth, but with a one hundred sixty-five-millimeter main gun, a forty mill coaxial autocannon, and four Apex ASM/G missile launchers, she can sure as hell settle almost any ground engagement." Hurley reached out and patted the Stalker's rock-solid armor plating. "Personally, I think she was designed with the three of you in mind, but that's way above my pay grade."

As Hurley led them away, Scales smiled—he wanted to use this thing the first chance he got. He looked the Stalker over from its wheels to the massive turret that sat atop it like a coronel, crowning it, in his mind, as the most powerful land assault craft the *Reveille* carried in her womb.

"The *Reveille* has several technicians, deckhands, a full CIC crew, officers of the watch for security, and two medical facilities with full staff," Hurley said as he led them through the halls of C deck. "There's housing quarters for all three hundred crew members aboard this ship, with room for fifty more. Commander, your cabin is located on A deck near the stern. Lieutenant Locke and Lieutenant Keller, you each have your own quarters on A, as well. Admiral Carr was very insistent you two be given private housing separate from the rest of the crew."

"This ship is amazing," Casey said.

"She is," Hurley agreed. "Beyond, in my opinion. I think I'd prefer her to any woman I've ever met—especially my ex-wife. But that's what you get for marrying a woman who sleeps with your sister the day after your wedding. Oh well, live and learn, right?"

Roy and Casey shared a glance. He smirked. She put her hand to her mouth to stifle a laugh.

"I cannot believe he just said that," Roy whispered.

Scales cleared his throat. "What other facilities do we have?" he asked, bewildered at his XO's choice to divulge that colorful tidbit of information.

"An armory, lab, firing range, barracks, gym, and an additional flight deck below the one you arrived in. There's also a communications and briefing room, a ready room for the pilots, a lounge, and a ward-room. Every facility any other ship in the fleet has, we do. In all, sir, the *Reveille* sports more armament than a frigate, despite the fact she's less than half the size. I think you'll find her to be equal to that of even a cruiser."

Hurley finished his tour as they stepped into CIC.

It was a circular room, about nine meters from wall to wall with twelve stations ringing its perimeter. Screens and displays decorated its walls and ceiling. A thick wall-to-wall viewscreen wrapped around the *Reveille*'s prow, giving all a lovely view of Electus Borealis several million kilometers in the distance. It winked at them with an amber eye. The marbled shades of browns, greens, and blues covering the surface of Katana were crystal clear through the glass of the stern-mounted viewscreen. There was a holotable in the center of the CIC, a private meeting room up three stairs on the portside, and a captain's chair in front of the prow viewscreen.

When Scales entered, someone called, "Commander on deck." Everyone rose and stood to attention.

"Carry on," Scales said.

Hurley strolled over to an ops station. He exchanged a few words with the officer and then turned to Scales. "Commander, Ops reports we're ready to get underway."

"Good," Scales said. "Ops, prepare to leave dock. Helm, plot us a course to the system's edge."

"Aye aye," they replied simultaneously.

There were a dozen loud clinks as the ship detached itself from Gamma Station Three's umbilical.

"We're in the green, Commander," a Vakari officer called from the operations station. "All systems check. Disengaging docking clamps. Atmosphere stabilized. Stand by…we're free. Ops station online."

"Navigations online," another officer called.

"Weapons online."

"Communications online."

"All stations online," the tactical officer—a woman with the single gold band of a junior lieutenant on her sleeve—turned and said.

"Excellent," Scales said. "Hurley?"

"Sir?"

"You have the deck. Casey, Roy, walk with me."

"See," Casey remarked to Scales as they left the CIC and sauntered the *Reveille*'s surprisingly well-lit corridors. "You're getting the hang of it already, sir."

"I was trained in ship navigations during my time at the Shelor'an Academy on Katana," Scales said. "I'm a little rusty. It's going to take some getting used to it. I'm going up to my quarters to review the briefing packet Carr left for us. Get settled in, grab a bite to eat, then meet me in briefing room A in two hours. If you get lost, I'm sure one of the crew can point you in the right direction."

"Aye, Commander." Casey said.

"Aye, sir." Roy said.

"See you soon."

They parted ways, and Scales made his way to a lift. He punched the button labeled "A deck" and the elevator doors closed. The lift began its climb up two decks. He consulted the holographic signs on the ceiling that told him where he was until he found his way to his cabin.

The bulkhead was at the end of a five-meter corridor. When Scales neared, the doors whispered open automatically. He stepped in.

It was surprisingly spacious. Against the immediate starboard wall was a wooden desk with several books and papers neatly organized on its surface. On the wall above hung a hand-painted picture of a famous Vakari Admiral, Grenethilus Sorvus. Down a flight of stairs, the room opened up. Two windows gave him a clear view of space on both the port and starboard sides; arrayed in front of the port window were three chairs. To the starboard, a wall-to-wall bookshelf was lined with books of all sizes and colors, along with a sitting area, three plush chairs, and a coffee table. Nestled in the starboard corner was a holo-terminal atop a beautiful oak desk. His private head and bedroom furnishings were through an archway two meters away and down a second set of steps.

Scales set his duffle down and put his hands on his hips. It was lovely in here, far more so than he thought he could ever get used to—the life of a Shadow was as far from plush living as one could get.

He went into his bedroom and saw the briefing folder sitting at the foot of the bed. Scales stowed his gear, then sat down at a desk in the corner of the room. He flicked on the desk lamp and opened the folder.

He read over it and smiled.

This was going to be a challenge.

CHAPTER TWENTY-TWO

"**S**o, , are you ever going to tell me what those rich kids back on your home planet did to piss you off so bad?" Casey asked.

They halted before the briefing room door.

Scowling, Roy hit the icon and it cycled open. "They used to beat me up," he replied tersely.

Casey couldn't help it. A burst of laughter escaped her mouth before she could stop it. "Aww," she said, "Roy, that's kind of cute."

They took their places at the table.

"Yeah," he said. "Real damn cute."

The bulkhead opened. Scales marched through in grey duty uniform. Casey and Roy arose to attention.

"At ease," Scales said coolly. "Sit." He settled in a chair across from them at the head of the ovular table. "Lights."

The room's illumination dimmed to amber. The holographic projector in the middle of the table warmed to blue before a cobalt planet blanketed in white fluffy clouds winked into existence ten centimeters above the surface. It slowly rotated on its axis. Two pitted moons hung in low orbit around it.

"This is planet Gorgoran in the Alpha Corinthus system," Scales said. He leaned forward and steepled his fingers. "It is largely uninhabited due to its frigid temperatures and wastelands of snow. The Colonial Affairs Administration has labeled it as a class-three hazard and ill-advises any form of colonization. Of course, that hasn't deterred a few hardheaded private organizations from leaving their mark. There are a dozen scattered settlements, and about twice as many research outposts. However, one of them has an unusual amount of incoming and outgoing activity." Scales licked his lips. "Bring up grid alpha-constellation one-four-niner by two-one-six," he ordered the projector.

The image complied. It dove through holographic clouds like a dive-bomber and came to a rest over a series of black structures from an eagle's eye view. The buildings stood out midnight black against the pure white of hundreds of kilometers of snow.

"This is Charybdis, a Muham experimental weapons facility. It stands alone, a staggering thirteen hundred kilometers away from any form of civilization to the north, south, east, and west. It's meant to be self-sustaining. It runs on pinch fusion reactors that are capable of providing necessary energy for several decades. It does require regular shipments of food for its staff, though, by way of shuttlecraft.

"Word is the Muham are researching some kind of new weapon, one rumored to dwarf a nuclear weapon in destructive capability. Obviously, this is something we can't afford to overlook. Our mission is to infiltrate Charybdis Facility, recover the research data, and then blow it on our way out. We are authorized to neutralize any targets that stand in the way of our objective."

Casey raised her eyebrows and shared a sideways glance with Roy. He sat with a stern look, but remained silent. She licked her lips. "Sir, permission to speak freely?"

"Of course, Casey."

"Sir, this seems a little … uh, extreme for a first mission. Are you sure we're ready for something like this?"

"Admiral Carr thinks you are, or he wouldn't have assigned it."

"Commander," Casey said and leaned forward, "with all respect to Admiral Carr intended, I'm not asking what he thinks. I'm asking if you think we're ready for something like this."

"Yes," he replied without missing a beat. The tone of his voice was laden with a heartening degree of confidence and uplifting encouragement. "After the way you two handled yourselves on Arcturus Septum, I think this will be a walk in the park, to be honest. What you two need to understand from here on out is that it was me who suggested to Admiral Carr that you two be inducted into the Shadows. If I didn't have faith in you, if I didn't think you two were capable of carrying out assignments like this, the thought would have never crossed my mind. Remember that. Plus," he added, settling back into his chair and folding his arms across his chest, "you're with me, and this isn't my first rodeo, as your human saying goes. I've been on plenty of missions like this."

"Of course, sir," she said. "Thank you. I apologize." She found herself oddly reassured. There was honesty in his reply, sincerity, and she didn't think him the lying type. He'd been utterly honest on Arcturus Septum, and there was no reason to start doubting him now.

"No apology necessary, Casey."

"What intel do we have on the Muham, sir?" Roy asked. "I don't think I've ever seen one in person."

"Yeah," Casey said. "Neither have I. I don't even know what they look like."

"I suppose they'd consider this comparison racist," Scales said, "But they look like giant beetles, more or less. They stand about two meters tall. They're brown and bipedal. They have six upper limbs and a triangular head with two antennae."

"Giant beetles," Roy said with disgust. "I hate bugs. What's their story, sir?"

"The Muham chose to leave the United Galactic Coalition three hundred and thirty years ago," he explained. "I have no idea why. Perhaps they thought the Council wasn't doing enough for them, figured maybe they could do better on their own. Since then, they've made themselves a crucial ally to merc bands, slavers, and even the Rebels. Muham are brilliant scientists, with minds capable of exceeding that of even an

Ura, in my opinion. For the right price, they provide their clients with pieces of technology that even the UGC doesn't possess. Weapons. Equipment. Advanced body armors. Things like that. Either way, the Muham supply the Rebels with the means to continue their war against us, and are therefore considered hostile by the military."

"Do you think we'll encounter any Rebels there with them?" Roy asked.

Scales considered the question for an instant before replying, "I long ago learned that anything is possible. Until we get out there, until we actually know for sure, hell, expect to encounter even the Vanguard. The first rule of the Shadows is to always expect the unexpected. That way you won't ever be caught off guard."

"Pretty practical," Casey said. "What's our next step?"

"Now we go over our plan of attack."

Scales tapped his display. Gorgoran flickered and vanished to give way to a solar system. A golden sun twice the mass of Sol burned bright at its center. Its gravity well held six planets in its grasp. The system was encompassed by an outlying asteroid belt, much like Sol. The only terrestrial planet swung round in an elliptical orbit one hundred and fifty million kilometers from the sun. It had brown and green mountainous continents smeared with blotches of hundreds of kilometers of forest and deep, unpolluted, clear blue seas.

A tab above the planet had it labeled as "Fortisan."

The solar system then shrunk into nonexistence, making room for an enlarged image of Fortisan. CAA records appeared and rapidly flashed information beside it: estimated population, major cities, geological surveys, shipping lanes, and L4 and L5 stations.

In all, the planet held a population of around five million.

"Intelligence has identified the location of Charybdis' supply shuttles as having come from here," Scales said. "As luck would have it, the next freighter bound for the facility—the *Orcanos*—leaves port from the planet's ODS *Pitch Black* two days from now. From there, it's a six-hour flight to Gorgoran.

"We are going to pose as members of the loading crew. Our false identities have already been fabricated, courtesy of OMI. Our names will show up on their records, should they check them.

"Now be warned. Fortisan isn't known to have a very strong allegiance to the UGC. Their population is thick with Rebels and sympathizers. For that reason, the *Reveille* will hang back while we take an unmarked shuttle to the *Black*, present our IDs, and board the *Orcanos*. Couldn't be simpler."

"How do we get inside the facility?" Casey asked.

Scales typed a few buttons on the display, and Fortisan disappeared. An overhead view of Charybdis snapped back into focus.

"As the crew begins unloading the cargo, we'll slip away and enter the facility through here—" he indicated a blinking red beacon thirty-five meters from the docks, "—a small auxiliary entrance, and find our way to the labs. If we're careful, quick, and quiet, we won't run into any patrols. Once we get to the labs, Roy, you're going to begin downloading the research data onto an OSD from this server room here, while Casey and I set the charges.

"The *Reveille* will have shadowed the *Orcanos* during its flight, and will be in orbit around Gorgoran by the time we arrive. After we set the charges, an Angel will pick us up at grid alpha five-five-zero by four-five-two at sixteen hundred sharp.

"We'll be arriving in the Fortisan system at oh-nine-hundred on the thirty-first. The *Reveille* will be running dark so as to avoid detection. Any questions?"

Roy was stroking his chin in deep contemplation.

Studying the projection, Casey leaned forward with her fingers steepled. "Sounds straightforward enough," she said. "How will we get the chance to slip away from everyone while they're loading cargo? Unless our kit came equipped with active camo generators, they are going to see us."

"Not active camo per se," Scales said mysteriously. "At least, not in the way you mean it."

"Would you care to elaborate, sir?" Roy asked.

"The *Orcanos* is going to arrive right in the middle of a snow storm. It'll be a complete whiteout. Visibility won't reach beyond two meters at the most. We wait for the loading crew to become engrossed in getting the cargo squared away so they can get out of the storm, then we give them the slip and make for the waypoint as quickly as we can."

"Won't they know they're a few people short?" Casey wanted to know.

"By that time, it won't matter. We'll be so far along that they won't be able to stop us."

"That's optimistic," she said.

"It has to be," Scales replied. "You have to believe with one-hundred and ten percent certainty that you will succeed in whatever assignment you're given, or you won't. Plain and simple."

"Again," she said, "practical."

"What's our kit going to consist of?" Roy asked. "And more importantly, how are we going to smuggle our weapons onto the *Orcanos*?"

"Shadows use a special type of body armor, a lot different than what you're used to. It's called Venerator armor. However, it would be too bulky to be worn underneath the work uniforms OMI provided us with. Instead, we'll be using Thermal armor, which would normally function as an under suit worn beneath a suit of Venerator. It provides significant small arms protection, as much as usual marine battle dress, and it will keep us warm in Gorgoran's frigid temperatures. It can also match our heat signatures to the tempature of the environment we're in, thereby hiding us from thermal or infrared sensors. We'll be carrying duffle bags with us that will hold our helmets, weapons, ammo, and equipment. They're lined with a coating that will hide our stuff from any sensors or metal detectors."

"Are we going in heavy?" Roy asked.

"Moderate. There are around a hundred and fifty guards inside Charybdis, so we'll need to pack accordingly. Roy, you and I are going in with assault weapons. Make sure to pack a sidearm, too. The armory has a nice selection of both, so take your pick. Casey, you're my marksman. Arm yourself with whatever precision weapon takes your fancy. Grab yourself a sidearm, too."

Casey gave him a curt nod. She could do marksman work. She'd done a wonderful job of it on Arcturus Septum, after all. "What kind of ordinance are we using to blow the facility?"

"A nuclear mine," Scales replied, a curious dash of enthusiasm bounding into his voice. "Forty kiloton yield. Should certainly make for a wonderful show once we're back up in orbit.

"Now listen, I want to make this clear. It's our job to complete this mission, and we have to do that no matter what. Think of the consequences if we fail. That weapon the Muham are building? How many people could it kill? No matter what. Understood?"

"Understood," they replied.

"I'd like you two to head down to the armory and familiarize yourself with your new armor when we've finished here," Scales said. "Venerator armor isn't that hard to get used to, but I want you to try it on and execute a few training exercises with our Master at Arms until you get a feel for it. At eighteen-thirty tonight, you two are invited up to my cabin for a drink and cigars. I have you both rostered off duty then, so don't consider it a formal occasion. I thought it might be nice to just unwind for a bit. Give us a chance to talk."

Casey raised her eyebrows. That took her a bit by surprise. For some strange reason, she hadn't considered Scales to be the sociable type—but then, she hadn't thought herself to be combat material, either.

She'd been dead wrong about that.

"I'd never turn down a drink, sir," Roy chirped.

"Thank you, Commander," Casey said.

"Of course," Scales said. "I've sent the mission specs to your quarters. You're free to review them at your leisure. See you at eighteen thirty."

Casey arose and stood to attention. Roy joined her. With a brisk nod, Scales turned and left.

Gunnery Officer Maneeus Tok was speaking to Scales over the coms when Roy and Casey walked through the doors of the armory.

"Operatives Keller and Locke are going to be coming down and trying on the new Venerator armor. Run them through a few tests and send me a performance evaluation afterwards."

"Wilco, Commander," the gunnery officer replied. "They just arrived. I'll see that they get suited up immediately."

The channel clicked off.

Tok snapped off a lazy salute. "Sir. Ma'am."

"At ease, Gunnery Officer," Roy said. "Let's see what this armor is all about." He turned to Casey. "Ladies first."

"Oh, how polite of you," she said impishly. "You're such a gentleman, Roy."

"Please stand here, Lieutenant Keller," Tok motioned to the middle of the floor. "Try to remain as still as you can."

He called in a few technicians. They cracked the lid of a huge crate open and began taking out components of black, sleek-looking armor and laying them out atop a nearby table. Three of the techs helped Casey get into a skin-tight, black under suit. When it touched her skin, a cold inner layer of gel made her shiver. An instant later, the gel warmed to her body temperature.

"This is the Thermal suit," Tok said. "It's worn beneath your armor, usually over the body suit."

So this was the Thermal suit Scales had mentioned. It was comfortable and significantly flexible. She wondered how well it would do against small arms fire, though. Surely something this light couldn't stop a bullet.

"I think that's a good look for you, Casey," Roy quipped. "That suit really …um … accentuates your figure."

"Shut up."

Tok said, "The Thermal suit is airtight and vacuum rated. Along with a helmet, it provides you with a full sixty minutes of oxygen to perform any EVA or underwater operations."

"Feels cozy," Casey said to Roy, who stood leaning against the wall with his arms folded across his chest. He was visibly impressed … though whether he was impressed with the under suit or the way she looked in it was open for debate.

The techs started fitting Casey with the various pieces of armor. Though it looked heavy, the armor was surprisingly lightweight.

Over her gloved hands, they slid on an armored gauntlet. They sealed the locking collar, and she wriggled her fingers. There were armor caps on all her fingers except her trigger finger and thumb.

One of the techs handed Casey a fully enclosed helmet. She could see her reflection in its bluish-silver visor. She pulled it over her head, and with a hiss, the airtight seals locked into place.

In the upper right-hand corner of the helmet, a holographic orange circle appeared. Instinctively, Casey looked at the image, which morphed into a square and expanded across her right eye. "Gunny, something happened." Her voice sounded unmolested and clear through the helmet's speakers. "Some kind of holo projection just appeared."

"It's okay," Tok said. "It's supposed to. What you're seeing in front of you is the beginning of your suit's diagnostic cycle. Give it a moment."

Text scrolled across Casey's vision so quickly it was a blur. A schematic of the armor snapped up, different sections blinked red, then green. It faded. In the left-hand corner of her visor, her biomonitor winked to life. Then the words "Armor Diagnostic Complete" and "Venerator Armor Online" flashed in front of her eyes. The square changed back into an orange circle and took its place back in the right-hand corner.

"When do I get to play?" Roy asked.

"In a minute," Tok said over his shoulder. "Ok, Lieutenant Keller, what you are seeing now is your suit's basic Heads-Up-Display. Everything you need to know, from mission reports, team positions, to topographic maps, will be displayed in front of your eyes whenever you call it up. When I tell you to, I want you to look at the orange circle again. When you do, scroll your retinas from the right to the left until you find the option to pull up the schematics for the *Reveille*. Do it now."

Casey did. The circle transformed into a blue square, moved in front of her right eye, and displayed a series of texts. She moved her eyes right to left and scrolled through the information selections until she found the option to bring up the blueprints for the *Reveille*.

"Okay," she said. "What now?"

"I want you to look at the option and blink your right eye."

When she blinked, the schematics file opened, and a small holographic display of the ship's decks snapped up and wrapped around her field of vision. A small blue box lit up on the inside of the holographic ship. Wherever she moved her eyes, it followed.

"Venerator armor has neurological hardware that links up directly with your brain. Now, with your eyes, use the blue indicator to navigate the ship and find the armory on B deck," Tok said. "Then zoom in by gradually widening your eyes."

With her eyes, she moved the box to the armory. She widened her eyes as she was instructed. It seemed like a foolish action, but the image enlarged and zoomed, and she saw a frame outline of the armory's walls. Inside, twelve red silhouettes stood around the room. They mirrored the exact positions she, Roy, Tok, and the techs stood in.

"I can see you, Roy," she said. "You're hot."

"Well thank you," he smirked. "You're pretty hot yourself."

"I meant your heat signature, ass."

"Your helmet is perhaps the most important component to this entire suit," Tok said. "It has air filters; imaging, sensor, and video suites; and communications modules. There are nearly limitless amounts of battlefield and tactical information you can pull up—even more if you've got the proper clearance. Anything in the UGC database that you have access to can be brought up for your viewing by the same method. All you have to do is move your eyes. The suit's onboard computer will do the rest. Now, let's get Lieutenant Locke situated. Lieutenant Keller, go over to the firing range and try out your new HUD's targeting uplinks to hit a few targets in the meantime."

Roy eagerly stepped forward to be suited up.

Casey strolled gingerly over to a field armory. The armor wasn't bulky, but it did take her time to get used to walking in it. She took a Talon Battle Rifle off the rack and loaded it with an armor-piercing clip. She stood at the range and pressed the stock against her shoulder.

On her HUD, a holographic targeting reticle appeared, along with the weapon's ammunition counter across the top of her visor.

The sensors in her gauntlets were projecting the weapon's information directly onto her HUD.

She clicked the Talon's magnification to 2X zoom. Her HUD picked it up right away. Her vision sharpened and the target leapt forward right before her eyes.

It was incredible. She'd never witnessed anything like it.

She sighted down on the target dummy's head and squeezed the trigger. A four-round burst caught it right between the eyes. She sighted down the second, four meters downrange of the first. The Talon coughed and hit the next target center mass. The last target was farther away.

She aimed … steadied her breathing … and fired. The rounds found their mark between its eyes.

Impressed with her skill, she lowered the Talon. The armor's targeting uplink suite would boost her already exceptional marksman skills tenfold.

Roy joined her. He hit the targets right on the mark, too. Tok ran them through a series of scenarios—sprinting, vaulting over cover, hand-to-hand combat. In two hours, they had adapted well to the Venerator Armor and learned to implement it into their training.

Roy reluctantly allowed the technicians to undress him. "I can't wait to try this out in combat."

"Take it easy, Lieutenant," Tok said. "You two adapted well to the armor. Here are your access chips. Use them to open your armor storage lockers whenever you need to. Now, if you don't mind, I've got a lot of weapon crates that need to be inventoried, so with all due respect, scat."

Trailing behind Casey as they left the armory, Roy stole one final glance at the armor being placed in his locker.

"God," she said. "I'll bet you're just bursting with excitement right now."

"Damn right," he replied. "If I'd had armor like that on Arcturus Septum, I may have come back a little less beat up."

"A bolt of liquid metal hit Scales dead center in the chest, remember? The Venerator armor didn't do much to stop that."

"Don't think it was supposed to, Casey. How can you make a body armor resistant to weapons you've never encountered before?"

"Ouch, touché," she said. "I'll catch you later. I'm going up to my quarters and take a nice, hot shower. See you later tonight."

The fine Eruvan glass decanter was three-quarters of the way full of amber-colored brandy. A matching set of three glasses and three cigars encased in long silver tubes added quite the compliment to the silver Borean-crafted tray Scales set down on the coffee table. After pouring Casey and Roy a glass, he raised his own in a toast.

"To new friends," Scales said. "To Nova Team. And to all our fallen friends and comrades who didn't make it off Arcturus Septum."

Casey found herself surprised Scales would offer such a heartfelt sentiment. It just seemed so … out of character for him. She was beginning to see a different side of him today. Perhaps, like her, there was more to him than met the eye.

"Aye, aye," she said.

Roy paused for a moment. Casey guessed he was thinking of Lister and the others. "Aye."

Casey took a sip of the liquor and coughed. "God." Her voice was strained. "What is this?"

Scales smiled. "It's human," he said. "Roman Red. I've developed quite the taste for it over the years."

Casey coughed again. Her eyes brimmed with tears. "It's really strong."

Scales chuckled. "You get used to it after a while."

As they drank and talked, Scales' demeanor took an unexpected one hundred eighty degree spin, and Casey began to see in him the lighter side to the stoic soldier she had known. He joked and laughed with them, told them hilarious stories that had happened to him during the course of his long, eventful life. It turned out he possessed a very likable personality. She realized there was so much more to him than a man programmed for combat, a man on autopilot who had no sense of … well, she would have called it humanity, but … well, perhaps that was the best word to describe it for now. She found it comforting, reassuring to know that this inhuman being had a very human side … and one she could most definitely relate to and respect.

"So how did you become a Shadow?" Casey asked sometime later. "What made you want to join?"

Scales considered the question before speaking. "I had been on Axios during the Long Winter. That was when the Rebels had allied themselves with damn near every mercenary and slaver in the Vror Sector. I was assigned to Special Reconnaissance Group Four. Our mission was to defend a spaceport while the civilians were being evaced off-planet. The only problem was there were sixty of us against seven-thousand Rebel troops. They had armor, artillery, air support—the works. We had help from the Twenty-Third and the Fifty-Fourth Marine Tactical, but we were still outnumbered.

"They swarmed the space port. We were able to hold them off at first, but then they started throwing tanks and rapid-assault vehicles at us to no end. It didn't take long for our numbers to dwindle. On the second day, they breached our first defensive line, completely blew through the second, and almost plowed through the third. After my company CO died, I assumed command. We held out until the evacuation shuttles finally lifted off, but by that time our combined forces totaled a hundred and fifty men. We didn't have the numbers to continue a prolonged battle, so I came up with a plan.

"The enemy was using a staging area to drop off troops and supplies about thirty kilometers north-west of us. I lead a group of four men to the site and we were able to fight our way into the base. We armed a nuclear mine, planted it, and bugged out. When the smoke finally cleared, all that was left of the staging area was a smoldering crater about half a kilometer deep.

"I kept my team alive during that last improvised mission. When UGC reinforcements finally showed up, we knew we'd won. Shortly after, HighCom called me in for one of their famous debriefings, gave me an earful about how I had endangered the lives of my men on a suicide mission, threatened to court martial me for leaving my post, then gave me a medal and promoted me, told me about the Shadows, and offered me a place. I accepted."

"Jesus," Roy said. He shook his head. "If every time you walked into a bar you told that, shit, sir, you wouldn't ever have to buy yourself a drink again."

"Roy, Casey, enough with the sir stuff, okay? When we're together, we Shadows aren't that formal. Scales will suffice. Plus, I've never liked my friends getting formal on me, anyway."

"Ah-ooh." Roy raised his glass in a toast and downed the rest of its contents.

But something about that statement, the part about Scales calling them his "friends," gave Casey pause. They'd toasted to new friends earlier, but she had never actually thought that the commander, a man who was so far above and beyond any soldier she could ever hope to be, would consider her his friend. She didn't know what that meant to Roy, but to her it meant everything.

"That's going to take some getting used to," Casey said. She smiled. "But I'll try … Scales."

With a wink, Scales drained his glass and set it down. "Now, I don't know if you two know a whole lot about tobacco, but these cigars are rolled from the finest, sweetest leaves on Katana." After giving each of them one, he unscrewed the lid on his own metal tube and tapped the long cigar out onto his palm. "They are considered by many to be the finest cigars in the whole of the Milky Way." Scales struck a match, lit his cigar, and puffed it twice. He slowly exhaled a curl of grey smoke.

Roy joined in. "They are sweet," he said. "Smooth, too."

Casey was still struggling to get the cigar out of its case.

"Here," Roy took it and tapped it out. He handed it back to her.

"You made that look so easy," she quipped. She stuck it in her mouth, lit it, and inhaled a lung full. The resulting episode of coughs and hacks prompted smirks and snide side comments from Roy and Scales.

"You're not supposed to inhale," Roy jabbed, patting her on the back. "Just puff."

Tears were streaming down Casey's cheeks as she coughed so violently she gagged. "Gee, thanks for telling me that now." She set the cigar down on the tray. "I think I've had enough of that." She cleared her throat. That was one experience she could say she honestly never wanted to have again. "How do people find that enjoyable?"

"All depends on what you like, I guess," Scales replied. "You poor thing," he chuckled. "Refill?"

"Okay," Casey said, "but only a little. I'll be drunk off my ass if I drink much more of that stuff."

Scales picked up the half-empty decanter and poured Casey another round.

"Casey," Roy said and exhaled a mouthful of smoke. "I'm curious, why did you join the military?"

Casey sat back comfortably in her chair and sighed deeply. She took a sip of liquor. "My parents abandoned me on the steps of an orphanage when I was four months old. I was bounced around foster care until I was sixteen. That's when I decided I could take care of myself and started living out of a car. I parked in this really nice neighborhood near my school, a lot of the richy-rich kids lived there. The houses were so huge, it was incredible. I'd wait outside of a house in the morning and watch to see when everyone left. Then, hopefully, I'd find an unlocked window so I could sneak in and get a shower before class started.

After I graduated, I started thinking that maybe I could really make a difference on my home planet, or at least in the city I lived in. That's when I decided I'd join the military. The plan was to enlist, serve my term, then go to secondary school and major in business. I wanted to start a children's home, one that I could run myself, one that would give kids who had to grow up like me someplace they actually wanted to call home. But then I thought that if I went to an academy and graduated an officer, an officer's pay would give me enough of a financial boost to put a down payment on some property after I got out of secondary school. Sounded better than working some fast food joint for ten years and trying to save up that way. I'd made top marks in school, so it wasn't hard to get into the academy. When I graduated, I decided to go into the navy. I'd watched so many romantic vids in my dorm about a soldier serving on a ship in deep space, and I don't know, I thought maybe my experience would be like that. But when I was commissioned, they posted me on Arcturus Septum. That's when I met Penny. I'd been there a few months when the Vanguard attacked. You know the rest." She looked at Roy. "Far from the life of a princess, wouldn't you say?"

He didn't respond immediately—and surprisingly, neither did Scales. Shadows were trained to expect the unexpected … but that was one thing neither man had expected to hear.

"You know, I think I could use one more round," she said. "What about you guys?"

Roy stared at her. There was something in his eyes. Something she hadn't seen before.

He smiled. "If you promise me you're going to start that children's home when all this is over," he said, "I'd love one."

"Deal."

Scales picked up the half-empty decanter. "I'll drink to that."

Section VI:

A Shadow from the Past

CHAPTER TWENTY-THREE

C asey slid her hand into the Thermal armor's layered gauntlet. The warm gel layer adjusted to her body temperature. She locked the collar and wriggled her fingers. The armor's padding could nearly stop a bullet, but it was as light as a feather. Her fingers felt free, unencumbered.

She scanned over a wide assortment of precision weapons the field armory offered and found one that took her fancy.

She hefted a M464 Sketh Designated Marksman Rifle. She peered through the scope and made a few adjustments. It had three modes of fire—single-shot, three-round burst, and full auto, and fired a clip of thirty ten-millimeter rounds. The DMR was highly accurate, and it would well serve her needs as marksman on this mission.

Roy took a Razor off the weapons rack. He grabbed six clips of ammunition—four AP and two Shredder—and stowed them and two HE frag grenades in his duffle. He lifted it to test its weight and nodded to himself in approval.

Scales watched with a keen eye while he stuffed a MAR-5 and SIB7 energy pistol into his duffle. Casey and Roy were ready for this. If their performance on Arcturus Septum was any indicator for the future, then they could probably pull this off without a hitch.

Three words Shadows lived by were observe, absorb, and adapt. There were always new tactics for one to learn and new techniques to implement into one's battle strategy. Scales made sure he'd gotten that point across to Roy and Casey.

"ETA to drop-off point twenty minutes, Commander," Hurley said over the coms. "Mako shuttle is prepped and waiting for takeoff."

"Roger, XO," Scales replied, then to Roy and Casey, said, "Double time, guys. Don't forget to pack those SIBs. They're light and easy to maintain, but most importantly they're silent, and stealth is going to play a large part in this assignment."

With that in mind, Nova threaded silencers onto the barrels of their rifles. Scales tucked his helmet in his bag along with his equipment— two flashbangs, extra mags, a fiber optic probe, an EMP grenade, and a smoke canister.

"All packed and ready to go," Roy reported.

Scales turned to Casey. "Ready?"

"Affirmative," she said.

During the elevator ride down to F deck and their trip through the ship's corridors to the hangar bay, Scales reviewed the plan with them one more time.

"You two can handle this," he added. "Just remember that when we're on the *Orcanos*, don't initiate conversation with any of the crew. We need to keep a low profile."

Sitting atop a crate, CAG (Commander of the Air Group) Captain Samantha "Torch" Rawley was reading her datapad when Nova strolled into Hangar Bay 2. Her head snapped up from her lap when she heard approaching footsteps. She stood and snapped smartly to attention. "Commander, sir."

"As you were, Captain. Are we ready?"

"Affirmative, sir." She made a gesture toward the Mako behind her. "She's been disguised to look like a civilian craft," she said. "Ain't spacious, though. Only holds five." Leading Scales through the airlock, she explained in great detail how the shuttle would appear as a civilian registered boat should the folks at Fortisan decide to run a thorough scan on her.

Rawley had been chosen by Carr personally as the commander of the Air Group aboard the *Reveille*. Before that, she had been a pilot for the 186th Marine Hellburners—one of the most notorious and toughest divisions of marines in the service. They all carried with them no small degree of pride and had exceptional loyalty to the Corps.

One of the best pilots in the service, Rawley had flown marines into and out of hot-zones, maneuvered an Angel in flak-thick atmosphere like no one had ever seen, and evaced marines off the battlefield, even against orders. She had been threatened with several court martials, been demoted twice, and had more medals and commendations for valor and honor than an entire platoon of marines. She was a natural choice as CAG.

The *Reveille* needed someone with Rawley's skills leading the charge—someone who wasn't afraid to face the consequences if it meant saving a life.

That was something Scales could relate to.

Nova stowed their duffels into overhead compartments while Torch went into the cockpit. She took her seat at the controls and performed a series of pre-flight checks. "We're green across the board. Preparing for liftoff. Strap in."

Hurley's voice crackled over the coms. "Approaching drop point," he said.

Scales plopped down in a jump seat across the tiny aisle from Roy and Casey in the passenger bay and buckled his harness.

Like Torch had said, the interior of the Mako wasn't spacious in any sense of the word. In fact, Scales' feet were almost touching the tips of Casey's and Roy's. Flight gear and other equipment hung down from straps or was stored onto the overhead webbing. The only giveaway that this was a military vessel was the titanium weapons locker on the port side of the airlock that held a small arsenal of guns, ammo, and explosives.

Illuminated only by four overhead, pale golden lights, the interior of the cabin was dark. Scales could barely see the faces of his teammates.

The Mako's engines rumbled with excitement as Torch pressed the ignition button. Their slight hum quickly grew into a roar.

Outside, the lights in the bay flashed red three times and a warning alarm sounded.

The deck crew cleared the area. The *Reveille*'s aft hangar doors hissed open. The bay's atmosphere vented with a gasp as it was sucked out into the void of space. The Mako dropped out of the belly of the *Reveille* as she moved into position several hundred thousand kilometers distant from Fortisan. Per Scales' orders, the ship was running dark—she'd have a much easier time shadowing the *Orcanos* and avoiding detection that way.

"Here we go," Scales heard Casey mutter.

He nudged her foot with his and gave her a reassuring thumbs up—a gesture he'd learned from spending so much time around humans.

Starboard side of the cockpit door, a holographic screen showed their fast approach to Fortisan's ODS—*Pitch Black*. She wasn't a third as large as the ODS's in-station around Katana, or even Tanto, but she could still berth around thirty medium-tonnage ships.

Scales shut his eyes and breathed, deep inhales and slow, controlled exhales—a mental exercise he'd learned in training. Focusing on the mission and his objectives, he purged his mind of all preoccupations. His every worry, his doubts, his roaming thoughts faded away—growing dimmer and dimmer, until they winked out of existence, banished.

He was ready.

Roy and Casey had steeled themselves as best they could. If they followed his orders, remembered their training, kept a cool head, and focused on completing the mission, as Scales had told them, this would go off without a hitch.

As the Mako neared the *Black*, Torch sent an automated signal requesting to dock. Fortisan Control hailed them an instant later. The tri-vocal voice of a Vakari came in over the coms. "Mako shuttle Bravo-Bravo-Tango One-Four-One, this is Fortisan Control. You are cleared to dock. Move toward hangar bay Constellation on approach vector three-one-seven point oh-four-one. How copy?"

"Solid copy, Control," Torch said with her heavy southern twang. "Moving toward hangar bay Constellation, vector three-one-seven point oh-four-one. Beginning our approach."

The coms snapped off. The Mako slid into the *Black's* open hangar bay doors and through a containment field—a curtain of energy that kept the bay's breathable atmosphere from escaping into space—fluidly, thanks to Torch's skills. She tapped her display and engaged the landing gear. There was a bit of a jolt when the Mako's RCS thrusters fired and leveled out her pitch. Torch gently set the shuttle down on her struts.

She flipped a few overhead switches. "All right, Commander," she said. "We're in. Grab your kit quickly. Don't want to linger here longer than I have to in case they get suspicious and decide to search us."

"Roger that, Torch."

Nova removed their duffels from the overhead compartments.

Scales moved toward the airlock and was about to touch the open key when he spun round to Roy and Casey. Roy had his mask on; that typical marine combat attitude, ready for anything. Casey's eyes were narrowed, her lips drawn into a tight line. They were both nervous, but Casey more so than Roy.

"Relax, guys," Scales said. "Don't want to blow our cover. This is the simple part. We show our IDs to the *Orcanos* security team and board. Then we go to the crew quarters, stow our gear, and do whatever they tell us until we get to Gorgoran. Okay?"

"Okay," Casey replied with a curt nod.

"Got it," Roy said and shifted his weight. "Let's do this."

Scales touched the keypad. The airlock cycled open. He took the lead and plodded out of the Mako and across the ODS's hangar bay.

Several civilian craft much larger than the Mako were docked along with a corvette-class warship—no doubt stolen from the UGC. Scales made a mental note of that.

A labyrinth of gantries and catwalks wound round the circular station several stories high.

Scales, Roy, and Casey did their best to blend into the crowds of rebels and mercenaries that brushed past them. Someone bumped Roy's shoulder and didn't stop to apologize. Roy kept walking.

The *Orcanos*—a Mercury-class freighter—was docked on the station's far side. At three hundred meters long, she was easily the largest ship in the hangar. A few deckhands with power-loader mechs hurried to finish stocking her with cargo.

There was a line of people already waiting to get into the ship. Nova fell in file casually behind them. Half an hour later, Scales presented his ID to the guard and was admitted, then Casey, and then Roy, and the three of them made their way through the *Orcanos*.

The deck was constructed of steel plates and grated flooring. The bulkheads were dull gunmetal grey. A strong odor of grease permeated the air. Overhead, flickering tube lights illuminated the interior.

Nova passed by three deckhands welding a few centimeters of titanium plating onto one of the bulkheads. The corridors were so tight and narrow the sparks jumped across Scales' boots and bounced off the opposite wall.

The overhead coms crackled. "This is the Captain. To all crew: find your bunks, stow your gear, and report to the mess for a briefing in fifteen."

"Don't let anyone near your bags," Scales told Roy and Casey. "If we get busted, it's going to be a hell of a job shooting our way out of here."

Roy wiped his greasy, grimy hands on his coveralls.

After the mess briefing, the Captain had assigned them all tasks. Roy had been given a plasma torch and told a few pipes needed to have plates welded onto them.

He drew the back of his hand across his sweaty forehead. He didn't have any experience with welding, but he decided the job he'd just performed would be fine. Not like he was going to be living on this ship, after all. He picked up the toolkit and started down the corridor toward the storage room.

With the exception of his gloves and boots, the grey coverall work uniforms OMI gave them for this mission completely hid his Thermal armor from view.

Roy heard a raised male's voice up ahead. The man was cursing. It was coming from the crew quarters. Roy decided to investigate. When he entered, he saw two men backing a woman into the wall—Casey. One of them had their hand on her arm.

"What's a pretty thing like you doing on a ship like this?" the Borean holding Casey's arm asked.

"I said *back off!*" Casey yelled. "And get your damn hand off my arm."

"Oh," the second man said when she shrugged him off. "This one's a bit feisty. Maybe we can put all that fire to good use, eh? What's in this bag, then?" He moved to the duffle bag on the top of Casey's bed. "What kind of panties do we have in here?"

He managed to unzip it halfway before Roy dropped his toolkit to the deck. The resulting clatter succeeded in halting him from seeing the duffel's true contents.

"Hello, gentlemen," Roy said. "There a problem?"

"Roy," Casey said with no small amount of relief.

The Borean—Shavvar—sneered.

"Keep walking there, pretty boy. This ain't none of your business."

"I believe the lady told you to back off."

Shavvar looked at his friend—Leonard—and smiled. "Get a load of this asshole, Len," he said. "He really thinks he's something, don't he? I think we ought to teach him to mind his own fucking business, don't you?"

Leonard punched his palm. "Last chance, pretty boy."

"You're right about that," Roy said. "This *is* your last chance. Now *back* the *fuck* off."

Shavvar stepped forward. "Or what?"

Roy delivered a punch right to the man's nose, staggering him. He stumbled backward, blood running down his face. Casey put her hand on his shoulder, spun him around, and kneed him in the groin. As he fell to his knees, she followed with a prompt uppercut to the chin. He fell backward onto the deck.

Leonard bounded forward and lunged at Roy. As his friend fell to the floor unconscious, Leonard threw a right hook that struck Roy's temple.

The man had strength, enough of it to cause stars to explode across Roy's vision. He stumbled backward a few paces, tripped over a foot-locker, and fell on his back.

Leonard raised his foot to stomp on Roy's stomach when Casey hit him from behind. He dropped to the floor. In a daze, he rolled onto his back. Roy seized the opportunity and sprung up. As Roy leapt forward to pin Leonard with his weight, the man regained his senses and rolled to his left and onto his feet.

Fists raised, Roy and Casey both took positions in front of the man—ready to beat him to a pulp.

Leonard raised his own fists. Backtracking, he collided into Casey's bunk and fell backward. During his fall, he knocked her duffle bag to the floor and spilled its contents.

When he saw the guns, ammo, and helmet tumble out onto the deck, he gazed at the Shadows. "You're military," he said in realization. "Spies! Somebody come in here quick! We've got UGC on board and—"

Neither Roy nor Casey saw or heard Scales enter until he suddenly appeared behind the man, grabbed his head, and yanked. Leonard went limp and fell in a heap; neck broken.

With a liquid grace, Scales bounded forward, swooped down, and broke the unconscious Shavvar's neck, as well. He looked up at a bewildered Roy and Casey—still in their fighting stance—with a stone-serious glare.

Scales was in combat mode.

"Casey, stuff your gear back into your duffle quick, before anyone comes in. Roy, help me hide the bodies."

While Casey grabbed her gear and stuffed it back into her bag, Roy and Scales dragged the lifeless forms of Leonard and Shavvar to the far end of the room. Scales took out a combat knife and used it to remove the screws bolting the grate to the wall. He and Roy stuck the bodies of the two men into the ventilation duct. Scales secured the grating back onto the wall and twisted the screws back into place.

"Are you two okay?" he asked when he stood.

Roy nodded. "Fine. Casey?"

She finished zipping her bag. "Fine, too. I'm not sure what I would have done if you hadn't come in, Roy. God. Thank you." She looked at Scales. "Nice timing, Scales."

Scales nodded. "That vent will hide them until we land." He turned to leave. "Let's go to the mess and grab a bite to eat. We're going to need the energy. We land in an hour."

CHAPTER TWENTY-FOUR

1546 hours, May 31, 2343

*Aboard Mercury-class freighter **Orcanos***

Civilian Registry CF3-1147

Alpha Corinthus System, near planet Gorgoran

In his stomach, Scales felt the *Orcanos* decelerate. He heard the hull groan and ping from stress.

The Captain's voice came in over the coms.

"Loading crew, report to the cargo bay. I repeat, all loading crew, report to the cargo bay at once. Fifteen minutes to touchdown."

The ship's corridors quickly became choked up with people hurrying to the ladders and lift. As planned, Casey and Roy met up with Scales near the crew quarters. They grabbed their duffels and made their way to the starboard ladder.

"All right," Scales said as he nudged past people constricting the corridor right outside the cargo bay. "Stay together. Try not to get separated. Remember, we slip away the first chance we get."

The cargo bay was a three-story high, two hundred fifty-meter long room stocked floor to ceiling with crates, steel containers, drums, and tanks of water. Automated tram systems and loading mechs raced around the bay and through the aisles, inspecting the cargo to ensure nothing had fallen or come out of place during the journey.

Scales felt the deck buck slightly under his boots when the *Orcanos* settled on its struts. There was a hiss as the internal pressure stabilized with Gorgoran's nitrogen-oxygen atmosphere.

Scales nodded to a bulkhead thirty meters to port, almost hidden at the end of a tiny aisle, a small canyon enclosed left and right by sheer cliff walls of titanium cargo containers. If they were lucky, Scales thought, the hatch—an auxiliary exit—wouldn't be guarded at all.

Silently, Nova made their way to it swiftly. Checking in every direction, they surveyed the bay to make sure none of the four-hundred dock workers looked their way. They marched into the aisle and down its dim length.

A deafening hiss heralded the opening of the ship's port hangar bay doors. They rumbled apart, granting entrance to a violent gust of gelid wind and snow that rushed through the bay.

The snowstorm was already battering Charybdis, locking the facility in its vice-like grip of snow, ice, and cold.

Nova reached the bulkhead.

Scales set his bag on the floor and unzipped it. He, Casey, and Roy shed their coveralls and put their helmets on. Scales shouldered his MAR and tucked his SIB into a thigh holster. He used a magnetized strip on his suit's left thigh to hold the nuclear mine.

He could hear the dockworkers milling around the bay, going about their business. Men were barking orders, loaders and trams were beeping, and heavy resonate thumps were credence to the loading mechs thumping across the deck.

There was motion at the entrance of the aisle; Nova snapped their weapons up and sighted down as two men walked by. Talking to each other, they passed.

Casey let out an audible sigh of relief. Roy placed a steadying hand on her shoulder and gave it a squeeze. Scales turned and opened the bulkhead. It creaked as he pulled it open, but there was so much noise in the bay he didn't think anyone would notice it. He turned and crouched, MAR shouldered, and jerked his thumb toward the door. Roy slinked through first, then Casey. Satisfied that they had made good on their escape, Scales backed out slowly.

He passed through and into the freezing cold. Thankfully, his Thermal armor kept him warm. The temperature readout on his helmet's HUD read -50° C.

Fifty meters to his left, the dockworkers and loading crew had already begun transferring the cargo from the *Orcanos* onto trucks, trams, and Muham-operated mechs, although he didn't actually have line of sight on them—the winter storm was a total whiteout.

Scales closed the bulkhead behind him. He clicked his com on. "Okay," he said. "I'm uploading a NAV beacon to your HUD. There. That's our way into Charybdis. Remember, eyes on. Move out."

Scales took point, Roy walking drag. A priority transmission from the *Reveille* hailed Scales' coms. He opened the uplink, and Hurley's face popped up on a video feed on the left-hand corner of his HUD.

"Commander, the *Reveille* is in position, In station around Gorgoran like we planned."

"Music to my ears, Hurley," Scales replied.

"Captain Rawley will pick you up at evac coordinates oh-four-one by six-seven-niner at eighteen sharp. Good luck, sir. Hurley out."

The feed cut to static, and the link snapped off.

Keeping as far to the outer perimeter as they could, Nova Team avoided golden beams of light courtesy of the tall light posts spaced all around the perimeter of the LZ as they neared their auxiliary entrance.

Though they were staggered less than two meters behind him, when Scales glanced over his shoulder, he couldn't see either Roy or Casey. If not for the FOF locators on their HUDs, Nova would lose each other in this storm and become hopelessly separated for sure.

They were fifteen meters from target when Scales saw movement. He immediately held up his fist and crouched. Casey and Roy halted.

The dark, bipedal form of a Muham guard silhouetted by the snow passed in front of them two meters ahead.

Scales held up a finger, then pumped his fist—the signal for "single contact, do not engage."

They waited until the guard moved on before Scales motioned them forward again.

There was a raised concrete ledge bordering the facility. Without breaking stride, Scales bounded up onto it in a single leap and kept moving. Nova followed the ledge for several meters, rounded a corner, and found the door.

Casey and Roy stacked the door—she took position on the left, Roy on the right. Scales typed in a series of codes on the holopad. The door slid open. Weapon shouldered, Roy swung round the frame and entered the facility. Scales and Casey followed him.

They found themselves in a tunnel. It was a maintenance access-way that ran adjacent the reactor room. The map on Scales' HUD indicated it ran the perimeter of the facility. Eventually it would lead them to their destination—the labs.

Scales sealed the door behind them. Roy took point.

They moved down the corridor. Scales dialed his motion sensor up to its maximum detection range of fifty meters. Nothing moved ahead of them. When they reached the corner they halted and crouched. Scales passed the fiber optic probe to Roy.

Roy uncoiled it and plugged the end into his helmet's port. He snaked it around the bend. There was no movement. "Clear," he said.

"Move up," Scales said. "But keep alert."

The Shadows turned the corner.

They followed the maintenance corridor for another five hundred meters. The flashing red beacon on Scales' HUD that represented the back door into the labs grew closer and closer.

Thirty meters.

Fifteen.

Ten.

Roy reached it first. He tapped the holopad, but nothing happened. He looked at Scales and shook his head.

"Damn," Scales muttered.

It was sealed. He could hack the system from his TACTICOM, but it would take him a minute.

"Eyes," he said.

Roy and Casey took defensive positions while he began to process.

Scales worked at it for thirty seconds, bypassing and hacking several security codes until at last the red light over the doorway lit green. Nova moved through with Scales on point.

Beyond, a corridor stretched several dozen meters. Doors and other hallways branched off on either side.

There were too many places for an enemy to hide.

The server room was ahead and off to the right. Careful not to make any sound, Nova crept through the corridor at a slow crouch.

They halted.

Scales slid the probe under the server room door. A maze of massive rectangular hard drive towers stretched from the floor to the ceiling. There were three Muham, all scientists, tending to them.

He retracted the probe and relayed the information to Roy and Casey.

They stacked the doorway. Scales moved off to the side and typed in the access code on the keypad. The door slid apart.

The Muham turned.

Casey swung round left and high, Roy right and low.

The muzzles of their weapons flashed. Three dead Muham fell to the ground.

Roy shuffled through and swept the area for any more contacts. "Clear," he said over the coms.

"Let's get down to business," Scales said. "Roy, start downloading the data, then wipe the hard drives."

"Roger that."

"Casey, on me. Remember what I told you two—we complete this mission no matter what."

Roy moved to the array of terminals and screens bolted to the wall. He removed the small blue OMI pentagon-shaped OSD from his pouch and plugged it into one of the mainframe's ports.

The words—**"Data Transfer Initiated"**—flashed across his HUD. "Files downloading," he said over the coms.

"Acknowledged," Scales replied. "Keep one eye on your motion tracker. Those bugs can be pretty tricky."

"Those things give me the creeps."

"I hear you," Casey said. "I don't even like cockroaches that crawl. Ones that can walk … that's just wrong."

Scales and Casey rounded the bend.

The lab room door was at the end of the corridor. As before, Scales slid the probe underneath the bulkhead and swept the area. He didn't see any contacts. His motion tracker didn't pick up any movement.

He nodded, and Casey took position. Scales tapped the holopanel. Casey went in first; Scales followed right behind her. They fanned out and scanned the room to make sure they were alone.

They were.

The labs were stuffed with equipment: tables, computer terminals, holoscreens, lab instruments, and jars and beakers half full with a rainbow of colored liquids.

Casey moved in between a row of massive glass tubes that pulsed with a sick green substance. Conduits ran from the tops of them and disappeared into the floor. She slung her DMR. Scales handed her the nuclear mine.

She used its adhesive strip to attach it to the back of one of the tanks. She input the firing codes and primed the device. "Bomb armed," she said over the com.

While Roy waited for the data to download onto the OSD, he opened a link to the computer system and read the file names as they flashed up on his HUD. They were curious. It was probably highly classified information. He read them as they appeared anyway:

PROJECT: RAGNAROK

DATA RECOVERED 23/12/2320 FROM PLANET SOLOMON; RUINS OF REBEL FACILITY CODENAMED: KRONOS

DR. ARUV T'MORTI – PROJECT OVERSEER

REFERENCE CODE AA2.342-123455/W22SSF-411-02RED/ BETA/BETA

ACCESS CODE: THEENDOFALL

ORIGINAL CREATOR AND HEAD RESEARCHER: DR. JAMES LOCKE

"Whoa," Roy said in surprise. He isolated that last file and pulled it up on his HUD.

ORIGINAL CREATOR AND HEAD RESEARCHER: DR. JAMES LOCKE

"What?" he muttered.

This didn't make sense.

Roy knew that name, James Locke, and he knew it well. He didn't understand. That man had died a long time ago. What were files on him doing in a Muham facility? What did *original creator* and *head researcher* mean? And what could they have possibly had to do with James? And what *the hell* did the file mean by ruins of a *Rebel* facility?

"Bomb armed," he heard Casey say over the com.

"How's the data coming, Roy?" Scales asked.

"Um ... " Roy was still trying to piece all this together. "I uh—"

There was a blip on his motion tracker.

Then two.

"Oh, fuck," Roy said. "Contacts. Two of them."

Roy shouldered his Razor and stepped out into the hallway. He swept the corridor with his carbine, but it was mysteriously empty.

"Where, Roy?"

He double-checked his motion tracker. The red dots blipped once—and were gone.

"Roy, damn it," Scales growled. "Where are they?"

"I don't know."

"What?"

"I don't know. They're gone."

"What do you mean gone?"

"Roy," Casey said over the coms. "Are you okay?"

A single blip reappeared on his motion tracker. Roy saw a shadow dart behind a doorway ahead.

"Roy," Casey said again.

"I'm fine, Casey. I've got the bastard, Scales. I see him. Heading to investigate now."

Roy started for the doorway. "I see you," he muttered.

"Casey," Scales said. "We've got trouble."

She shouldered her DMR and crept across the room. She and Scales took up position on either side of the doorframe.

She looked at him. He nodded. They swung round the frame: Scales right, Casey left.

Nothing.

"Roy," Scales whispered over the com. "Roy, respond."

He waited one heartbeat.

Two …

Three …

Silence.

"Goddamn it," he muttered.

"Why isn't he answering?" Casey whispered.

"I have no idea. Ping his IFF transponder once."

"Roger."

A map overlaid on Scales' HUD. Casey's ping illuminated Roy's transponder and showed his location. He was in an office some ways down the hallway.

But something wasn't right.

And then Roy's IFF winked off.

Scales' heart fluttered. Roy couldn't just turn his transponder off like that. Scales opened a link to his com. "Roy, respond immediately. That is an *order*! Roy—"

There was a loud clatter behind them. Something in the labs crashed to the tiled floor. Casey and Scales both swung about, weapons raised.

"What the hell was that?" she whispered.

Scales shook his head. "I don't know. Let's check it out." He crouched low and started forward.

"*Merde,*" Casey muttered under her breath. She followed Scales. "Scales, I don't like this."

"Neither do I."

They entered the labs—fully ready to face Muham resistance.

They found nothing.

Everything was just as they'd left it. There wasn't one instrument, one beaker, or one speck of dirt out of place.

"What the hell is going on?" Casey hissed.

"Somehow this all seems familiar," a voice boomed.

Scales and Casey immediately dropped into crouches. They desperately scanned everywhere, everything. The lights in the lab dimmed, leaving only a few overhead amber beams to splash the white-tiled floor.

"I do so hate déjà vu, don't you?"

Scales' heart completely stopped. A shiver ran down his spine.

That voice.

He knew that voice. He remembered it every day, and the very last time he'd ever heard it.

But no. No. That was impossible. That man was ... *dead!*

A figure stepped out of the shadows, directly into Scales' and Casey's line of fire: a Vakari fully encased in a black suit of combat armor, except for his head.

Scales lowered his weapon.

He saw the Vakari's face.

Scales' mouth dropped open and went dry.

"Nakolus Aaragon?"

The figure smiled and gave a slight nod.

It was him.

It was Nakolus Aaragon.

"You do remember," Aaragon said. "Even after all these decades?"

Scales tried to find his voice. " I ... I saw you die," he whispered. "How? How are you—"

"Back from the dead?" Aaragon interjected. "One cannot return if they were never dead to start with."

Movement caught Casey's eye, and she turned her head. The shadows around her were moving.

Black moving on black.

She and Scales were surrounded, and the shadows were closing in around them. Only they weren't shadows. They were figures—Vakari, humans, Asgards—in black combat armor.

"Scales? Scales, we need to go. Right. Now."

If he heard her, he didn't answer.

"But I *saw* you die!" Scales said. "I *watched* you die!"

"No," Aaragon corrected. "You saw my heart rate monitor flat line, but you didn't bother to check my pulse, just to be sure."

The flashback of that day replayed in Scales' head on a continuous loop. There were so many thoughts swimming in his brain he couldn't think straight. Why hadn't he bothered to check his pulse? If what Aaragon had said was true, then he had made the biggest mistake of his life.

"Nakolus ... I—"

"No apology needed," Aaragon said. "That's what we Shadows are trained for, are we not? To complete the mission no matter the cost? And you did complete your mission, didn't you, regardless of any *obstacle* that was thrown your way. You've always been able to do that. Always had that *gift* to just turn off your emotions so no matter what—you can complete your mission. That's one of the things I've always admired about you."

Aaragon turned his gaze to Casey. "That's what you told this one, is it not? Complete the mission no matter what?"

Scales and Casey shared a glance.

"Oh," Aaragon chuckled. "Of course it is. Nothing can stop the great Kileeus Scales from completing his mission. Not even the death of a teammate. Not even when that teammate was his *best friend*. His *Shirum.*"

"What are you doing here, Nakolus?" Scales asked.

"It seems we're after the same thing," Aaragon answered. "This device, this research project the Muham are occupying their ugly beetle minds with. We have a truce with them, you know."

"*We?*" Scales stomach dropped into the bowels of his feet. "Nakolus ... you're with the *Rebels.*"

Aaragon laughed. "Took you that long to figure it out? Damn, you're not as sharp as you used to be. Yes, Scales. I'm with the *Rebels*, as you Coalition types call us. Our government has a truce with the bugs. They leave us alone, we leave them alone. Because of that, we were at a loss as to how we could obtain the data to make their Ragnarok project *our* Ragnarok project. Then the Coalition dropped the answer-right in our lap: you. So we waited, waited until you were inside, and then moved in to claim our prize. You made this pretty easy on us."

"The Muham are never going to let you leave this facility with the data on Ragnarok," Scales said. "Not alive."

"That would probably have been true if my men weren't outside finishing off the last of those bugs and everyone else on that freighter. We're also going to nuke the site from orbit—just to be sure. Time's wasting and we need to wrap this up. My ship leaves in ten minutes. I invite you to come aboard!"

Scales raised his rifle. His trigger finger tensed.

He felt something hit him over the head from behind.

Everything went black.

Chapter Twenty-Five

1800 hours, May 31, 2343
Electus Borealis System, planet Katana
UGC Headquarters Complex, Zenith Tower
675th Floor, Executive Apartments
Apartment B117-A

"*Shit,*" Katherine muttered as the smell of burnt toast filled her nostrils.

She jumped up from behind her desk and ran to the kitchen. In the process, she knocked over her chair. The toaster belched black smoke. The apartment's fire alarm started screeching.

"Oh, shut up," she yelled.

As if the fire alarm would stop screaming at her on command.

She took the toast out of the toaster with a pair of tongs and set it on the counter. The slices were as black as coal. She grabbed her datapad and started using it to fan the air around the fire alarm system. After the alarm stopped and everything had settled down, she ran her hands through her hair and sighed.

For the last seven hours, she'd been sitting at her desk, doing exactly what Admiral Carr had asked her not to do: work. In the minute or so it took the toast to crisp, she'd gotten engrossed in her work and completely forgotten about it.

Carr had given her a few days' leave yesterday. He claimed she really needed some time to wind down and just relax. She did, it was true, but how could she relax when there was so much work to do, so many questions to be answered?

God. That burnt toast smell was going to permeate her apartment. She *hated* that smell.

Katherine went back over to the desk in her office. After righting the chair, she glanced at the computer screen and frowned.

Her essay to the Council on her theory about the origins of the Vanguard seemed a little too ... hallow. She wished there had been more evidence to support her theory that they had been created by another species. But as a form of ... what? Why would a species advanced enough to actually create hybrid synthetic-organics like the Vanguard want to do that? What purpose would the Vanguard serve?

She sighed.

A theory was a theory, but she still needed a few solid reasons for their motive. It frustrated her that she didn't have those reasons right now.

Maybe she should take a break. This could wait for an hour or two. The toast was testament to that.

Hmm. A cup of coffee sounded good. Maybe she could sit down and try to *actually* relax for a bit, like Admiral Carr had suggested. She had to admit that she had been pretty strung out these last few months. How could she not have been? With all that had happened, she was lucky she hadn't had a nervous breakdown.

Hopefully I won't forget about the damn coffee. Sometimes she really became too engrossed in her work for her own good.

There was a knock at the front door just as she stepped into the kitchen.

Katherine debated on whether or not to answer it. *I look horrible.* Her hair was in a ponytail, she was wearing the shortest pair of shorts she had, tank top, no makeup. *Oh, screw it. I guess I could look worse. Besides, it could be important.*

Whoever was knocking rapped on the door again.

"Coming," she yelled.

She was not prepared to find Admiral Carr standing on her welcome mat in full dress uniform when she opened the door. He had his cap tucked under his arm.

"Oh," she said and straightened her posture. "Admiral Carr, sir."

"Hello, Katherine," he said. "Mind if I come in?"

"Of course not, sir." She stood aside so he could walk through the door.

She blushed. *Maybe I should have put a robe on.*

"Can I make you a cup of coffee?" She shut the door.

"No, thank you," he replied. "I was wondering if I could have a moment of your time. I know you're off duty, but this won't take long."

"Certainly, sir." She gestured to the living room. "You're welcome to sit."

"Something smells like burnt toast." Carr sniffed the air.

"Yeah, that was my fault. I forgot it was in the toaster because I was so engrossed in my essay paper—" She clasped her hand over her mouth.

The faintest hint of a smile touched Carr's lips.

"Sorry, sir," she said. "I had to. I had so much on my mind that it couldn't wait."

"I know the feeling, but you should have rested while you had the chance, because I know you won't be able to pass this up."

"Sir?"

"We just got word from the team stationed on Mars, at your old Monolith Project. Seems they've stumbled across something they aren't sure how to handle."

"What do you mean?"

"They found some sort of chamber deep underneath the roots of the artifact. When they tried to enter, it kind of came to life, put up some sort of shield around the entrance to the room so no one can get in. They have no idea how to proceed. I told them you might be able to help."

"Admiral, you can sure hit me with some whammies, I'll give you that." She smiled. "When do we leave?"

"As soon as you're ready. How long do you need?"

"Give me ten minutes."

"Excellent. I'll leave you to it, then."

"Oh, okay. You can um … stay here, if you'd like." She let out a nervous laugh. "Find a book to read, or something. Or maybe I can make you that cup of coffee? Drink it while you wait?"

"That sounds nice," Carr said. "Thank you. And Katherine, you can call me Terrence when it's just us if you'd like. I've never been one to stand on fierce formality. Besides, we're partners, are we not? Friends?"

Katherine gazed deep into Carr's eyes. That had touched her, those words. Touched her deep down in her soul. She really liked Carr. He had been so kind to her ever since she had met him on Earth. He was almost like a father figure.

It was nice for a man like him to think of her as his equal. To call her his partner. His *friend*.

She smiled warmly. "Yes, sir," she said. "We are."

CHAPTER TWENTY-SIX

1603 hours, May 31, 2343

Alpha Corinthus System, planet Gorgoran

Muham Research Facility TT043-5R

Designation: Charybdis

"I see you," Roy muttered under his breath. He started slowly for the doorway a few meters down the hall. His finger was a hairsbreadth away from the trigger; one twitch was all it would take.

He crept up to the door. He braced his back against the wall and swung round into the room. He scanned the tiny office with his Razor.

Nothing. There was no place for an enemy to hide.

I know I saw something.

His motion tracker blipped again—the ghost contact appeared again. Roy rushed back out into the hallway and saw a shadow flit round the corner.

He shouldn't be going this far away from Scales and Casey, lest the worst happen, but he had to find the enemy and neutralize him before he tripped the alarm, or else their cover would be blown and the mission would fail.

He couldn't let that happen.

Complete the mission no matter what.

Roy pursued the ghost contact down the hall and round the bend. He saw it again—a black shadow, a moving darkness that darted into a storage room.

Roy gave chase. He worked his way down the hallway quietly. The patter of his boots was surprisingly soundless on the tiled floor. The storage room was four meters ahead; three, two—he got ready to stack the doorway.

Something hit the back of his head. Stars exploded across his vision and he fell forward. His Razor left his grasp and slid across the floor.

He felt a hand grab his leg and pull him into the storage room.

He tried to resist, tried to wrestle with his attacker, but his head was swimming.

Roy tore off his helmet. The visor was cracked. He blinked rapidly. Black dots soared across his blotchy vision, but he saw the outline of a being drag him behind some shelves.

Then the man raised his rifle high into the air, butt down, ready to deliver the killing blow.

Roy rolled out of the way.

The man missed. The butt of the rifle hit the tile. It cracked.

Roy jumped to his feet. Vertigo slammed into him hard. Teetering, he fought to regain his balance.

His attacker landed a punch to his abdomen.

The wind flew out of Roy's stomach and he doubled over in pain.

The man delivered an uppercut.

Roy reeled backward and hit the wall. He slid down to the floor. The taste of blood was fresh in his mouth. He fought against the dizziness and shook his head to clear his vision. He regained enough awareness in time to dodge a kick. The man's boot put a hole in the wall where his head had been only a second ago.

Roy snapped out of it, his vision cleared. His adrenaline kicked in—and instinct took over.

He lunged at his armored attacker and tackled him across his abdomen. They both fell to the floor. Roy used his weight to his advantage and straddled the man. He grabbed the man's helmet and yanked it off.

The slitted pupils of an Asgard's eyes locked with his. Only it wasn't a man—it was a woman.

Roy didn't give her any time to recover. He delivered two rapid strikes to her face.

She grabbed him by the collar of his thermal suit and pulled him forward. As he lost his balance, she thrust her powerful hips upwards, pulled his left arm back, and tossed him sideways off of her.

Roy rolled to his feet.

So did the Asgard. She lunged.

He met her with a solid kick to her chest.

It knocked her off balance and she staggered backwards.

Roy bounded forward and hit her with three lightning-quick jabs to the face, then a right hook to her temple.

She clocked him with a heavy backhand. He staggered. She used the second it took for him to recover to her advantage and landed a series of quick, rapid punches to his face. The last one broke his nose.

Pain blinding him, he swayed precariously. Blood ran down his face and dripped off his chin. She threw another punch, but somehow Roy found it in him to block it by crossing his forearms.

He countered with a blow of his own. He put all his weight and power behind a single punch and landed it square on her beak.

It cracked and splintered like brittle bone.

Her dark purple blood spattered across his face.

Stunned, she reeled backward. She covered her face with her hands and Roy let her have it. He landed four powerful strikes. She fell up against the wall, her arms—and her guard—wide open.

He grabbed her head and kneed her in the face once, twice, three times. She went limp and toppled forward. She managed to catch herself with her forearms at the last second. Roy took a step back, braced himself, and struck her with the toe of his right boot in an uppercut. Her neck snapped backward and she slumped unceremoniously to the ground.

He checked her body—her neck was broken.

Roy exhaled explosively. He bent down and put his hands on his knees to catch his breath.

"Jesus Christ," he muttered.

Blood ran from his nose and dripped from his mouth, leaving shapeless splotches of crimson on the white tiled floor.

He glanced back at the body.

The Asgard was clad in black combat armor, somehow both similar and dissimilar to Venerator armor. He noticed a sigil on her pauldron. He went over and crouched down next to her to examine it.

A snake—a cobra—coiled around a bolt of lightning with the Rebel's flag in the background.

He'd never seen that symbol before. Whoever she was—whatever she was—she was well trained. She knew hand-to-hand combat probably better than he did. She might have beaten him had he not gotten in a couple of lucky shots.

He wiped his nose with the back of his hand and went over to where his helmet lay. He picked it up and put it on. The HUD flashed on and off. He tried to raise Scales and Casey on the com, but all he got was static.

Damn. That woman really must have hit him hard to damage his helmet that badly. Roy cursed and tossed it aside. As he stooped down to pick up his Razor, he heard footsteps echoing down the hall. They were followed by voices.

He scooped up his helmet and the woman's assault rifle that lay in the middle of the floor out in the open, and hid himself behind some shelves.

He peeked through a gap in the stacked boxes and saw six armored men march past the doorway, each holding a MAR. They all had helmets on. He was certain they were Rebels.

What he saw next made his blood run cold.

Four men carried two bodies between them—one was Scales, the other, Casey.

Roy almost sprung out of cover right then and there. The only thing that kept him rooted behind those shelves was this sobering thought:

He had to be smart about this.

Roy wanted to rescue his friends, but to charge into the hallway and engage all those men alone was suicide.

He was good, but he wasn't *that* good.

He remembered the data chip he still had plugged into the main-frame back in the server room.

Damn it!

He needed to follow the Rebels and see where they were taking his friends, but he had to grab the chip first.

Complete this mission no matter what.

"Yes," Roy heard someone say as the men passed. "We've got them and the data. Get ready for liftoff and arm the nuke."

A Vakari strolled casually past the door. He wasn't wearing a helmet and had his finger plugged into his ear as he listened to whoever was on the other end of his microbead.

He must be the head asshole for this group.

The Vakari moved on.

Roy waited almost a full minute before he risked inching toward the door. He poked his head out and checked left, then right. The coast was clear. He made a beeline for the server room as quickly as he possibly could while still remaining quiet. He bounded through the door and hastily swept the room. When he got to the mainframe, his chip was gone.

"Mother *fuck,*" he hissed through clenched teeth. "Fuck, fuck, *fuck!*"

The Rebels had taken it. They'd taken the data.

And now they were going to nuke the facility.

He had to get the hell out of here, and fast.

It would take them a couple of minutes to get into orbit. He was on the clock.

Roy made his way out of Charybdis Facility. When he stepped outside, he saw the running lights of a ship through the blizzard as it fired RCS thrusters and lifted off into the sky.

The temperature was well below zero. Ice crystals began to form on the blood on his face after only a few seconds.

How was he going to get out of here?

Torch!

Captain Rawley was supposed to pick them up at the RZ coordinates. But without the aid of his helmet's TACTMAP, he had no idea how he would find them, especially not in this whiteout.

He glanced around desperately for something—anything. Time was running out. The Rebels would be in orbit any minute. He saw lights in the distance.

The *Orcanos!*

The poor bastards had never even had a chance to leave.

Roy had never been so happy to see a merc ship in his life.

He sprinted across the lot toward the freighter. Dozens of bodies littered the area. The snow was already hard at work swallowing their bodies, effectively erasing all signs that they had ever been there.

The *Orcanos'* cargo bay doors were still open. Roy ran inside. The freighter's internal temperature was plummeting. His thermal suit would do its best to keep his body warm, but if he stayed out in this weather too much longer without his helmet, it wasn't going to matter.

He made for the bridge. Every corridor he passed was littered with dead bodies. The Rebels had killed everyone. Their nuke would wipe away all trace of their actions.

Roy burst through the bulkhead and onto the bridge. He ran to the coms station. It was an archaic piece of equipment. It had dials and buttons all over it. However, he knew it still had the same basic operating principals. He thumbed a button, flipped two switches, and put the headphones on. He couldn't hack into the UGC priority channel from here, but if he could send out an emergency broadcast, maybe, just maybe, the *Reveille* would pick it up.

So would the Rebels if they were monitoring radio traffic for any survivors. That could prompt a premature detonation.

He had to risk it or burn.

"This is Lieutenant Locke to the *Reveille*," he said into the headset's boom mic. "This is an emergency. Respond."

One second.

Five.

"Hurley, if you're listening to this respond. For Christ's sake, please respond."

Two more seconds.

"Locke, this is Hurley."

Roy sighed explosively and smiled.

"Goddamn it's good to hear your voice, Hurley. The mission has been compromised. Scales and Casey have been captured by Rebel forces. The bastards stole the research data and are planning to nuke the site from orbit. I need a ride out of here and fast."

"Shit. We're in orbit now, but it'll take at least five minutes to ready a bird and another five to get down there. You're going to have to find your own ride out of there. Coms reports this transmission is coming from inside *Orcanos*. That accurate?"

"Yes. I'm on the bridge."

"Okay. Freighters usually have a few two-man crafts used for equipment ferrying and orbital drop-offs. Get down to the hangar bay and see if you can find one."

"Hurley, I have no idea how to fly one of those."

"I'll think of something, Locke, but you need to get there quick. Contact me once you're in the cockpit on emergency frequency REDBLIND. Go!"

Roy tore off the headset. He barely remembered to grab his Razor on the way out as he thundered through the halls toward the hangar bay. He only had a few minutes left before the Rebels would be in the sky. He had to hurry.

Why is time never on my side?

The hangar was two decks below him and right above the cargo bay they'd snuck out of. The quickest way down was to use the access ladders on each deck. Roy slung his Razor and mounted the ladder. He gripped both sides and slid down to the deck below.

He ran for the next set of ladders two compartments over. He slid down and landed on the hangar deck. He didn't even bother sweeping the area with his weapon. There wasn't time, and if anyone was left alive, he was pretty sure they'd have had this ship in the air by now.

Roy spotted the two-man utility craft.

He sprinted for it as fast as he could. He threw open the canopy and jumped into the pilot's seat. As the canopy closed, he typed in the frequency code on the radio. "Hurley, it's Locke. I'm inside. Now what?"

"I read you, Lieutenant. We just got a ping on the radar—the Rebel ship has broken orbit. Radiological alarm just went off—they're preparing to fire. I want you to tap the control panel. When the orange button appears, double tap it. Make sure the cockpit is pressurized."

The canopy closed. Roy pressed a button and it sealed. He looked at the holographic panel in front of him. He tapped it.

The panel lit up like a Christmas tree. Readouts appeared on the starboard and port screens. A large orange circle flickered to life on the middle of the panel. Roy tapped it twice.

"Okay, Hurley. Now what?"

"Do you see the switch that says 'Remote Pilot?'"

"Yeah."

"Flip it and enter this code exactly: 023-45532RR-FRM/02."

Roy flipped the Remote Pilot switch. A number pad materialized above his lap. He muttered the code under his breath as he put it in.

"Okay, got it."

"Press the button that says 'Initiate.'"

He did.

Suddenly, the engines rumbled to life and the utility craft turned port all by itself.

"What the hell is going on?" Roy yelled in surprise.

The craft's thrusters lifted it vertically off the deck.

"Strap in, Locke. The code you entered gave Lieutenant Hoshi remote control from here in the CIC. She's going to pilot you out of there."

Roy raised his eyebrows. "Okay …"

The hangar bay doors hissed open as Hoshi accessed their controls from the *Reveille's* CIC. Snow and wind blew in with hurricane force.

"Locke, the Rebels just launched an Arkus nuke. Impact in four minutes. But you'll be well out of there by then. Now hang on."

The UT craft's engines flared and she shot out of the hangar bay like a bullet.

The gees forced Roy back into his seat. Vertigo hit him hard. He tried to control his breathing to stop the rapid beating of his heart.

Hard snow crystals pounded against the canopy as the UT craft flew higher and higher into Gorgoran's atmosphere. They halted all at once as the craft flew through, then over the clouds.

The greyness outside the glass faded to blackness. Roy saw small specks of light twinkling in the distance. He'd broken through the atmosphere. The craft was in space.

"Impact in five …" Hurley said over the radio.

Hoshi spun the craft "upside down" so Roy could get a look at Gorgoran through the canopy.

It was an icy blue ball in the night.

"Four, three, two … one."

A sphere of brilliant white light winked into existence on Gorgoran's surface. A cloud of dust, dirt, and earth bellowed high into the sky. Roy sighed slowly and closed his eyes.

Never in his life had he felt so close to dying.

"Locke," Hurley said. "You with me?"

"Yeah," Roy replied.

"Sit tight. We've triangulated the UT craft's transponder and are on our way to pick you up."

"What are we going to do about Scales and Casey?" Roy asked. "Please tell me you can track that ship."

"We've got it, Locke. Don't worry. I'll be damned if I let those sons-a-bitches slip away from me."

Roy nodded. "Good," he whispered. The channel clicked off. "Good."

He eased his posture and rested his head against the seat's padded headrest. "I'm coming for you, Casey," he whispered. "For both of you. I promise."

CHAPTER TWENTY-SEVEN

2002 hours, May 31, 2343
Unknown location

"Scales," a distant voice said.
       It was female. Desperate. Pleading.
       "Scales, please wake up."
Scales sluggishly opened his heavy eyelids.

He was looking up at the outline of a white face, framed with tousled, bright red hair. Her pretty green eyes were wide, blood ran from her nostrils and down the left side of her face. Her white teeth were bared as if in pain.

"Scales," she said again. "Can you hear me?"

"Casey," he whispered and licked his lips. He touched the back of his head and felt something sticky. His hand came back covered in blue blood. "Where are we?"

"I have no idea," she whispered. "Take a look."

Scales blinked black dots away. He realized he was lying across Casey's lap in the back seat of a car. He struggled to right himself. When he did, he had an intense feeling of vertigo. Something tugged at his right arm—he was handcuffed to Casey's left.

"What happened?"

"I saw you go down," she said. "And then I woke up in the back of this car with you unconscious in my lap."

"Did Roy make it?"

"I haven't seen him."

"Are you hurt?"

"One of those guys hit me really hard. I think my nose is broken. Who was that Vakari you were talking to?"

He huffed. "I don't even know where to begin. He and I were in the same unit together on Axios. He was one of the men I led on the suicide mission. We became partners when we joined the Shadows. Our mission to destroy a Rebel facility got botched, and he died. Or at least I thought he did."

"He said you were his *Shirum?* What's that?"

"*Shirum* is a Vakari term that means bond-brother. It's used for two men who aren't related, but share a bond as strong as if they were blood relatives."

"Okay, great. Why is he so pissed off?"

Scales shrugged. "Now that, I don't know. Or why he's working with the Rebels."

"Is this the end of the line?" she asked.

Scales tried hard to focus on her face; black dots still flecked his vision. "Casey, listen to me. I promise I will get you out of here safely. I promise." He averted his gaze to look back out of the windshield. "I'm not losing any more friends."

She rested her free hand on top of his. "Whatever happens, I'm glad you're with me." She smiled.

There was a bump in the road that tossed Casey into the door and nearly knocked Scales off his seat.

The car passed through a security checkpoint and in through tall iron gates. Out of the windshield, a building came into view. It had to be at least a hundred meters high, with windows as tall as a person on each floor. It was a manor of some sort; it had a courtyard paved with flagstone and green lawns extending out kilometers in every direction. Hanging above the door was the unmistakable Rebel flag: an Aquila clasping lightning bolts in one foot and a MAR in the other; a golden sun rose in its background.

Wherever they were, whatever planet this was, it was night-time. The only illumination came from tall floodlights spaced in a semi-circle around the courtyard and the light of a small moon hanging in the sky.

Scales' mind was still a bit cloudy, but he wondered how he could get an SOS out to the *Reveille*.

The car traveled down a steep decline and rolled into an under-ground parking lot. The driver stopped the car and six men with MARs hauled Scales and Casey out of the car. They marched them through the garage and into the manor.

Scales and Casey descended the stairs leading into the manor's base-ment. At their slightest hesitation, the guards yanked and tugged at the chain linking their cuffs, constricting their shackled wrists.

They were hurried down a long corridor with a single, ancient non-automated door at the end. It was gunmetal grey and window-less. It looked as cold as the hearts of the men who pushed Scales and Casey into the room on the other side. Its only features were a single table and three chairs: two to one side, one to the other.

This was an interrogation room. Scales had a pretty clear idea of who would be doing the questioning.

The guards locked the door behind them. With nothing left to do, Scales and Casey took a seat in the hard, cold iron chairs.

After what seemed like an eternity, Scales heard a key being inserted into the door's lock and a click as it was turned. It creaked open.

He wasn't surprised to see Aaragon stroll through. A duet of guards came in after him and unlocked the shackles around Scales' and Casey's wrists. Scales rubbed at his raw skin.

"Ah sh'bah la no kee selai," Aaragon said to the guards and jerked his head toward the door. They saluted and left the room. The door shut with a resonate *bang*.

Aaragon un-holstered a K2 magnum from his side and set it on the table square between Casey and Scales. He sat down and smiled. With meshed fingers he leaned forward.

He took his time to study Scales, and then Casey, and then back to Scales again. Finally, he spoke.

"I wonder what the UGC would pay to have you both back?" He laughed to himself. "Oh yeah, I forgot. You're Shadows! You're merely tools to be used, discarded, and forgotten. Like I was."

"You know that's not true," Scales muttered. He snorted in disgust. "But I'm not going to change your mind. I'll save my breath. You always were hardheaded. Tell me, what are you going to do with us, Nakolus? What's your game plan? If you knew we'd be at Charybdis, then you know far more than any amount of torturing us could get you."

"True, though I would like to do it for the pleasure. But that's another matter. The matter at hand is this: the other member of your team."

"What about him?"

"He's a slippery one, he is. My men couldn't find him. I'm surprised he was able to give us the slip and get away. He really brings new meaning to the word *Shadow*, now doesn't he? That's beside the point. I want you to tell me who he is."

Scales was exhausted, spent, but he managed a smile. "You know we're not going to tell you anything."

"You won't." He pointed a finger to Casey. "But she might, under the right circumstances."

Casey answered by spitting in Aaragon's face.

He calmly wiped away her mix of blood and saliva with a rag he had stuffed in his pocket. "Kileeus, I already know who he is. First Lieutenant Locke, Roy J. Service Number 9925475-441RL. Born to Hannah and James Locke on April 7, 2317, on planet Sepprus Mora. It's my job to know these things. I'm the chief intelligence officer for the Republic. I'm asking if you know who he is."

"Surprise me," Scales said.

"That data you were sent to recover from Charybdis was the blueprints to a weapon of mass destruction. Though they were researching it, the Muham were not its original creators. It was invented by the same man you and I were sent to assassinate all those years ago, the scientist back on Solomon at the Kronus facility. But the interesting fact about that is that man, James Locke, was your friend Roy's father." He snorted. "And the poor sod still isn't aware that his beloved daddy was in fact an undercover agent working for the Republic ... or the fact that it was you who killed him. How's that for a surprise?"

Casey looked at Scales, mouth ajar, as if expecting him to have an answer—some witty remark about how he already knew this and that it was old news.

Scales didn't. He shook his head to clear his mind. He had to play Aaragon's game. If he knew it was getting to him, Aaragon would exploit it. He needed to change tact and take the fight to him.

Before Scales could speak, Aaragon took something out of his pocket and set it on the table.

It was a small pentagonal data chip. That was when Scales realized it was the one Roy had used to download the data in the server room at Charybdis.

"By the way," Aaragon said. "Thank you for getting this for me. The data on this Ragnarok project is going to do wonders for us." He plucked it from the table and put it back in his pocket.

He looked at Casey. "Tell me, Lieutenant Keller, did Kileeus here promise to keep you safe? To get you out of here? You know he once said the same to someone else. She ended up getting killed anyway. Have you told her about your foolish love affair with that human, Kileeus? That whore of a woman." He leaned in closer. "She died because she put her faith in you."

Scales tensed up. He balled his fists. Rage welled up inside of him—a flood of fury that was very near too much to control. As he glared into the eyes of his former bond-brother, he remembered the pistol still on the table.

He didn't dare look at it, lest it betray his plan. Scales was faster than Aaragon—always was. It was a gamble with both his life and Casey's, but he bet he could make a move for it before Aaragon could stop him.

"You're an arrogant, egotistical *son-of-a-bitch,* Nakolus," Scales said. "You always were. Why is it you're so upset, anyway? What has gotten you so pissed off that you'd turn your back on everything we stood for, everything you stood for, and side with the very people that seek to destroy us? Are you really mad that I followed orders and left you there to drown in your own blood? Is that it?" He leaned forward. "Or is it because you know, deep down, that I'm better than you."

Scales didn't give Aaragon any time to respond. He put all of his strength behind his fist and clobbered Aaragon in the face.

The blow sent him reeling backward.

Scales made a grab for the pistol. He felt the grip brush against his fingertips, felt the cold metal touch his palm.

Aaragon jumped to his feet and sprung forward. He grabbed Scales' wrist and twisted.

Before his bones broke, Scales balled up the fist on his free hand and thrust it into Aaragon's face.

Aaragon anticipated the move. He saw it coming and grabbed Scales' fist in midair, stopping the blow.

They were at a stalemate. Scales couldn't move. But neither could Aaragon. They were too evenly matched … until Casey settled the matter for them.

She grabbed her chair.

"Asshole!" She screamed and bludgeoned Aaragon over the head with it.

His strength weakened enough for Scales to head-butt him, knocking him off balance. In a blur of motion, he grabbed the pistol, pointed it at Aaragon, and pulled the trigger.

The K2 crackled, but Aaragon moved a fraction of a second early. The bullet lodged itself in his shoulder instead of his chest. He bellowed in pain and leapt over the table, tackling Scales to the floor.

The pistol flew out of Scales' grasp.

Casey made a dive for it, but Aaragon used his legs to sweep her feet out from under her. She fell on her stomach.

Scales punched his temporarily unguarded mouth, knocking free a few teeth. Aaragon fell backwards off him. Scales sprung up and got his stance—and so did Aaragon. They stared each other down, and then Aaragon lunged and threw a punch at Scales' face. Scales parried, then countered with a punch of his own. Aaragon snatched it out of the air.

In order to break the second stalemate, both men threw their heads forward in a head-butt. Releasing their hold of one another, both Shadow and ex-Shadow staggered backward.

Scales stumbled and nearly tripped over one of the chairs before regaining his balance.

Casey again went for the pistol. She grabbed it, spun round, and pointed it at Aaragon. In one leap, he bounded forward and knocked it from her grasp. She tried to punch him, but he sidestepped the blow, grabbed a fistful of her hair and with his other hand, delivered a strong punch to her face. She collapsed.

Scales threw a side kick that struck Aaragon in the chest. The ex-Shadow fell up against the wall, his guard momentarily open.

Scales didn't hesitate. He lunged forward, struck Aaragon on the nose with a right jab, a left hook across the chin; he delivered a powerful blow to his Solar Plexus.

Aaragon doubled over—Scales grabbed his head and slammed it against his kneecap once, twice—but Aaragon managed to block the third one.

He immediately tackled Scales across the midsection.

They toppled backward. Scales' guard was open—Aaragon seized the opportunity. He delivered two powerful jabs to his ribs.

Sharp pains stabbed through Scales' side, burned inside of him like fire—fierce. He heard bones crunch.

Aaragon straddled him and raised his fist.

Casey connected the ball of her foot to the back of his head.

It stunned him long enough to give Scales the second he needed.

Scales wrapped his arm around Aaragon's and used his weight to reverse the straddle so that he ended up on top. He threw a series of punches to Aaragon's face.

In a rage, Casey tried to kick him in the ribs, but Aaragon countered—looped his arm round her leg and used her uneven balance against her and threw her backward.

She toppled. Aaragon raised his knee to his chest and kicked a distracted Scales off of him.

Scales flew a meter backward and landed on his back, winded.

Aaragon jumped to his feet.

Scales was in agonizing pain, but he refused to let it affect him. He blocked it out—didn't allow himself to feel it. He got to his feet.

Bellowing in rage, Aaragon threw all of his weight behind one final haymaker.

Scales sidestepped it and open-palm struck the back of Aaragon's head.

The Vakari teetered.

It was time for this to end.

Scales grabbed a fistful of a stunned Aaragon's head-quills and, with a bellow of exertion, hauled him across the room and slammed him headfirst into the stone wall at a run. Blood spattered the stone. Aaragon went limp and collapsed.

The door opened and two guards burst in. They leveled their guns at Scales. He didn't have time to react.

The sounds of gunfire rang out, but they hadn't come from the guards.

Scales turned and saw Casey standing on the far side of the room, barrel of the K2 smoking.

Two dead bodies slumped to the floor.

"Come on!" Scales policed the guards' assault rifles and their ammo. He tossed one of their MARs to Casey. She shouldered up.

Scales crouched down to Aaragon's body. He plunged his hand into his pocket and rummaged around until he found the data chip. Scales stuffed it into his inside breast pocket.

Two more Rebel guards were thundering down the hallway toward them when they emerged from the interrogation room. Scales and Casey dropped into a crouch and sent a hail of rounds their way. The guards crumpled to the floor.

"We have to get to a radio," Scales said, "or some kind of com station. If we do, I can send a coded message to the *Reveille* and let them know we're in trouble. They'll triangulate the signal and pick us up. Thanks for saving my ass back there."

"Of course," she replied in a breathless tone.

"You okay?"

"Fine. Which way?"

"We'll figure it out as we go. Come on!"

CHAPTER TWENTY-EIGHT

2015 hours, May 31, 2343
Orvis System
*Aboard **UGC Glaive Reveille***
CIC, C Deck

Roy tapped his foot on the *Reveille's* rubberized deck. His eyes were glued to a wall-mounted holoscreen. Displayed on it were Casey's and Scales' transponder signals.

Somehow, Roy's had been damaged during his fight with the Rebel Asgard. But theirs were still pulsing.

They were still alive.

Hurley sighed. "Locke, you've been standing here staring at that screen for hours."

Roy said nothing. He was too occupied with his own thoughts to hear him.

Sighing again, Hurley went over to Roy and placed a hand on his shoulder. "Roy, you look like hell." His usual gruff tone was strangely gentle, but firm. "You need to get down to the medbay and get looked at. A shower and a shave wouldn't hurt you, either. Neither would a hot meal and a few hours' sleep."

Roy didn't break his gaze. "They're transponders haven't flat lined yet," he said evenly, "which means they're still alive. I'm not leaving the CIC until I know where they are."

Hurley nodded. "I understand that, Roy. I really do. And I admire it, but—"

"Jack," Roy finally tore is gaze away from the screen. He looked into Hurley's eyes. "Enough. I'm staying here."

Hurley lowered his gaze. "Okay," he relented. He gave Roy's shoulder a squeeze.

"Lieutenant Hurley," Lieutenant Myzaf said over his shoulder from communications. "I've got a signal! Very faint, but it's definitely there!"

"Where's the source?" Hurley asked.

"Let me triangulate … there. Got it. I'll put the coordinates up on the holotable."

Hurley and Roy made their way to the chart table. "Let's go over what we know."

Lieutenant Restov tapped the control panel.

The ghostly holographic image of a planet faded in, hovering a few centimeters above the table's surface. It was about the size of Pluto. There were white clouds in its blue skies. Alpine forests stretched from one end of a continent to the other. Snow covered its polar regions. A hurricane was forming in its seas.

"We've been following this Rebel ship's trail since it left Gorgoran," Hurley said. "The *Reveille* is twice as fast, but they did get a head start. The trail stops at this planet. It looks like they landed on it." He turned to Restov. "What do we know about it?"

"Planet Mintorium." Restov read from her datapad. "CAA records state that the planet has not yet been colonized due to intense hurricanes that batter its three continents almost constantly. There are no official colonies."

"Which makes it a perfect place for Rebels to hide," Roy said. "The signal we're picking up … What is it? IFF?"

"No, sir," Restov replied. "It's a carefully coded seventy-six string code used by SpecOps groups."

"Scales," Roy said. "It has to be."

Hurley nodded in agreement. "Where precisely is the signal coming from?"

"We've triangulated it to a small island in the northern hemisphere," she said. "We're working hard to pinpoint the signal's exact location, but it's faint. We need to get closer to the planet."

"All right," Hurley said. "Call the ship to battle stations."

"Aye aye,"

Warning klaxons sounded throughout the ship. Red lights flickered in the CIC.

"Lieutenant Myzaf," Hurley called. "How long do you need to triangulate the signal?"

From his coms station, Myzaf replied, "Signal will be precisely located in six minutes."

"Can we send a counter response?" Hurley asked.

"Yes, sir," Restov answered. "But there's a chance we may alert the Rebels to our arrival."

"I don't care," Hurley said. "Do it. Let them know we heard them."

"Aye aye."

Stress creased Roy's features. His eyes were narrowed, locked on the holograph of Mintorium. A frown tugged at his mouth.

Hurley saw the desperation in Roy's eyes. He knew what he was thinking: Would Scales and Casey make it six more minutes? Hurley knew what the possibility of losing friends felt like all too well.

"They're going to make it, Roy," he said. "Remember, she's with him. He's not going to let anything happen to her. If anyone can pull themselves out of a tight jam, it's you three."

Roy nodded in acknowledgment.

"Lieutenant Hurley," Hoshi cried, "Ship signatures detected! I count three! Signatures match the profiles of Rebel ships—two Defiance-class frigates and a Vengeance Cruiser! They just peeled away from Mintorium's orbit and are on an intercept course with the *Reveille*."

Hurley and Roy shared a glance.

"Time to finally put the girl through her paces," Hurley said and smiled. "Listen up," he said to the CIC crew. Most of them wore anxious expressions. The *Reveille* was a good ship. She could hold her own, but two rebel frigates was one thing ... two frigates and a Vengeance cruiser were an entirely different playbook book all together. "This is our trial by fire. Sink or float, it's on us. Ops, clear all personnel from all non-essential decks, then seal them."

"Aye, sir."

"Lieutenant Mantum?"

"Sir?"

"Warm up our Maelstrom capacitors and all offensive batteries. Arm Rapture missile pods oh-one through ten. I want a firing solution on the lead ship, and I want it yesterday."

"Aye, aye. Maelstrom capacitors warming up, climbing twenty percent per second. Helix, Kestrel, and Rapier railguns are spun up and ready to fire. Rapture pods oh-one through ten armed and ready. Maelstrom cannon is hot and ready, sir."

"I want the Air Guard on standby," Hurley told someone at Ops. "Tell Torch I want all pilots ready to go as soon as I give the order."

"Aye, sir."

"Firing solution plotted, sir," Mantum said.

"Enemy frigates are speeding up, sir," Hoshi reported. "They're pulling away from the Vengeance Cruiser. Cruiser is hanging back."

"Send them our regards," Hurley said. "Fire Maelstrom."

"Aye. Maelstrom cannon firing."

A flash of white light saturated the main viewscreen. There was a muffled pang as a one hundred ton ferrous-tungsten round was propelled at tremendous speed out of the Maelstrom cannon's barrel.

It tore across the abyss and impacted the lead enemy frigate on its prow.

The hull shattered under the force of the impact, and the ship was knocked into an erratic spin, belching fire and smoke. Its running lights winked on and off several times—then died. With no RCS thrusters to correct her spin, she started to roll.

She was dead in space.

"Fire all primed Carrion missiles at that frigate," Hurley barked.

"Aye aye," Mantum replied. "Missiles away."

Dull thumps echoed throughout the *Reveille* as a barrage of high-explosive missiles left their silos. They snaked toward the frigate. Their exhausts left bold streaks of grey against the midnight black of space.

The missiles tore gaping wounds into the ship's hull. Fire ballooned outward. Smoke and plasma bellowed from her cratered armor.

Two massive explosions burst from the frigate's port and starboard hull like twin solar flares, and she detonated. Glittering fragments of her hull shot in all directions, leaving tiny, swirling trials of smoke in their wake.

"One down," Roy muttered.

"Contact!" Restov screeched. "Contact! Inbound Carrion missiles fired from second enemy frigate! Impact in thirty seconds."

Carrion missiles had homing devices on them. Hurley paused for a moment. He nodded. He was going to use that to his advantage. "Helm," he said, "Heading zero-three-five. Engines all ahead full."

"Aye aye," Hoshi replied. "Heading zero-three-five. Answering all ahead full."

Reveille's engines flared, blasting her into a sharp sloping incline. The three dozen Carrion missiles chasing her lazily arched upward and continued their pursuit.

Hurley crunched some numbers on the commander's personal datapad. He figured up the equation. "Course correction," he said, "Declination minus four-seven point niner, heading one-five-zero."

"Course correction, aye. Declination minus four-seven point niner, heading one-five-zero."

The *Reveille* tilted her nose downward—and then plunged straight down at incredible speed.

The Carrion missiles trailing her had to adjust their trajectories. They corrected their approach vectors and continued to give chase.

"Carrions are matching our speed," Restov reported. "Missiles will impact in thirty seconds."

"Helm," Hurley said, "course four-one-eight by seven-niner. Bow thirty-nine degrees starboard."

On the prow viewscreen, the image of space turned and suddenly centered on the top-side of the second Rebel frigate. At this distance, it was a speck in the blackness—but it was growing closer.

"Course corrected," Hoshi replied. "Be advised, sir, we are now on a collision course with Rebel frigate. Collision in twenty-five seconds."

"Noted," Hurley said. "Course correction on my mark: bow twenty-three degrees starboard, course one-eight-zero. Stand by to fire emergency portside thrusters on my order."

Hoshi and her navigations team swapped uncertain glances, but then Hurley's plan hit them. Hoshi sat straighter and said, "Aye aye."

"Collision with frigate in nine seconds," Restov announced.

"Sound collision alarms," Hurley ordered. "Everyone strap into your seats!"

Roy and Hurley gripped the sides of the holotable, bracing themselves.

"Carrion missiles closing—eight seconds to impact!"

The *Reveille*'s nose was seconds away from smashing into the frigate's dorsal hull. This was a risky move, but if it worked …

"Mark!" Hurley yelled. He waited exactly one heartbeat then said, "Fire thrusters!"

There was a deep bang as the *Reveille*'s portside thrusters fired. Hurley and Roy flew sideways. A boom reverberated along the length of *Reveille*'s hull. The portside thrusters blasted her off-course at the last second. Her port armor nearly scraped the frigate's hull as she passed centimeters beside it.

The Carrions held their course. At this speed and distance, there was no time for their targeting computers to correct their vectors and adjust their course …

Thirty-six missiles slammed into the dorsal surface of the Rebel ship's hull. The explosions ripped her open like a tin can. Sections of the hull drifted apart, silently tumbling in uncontrollable spins in the vacuum of space.

Roy and Hurley picked themselves up off the deck. Roy slapped Hurley on the back. "Nice, Jack. Damn nice."

"We've still got one more to deal with," Hurley replied. "That Vengeance Cruiser is a lot tougher than those frigates, and has the firepower to match. Mantum, arm Rapture pods eleven through twenty-five. Prepare to fire Maelstrom cannon on my order"

"Aye aye, sir. Pods armed. Maelstrom ready to fire on your command."

"Sir," Restov said. "Enemy cruiser has just released a squadron of Scythe fighters and four Black Raiders."

"Scramble our pilots," Hurley said. "Helm, course three-one-five by one-seven-niner, inclination four-seven point one-niner. Engines to two-thirds power."

"Aye, sir. Course three-one-five by one-seven-niner, inclination four-seven point one-niner. Answering two-thirds power."

On the viewscreen, the Vengeance Cruiser—the *Ordatl*—fired up her engines and headed toward the *Reveille*.

Her strike craft accelerated ahead.

"Pilots in the air," Restov reported.

"*Reveille* actual," a woman said over the coms. Roy recognized her accent. "This is Torch."

"Go ahead, Torch," Hurley said.

"The enemy fighters outnumber us three to one, sir."

"Too much for you to handle, Captain?"

"Hell no, sir. I was about to say I feel sorry for the bastards. Maybe if they stacked the odds five to one I'd say we were even, but they don't stand a chance. Do you want us to engage or cover the *Reveille*?"

"I want you to break your wing up and concentrate on taking out their Scythes. If I know pilots, those Raiders will ignore you and head straight for us. Let me handle them. Understood?"

"Understood, sir. Torch out."

The overhead coms snapped off.

"Pull up fore camera feed on viewscreen four," Hurley said.

"Aye aye," someone replied from Ops.

On the screen, Torch and the *Reveille*'s other seven Lancer fighters accelerated straight toward the enemy fighter line.

The two lines opened fire. Cannons flashed.

Reveille's squadron broke formation. Eight puffs of fire lit up the night as a matching number of Rebel Scythe fighters detonated.

The squadrons overpassed each other. The remaining sixteen Rebel fighters fired recursive thrusters and came about. Torch and her Wing did the same.

As Hurley had predicted, the Raiders blew past *Reveille*'s Lancers and made a beeline for the *Reveille* itself.

"Four Raiders inbound, sir," Restov said.

"Fire up our point defense system," Hurley said. "As soon as they come in range, open up."

"Aye aye," Mantum tapped his screen. His fingers danced across the keypad and he said, "Point defense batteries online. Raiders will be in range in three … two … one. Firing!"

The *Reveille*'s quad-barreled 50mm point defense cannons strobed the night with rapid flashes of gunfire. The heavy slugs found their mark—two Raiders exploded in a blaze of fire, a puff of smoke—and vanished.

The two remaining Raiders opened fire. Their heavy main guns barked and raked the *Reveille*'s hull with a dozen 100mm depleted uranium slugs.

"Taking fire!" Restov said.

The *Reveille*'s 50mm cannons continued to flash. The Raider pilots did their best to weave their craft in and out of the intense firestorm of gunfire.

Their main guns fired again.

Specks of fire erupted across the *Reveille*'s hull.

A dozen shells found the third Black Raider, punctured its armor, and tore through its vital systems and reactor. It exploded.

An instant later, the last strike craft succumbed to the barrage.

"All Raiders destroyed," Restov reported.

On the viewscreen, Torch and her Wing were mopping up the last of the *Ordatl*'s Scythes.

When the last craft exploded, Torch's voice came in over the coms. "*Reveille* actual, Rawley."

"This is actual," Hurley replied. "Go ahead, Captain."

"The enemy fighters are toast, sir."

"Glad to hear it. Now hang back and keep out of the *Ordatl*'s firing range. Leave that bastard to me."

"Roger that," Torch said. "Send our regards."

"Will do. Actual out."

Hurley turned to Mantum. "Lieutenant Mantum, get me a firing solution for our primed Raptures. Ready our plasma batteries. Let's see how that ship's armor stands up against those."

"Aye aye. Firing solution plotted, sir," Mantum replied. "Plasma capacitors are warmed up and ready to go."

"Fire missiles at will, Lieutenant."

Mantum nodded. "Aye, firing."

A hail of missiles launched from their silos and streaked toward the *Ordatl*.

"Fire plasma cannons," Hurley barked.

"Aye aye."

The firing channels on the *Reveille*'s port and starboard plasma cannons warmed to blue, then red—motes of light appeared and collected along the channels.

With a flash of light, they discharged.

They tore across the midnight sea.

An instant later, they hit their target.

Fire splashed across the *Ordatl*'s bow. The superheated plasma burned through her armor, which bubbled and completely boiled away. Her foredecks were set ablaze.

An explosion tore through the cruiser and burst from her portside hull. Debris and a half-dozen large hull fragments scattered into space.

The inbound Rapture missiles closed in on their target.

The *Ordatl* fired up her point defense system. The fifty millimeter rounds blew two-thirds of the advancing Rapture barrage to pieces.

The remaining ones hit.

Chains of fire erupted across the ship's hull. Fire tore through her insides.

But she was still in the fight. The remaining Raptures hadn't been enough to deliver the knockout blow Hurley intended.

Her skeletal frame exposed in various places, wounds coughing smoke, the *Ordatl* accelerated.

"I'll teach you to charge at me, you son-of-a-bitch," Hurley muttered. "Engines all ahead full!"

"Aye, sir," Hoshi replied. "Answering all ahead full."

"Restov," he said, "all fire-fighting crews to stand-by. Ready all emergency personnel. And tell medbay they're about to get very busy."

"Yes, sir."

Hurley strapped himself into the commander's chair. "Roy," he said, turning to him, "I'd find a seat if I were you." He tapped the chair's arm-panel and opened the ship-wide com. "All hands: this is the XO. Prepare to broadside."

The space between the two warships was rapidly closing.

On her portside, ventral, and dorsal hull, *Reveille*'s offensive railguns came about.

Starboard, *Ordatl*'s two dozen heavy 100mm Mazur rail batteries did the same.

Hurley watched the ship grow in size on the prow viewscreen. He gripped the arms of the chair. The Rebel Vengeance Cruiser was nearly twice *Reveille*'s size.

"Prepare to fire!" Hurley said.

The two ships decelerated. Their noses passed each other.

"Fire!"

Both ships opened up.

Aboard the *Reveille*, the CIC's lights flickered. The ship shook violently as heavy slugs thudded against her flank. Pinpricks of fire erupted across her hull.

Her cannons spit shells that slammed against the *Ordatl*'s side. The Rebel ship's running lights flickered. A thousand explosions blossomed across its hull.

Debris from both ships impacted against the other.

The section of space between the two vessels flashed alight with fire.

After another ten grueling, brutal seconds, the two ships passed one another. The firing stopped as they both flew out of range.

"Status!" Hurley called.

Lieutenant Forrus wiped a trickle of blood from his nose. His head had slammed into the console during the fight.

"DCON reports fires on all decks, sir." He tapped his screen. "No major casualties reported, though. Damage to decks is contained and fire crews are handling the fires now, sir."

"Looks like that new armor plating really saved our asses," Hurley said. He unbuckled his harness and stood in front of the viewscreen. "Aft camera on the main."

"Aye."

On the window, a display of the *Ordatl* faded into existence.

The Vengeance Cruiser had taken a beating. Smoke and atmosphere vented from two hundred breaches to her decks. There were two gaping holes in her midsection—her Carrion missiles had detonated in their tubes. She listed to starboard as she flew.

"The bitch is still flying." Roy ambled over next to Hurley. He put his hands on his hips. "Those Rebel ships are tough, I'll give them that."

"Helm," Hurley said, "come about. Weapons, is our Maelstrom still charged at one hundred percent?"

"Capacitors still hot and ready, sir," Mantum replied.

"Good. Ready three consecutive rounds and get ready to fire on my command."

"Aye, sir."

"Coming about," Hoshi said from her navigations station.

Reveille spun round to face the wounded Rebel ship as it turned toward them.

But her wounds were great, and she was slow.

The *Reveille* completed her spin. The cruiser centered on the main viewscreen.

"Fire Maelstrom," Hurley commanded.

"Firing!"

Thunder rumbled from below decks and a flash of white light obscured the main viewscreen. Two seconds later, another round fired … and another two seconds after that.

The Rebel ship was so slow in her spin her flank was presented to the *Reveille* like an open invitation.

The white-hot Maelstrom rounds gave their RSVP.

They slammed into her.

The impact tore the *Ordatl* apart—she was severed amidships. Her engines flickered, flared, and died as the aft section drifted away.

The fore section tumbled once in the silent vacuum, bleeding bodies and debris into oblivion before it was ripped to bits by a series of internal detonations.

Hurley sighed.

Roy realized he'd been holding his breath. He exhaled.

"Final target destroyed," Lieutenant Restov announced.

The crew erupted into cheer.

Hurley let them have a few seconds to congratulate each other. They deserved to be proud, to be happy. The *Reveille* had survived her first official battle—and had emerged the victor.

"All right," Hurley yelled. "Shut up and sit your asses back down. We're not out of the fire yet, not until the commander and Lieutenant Keller are back on board. Lieutenant Myzaf, you better have that signal triangulated by now."

He sat straighter. "Yes, sir." He rapidly typed away at his keyboard. "Uploading coordinates to the holotable."

Hurley made his way over.

"There." Roy pointed to the flashing red beacon overlaid onto the image of Mintorium. "We've got them."

"Restov," Hurley said, "Call Torch and our flyboys back."

"Aye aye, sir."

Roy tapped his foot.

Hurley placed a hand on his shoulder. "They'll make it, Roy."

"All Lancers back onboard," Restov said. She pressed her finger to her headset. "Captain Rawley says all pilots report one hundred percent status."

"Then Lieutenant Forrus," Hurley called. "I want our engines running at two hundred percent. Divert power from whatever systems you have to."

"Aye aye," Forrus replied from Ops. "Diverting power from Maelstrom capacitors to super-charge our drive core. Drive core red-line in four minutes."

"What's our best ETA?" Hurley asked.

"ETA to target zone five minutes," Hoshi replied.

"Hurley," Roy asked, "are we in range to hail Scales or Casey on their microbeads?"

"We will be in three minutes," he answered.

CHAPTER TWENTY-NINE

"**G**ot it!" Scales said over his shoulder to Casey.

She stood watch across the room, near the doorway. She was crouched behind a table turned on its side for what little cover it would provide. Her MAR was leveled right at the door.

Six dead guards lay sprawled on the com room's floor in pools of blood.

"Signal sent," Scales said. "Wait one."

"How long?"

"This is a short range station. It's not meant to send signals as far out as we're trying to. Let's hope Hurley picks it up soon."

Casey blinked and wiped a fresh trickle of blood from her nose. She switched her stance to a more comfortable position.

"How are we looking, Casey?"

"Hallway's clear. But it's not going to take them long to find out where we are. They have to know we've escaped. And it won't be hard to find us. All they need to do is follow the bodies. I'm down to my last clip. You think he's dead?"

"Who?"

"Aaragon."

"He looked dead to me."

"Isn't that what you thought last time?"

"Point taken," Scales said. "But it's too late to go back now. There! The *Reveille* just sent the counter-response. They're on their way. Now we just need to get outside." He picked up the MAR he'd propped up against the coms station. "If we can ever manage to find our way out of this place, that is," he added. "I'll take point."

He and Casey left the com room through a side door, which took them into a map room. Casey stopped to look around while Scales continued on and made for the thick oak door at the far end.

"Wait," she said.

Scales turned.

"What?"

She pointed to the chart table. A data tablet had been set on its edge. Casey grabbed it and slung her MAR.

"What are you doing?"

She tapped the screen. Without looking up, she said, "If I find some kind of layout of this place, it'll make getting out of here a hell of a lot easier."

"Smart thinking, Casey. I'll cover the door. Hurry."

"You know, I've never worked well under pressure," she said. "So, for calm's sake, let's just pretend there aren't a hundred armed guards trying to track us down and fill our bodies with a million holes."

"If we're *pretending*," Scales said, "then let's *pretend* I actually have five mags and a pistol instead of two and no back up weapon. That being said—hurry."

"You were never good at make believe when you were a kid, were you, Scales?"

"Casey."

"I know, I'm hurrying. Give me another minute to access …" Her hands trembled. She tapped the enter key, thumbed the holographic spacebar, but she hit backspace instead of enter again. The error took her back to the previous screen. *"Merde,"* she breathed through clenched teeth.

She typed in the commands more carefully. "There," she said. "I got the layout. The building we're in is some kind of manor. It's part of a larger complex. We're right at the edge of it."

Her eyes scanned back and forth, and she took it all in; quickly memorized the path through the maze of corridors to the outside. "Got it." She tossed the pad aside.

When Scales cocked an eyebrow in her direction, she tapped the side of her head. "I have a good memory." She unslung her MAR and shouldered up. "I've got point."

Outside the map room, the corridor was long and dim. Doors lined either side. Expensive red carpeting covered the floor. Paintings hung neatly on the paneled walls.

"Here." Casey stopped and opened a door on the left. "Through here. There's a door on the other end that leads out into an outside courtyard."

She went through first and swept the room. It was a sitting room furnished with couches and chairs and tables situated around a fireplace.

Scales gave the hallway one last check and backed into the room. He shut the door and locked it. He and Casey grabbed one of the sofas and slid it in front of the wooden door. "That should give us a few good seconds," he said. "On you."

There was a hinged iron door on the room's far side. Casey unlatched the archaic lock and pulled the heavy thing open. She and Scales slinked through. They emerged into a courtyard on the manor's east side.

No guards were in sight.

In a second, Scales took in his surroundings. There were kilometers of green fields outside the courtyard walls.

That was where they needed to get to—an open, clear, treeless field.

Casey moved across the stone yard toward the gate.

"No," Scales said. "We'll never make it on foot." He nodded to a small collection of vehicles. Parked in several neat rows were pristine-looking, shiny new Ranger LCVs that were no doubt stolen.

"We need to put some distance between ourselves and this place before the *Reveille* shows up," he said. "If there are any AA batteries, which I'm sure there are, pick up is going to be hell. You're driving."

He hopped up onto the back of one of the Rangers. Casey threw her MAR into the passenger seat and jumped behind the wheel as Scales snapped the charging lever back on the Ranger's M66 20mm cannon.

"Go!" he yelled.

Casey pushed the ignition button. With a rumble, the Ranger's hydrogen-convertor ICE sputtered to life. She stomped down on the pedal and the tires squealed, throwing up a geyser of dirt and bits of loosened flagstone.

The Ranger leaped forward. Casey turned the wheel to the left. The vehicle swung round as it spun ninety degrees.

Scales braced himself and swung the turret round to target the other Rangers. They were stolen, and their destruction meant that much less for the UGC to deal with. The M66 roared—it shook the teeth in his head. A hail of rounds tore into the parked Rangers and peppered their side armor, their windshields and tires, chewing them to bits.

The Ranger accelerated through an opening in the encompassing stone wall as a dozen armored guards burst out of the door Scales and Casey had used and ran into the courtyard. They leveled their guns and fired at the vehicle, but their MARs had no effect on the Ranger's plate armor.

Scales answered with a sustained burst from the cannon. The firestorm of large caliber rounds blasted the guards apart.

Casey took the Ranger out into the open grass. Its rear tires chewed through the blades of short turf and spit it out the back. The Ranger's speed climbed quickly.

Scales heard the whine of aircraft engines and saw an Arrow Gunship liftoff from somewhere behind the manor. Its thrusters fired a corrective burst and it came about to face them.

"Shit! Casey, we need to go faster!"

"I've got the pedal to the floor!" she yelled over the howl of the engine.

The Arrow's engines flared and she gave chase. Her speed was climbing rapidly. She would eventually overcome them.

Scales opened up with a sustained burst from the M66.

The Arrow banked hard to port.

The rounds cleanly missed it.

A rocket shot out from its wing-mounted pod and streaked for the Ranger. Casey saw it in the rearview mirror and swerved the Ranger to the right.

Scales saw the rocket whizz past them—heard it, felt the heat from its exhaust. It cratered the ground three meters in front of them. Dirt, rocks, and grass showered them. Casey steered the Ranger farther to the right, out of the Arrow's firing line.

Static burst in Scales' ear. "Hurley to Nova-One," a voice said over his microbead com. "I repeat, Hurley to Nova-One. Please respond."

Scales took one hand off the M66 and pressed it firmly to his ear.

"*Shiala,* Hurley, it's good to hear your voice. Lieutenant Keller and I are in a Ranger a few klicks away from a large manor complex— traveling north. Can you get a fix on my transponder?"

"Already done, Commander. I've got you. Can you see us?"

Scales twisted around and looked up at the sky.

A ball of red light appeared in the black, cloudless night sky. Scales watched it grow larger and larger until he could make out the shape of a sleek ship.

The *Reveille* had come.

But the Arrow gunship was still in pursuit.

It had corrected its path and was on an intercept vector with the Ranger. Two rockets sailed out from under its wings. Casey again veered the car sideways, this time to the left. The rockets missed, but one impacted too close to the back of the Ranger.

Scales was jolted by the concussive blast and felt the heat wave wash over him. He blinked a few times to clear his vision and saw the rear of the Ranger was in flames. Fire licked at his feet and the M66's barrel. "Hurley, do something about that gunship!"

"Aye aye. Get clear, Commander."

There was a boom, a flash of light. A lance of fire shot out from the *Reveille*'s underside hull.

The 50mm slug hit the Arrow. It burst into flames and smoke. The ruined hulk crashed and skidded several dozen meters forward, gouging a canyon in the earth.

"All clear," Hurley said. "We're sending down the cargo lift."

Casey steered the Ranger toward the descending cargo elevator and up onto the platform. Scales jumped down off the turret. As the lift ascended, he watched the manor until it disappeared from view.

Roy and Hurley were waiting in the hangar for them. Roy smiled at Scales and nodded respectfully.

Smiling, Scales nodded back. He reached into his pocket and pulled out the chip. He held it up for Roy to see.

Roy grinned. "No matter what," he said.

"No matter what," Scales agreed.

Casey climbed out of the Ranger's driver seat and beamed Roy a huge grin and then teetered. Roy rushed over to help her.

Hurley gave Scales a crisp salute.

Scales returned it, and extended his hand. "Nice job, Jack," he said.

Hurley nodded and shook it firmly. "Thank you, sir."

"Here," Roy said to Casey and helped her off the lift. "Sit down on this crate."

"Roy … "

"Shh," Roy whispered. "Later." He took her face into his hands. He peered into those pretty, emerald eyes. Roy gave her a big toothy smile—and kissed her on the lips.

It lasted for several long, sweet seconds.

"I was so worried you were dead," she whispered as she pulled back. "How did you get here?"

"If you want to hear that story," he said in a sly tone, "then you'll have to let me buy you a drink."

Casey smiled. "That sounds like a plan."

Back in the CIC, the crew gave Scales and Casey an honorary stand-to. Scales acknowledged them with a nod.

"Okay, okay," Hurley snapped. "Get back to your stations!"

The crew moved like they had been electrified.

"Lieutenant Hoshi?" Scales called.

"Sir?"

"Move us into orbit."

"Aye aye, sir," she replied.

"What are we going to do about that base, Scales?" Casey asked.

"We need to make sure we destroy that entire area," Scales said. "Deny those bastards every asset down there. Lieutenant Mantum?"

"Yes, sir?"

"Arm and release the safety interlocks on one of our Arkus nukes. Target the Rebel base and prepare to fire on my mark."

"Aye aye, Commander," Mantum typed in several commands on his keyboard and tapped his screen a few times. "Nuke interlock safeties removed. Target locked on and ready to fire."

Scales paused.

He thought of Aaragon; his partner, best friend, his *shirum*, and of all the missions they had been on together. He thought of his return from the grave ... and then of his new allegiance with the Rebels. One word came to mind.

"Fire."

"Missile away," Mantum answered.

There was a thump as the nuke left its silo.

"Bring up the area of impact on viewscreen four," Scales said.

"Aye aye."

Scales watched the screen.

"Ten seconds to target," Mantum reported.

Scales counted down the seconds. He didn't even blink when the nuke hit and obliterated everything within thirty kilometers.

He exhaled.

It was done.

"Sir?" Hoshi piped. "I'm picking up a contact on the scanners, a chiropter-class dropship. Heading indicates it left the Rebel base just before the nuke hit."

Scales let out an amused huff. "So," he muttered. "You're still alive, you slippery little shit."

"Chiropter hailing us on channel two, sir," Lieutenant Myzaf reported.

"Patch it through," Scales said.

Casey rolled her eyes. "This ought to be good."

The speakers exploded with static, then Aaragon's voice came in loud and clear.

"Too slow, Kileeus," he teased. "Better luck next time."

The channel went dead, and the dropship's transponder vanished from the sensors.

Six hours later

Roy exhaled and pressed the button that would route his uplink to Lord Carr's personal Quantum Entanglement Communicator (QEC).

A few seconds later, Carr's full body apparition appeared in front of him.

Roy snapped to attention and saluted. "Sir."

"At ease, Roy. What can I do for you?"

Roy spread his legs a shoulder's width apart and clasped his hands behind his back in the "parade rest" position.

"Admiral …" Roy stopped and lowered his gaze. He wasn't quite sure how to say it without sounding disrespectful.

"You're wondering why I didn't tell you your father was tied into this mission," Carr finished.

Roy looked up suddenly. He was shocked. It showed on his face. "Sir … how did you know I was calling to ask about that?"

"Roy, I've been in this job a long time," Carr said. "I know my Shadows. Now, would you like me to start from the beginning?"

"I would very much appreciate that, sir."

"You were brought up believing James Locke worked as an intelligence liaison with the military. After all, you were told he died when Rebels attacked the UGC base he was stationed at—Kronus Facility. I'm not sure why that's the story your mother gave you, but perhaps in the end she realized that what James was doing, what he was involved in, was wrong. Your mother did everything she could to guide you down a different path so that you wouldn't follow in his footsteps. Nothing on Heaven or Earth could have swayed you from your decision to enlist in the Coalition and avenge your father's death.

"What would you have done had I told you your father, the main reason you joined the Marine Corps, had been the very enemy you were fighting? Just as nothing could have swayed you from your determination to join the military, nothing I could have told you about your father would have convinced you of the hard, disappointing truth. Instead, you had to find out for yourself. And from what I know of you, Roy, that was the only way you'd ever believe your father was actually the head researcher for a weapon that was going to kill millions of innocent people.

"That's why Scales and Aaragon were sent to kill him all those years ago. I can understand if you're feeling anger towards Scales. He was the one who took your father from you. But ask yourself this—had events turned out differently, had your father not been assassinated, had that bomb been used to kill all those people ... what kind of man would you be today? Where would your heart truly lie: with the government your parents hated so much, or with the radical terrorist organization that will stop at nothing to bring it down?

"I'm sure you understand that Scales was simply following his orders, and he had no idea up until a few hours ago that you and his target were related. Now, with knowing that your commanding officer did kill your father, for whatever reason, are you going to request a transfer from me?"

Roy smiled. "The thought never crossed my mind, sir. My place is here, in the Shadows, next to Casey, and under the command of Kileeus Scales."

"Glad to hear it. I was very pleased to hear of Nova Team's success in recovering the Ragnarok data. It's now safely out of the Rebel's hands. You three saved a lot of lives today, son. Now, is there anything else?"

"No sir," Roy said, then, "well wait, actually there is. In the Charybdis facility I fought an Asgard Rebel. She was good. Better than I was. There was this symbol on her pauldron. A cobra coiled around a bolt of lightning with the Rebel flag in the background."

"A snake," Carr said. "Snakes are Rebel counter-operatives, very much like Shadows. They're very well trained, and, to make matters worse, some of them are even ex-Shadows. You're lucky to have survived that encounter. Not many newly recruited Shadows could hold claim to engaging a Snake in hand-to-hand and come out on top. Well done."

"Thank you, sir," Roy said.

Carr nodded. "Take care, Lieutenant, and congratulations on completing your first assignment as a Shadow. Carr out."

Scales poured himself his thirteenth glass of whiskey.

He sat at the bar in the wardroom, alone. The whiskey wasn't doing a good job of drowning his sorrows tonight. He downed his glass in one gulp. Hmm. Maybe he needed more.

As he poured another glassful, he heard footsteps behind him. Casey took a seat on one of the stools next to him.

"Hey," she said cheerfully, and smiled.

He cleared his throat and licked his sour lips. "Hey," he said. "Can I pour you a glass?"

"No, thanks." She shook her head. "I'm not really in the mood for a drink right now. But I um…I wanted to say thank you for saving my butt down there. Really, Scales, from the bottom of my heart." She leaned over and rested her head on his shoulder.

He put his arm around her shoulder and squeezed. "You're welcome," he whispered. "And thank you for trusting me."

"I'm sorry about your friend."

"Yeah. So am I."

She looked up at him.

"You loved her, didn't you?"

He scrunched his forehead. "What?"

"That human Aaragon talked about. The woman."

Scales' gaze drifted away to the far wall. He stared at it a long while before he answered. "Yes. I did."

"What was her name?"

Scales smiled weakly. "*Miranda*."

"That's really pretty. Maybe you can tell me about her someday."

"Someday."

Another set of footsteps caused Scales and Casey to turn around.

Roy stood a few paces behind them with his hands clasped behind his back. "Hey," he said. "Not interrupting, am I?"

Casey stood. "I think I'll give you two some time to talk alone," she whispered to Scales. She winked at Roy on her way out.

Roy took the stool she had been sitting on.

"Roy," Scales began. "There's something I need to tell you."

"No, there's not," he said. "I know."

"You know?"

"Yeah. I took a look at those files we downloaded in Charybdis. I saw that my father was involved with the Rebels somehow, but I didn't know the whole story. So I asked Carr about it, and he told me everything—who my father was, what he was trying to do—everything. I know you did what you had to do when you killed him. No hard feelings, okay?" He extended his hand.

The gesture warmed Scales' heart. He grasped Roy's hand and squeezed.

"So," Roy grabbed a glass. "I bet you anything I can drink your alien ass under the table."

There was a lot on Scales' mind. Aaragon was still alive. He was going to be a problem in the future. The Vanguard were still out there, the possibility of war with them growing ever brighter with each passing day.

But today, now, he decided he was going to do something he hadn't done in years: relax. He was going to enjoy this moment, savor it.

For he sat in the company of a fellow Shadow, a fellow soldier … and a friend.

Scales shot Roy a hearty grin. "You're on."

Epilogue

1800 hours, June 2, 2343
Sol System, planet Mars
OMI Archeological Excavation Facility 007125-22F
Codename: "Leonidas"

As soon as Katherine and Carr stepped off the shuttle on the landing pad inside the facility's perimeter, a human in a white lab coat ran up to greet them.

"Lord Carr, sir," he said and extended his hand. "A pleasure to meet you. Both of you." He shook Katherine's hand. "Dr. Samuel Portenelli, Chief Analyst at Leonidas Facility."

Amused, Katherine cocked her eyebrow. *This is who replaced me? He's not even military. And damn, he's hyper. Like a terrier on coffee.*

"A pleasure, doctor," she said, and forced a smile. "What seems to be the problem?"

"I'll explain on the way." He gestured toward the main entrance to the facility. They followed him into the lobby, past the security checkpoint, and down a flight of stairs to a sublevel that hadn't been there the last time Katherine had.

"We were doing some tests," he explained while they walked through a seemingly endless corridor that began to steeply decline. "When suddenly the whole artifact lit up like a Christmas tree. Every hieroglyph on the Monolith's surface started glowing with a blue light. We had no idea what caused it, but we detected an energy spike originating from somewhere below the facility. It took some time to dig it out, but we eventually found a doorway leading somewhere. When we touched the symbols on the door, it slid back and *disappeared*. That's when we found the antechamber. For being buried for over a hundred and fifty *million* years, it looks like it was made yesterday. There's no dust, no dirt, not one damn speck in the whole place. When one of the scientists tried to enter, this blue energy barrier materialized in front of the entrance. We haven't been able to get inside, no matter how hard we try. There are dozens of hieroglyphs scattered around the entrance, the same kind of mica inclusions that are on the Monolith."

He finished his account as they stepped into the ancient alien antechamber's lobby. They stood a few meters before the barrier. Several floodlights illuminated the area while a group of scientists studied the shield. Six marines armed with MARs stood guard, in case they were needed.

"How far are we below the surface?" Katherine asked.

"A kilometer," Portenelli answered.

Katherine turned to Carr. "May I, sir?"

"By all means."

She stepped closer to the shield. It was a risky move, but she brushed two fingers across its surface. The shield was as hard as iron.

Katherine stepped back and put her hands on her hips while she studied the various hieroglyphs on the walls. She was looking for a pattern.

There. She found it. She stepped in closer to it. It was a symbol she had seen on the Monolith that repeated itself far more than any of the others.

Against her better judgment … she reached out and touched it.

It lit up, gold, then a pale blue. Gasping, she took a step back. The blue light traveled outward, danced across the entire wall, and then moved on until every symbol glowed blue. The one she touched then warmed to gold again, and the shield dissipated.

"Well I'll be damned," Portenelli muttered. "Why didn't I think of that?"

"Yes," Katherine muttered. "Why didn't you."

The marines shouldered their weapons and closed in around Carr and Katherine in a tight shield formation. They aimed their MARs at the entrance to the main chamber.

"Stand down," Carr said.

They lowered their weapons—slightly.

"Shall we?" Katherine said to Carr.

He cast her a weary glance, but then nodded. "Sweep it good, marines."

They shuffled into the chamber while everyone waited outside. The anticipation was so thick Katherine could have cut it with a knife.

The Marine NCO stuck his head out and said, "All clear, sir."

Katherine almost ran forward, but Carr grabbed her arm. "Take it easy, Katherine. We don't know what's in there yet. Let me go first."

She nodded. "Yes, sir."

"Everyone wait out here." He went into the chamber with Katherine following on his heels.

The chamber was ovular in shape, walls curving upward into a ceiling that disappeared from view. There was a raised dais surrounded by four pillars that danced with glowing hieroglyphs. As Katherine and Carr stepped onto the dais, a ball of blue light materialized in front of them.

Immediately, Carr stepped in front of Katherine to shield her, but she said, "Wait! I don't think it's a weapon." She patted his shoulder. With a sigh, he allowed her to inch closer.

The blue ball of light hovered, perfectly still. It warmed to purple.

"Potest intelligere te me?" the ball said. Its voice sounded male, disembodied, but far from artificial.

"What did it say?" Carr asked.

Katherine furrowed her brow. "I think it's trying to communicate in a root language. It spoke Latin, but how it knew to do that is beyond me."

"Potest intelligere te me?" it said again.

"Can you communicate with it?" Carr asked.

"I can try." She cleared her throat. *"Etiam possum,"* she said. *"Quid es?"*

"Plecere expectare momento," it replied. *"Nomina tua vocalis exemplaria ..."*

"It said to wait a moment," Katherine told Carr. "It's analyzing our vocal patterns."

"Hello," the ball said in clear, flawless English. "My sensors have analyzed your speech patterns so that I may communicate with you in the same manner as you do with each other. My name is Solsulin, or Sol, if you prefer. Who might you be?"

"All yours, sir," Katherine muttered and took a step back.

"I am Lord Fleet Admiral Terrence Carr of the United Galactic Coalition. What are you?"

"I am what you would call an Artificial Intelligence, though far more advanced than you could ever imagine."

"Did the Vanguard create you?" Carr asked.

Sol laughed. "Heavens, no. I was created by a race that predated you by many millions of years. In your language, the closest translation of their name would be the Antecessors."

"Did the Antecessors build these ruins?" Katherine asked.

"I would hardly call them ruins," Sol said. "Yes, the Antecessors built this installation and many others."

"Where are they?" Katherine asked.

"I don't know. I assume they died in the War."

Carr asked, "What war?"

"The war with the Vanguard."

"Please explain," Katherine said.

"One hundred and fifty million years ago, my creators had an empire that spanned the length of this galaxy and one other. At the pinnacle of their civilization, the Antecessors made contact with an unknown species, a race they would come to know as the Vanguard. A conflict between the two erupted. This conflict quickly evolved into a full-scale war that engulfed the entirely of the Antecessor Plathara. When it was over, the Vanguard emerged as the victors. The Antecessors did not survive."

Katherine and Carr exchanged troubled glances. Both were thinking the same thing: if the Vanguard were powerful enough to defeat a race as advanced as these Antecessors, then the UGC was in a lot of trouble.

"What are the Vanguard?" Katherine asked.

"I don't know," Sol said. "Near the end of the War, there were many theories as to their origins, but nothing could ever be proven. The Vanguard are shrouded in complete mystery. The Antecessors never knew where they came from, how they came to be, or what their purpose for attacking the Plethara was. However, it was widely believed the Vanguard were as old as the Antecessors themselves, which, at the time the War started, would have put their age at one point three billion years old."

"Could they have come from another galaxy?"

"Extragalactic origins were a possibility the Antecessors explored," Sol said. "But as I said, nothing could ever be proven."

"Why did they attack us?" Carr asked.

"I imagine it has something to do with the crystals."

"You know about the crystals?" Katherine asked. "What are they?"

"Information."

"We've found two," Carr said. "Are there more?"

"Yes. There are three."

"Where do we find the last one?" Katherine asked.

"I do not know," Sol replied solemnly. "The Antecessors, in their infinite wisdom, saw it prudent to limit my knowledge on such matters. I suspect in case I was ever captured by the Vanguard."

Katherine shook her head. "What is your function, Sol?"

"I am the Observer. It is my job to monitor all forms of intelligent life, to study you and your civilization, and transmit that data back."

"Transmit it back?" Carr said. "To who?"

"I do not know, though I assume it is a fruitless effort now that all my creators are dead."

"Then why do it?"

"Because that is the job I was created to do. I am the Observer."

"When the Monolith … when this *installation* powered up," Katherine said, "What was that?"

"That was me beaming the data at superluminal speeds to this cycle's designated coordinates."

"What coordinates do you transmit the data to?" Katherine asked.

"It is different every cycle," Sol said. "But I will not share that information with you. Any attempt to access any information regarding that or anything else from my matrix will result in my destruction, as well as the destruction of this facility. The blast radius would equal twelve kilometers, so I would not advise that. You have been warned."

Katherine shifted her weight. Now she wanted to ask the big question.

"How do we defeat the Vanguard, Sol?"

"That information was purposely blocked from my data matrix," he replied. "I do not know, nor can I obtain that information. However, you should have no problem in doing so. Have you learned nothing from the information stored in the crystals you've found?"

"The crystals have information stored inside them?" Carr asked.

"No," Sol replied. "They *are* information, as I said before. But if you did not know that, then you have not found the Occulary."

"What is that?"

"A device that will allow you to access the crystals' information," Sol said. "I do not have any more information than that, I'm sorry."

"I'm guessing you have no idea where that is, either, right?" Carr asked.

"That is correct. But there are clues that will lead you to it."

"Clues?" Katherine said.

"Yes. The Antecessors knew there would, undoubtedly, be others that came after them. They knew the Vanguard would return eventually to finish what they started, to destroy any intelligent life that would pose a threat to them. Therefore, my creators left behind clues that would help you learn what they knew of the Vanguard ... and how to defeat them. I cannot tell you more, but I can, however, give you two valuable pieces of information. This is the first."

Above Sol's ball of light, a holographic projection winked to life. It took the form of a star map. There was a blinking red beacon over one of the planets, and its relative coordinates to the system's sun popped up beside it.

"That's the Electus Borealis system." Katherine gazed intently at the map. "And that blinking beacon is … *Katana*. Right, Admiral?"

His hands on his hips, Carr was studying the projection. "Yeah," he muttered. "It is."

Katherine gave an irritable huff. She tore her focus away from the map and glared at Sol's ball. "What's on Katana?"

"The next clue," he said simply. "As for precisely where on the planet it is, I cannot say."

"We've got a lot of work to do," Carr said.

"What's the second piece of information you have?" Katherine asked Sol.

"Only this," Sol said. "The Vanguard will do everything they can to stop you from discovering the secret to their defeat. The path ahead of you will be an arduous one, but you must prevail in your quest to find the remaining crystal and get them all to the Occulary. The clue on the planet you call Katana will aid you. Know this: the events over the horizon are coming fast, and one way or another, they will alter the course of life in this galaxy. Your very existence hangs in the balance. I must now report on these events and send a transmission, so if you will excuse me, I will be going now. I wish you the best of luck. I will speak to you again soon."

"Wait, no!" Katherine protested, but Sol's ball winked out.

However, the star chart of Electus Borealis remained.

"Damn it," she muttered.

"We'd better get back to HighCom," Carr said. "We've got a lot to tell the Council."

Katherine stared at the space that had been occupied by Sol's avatar just moments ago, glaring at it, willing him to return.

But he didn't.

There were so many questions she needed answered. But she had enough to process for now. She needed to write it all down so she wouldn't forget it. She followed Admiral Carr out of the chamber. Thinking about what Sol had said, she gazed out of the shuttle window while they rode back to the ODS.

His last words chilled to her to bone.

This was just the beginning.

The Vanguard were coming.

GLOSSARY

Asgards: The Asgards resemble humanoid raptors due to their distinctive avian features. They are from planet Kathajora, a world known for its lush, green continents and great emerald seas. They have keen eyesight and smell. Their bodies are covered in fine scales, and their thick digits and opposable thumb are tipped with talons.

Ah-ooh: The Marine Corp's battle-cry.

Battlenet: The Battle Network is the UGC military's galaxy-wide communication network.

Boreans: Boreans are very serpentine in appearance and have long, graceful necks. They typically stand as tall as the average human.

Carbite: Carbite is a titanium-based alloy used as either ablative plating aboard UGC starships, or as the primary armor plating on military combat vehicles. It is nearly impervious to small arms fire.

Chixil: A humanoid alien race with two sets of eyes.

Eka: The Eka are humanoid in appearance, with six-fingered hands and semi-flexible horns that sweep backward off their heads. The defining feature of the Eka is that the male half of the species has grey skin, while females seen with tones of grey, blue, green, purple, and even crimson, are common.

FTL: Faster Than Light travel is a ship's ability to travel faster than the speed of light. As star systems are often flung many, many light years from one another, FTL travel allows a ship to traverse a distance that would take months in mere hours.

FleetCom: Fleet Command is the ruling branch of the navy that co-ordinates the Coalition's vast fleets. It is commanded by the navy's top officials, referred to as the Admiralty.

GroundCom: Ground Command is the commanding branch of the Coalition Marine Corps.

HighCom: High Command is the supreme, ruling branch of the military to which both FleetCom and GroundCom answer.

Humans: Humanity hails from the terrestrial world called Earth. Humans have been attributed with both stubbornness and persistence. They are the newest species to join the galactic community, and the most recent race to seek membership into the UGC.

Microbead: A microbead is a short-range communication device that is inserted into the ear canal. Marines, pilots, and any other naval person-nel expecting to go aground are required to carry them.

ODS: An Orbital Docking Station is a space station that serves as a docking platform for starships, whether they be civilian craft or war-ships. They typically orbit settled planets where the influx of traffic is heavy. ODSs range in size from a few hundred meters in diameter to dozens of kilometers.

OWP: Orbital Weapon Platforms are titanic magnetic accelerator can-nons that defend heavily settled UGC worlds and colonies in the event of an attack from space-borne targets. Point defense weapons protect them against boarding craft, and the platform itself is host to a large sta-tion, which can house several hundred marine and navy personnel.

TACTICOM: Short for Tactical Command interface, a TACTICOM is a wrist-mounted device soldiers carry on the battlefield that provides them with tactical information.

Tetriite: Tetriite is the strongest metal known to the denizens of the Milky Way. It serves as the primary armor plating aboard UGC warships.

Tiberan: The Tiberan are the most alien looking of all the Coalition's races. They are tall, broad-shouldered, and unbelievably strong. Tiberan are tribal by nature and hail from the high-gravity planet Ghinko. However, despite their very hostile appearance, they are actually the most peaceful of the Coalition's races.

Tomlyns: This race of canine-like beings hail from the farthest home-world in Coalition space. They have patches of fine pink, white, or brown fur on their faces, necks, hands, and feet.

Ura: Ura are tall, slender aliens that resemble the greys of human myth. The have large, ovoid eyes nestled in egg-shaped heads that sit on skinny necks.

Vakari: The Vakari are a proud, militaristic race of bipedal saurians from the planet Katana. Their numbers make up the largest percentage of soldiers serving in the military, and, as such, they are some of the best. They are highly respected by the other UGC-affiliated races.

About the Author

Victor Nieves lives in West Virginia. He enjoys writing, reading, and is a huge horror movie fan, zombies in particular. At the young age of twenty-one, he found a way to communicate his ideas and imagination with others through writing, which he plans on doing it the rest of his life.